ALSO BY CASEY McQUISTON

RED, WHITE & ROYAL BLUE

Casey McQuiston

ONE

LAST
STOP

ST. MARTIN'S GRIFFIN
NEW YORK

First published in the United States by St. Martin's Griffin, an imprint of St. Martin's Publishing Group

ONE LAST STOP. Copyright © 2021 by Casey McQuiston. All rights reserved. Printed in the United States of America. For information, address St. Martin's Publishing Group, 120 Broadway, New York, NY 10271.

Designed by Anna Gorovoy

ISBN 978-1-64385-983-5

For queer communities past, present, and future

And for Lee & Essie, whose love
cannot possibly fit on a dedication page

ONE LAST STOP

1

Taped to a trash can inside the Popeyes Louisiana Kitchen at the corner of Parkside and Flatbush Avenues.

SEEKING YOUNG SINGLE ROOMMATE FOR 3BR APARTMENT UPSTAIRS, 6TH FLOOR. $700/MO. MUST BE QUEER & TRANS FRIENDLY. MUST NOT BE AFRAID OF FIRE OR DOGS. NO LIBRAS, WE ALREADY HAVE ONE. CALL NIKO.

"Can I touch you?"

That's the first thing the guy with the tattoos says when August settles onto the rubbed-off center cushion of the brown leather couch—a flaking hand-me-down number that's been a recurring character the past four and a half years of college. The type you crash on, bury under textbooks, or sit on while sipping flat Coke and speaking to no one at a party. The quintessential early twenties trash couch.

Most of the furniture is as trash as the trash couch, mismatched and thrifted and hauled in off the street. But when Tattoo Boy—Niko, the flyer said his name was Niko—sits across from her, it's in a startlingly high-end Eames chair.

The place is like that: a mix of familiar and very much not familiar. Small and cramped, offensive shades of green and yellow on the walls. Plants dangling off almost every surface, spindly arms reaching across shelves, a faint smell of soil. The windows are the same painted-shut frames of old apartments in New Orleans, but these are half covered with pages of drawings, afternoon light filtering through, muted and waxy.

There's a five-foot-tall sculpture of Judy Garland made from bicycle parts and marshmallow Peeps in the corner. It's not recognizable as Judy, except for the sign that says: HELLO MY NAME IS JUDY GARLAND.

Niko looks at August, hand held out, blurry in the steam from his tea. He's got this black-on-black greaser thing going on, a dark undercut against light brown skin and a confident jaw, a single crystal dangling from one ear. Tattoos spill down both his arms and lick up his throat from beneath his buttoned-up collar. His voice is a little croaky, like the back end of a cold, and he's got a toothpick in one corner of his mouth.

Okay, Danny Zuko, calm down.

"Sorry, uh." August stares, stuck on his question. "What?"

"Not in a weird way," he says. The tattoo on the back of his hand is a Ouija planchette. His knuckles say FULL MOON. Good lord. "Just want to get your vibe. Sometimes physical contact helps."

"What, are you a—?"

"A psychic, yeah," he says matter-of-factly. The toothpick rolls down the white line of his teeth when he grins, wide and disarming. "Or that's one word for it. Clairvoyant, gifted, spiritist, whatever."

Jesus. Of course. There was no way a $700-a-month room in Brooklyn was going to come without a catch, and the catch is marshmallow Judy Garland and this refurbished Springsteen who's probably about to tell her she's got her aura on inside out and backward like Dollar Tree pantyhose.

But she's got nowhere to go, and there's a Popeyes on the first floor of the building. August Landry does not trust people, but she trusts fried chicken.

She lets Niko touch her hand.

"Cool," he says tonelessly, like he's stuck his head out the window to check the weather. He taps two fingers on the back of her knuckles and sits back. "Oh. Oh wow, okay. That's interesting."

August blinks. "What?"

He takes the toothpick out of his mouth and sets it on the steamer trunk between them, next to a bowl of gumballs. He's got a constipated look on his face.

"You like lilies?" he says. "Yeah, I'll get some lilies for your move-in day. Does Thursday work for you? Myla's gonna need some time to clear her stuff out. She has a lot of bones."

"I—what, like, in her body?"

"No, frog bones. Really tiny. Hard to pick up. Gotta use tweezers." He must notice the look on August's face. "Oh, she's a sculptor. It's for a piece. It's her room you're taking. Don't worry, I'll sage it."

"Uh, I wasn't worried about . . . frog ghosts?" Should she be worried about frog ghosts? Maybe this Myla person is a ritualistic frog murderer.

"Niko, stop telling people about frog ghosts," says a voice down the hall. A pretty Black girl with a friendly, round face and eyelashes for miles is leaning out of a doorway, a pair of goggles shoved up into her dark curls. She smiles when she sees August. "Hi, I'm Myla."

"August."

"We found our girl," Niko says. "She likes lilies."

August hates when people like him do things like that. Lucky guesses. She *does* like lilies. She can pull up a whole Wikipedia page in her head: *lilium candidum*. Grows two to six feet tall. Studied diligently from the window of her mom's two-bedroom apartment.

There's no way Niko should know—no way he *does*. Just like she does with palm readers under beach umbrellas back home in Jackson Square, she holds her breath and brushes straight past.

"So that's it?" she says. "I got the room? You, uh, you didn't even ask me any questions."

He leans his head on his hand. "What time were you born?"

"I . . . don't know?" Remembering the flyer, she adds, "I think I'm a Virgo, if that helps."

"Oh, yeah, definitely a Virgo."

She manages to keep her face impartial. "Are you . . . a professional psychic? Like people pay you?"

"He's part-time," Myla says. She floats into the room, graceful for someone with a blowtorch in one hand, and drops into the chair next to his. The wad of pink bubblegum she's chewing explains the bowl of gumballs. "And part-time very terrible bartender."

"I'm not that bad."

"Sure you're not," she says, planting a kiss on his cheek. She stage-whispers to August, "He thought a paloma was a kind of tumor."

While they're bickering about Niko's bartending skills, August sneaks a gumball out of the bowl and drops it to test a theory about the floor. As suspected, it rolls off through the kitchen and into the hallway.

She clears her throat. "So y'all are—?"

"Together, yeah," Myla says. "Four years. It was nice to have our own rooms, but none of us are doing so hot financially, so I'm moving into his."

"And the third roommate is?"

"Wes. That's his room at the end of the hall," she says. "He's mostly nocturnal."

"Those are his," Niko says, pointing at the drawings in the windows. "He's a tattoo artist."

"Okay," August says. "So it's $2,800 total? $700 each?"

"Yep."

"And the flyer said something about . . . fire?"

Myla gives her blowtorch a friendly squeeze. "Controlled fire."

"And dogs?"

"Wes has one," Niko puts in. "A little poodle named Noodles."

"Noodles the poodle?"

"He's on Wes's sleep schedule, though. So, a ghost in the night."

"Anything else I should know?"

Myla and Niko exchange a look.

"Like three times a day the fridge makes this noise like a skeleton trying to eat a bag of quarters, but we're pretty sure it's fine," Niko says.

"One of the laminate tiles in the kitchen isn't really stuck down anymore, so we all just kind of kick it around the room," Myla adds.

"The guy across the hall is a drag queen, and sometimes he practices his numbers in the middle of the night, so if you hear Patti LaBelle, that's why."

"The hot water takes twenty minutes to get going, but ten if you're nice."

"It's not haunted, but it's like, not *not* haunted."

Myla smacks her gum. "That's it."

August swallows. "Okay."

She weighs her options, watching Niko slip his fingers into the pocket of Myla's paint-stained overalls, and wonders what Niko saw when he touched the back of her hand, or thought he saw. *Pretended* to see.

And does she want to live with a couple? A couple that is one half fake psychic who looks like he fronts an Arctic Monkeys cover band and one half firestarter with a room full of dead frogs? No.

But Brooklyn College's spring semester starts in a week, and she can't deal with trying to find a place *and* a job once classes pick up.

Turns out, for a girl who carries a knife because she'd rather be anything but unprepared, August did not plan her move to New York very well.

"Okay?" Myla says. "Okay what?"

"Okay," August repeats. "I'm in."

In the end, August was always going to say yes to this apartment, because she grew up in one smaller and uglier and filled with even weirder things.

"It looks nice!" her mom says over FaceTime, propped on the windowsill.

"You're only saying that because this one has wood floors and not that nightmare carpet from the Idlewild place."

"That place wasn't so bad!" she says, buried in a box of files.

Her buggy glasses slide down her nose, and she pushes them up with the business end of a highlighter, leaving a yellow streak. "It gave us nine great years. And carpet can hide a multitude of sins."

August rolls her eyes, pushing a box across the room. The Idlewild apartment was a two-bedroom shithole half an hour outside of New Orleans, the kind of suburban built-in-the-'70s dump that doesn't even have the charm or character of being in the city.

She can still picture the carpet in the tiny gaps of the obstacle course of towering piles of old magazines and teetering file boxes. *Double Dare 2000: Single Mom Edition.* It was an unforgivable shade of grimy beige, just like the walls, in the spaces that weren't plastered with maps and bulletin boards and ripped-out phonebook pages, and—

Yeah, this place isn't so bad.

"Did you talk to Detective Primeaux today?" August asks. It's the first Friday of the month, so she knows the answer.

"Yeah, nothing new," she says. "He doesn't even try to act like he's gonna open the case back up anymore. Goddamn shame."

August pushes another box into a different corner, this one near the radiator puffing warmth into the January freeze. Closer to the windowsill, she can see her mom better, their shared mousy-brown hair frizzing into her face. Under it, the same round face and big green bush baby eyes as August's, the same angular hands as she thumbs through papers. Her mom looks exhausted. She always looks exhausted.

"Well," August says. "He's a shit."

"He's a shit," her mom agrees, nodding gravely. "How 'bout the new roommates?"

"Fine. I mean, kind of weird. One of them claims to be a psychic. But I don't think they're, like, serial killers."

She hums, only half-listening. "Remember the rules. Number one—"

"Us versus everyone."

"And number two—"

"If they're gonna kill you, get their DNA under your fingernails."

"Thatta girl," she says. "Listen, I gotta go, I just opened this shipment of public records, and it's gonna take me all weekend. Be safe, okay? And call me tomorrow."

The moment they hang up, the room is unbearably quiet.

If August's life were a movie, the soundtrack would be the low sounds of her mom, the clickity-clacking of her keyboard, or quiet mumbling as she searches for a document. Even when August quit helping with the case, when she moved out and mostly heard it over the phone, it was constant. A couple of thousand miles away, it's like someone finally cut the score.

There's a lot they have in common—maxed-out library cards, perpetual singlehood, affinity for Crystal Hot Sauce, encyclopedic knowledge of NOPD missing persons protocol. But the big difference between August and her mother? Suzette Landry hoards like nuclear winter is coming, and August very intentionally owns almost nothing.

She has five boxes. Five entire cardboard boxes to show for her life at twenty-three. Living like she's on the run from the fucking FBI. Normal stuff.

She slides the last one into an empty corner, so they're not cluttered together.

At the bottom of her purse, past her wallet and notepads and spare phone battery, is her pocketknife. The handle's shaped like a fish, with a faded pink sticker in the shape of a heart, stuck on when she was seven—around the time she learned how to use it. Once she's slashed the boxes open, her things settle into neat little stacks.

By the radiator: two pairs of boots, three pairs of socks. Six shirts, two sweaters, three pairs of jeans, two skirts. One pair of white Vans—those are special, a reward she bought herself last year, buzzed off adrenaline and mozzarella sticks from the Applebee's where she came out to her mom.

By the wall with the crack down the middle: the one physical book she owns—a vintage crime novel—beside her tablet containing her hundreds of other books. Maybe thousands. She's not sure. It stresses her out to think about having that many of anything.

In the corner that smells of sage and maybe, faintly, a hundred frogs she's been assured died of natural causes: one framed photo of an old washateria on Chartres, one Bic lighter, and an accompanying candle. She folds her knife up, sets it down, and places a sign that says PERSONAL EFFECTS over it in her head.

She's shaking out her air mattress when she hears someone unsticking the front door from the jamb, a violent skittering following like somebody's bowled an enormous furry spider down the hallway. It crashes into a wall, and then what can only be described as a soot sprite from *Spirited Away* comes shooting into August's room.

"Noodles!" calls Niko, and then he's in the doorway. There's a leash hanging from his hand and an apologetic expression from his angular features.

"I thought you said he was a ghost in the night," August says. Noodles is snuffling through her socks, tail a blur, until he realizes there's a new person and launches himself at her.

"He is," Niko says with a wince. "I mean, kind of. Some-times, I feel bad and take him to work with me at the shop during the day. I guess we didn't mention his, uh—" Noodles takes this moment to place both paws on August's shoulders and try to force his tongue into her mouth. "Personality."

Myla appears behind Niko, a skateboard under one arm. "Oh, you met Noodles!"

"Oh yeah," August says. "Intimately."

"You need help with the rest of your stuff?"

She blinks. "This is it."

"That's . . . that's it?" Myla says. "That's everything?"

"Yeah."

"You don't, uh." Myla's giving her this look, like she's real-izing she didn't actually know anything about August before agreeing to let her store her veggies alongside theirs in the crisper. It's a look August gives herself in the mirror a lot. "You don't have any furniture."

"I'm kind of a minimalist," August tells her. If she tried, August could get her five boxes down to four. Maybe something to do over the weekend.

"Oh, I wish I could be more like you. Niko's gonna start throwing my yarn out the window while I'm sleeping." Myla smiles, reassured that August is not, in fact, in the Witness Pro-tection Program. "Anyway, we're gonna go get dinner pancakes. You in?"

August would rather let Niko throw *her* out the window than split shortstacks with people she barely knows.

"I can't really afford to eat out," she says. "I don't have a job yet."

"I got you. Call it a welcome home dinner," Myla says.

"Oh," August says. That's . . . generous. A warning light

flashes somewhere in August's brain. Her mental field guide to making friends is a two-page pamphlet that just says: *DON'T.*

"Pancake Billy's House of Pancakes," Myla says. "It's a Flatbush institution."

"Open since 1976," Niko chimes in.

August arches a brow. "Forty-four years and nobody wanted to take another run at that name?"

"It's part of the charm," Myla says. "It's like, our place. You're from the South, right? You'll like it. Very unpretentious."

They hover there, staring at one another. A pancake stand-off.

August wants to stay in the safety of her crappy bedroom with the comfortable misery of a Pop-Tarts dinner and a silent truce with her brain. But she looks at Niko and realizes, even if he was faking it when he touched her, he saw something in her. And that's more than anyone's done in a long time.

Ugh.

"Okay," she says, clambering to her feet, and Myla's smile bursts across her face like starlight.

Ten minutes later, August is tucked into a corner booth of Pancake Billy's House of Pancakes, where every waiter seems to know Niko and Myla by name. The server is a man with a beard, a broad smile, and a faded name tag that says WINFIELD pinned to his red Pancake Billy's T-shirt. He doesn't even ask Niko or Myla's order—just sets down a mug of coffee and a pink lemonade.

She can see what they meant about Pancake Billy's legendary status. It has a particular type of New Yorkness to it, something she's seen in an Edward Hopper painting or the diner from *Seinfeld,* but with a lot more seasoning. It's a corner unit, big windows facing the street on both sides, dinged-up Formica tables and red vinyl seats slowly being rotated out of the busiest sections as they crack. There's a soda shop bar down the length of one wall, old photos and Mets front pages from floor to ceiling.

And it's got a potency of smell, a straight-up unadulterated olfactory turpitude that August can feel sinking into her being.

"Anyway, Wes's dad gave them to him," Myla says, explaining how a set of leather Eames chairs wound up in their apartment. "A 'good job fulfilling familial expectations' gift when he started architecture school at Pratt."

"I thought he was a tattoo artist?"

"He is," Niko says. "He dropped out after one semester. Bit of a . . . well, a mental breakdown."

"He sat on a fire escape in his underwear for fourteen hours, and they had to call the fire department," Myla adds.

"Only because of the arson," Niko tacks on.

"Jesus," August says. "How did y'all meet him?"

Myla pushes one of Niko's sleeves up past his elbow, showing off the weirdly hot Virgin Mary wrapped around his forearm. "He did this. Half-price, since he was apprenticing back then."

"Wow." August's fingers fidget on the sticky menu, itching to write it all down. Her least charming instinct when meeting new people: take field notes. "Architecture to tattoos. Hell of a leap."

"He decorated cakes for a minute in between, if you can believe it," Myla says. "Sometimes, when he's having a good day, you come home and the whole place smells like vanilla, and he'll have just left a dozen cupcakes on the counter and dipped."

"That little twink contains multitudes," Niko observes.

Myla laughs and turns back to August. "So, what brought you to New York?"

August hates this question. It's too big. What could possess someone like August, a suburban girl with a swimming pool of student loan debt and the social skills of a Pringles can, to move to New York with no friends and no plan?

Truth is, when you spend your whole life alone, it's incredibly appealing to move somewhere big enough to get lost in, where being alone looks like a choice.

"Always wanted to try it," August says instead. "New York, it's . . . I don't know, I tried a couple of cities. I went to UNO in New Orleans, then U of M in Memphis, and they all felt . . . too small, I guess. I wanted somewhere bigger. So I transferred to BC."

Niko's looking at her serenely, swilling his coffee. She thinks he's mostly harmless, but she doesn't like the way he looks at her like he knows things.

"They weren't enough of a challenge," he says. Another gentle observation. "You wanted a better puzzle."

August folds her arms. "That's . . . not completely wrong."

Winfield appears with their food, and Myla asks him, "Hey, where's Marty? He's always on this shift."

"Quit," Winfield says, depositing a syrup dispenser on the table.

"No."

"Moved back to Nebraska."

"Bleak."

"Yep."

"So that means," Myla says, leaning over her plate, "you're hiring."

"Yeah, why? You know somebody?"

"Have you met August?" She gestures dramatically to August like she's a vowel on *Wheel of Fortune*.

Winfield turns his attention to August, and she freezes, bottle in her hand still dribbling hot sauce onto her hashbrowns.

"You waited tables before?"

"I—"

"Tons," Myla cuts in. "Born in an apron."

Winfield squints at August, looking doubtful.

"You'd have to apply. It'll be up to Lucie."

He jerks his chin toward the bar, where a severe-looking young white woman with unnaturally red hair and heavy eyeliner is glaring at the cash register. If she's the one August has to scam, it looks like she's more likely to get an acrylic nail to the jugular.

"Lucie loves me," Myla says.

"She really doesn't."

"She loves me as much as she loves anyone else."

"Not the bar you want to clear."

"Tell her I can vouch for August."

"Actually, I—" August attempts, but Myla stomps on her foot. She's wearing combat boots—it's hard to miss.

The thing is, August gets the sense that this isn't exactly a normal diner. There's something shiny and bright about it that curls, warm and inviting, around the sagging booths and waiters spinning table to table. A busboy brushes past with a tub of dishes and a mug topples from the pile. Winfield reaches blindly behind himself and catches it midair.

It's something adjacent to magic.

August doesn't *do* magic.

"Come on, Win," Myla says as Winfield smoothly deposits

the mug back in the tub. "We've been your Thursday nighters for how long? Three years? I wouldn't bring you someone who couldn't cut it."

He rolls his eyes, but he's smiling. "I'll get an app."

"I've never waited a table in my *life*," August says, when they're walking back to the apartment.

"You'll be fine," Myla says. "Niko, tell her she'll be fine."

"I'm not a psychic reading ATM."

"Oh, but you were last week when I wanted Thai, but you were sensing that basil had *bad energy for us*. . . ."

August listens to the sound of their voices playing off each other and three sets of footsteps on the sidewalk. The city is darkening, a flat brownish orange almost like a New Orleans night, and familiar enough to make her think that maybe . . . maybe she's got a chance.

At the top of the stairs, Myla unlocks the door, and they kick off their shoes into one pile.

Niko gestures toward the kitchen sink and says, "Welcome home."

And August notices for the first time, beside the faucet: lilies, fresh, stuck in a jar.

Home.

Well. It's *their* home, not hers. Those are *their* childhood photos on the fridge, *their* smells of paint and soot and lavender threaded through the patchy rugs, *their* pancake dinner routine, all of it settled years before August even got to New York. But it's nice to look at. A comforting still life to be enjoyed from across the room.

August has lived in a dozen rooms without ever knowing

how to make a space into a home, how to expand to fill it like Niko or Myla or even Wes with his drawings in the windows. She doesn't know, really, what it would take at this point. It's been twenty-three years of passing through, touching brick after brick, never once feeling a permanent tug.

It feels stupid to say it, but maybe. Maybe it could be this. Maybe a new major. Maybe a new job. Maybe a place that could want her to belong in it.

Maybe a person, she guesses. She can't imagine who.

August smells like pancakes.

It just doesn't come *off,* no matter how many showers or quarters wasted at the twenty-four-hour laundromat. She's only been working at Billy's for a week, and greasy hashbrowns have bonded with her on a molecular level.

It's definitely not coming off today, not after a graveyard shift with barely enough time to haul herself up the stairs, shrug on a clean shirt, cram the tails into a skirt, and throw herself back down them again. Even her coat smells like bacon. She's a walking wet dream for three a.m. stoners and long-haul truckers, a pancake-and-sausage combo adrift on the wind. At least she managed to steal a jumbo coffee.

First day of classes. First day of a new school. First day of a new major.

It's not English (her first major), or history (her second). It's kind of psychology (third minor), but mostly it's the same as everything else for the past four and a half years: another *maybe this one,* because she's scraped together just enough course credits and loans, because she's not sure what to do if she's not living blue book to blue book until she dies.

Sociology it is.

Monday morning classes start at eight thirty, and she's already memorized her commute. Down the street to the Parkside Ave. Station, Q toward Coney Island, off at Avenue H, walk two blocks. She can see the bubbles of train letters in her head. She's hopeless with people, but she *will* force this city to be her goddamn friend.

August is so focused on the subway lines unfolding in her brain that she doesn't notice the patch of ice.

The heel of her boot skids, and she hits the ground knees first, tights ripping open, one hand catching the concrete and the other crushing her coffee into her chest. The lid pops off, and coffee explodes across the front of her shirt.

"Christ on a fucking *bike*," she swears as her backpack spills across the pavement. She watches helplessly as a woman in a parka kicks her phone into the gutter.

And, well. August does not cry.

She didn't cry when she left Belle Chasse or New Orleans or Memphis. She doesn't cry when she gets in fights with her mom, and she doesn't cry when she misses her, and she doesn't cry when she doesn't miss her at all. She hasn't cried once since she got to New York. But she's bleeding and covered in hot coffee, and she hasn't slept in two days, and she can't think of a single person within a thousand miles who gives a shit, and her throat burns sharply enough to make her think, *God, please, not in front of all these people.*

She could skip. Drag herself back up six flights, curl up on her twin-size air mattress, try again tomorrow. She could do that. But she didn't move across the country to let a skinned knee and a coffee-soaked bra kick her ass. As her mom would say, *Don't be a little bitch about it.*

So she swallows it down. Scoops up her things. Checks her phone for new cracks. Shoulders her bag. Tugs her coat around her.

She's gonna catch her stupid train.

The Parkside Ave. Station is above ground—big red columns, mosaic tiles, ivy creeping up the brick backs of the apartment buildings that shade the tracks—and it takes August four swipes to get through the turnstile. She finds her platform right as the Q pulls up, and she's shouldered and elbowed onto a car with a few mercifully empty seats. She slides into one.

Okay.

For the next ten minutes, she knows exactly where she is and where she's going. All she has to do is sit and let herself get there.

She hisses out a breath. Back in slowly through her nose.

God, this train *reeks*.

She's not going to cry—she's *not* going to *cry*—but then there's a shadow blocking the fluorescent lights, the staticky warmth of someone standing over her, bracketing her with their body and attention.

The last thing she needs is to be harassed by some pervert. Maybe if she does start crying, a full-scale Wes-dropping-out-of-Pratt level meltdown, they'll leave her alone. She palms her pocketknife through her coat.

She looks up, expecting some scraggly man to match the long legs and ripped jeans in front of her, but instead—

Instead.

Long Legs is . . . a girl.

August's age, maybe older, all devastating cheekbones and jawline and golden-brown skin. Her black hair is short and swoopy and pushed back from her forehead, and she's quirking an eyebrow at August. There's a white T-shirt tucked into the ripped jeans and a well-loved black leather jacket settled on her shoulders like she was born in it. The set of her smirk looks like the beginning of a very long story August would tell over drinks if she had any friends.

"Yikes," she says, gesturing at August's shirt, where the coffee stain has soaked in and spread, which is the last possible reason August wants this girl to be looking at her boobs.

The hottest girl August has ever seen just took one look at her and said, "Yikes."

Before she can think of anything to say, the girl swings her backpack around, and August watches dumbly as she unfurls a red scarf, shoving down a pack of gum and some vintage-looking headphones.

August can't believe she thought this motorcycle jacket model was a subway pervert. She can't believe a tall butch subway angel saw her crying into her coffee tits.

"Here," the girl says, handing the scarf over. "You seem like you're going somewhere important, so." She gestures vaguely at her neck. "Keep it."

August blinks up at her, standing there looking like the guitarist of an all-girl punk rock band called Time to Give August an Aneurysm.

"You—oh my God, I can't take your scarf."

The girl shrugs. "I'll get another one."

"But it's cold."

"Yeah," she says, and her smirk tugs into something unreadable, a dimple popping out on one side of her mouth. August wants to die in that dimple. "But I don't go outside much."

August stares.

"Look," the subway angel says. "You can take it, or I can leave it on the seat next to you, and it can get absorbed into the subway ecosystem forever."

Her eyes are bright and teasing and warm, warm forever-and-ever brown, and August doesn't know how she could possibly do anything but whatever this girl says.

The knit of the scarf is loose and soft, and when August's fingertips brush against it, there's a pop of static electricity. She jumps, and the girl laughs under her breath.

"Anybody ever tell you that you smell like pancakes?"

The train plunges into a tunnel, shuddering on the tracks, and the girl makes a soft "whoa" sound and reaches for the hand-rail above August's head. The last thing August catches is the slightly crooked cut of her jaw and a flash of skin where her shirt pulls loose before the fluorescents flicker out.

It's only a second or two of darkness, but when the lights come back on, the girl is gone.

2

What's Wrong with the Q?

By Andrew Gould and Natasha Brown

December 29, 2019

New Yorkers know better than to expect perfection or promptness from our subway system. But this week, there's a new factor to the Q train's spotty service: electrical surges have blown out lights, glitched announcement boards, and caused numerous stalled trains.

On Monday, the Manhattan Transit Authority alerted commuters to expect an hour delay on the Q train in both directions as they investigated the cause of the electrical malfunctions. Service resumed its normal schedule that afternoon, but reports of sudden stops have persisted.

[Photo depicts commuters on a Brooklyn-bound Q train on the Manhattan Bridge. In the foreground is a mid-twenties Chinese American woman with short hair and a leather jacket, frowning up at a flickering light fixture.]

Brooklyn resident Jane Su takes the Q to Manhattan
and back every day.

Tyler Martin for the *New York Times*

"I've decided to dunk Detective Primeaux's balls in peanut
butter and push him in the Pontchartrain," August's mom says.
"Let the fish castrate him for me."

"That's a new one," August notes, crouching behind a cart
of dirty dishes, the only spot inside Billy's where her phone gets
more than one anemic bar. Her face is two inches from someone's half-eaten Denver omelet. Life in New York is deeply
glamorous. "What'd he do this time?"

"He told the receptionist to screen my calls."

"They told you that?"

"I mean," she says, "she didn't have to. I can tell."

August chews on the inside of her cheek. "Well. He's a
shit."

"Yeah," she agrees. August can hear her fussing with the five
locks on her door as she gets home from work. "Anyway, how
was your first day of class?"

"Same as always. A bunch of people who already know one
another, and me, the extra in a college movie."

"Well, they're probably all shits."

"Probably."

August can picture her mom shrugging.

"Do you remember when you stole that tape of *Say Anything*
from our neighbors?" she asks.

Despite herself, August laughs. "You were so mad at me."

"And you made a *copy*. Seven years old, and you figured out how to pirate a movie. How many times did I catch you watching it in the middle of the night?"

"Like a million."

"You were always crying your eyes out to that Peter Gabriel song. You got a soft heart, kid. I used to worry that'd get you hurt. But you surprised me. You grew out of it. You're like me—you don't need anyone. Remember that."

"Yeah." For half an embarrassing second, August's mind flits back to the subway and the girl with the leather jacket. She swallows. "Yeah, you're right. It'll be fine."

She pulls her phone away from her face to check the time. Shit. Break's almost over.

She's lucky she got the job at all, but not lucky enough to be good at it. She was maybe too convincing when Lucie the manager called her fake reference number and got August's burner phone. The result: straight onto the floor, no training, picking things up as she goes.

"Side of bacon?" the guy at table nineteen asks August when she drops off his plate. He's one of the regulars Winfield pointed out on her first day—a retired firefighter who's come in for breakfast every day for the last twenty years. At least he likes Billy's enough not to care about terrible service.

"Shit, I'm sorry." August cringes. "Sorry for saying 'shit.'"

"Forgot this," says a voice behind her, thick with a Czech accent. Lucie swoops in with a side of bacon out of nowhere and snatches August by the arm toward the kitchen.

"Thank you," August says, wincing at the nails digging into her elbow. "How'd you know?"

"I know everything," Lucie says, bright red ponytail bobbing under the grimy lights. She releases August at the bar and returns to her fried egg sandwich and a draft of next week's schedule. "You should remember that."

"Sorry," August says. "You're a lifesaver. My pork product savior."

Lucie pulls a face that makes her look like a bird of prey in liquid eyeliner. "You like jokes. I don't."

"Sorry."

"Don't like apologies either."

August bites down another *sorry* and turns back to the register, trying to remember how to put in a rush order. She definitely forgot the side of hashbrowns for table seventeen and—

"Jerry!" Lucie shouts through the kitchen window. "Side of hashbrowns, on the fly!"

"Fuck you, Lucie!"

She yells something back in Czech.

"You know I don't know what that means!"

"Behind," Winfield warns as he brushes past with a full stack in each hand, blueberry on the left, butter pecan on the right. He inclines his head toward the kitchen, braids swinging, and says, "She called you an ugly cock, Jerry."

Jerry, the world's oldest fry cook, bellows out a laugh and throws some hashbrowns on the grill. Lucie, August has discovered, has superhuman eyesight and a habit of checking her employees' work at the register from across the bar. It'd be annoying, except she's saved August's ass twice in five minutes.

"You are always forgetting," she says, clicking her acrylics against her clipboard. "You eat?"

August thinks back over the last six hours of her shift. Did she spill half a plate of pancakes on herself? Yes. Did she eat any? "Uh . . . no."

"That's why you forget. You don't eat." She frowns at August like a disappointed mother, even though she can't be older than twenty-nine.

"Jerry!" Lucie yells.

"What!"

"Su Special!"

"I already made you one!"

"For August!"

"Who?"

"New girl!"

"Ah," he says, and he cracks two eggs onto the grill. "Fine."

August twists the edge of her apron between her fingers, biting back a *thank you* before Lucie throttles her. "What's a Su Special?"

"Trust me," Lucie says impatiently. "Can you work a double Friday?"

The Su Special, it turns out, is an off-menu item—bacon, maple syrup, hot sauce, and a runny fried egg sandwiched between two pieces of Texas toast. And maybe it's Jerry, his walrus mustache suggesting unknowable wisdom and his Brooklyn accent confirming seven decades of setting his internal clock by the light at Atlantic and Fourth, or Lucie, the first person at this job to remember August's name and care if she's living or dying, or because Billy's is magic—but it's the best sandwich August has ever eaten.

It's nearly one in the morning when August clocks out and heads home, streets teeming and alive in muddy orange-brown. She trades a crumpled dollar from her tips for an orange at the bodega on the corner—she's pretty sure she's on a collision course with scurvy these days.

She digs her nail into the rind and starts peeling as her brain helpfully supplies the data: adult humans need sixty-five to ninety milligrams of vitamin C a day. One orange contains fifty-one. Not quite staving off the scurvy, but a start.

She thinks about this morning's lecture and trying to find a cheap writing desk, about what Lucie's story must be. About the cute girl from the Q train yesterday. Again. August is wearing the red scarf tonight, bundled warm and soft like a promise around her neck.

It's not that she's thought a lot about Subway Girl; it's just that she'd work five doubles in a row if it meant she got to see Subway Girl again.

She's passing through the pink glow of a neon sign when she realizes where she is—on Flatbush, across from the check-cashing place. This is where Niko said his psychic shop is.

It's sandwiched between a pawn shop and a hair salon, peeling letters on the door that say MISS IVY. Niko says the owner is a chain-smoking, menopausal Argentinian woman named Ivy. The shop isn't much, just a scuffed-up, grease-stained, gray industrial door attached to a nondescript storefront, the type you'd use for a *Law & Order* shooting location. The only hint to what's inside is the single window bearing a neon PSYCHIC READINGS sign surrounded by hanging bundles of herbs and some—*oh*—those are teeth.

August has hated places like this as long as she can remember.

Well, almost.

There was one time, back in the days of bootleg *Say Anything*. August tugged her mom into a tiny psychic shop in the Quarter, one with shawls over every lamp so light spilled across the room like twilight. She remembers laying her hand-me-down pocket-knife down between the candles, watching in awe as the person across the table read her mother's cards. She went to Catholic school for most of her life, but that was the first and last time she really believed in something.

"You've lost someone very important to you," the psychic said to her mother, but that's easy to tell. Then they said he was dead, and Suzette Landry decided they weren't seeing any more psychics in the city, because psychics were full of shit. And then the storm came, and for a long time, there were no psychics in the city to see.

So August stopped believing. Stuck to hard evidence. The only skeptic in a city full of ghosts. It suited her fine.

She shakes her head and pulls away, rounding the corner into the home stretch. Orange: done. Scurvy: at bay, for now.

On flight three of her building, she's thinking it's ironic—almost poetic—that she lives with a psychic. A quote-unquote psychic. A particularly observant guy with confident, strange charm and a suspicious number of candles. She wonders what Myla thinks, if she believes. Based on her Netflix watchlist and her collection of *Dune* merch, Myla's a huge sci-fi nerd. Maybe she's into it.

It's not until she reaches into her purse at the door that she realizes her keys aren't there.

"Shit."

She attempts a knock—nothing. She could text to see if anyone's awake . . . if her phone hadn't died before her shift ended.

Guess she's doing this, then.

She grabs her knife, flicks the blade out, and squares up, wedging it into the lock. She hasn't done this since she was fifteen and locked out of the apartment because her mom lost track of time at the library again, but some shit you don't forget. Tongue tucked between her teeth, she jiggles the knife until the lock clicks and gives.

Someone's home after all, puttering around the hallway with earbuds in and a toolbag at their feet. There's a bundle of sage burning on the kitchen counter. August hangs up her jacket and apron by the door and considers putting it out—they've already had one fire this week—when the person in the hall looks up and lets out a small yelp.

"Oh," August says as the guy pulls an earbud out. He's definitely not Niko or Myla, so—"You must be Wes. I'm August. I, uh, live here now?"

Wes is short and compact, a skinny, swarthy guy with bony wrists and ankles sticking out of gray sweats and a gigantic flannel cuffed five times. His features are strangely angelic despite the scowl they relax into. Like August, he's got glasses perched on his nose, and he's squinting at her through them.

"Hi," he says.

"Good to finally meet you," she tells him. He looks like he wants to bolt. Relatable.

"Yeah."

"Night off?"

"Uh-huh."

August has never met someone worse at first impressions than her, until now.

"Okay, well," August says. "I'm going to bed." She glances at the herbs smoldering on the counter. "Should I put that out?"

Wes returns to what he was doing—fiddling with the hinge on August's bedroom door, apparently. "I had my ex over. Niko said the place was full of 'frat energy.' It'll go out on its own. Niko's stuff always does."

"Of course," she says. "Um, what are you . . . doing?"

He doesn't say anything, just turns the knob and wiggles the door. Silence. It was creaky when August moved in. He fixed the hinge for her.

Wes scoops Noodles up in one arm and his toolbag in the other and vanishes down the hall.

"Thanks," August calls after him. His shoulders scrunch up to his ears, as if nothing could displease him more than being thanked for an act of kindness.

"Cool knife," he grunts as he shuts his bedroom door behind him.

Friday morning finds August shivering, one hand in the shower, begging it to warm up. It's twenty-eight degrees outside. If she has to get in a cold shower, her soul will vacate the premises.

She checks her phone—twenty-five minutes before she has to be on the platform to catch her train for class. No time to reply to her mom's texts about annoying library coworkers. She punches out some sympathetic emojis instead.

What did Myla say? Twenty minutes to get the hot water going, but ten if you're nice? It's been twelve.

"Please," August says to the shower. "I am very cold and very tired, and I smell like the mayor of Hashbrown Town."

The shower appears unmoved. Fuck it. She shuts off the faucet and resigns herself to another all-day aromatic experience.

Out in the hallway, Myla and Wes are on their hands and knees, sticking lines of masking tape down on the floor.

"Do I even want to ask?" August says as she steps over them.

"It's for Rolly Bangs," Myla calls over her shoulder.

August pulls on a sweater and sticks her head back out of her door. "Do you realize you just say words in any random order like they're supposed to mean something?"

"Pointing this out has never stopped her," says Wes, who looks and sounds like he stumbled in from a night shift. August wonders what Myla bribed him with to get his help before he retreated to his cave. "Rolly Bangs is a game we invented."

"You start by the door in a rolling chair, and someone pushes you down the incline of the kitchen floor," Myla explains. Of course she's figured out a way to use a building code violation for entertainment. "That's the Rolly part."

"I'm scared to find out what the Bangs are," August says.

"The Bang is when you hit that threshold right there," Wes says. He points to the wooden lip where the hallway meets the kitchen. "Basically catapults you out of the chair."

"The lines," Myla says, ripping off the last piece of tape, "are to measure how far you fly before you hit the floor."

August steps over them again, heading toward the door. Noodles circles her ankles, snuffling excitedly. "I can't decide if I'm impressed or horrified."

"My favorite emotional place," Myla says. "That's where horny lives."

"I'm going to bed." Wes throws his tape at Myla. "Good night."

"Good morning."

August is shrugging into her backpack when Myla meets her at the door with Noodles's leash.

"Which way you walking?" she asks as Noodles flops around, tongue and ears flapping. He's so cute, August can't even be mad that she was definitely misled about how much this dog is going to be a part of her life.

"Parkside Avenue."

"Ooh, I'm taking him to the park. Mind if I walk with you?"

The thing about Myla, August is learning, is that she doesn't plant a seed of friendship and tend to it with gentle watering

and sunlight. She drops into your life, fully formed, and just *is*.
A friend in completion.

Weird.

"Sure," August says, and she pulls the door open.

There's no ice to slip on, but Noodles is nearly as determined to make August eat shit on the walk to the station.

"He's Wes's, but we all kind of share him. We're suckers like that," Myla says as Noodles tugs her along. "Man, I used to get off at Parkside all the time when I lived in Manhattan."

"Oh yeah?"

"Yeah, I went to Columbia."

August sidesteps Noodles as he stops to sniff the world's most fascinating takeout container. "Oh, do they have a good art school?"

Myla laughs. "Everybody always thinks I went to art school," she says, smacking her gum. "I have a degree in electrical engineering."

"You—sorry, I assumed—"

"I know, right?" she says. "The science is super interesting, and I'm good at it. Like, really good. But engineering as a career kind of murders your soul, and my job pays me enough. I like doing art more for right now."

"That's . . ." August's worst nightmare, she thinks. Finishing school and not doing anything with it. She can't believe Myla isn't paralyzed at the thought every minute of every day. "Kind of amazing."

"Thanks, I think so," Myla says happily.

At the station, Myla waves goodbye, and August swipes through the turnstile and returns to the comfortable, smelly arms of the Q.

Nobody who's lived in New York for more than a few

months understands why a girl would actually like the subway. They don't get the novelty of walking underground and popping back up across the city, the comfort of knowing that, even if you hit an hour delay or an indecent exposure, you solved the city's biggest logic puzzle. Belonging in the rush, locking eyes with another horrified passenger when a mariachi band steps on. On the subway, she's *actually* a New Yorker.

It is, of course, still terrible. She's almost sat in two different mysterious puddles. The rats are almost definitely unionizing. And once, during a thirty-minute delay, a pigeon pooped in her bag. Not on it. *In* it.

But here she is, hating everything but the singular, blissful misery of the MTA.

It's stupid, maybe—no, definitely. It's definitely stupid that part of it is that girl. The girl on the subway. Subway Girl.

Subway Girl is a smile lost along the tracks. She showed up, saved the day, and blinked out of existence. They'll never see each other again. But every time August thinks of the subway, she thinks about brown eyes and a leather jacket and jeans ripped all the way up the thighs.

Two stops into her ride, August looks up from the Pop-Tart she's been eating, and—

Subway Girl.

There's no motorcycle jacket, only the sleeves of her white T-shirt cuffed below her shoulders. She's leaning back, one arm slung over the back of an empty seat, and she . . . she's got *tattoos.* Half a sleeve. A red bird curling down from her shoulder, Chinese characters above her elbow. An honest-to-God old-timey anchor on her bicep.

August cannot believe her fucking luck.

The jacket's still there, draped over the backpack at her feet, and August is staring at her high-top Converse, the faded red of the canvas, when Subway Girl opens her eyes.

Her mouth forms a soft little "oh" of surprise.

"Coffee Girl."

She smiles. One of her front teeth is crooked at the slightest, most life-ruining angle. August feels every intelligent thought exit her skull.

"Subway Girl," she manages.

Subway Girl's smile spreads. "Morning."

August's brain tries "hi" and her mouth goes for "morning" and what comes out is, "Horny."

Maybe it's not too late to crawl under the seat with the rat poop.

"I mean, sure, sometimes," Subway Girl replies smoothly, still smiling, and August wonders if there's enough rat poop in the world for this.

"Sorry, I'm—morning brain. It's too early."

"Is it?" Subway Girl asks with what sounds like genuine interest.

She's wearing the headphones August saw the other day, '80s-era ones with bright orange foam over the speaker boxes. She digs through her backpack and pulls out a cassette player to pause her music. A whole cassette player. Subway Girl is . . . a Brooklyn hipster? Is that a point against her?

But when she turns back to August with her tattoos and her slightly crooked front tooth and her undivided attention, August knows: this girl could be hauling a gramophone through the subway every day, and August would still lie down in the middle of Fifth Avenue for her.

"Yeah, um," August chokes out. "I had a late night."

Subway Girl's eyebrows do something inscrutable. "Doing what?"

"Oh, uh, I had a night shift. I wait tables at Pancake Billy's, and it's twenty-four hours, so—"

"Pancake Billy's?" Subway Girl asks. "That's . . . on Church, right?"

She rests her elbows on her knees, perching her chin on her hands. Her eyes are so bright, and her knuckles are square and sturdy, like she knows how to knead bread or what the insides of a car look like.

August absolutely, definitely, is not picturing Subway Girl just as delighted and fond across the table on a third date. And she's certainly not the type of person to sit on a train with someone whose name she doesn't even know and imagine her assembling an Ikea bed frame. Everything is completely under control.

She clears her throat. "Yeah. You know it?"

Subway Girl bites down on her lip, which is. Fine.

"Oh . . . oh man, I used to wait tables there too," she says. "Jerry still in the kitchen?"

August laughs. Lucky again. "Yeah, he's been there forever. I can't imagine him ever not being there. Every day when I clock in it's all—"

"'Mornin', buttercup,'" she says in a pitch-perfect imitation of Jerry's heavy Brooklyn accent. "He's such a babe, right?"

"A *babe,* oh my God."

August cracks up, and Subway Girl snorts, and fuck if that sound isn't an absolute revelation. The doors open and close at a stop and they're still laughing, and maybe there's . . . maybe there's something happening here. August has not ruled out the possibility.

"That Su Special, though," August says.

The spark in Subway Girl's eyes ignites so brilliantly that August half expects her to jump out of her seat. "Wait, that's my sandwich! I invented it!"

"What, really?"

"Yeah, that's my last name! Su!" she explains. "I had Jerry make it special for me so many times, everybody started getting them. I can't believe he still makes them."

"He does, and they're fucking delicious," August says. "Definitely brought me back from the dead more than once, so, thank you."

"No problem," Subway Girl says. She's got this far-off look in her eyes, like reminiscing about cranky customers sending back shortstacks is the best thing that's happened to her all week. "God, I miss that place."

"Yeah. You ever notice that it's kind of—"

"Magic," Subway Girl finishes. "It's magic."

August bites her lip. She doesn't do magic. But the first time they met, August thought she'd do anything this girl said, and alarmingly, that doesn't seem to be changing.

"I'm surprised they haven't fired me yet," August says. "I dumped a pie on a five-year-old yesterday. We had to give him a free T-shirt."

Subway Girl laughs. "You'll get the hang of it," she says confidently. "Small fuckin' world, huh?"

"Yeah," August agrees. "Small fucking world."

They linger there, smiling and smiling at each other, and Subway Girl adds, "Nice scarf, by the way."

August looks down—she forgot she was wearing it. She scrambles to take it off, but the girl holds up a hand.

"I told you to keep it. Besides"—she reaches into her bag and produces a plaid one with tassels—"it's been replaced."

August can feel her face glowing red to match the scarf, like a giant, stammering, bisexual chameleon. An evolutionary mistake. "I, yeah—thank you again, so much. I wanted—I mean, it was my first day of class, and I really didn't want to walk in looking like, like that—"

"I mean, it's not that you looked *bad*," Subway Girl counters, and August knows her complexion has tipped past blushing and into Memorial Day sunburn. "You just . . . looked like you needed something to go *right* that morning. So." She offers a mild salute.

The announcer comes over the intercom, more garbled than usual, but August can't tell if it's the shitty MTA speakers or blood rushing in her ears. Subway Girl points to the board.

"Brooklyn College, right?" she says. "Avenue H?"

August glances up— Oh, she's right. It's her stop.

She realizes as she throws her bag over her shoulder: she might never get this lucky again. Over eight and a half million people in New York and only one Subway Girl, lost as easily as she's found.

"I'm working breakfast tomorrow. At Billy's," August blurts. "If you wanna stop by, I can sneak you a sandwich. To pay you back."

Subway Girl looks at her with an expression so strange and unreadable that August wonders how she's screwed this up already, but it clears, and she says, "Oh, man. I would love that."

"Okay," August says, walking backward toward the door. "Okay. Great. Cool. Okay." She's going to stop saying words at some point. She really is.

Subway Girl watches her go, hair falling into her eyes, looking amused.

"What's your name?" she asks.

August trips over the train threshold, barely missing the gap. Someone collides with her shoulder. Her name? Suddenly she doesn't know. All she can hear is the whisper of her brain cells flying out the emergency exit.

"Uh, it's—August. I'm August."

Subway Girl's smile softens, like somehow she already knew.

"August," she repeats. "I'm Jane."

"Jane. Hi, Jane."

"The scarf looks better on you anyway." Jane winks, and the doors shut in August's face.

Jane doesn't come to Billy's.

August hovers outside the kitchen all morning, watching the door and waiting for Jane to sweep through like Brendan Fraser in *The Mummy*, rakish and windswept with her perfectly swoopy hair. But she doesn't.

Of course she doesn't. August refills the ketchup bottles and wonders what demon jumped up inside her and made her invite a hot stranger to tolerate her terrible service on a Saturday morning in a place where she used to work. Just what every public transit flirtation needs: old coworkers and a sweaty idiot dumping syrup on the table. What an extremely sexy proposition. *Really out here smashing pussy, Landry.*

"It's fine," Winfield says once he pries the source of her anxious pacing out of her. He's only barely paying attention, scribbling on a piece of sheet music tucked into his guest check pad. He has a penchant for handing out cards for his one-man piano and saxophone band to customers. "We get about a hundred hot lesbians through here a week. You'll find another one."

"Yeah, it's fine," August agrees tightly. It's fine. It's no big deal. Only carrying on her proud family tradition of dying alone.

But then Monday comes.

Monday comes, and somehow, in an insane coincidence Niko would call fate, August steps onto her train, and Jane is there.

"Coffee Girl," Jane says.

"Subway Girl," August says back.

Jane tips her head back and laughs, and August doesn't believe in most things, but it's hard to argue that Jane wasn't put on the Q to fuck up her whole life.

August sees her again that afternoon, riding home, and they laugh, and she realizes—they have the exact same commute. If she times it right, she can catch a train with Jane every single day.

And so, in her first month in the apartment on the corner of Flatbush and Parkside above the Popeyes, August learns that the Q is a time, a place, and a person.

There's something about having a stop that's hers when she spends most days slumping through a long stream of nothing. There was once an August Landry who would dissect this city into something she could understand, who'd scrape away at every scary thing pushing on her bedroom walls and pick apart the streets like veins. She's been trying to leave that life behind. It's hard to figure out New York without it.

But there's a train that comes by around 8:05 at the Parkside Ave. Station, and August has never once missed it since she decided it was hers. And it's also Jane's, and Jane is always exactly on time, so August is too.

And so, the Q is a time.

Maybe August hasn't figured out how she fits into any of the spaces she occupies here yet, but the Q is where she hunches over her bag to eat a sandwich stolen from work. It's where she catches up on *The Atlantic,* a subscription she can only afford because she steals sandwiches from work. It smells like pennies and sometimes hot garbage, and it's always, always there for her, even when it's late.

And so, the Q is a place.

It sways down the line, and it ticks down the stops. It rattles and hums, and it brings August where she needs to be. And somehow, always, without fail, it brings *her* too. Subway Girl. Jane.

So maybe, sometimes, August doesn't get on until she catches a glimpse of black hair and blacker leather through the window. Maybe it's not just a coincidence.

Monday through Friday, Jane makes friends with every person who passes through. August has seen her offer a stick of gum to a rabbi. She's watched her kneel on the dirty floor to soften up scrappy schoolgirls with jokes. She's held her breath while Jane broke up a fight with a few quiet words and a smile. Always a smile. Always one dimple to the side of her mouth. Always the leather jacket, always a pair of broken-in Chuck Taylors, always dark-haired and ruinous and there, morning and afternoon, until the sound of her low voice becomes another comforting note in the white noise of her commute. August has stopped wearing headphones. She wants to hear.

Sometimes, August is the one she hands a stick of gum to. Sometimes Jane breaks off from whichever Chinese uncle she's charming to help August with her armload of library books. August has never had the nerve to slide into the seat next to her, but sometimes Jane drops down at August's side and asks what she's reading or what the gang is up to at Billy's.

"You—" Jane says one morning, blinking when August steps

on the train. She has this expression she does on occasion, like she's trying to figure something out. August thinks she probably looks at Jane the same way, but it definitely doesn't come off cool and mysterious. "Your lipstick."

"What?" She brushes a hand over her lips. She doesn't usually wear it, but something had to counterbalance the circles under her eyes this morning. "Is it on my teeth?"

"No, it's just . . ." One corner of Jane's mouth turns up. "Very red."

"Um." She doesn't know if that's good or bad. "Thanks?"

Jane never volunteers anything about her life, so August has started guessing at the blanks. She pictures bare feet on hardwood floors in a SoHo loft, sunglasses on the front steps of a brownstone, a confident and quick order at the dumpling counter, a cat that curls up under the bed. She wonders about the tattoos and what they mean. There's something about Jane that's . . . unknowable. A shiny, locked file drawer, the kind August once learned to crack. Irresistible.

Jane talks to everyone, but she never misses August, always a few sly words or a quick joke. And August wonders if maybe, somehow, Jane thinks about it as much as August, if she gets off at her stop and dreams about what August is up to.

Some days, when she's working long hours or locked up in her room for too long, Jane is the only person who's kind to her all day.

And so, the Q is a person.

3

Location & Hours

MTA Lost and Found
34th St. and 8th Ave.

★☆☆☆☆ 1/21/2012

This service was NOT able to locate my lost items! I lost a very expensive hand-knitted red vicuña scarf on the Q train while visiting a friend in the city. I called the 511 number and told them exactly where I last saw the scarf, and they told me they didn't have any items matching its description and wouldn't even check the trains for it, even AFTER I told them how much the scarf was worth! The only helpful person I encountered in this EXTREMELY disappointing experience was a friendly passenger named Jane who helped me look for the scarf on the train. I can only assume it's lost forever.

The envelope is waiting on the kitchen counter when August steps inside Friday afternoon, finally free from class and work until Sunday. All she's thought about the whole walk home is mainlining YouTube eyebrow tutorials and passing out next to a personal pizza.

"You got something in the mail today," Myla says before August has even taken off her shoes in observance of Myla and Niko's strict No Shoes Indoors policy.

Myla's head pops up from behind the pile of mousetraps she's been disassembling for the last three days. Unclear if this is for the same sculpture as the frog bones. Her art is maybe beyond August's scope of appreciation.

"Oh, thanks," August says. "I thought you had work?"

"Yeah, we closed early."

By "we" she means Rewind, the thrift store responsible for her share of the rent. From what August has heard, it's extremely musty and extremely expensive and has the best selection of vintage electronics in Brooklyn. They let Myla take whatever doesn't sell home for parts. There's half a Nixon-era TV next to the microwave.

"Fuck a *dick*," Myla swears as one of the traps snaps on her finger. "Anyway, yeah, you got some huge envelope. From your mom, I think?"

She points at a thick plastic mailer next to the toaster. Return address: Suzette Landry, Belle Chasse, LA.

August picks it up, wondering what the hell her mom could have sent this time. Last week, it was half a dozen pecan pralines and a key chain mace.

"Yeah, for a second, I thought my mom sent some stuff for Lunar New Year?" Myla goes on. "I told you my mom is Chinese, right? Anyway, she's an art teacher and this year she got her kids to make Lunar New Year cards, and she was gonna send me one with some fah sung tong from this place—Whoa, what's that?"

It's not pralines, or self-defense paraphernalia, or a festive little Lunar New Year treat made by second graders. She doesn't have to open the manila folder to know it's full of archival documents, like the millions back home in August's mother's apartment, stuffed with public records and classified ads and phonebook entries. There's a note paperclipped to the front.

I know you're busy, but I found this friend of Augie's who may have ended up in New York, her untidy scrawl says. *Thought you might be able to look into it.*

"God, seriously?" August grumbles at the folder. The tattered edges peer back at her around the sides, impartial.

"Uh-oh," says Myla. "Bad news? You look like Wes when his dad sent the thing about cutting off his trust fund."

August blinks dumbly at her. "Wes has a trust fund?"

"Had," Myla says. "But, you . . . ?"

"I'm fine," August says, trying to shrug her off. "It's nothing."

"No offense, but it doesn't look like nothing."

"It's not. I mean, it is. Nothing."

"Are you sure?"

"Yes."

"Okay," Myla says. "But if you want to talk—"

"Fine, okay, it's my stupid dead uncle." August clamps a hand over her mouth. "Sorry, that—sounded fucked up. I just, uh, it's kind of a sore subject."

Myla's face has gone from curious to gentle and concerned, and it's almost enough to make August laugh. She has no idea.

"I didn't realize, August. I'm so sorry. Were you close?"

"No, I'm not, like, sad about it," August tells her, and a look of faint alarm crosses Myla's face. God, she's bad at explaining this. That's why she never tries. "I mean, it *is* sad, but he didn't die, like, recently. I never met him. I mean, I don't even technically know if he's dead?"

Myla sets the mousetrap she's been toying with down. "Okay . . ."

So, August guesses now is when she finally figures out how to tell someone what the first eighteen years of her life were like. This is where the whole charming single-mom-and-daughter, best-friends-forever, us-against-the-world bit breaks down. It's the thing that started August's cynicism, and she doesn't like to admit it.

But she likes Myla. Myla is surprising and funny and generous, and August likes her enough to care what she thinks. Enough to want to explain herself.

So she groans and opens her mouth and tells Myla the thing that's governed most of her life: "My mom's older brother went missing in 1973, and she's spent almost her whole life—*my* whole life—trying to find him."

Myla leans heavily against the refrigerator, nudging some photos out of place. "Holy shit. Okay. And so she sent you—?"

"A fuckload of information on some random person who *might* have known him and *might* have been in this area. I don't know. I told her I don't do this anymore."

"'Do this' as in," she says slowly, "look for a missing family member?"

When you put it that way, August guesses she does sound like a dick.

She doesn't know how to make anyone understand what it's like, how much she was hardwired to do this, to *be* this. She still memorizes faces and shirt colors, still wants to check the dust on every windowsill for handprints. Five years out, and her instincts still pull her back to this bootleg Veronica Mars act, and she hates it. She wants to be *normal*.

"It's—" She trips on her words and starts over. "Okay, it's like—one time, when I was in sixth grade, we had our end-of-the-year party at a skating rink. My mom was supposed to pick me up, and she forgot. Because she was at a library two parishes over looking up police records from 1978. I sat on the curb for hours, and nobody offered me a ride home because Catholic schoolgirls are really shitty to the poor latchkey kid with a weird hoarder conspiracy theorist mom. So I spent the first week of summer vacation with the worst sunburn of my life from sitting in the parking lot until seven o'clock. And that was just . . . *life*. All the time."

August puts the file back in the envelope, shoving it on top of the fridge between a case of LaCroix and a Catan box.

"I used to help her—take the bus by myself to the courthouse to file public records requests, do shady shit for information after school. It wasn't like I had friends to hang out with. But then I realized *why* I didn't have friends. I told her when I left for college that I was out. I don't want to be her. I have to figure out what the hell I'm supposed to be doing with my life and not, like, solving cold cases that can't be solved. And she can't accept it."

There's an extremely long pause before Myla says, "Whoa," and, "*that's* what it is."

August frowns. "That's what *what* is?"

"Your deal," Myla says, waving her screwdriver. "Like, what's going on with you. I've been wondering since you moved in. You're, like, a reformed girl detective."

A muscle in August's jaw twitches. "That's . . . one way to put it."

"You're like this hotshot film noir private eye, but you retired, and she's your old boss trying to get you back in the *game*."

"I feel like you're missing the point."

"Sorry, like, it's your life and all, but do you not hear how badass that sounds?"

And it *is* August's life. But Myla is looking at her like she doesn't care—not in the way people have for most of August's life—but like how she looks at Niko when he recites Neruda to his plants, or Wes when he stubbornly spends hours disassembling and rebuilding a piece of Ikea furniture someone put together wrong. Like it's another inconsequential quirk of someone she loves.

The whole story does sound kind of ridiculous. One of Myla's traps snaps shut and flips itself off the counter, skidding across the kitchen floor. It stops at the toe of August's sock, and she has to laugh.

"Anyway," Myla says, turning to open the freezer. "That sucks. I'm your mom now. The rules are, no Tarantino movies and bedtime is never."

She wrenches a tub of cotton candy ice cream from one of the overstuffed shelves and plunks it on the counter by the sink, then opens a drawer and throws down two spoons.

"You wanna hear about my mom's second graders?" she says. "They're nightmares. She had to get one off the roof the other day."

August picks up a spoon and follows her lead.

The ice cream is a radioactive shade of blue and horribly sugary, and August loves it. Myla talks and talks about her adoptive mom, about her clumsy but well-intentioned attempts at cooking waakye for Myla growing up so she could feel connected to her birth heritage, about her dad's woodworking

projects (he's making a guitar) and her brother back in Hobo-
ken (he's making his way through residency) and how their
main family bonding activity is marathoning old episodes of *Star
Trek*. August finds it soothing to let it wash over her. A family.
It sounds nice.

"So . . . all these mousetraps . . ." August nudges the one on
the floor with her foot. "What exactly are you making?"

Myla hums thoughtfully. "The short answer? No idea. It was
the same with the frog bones, dude. I keep trying to figure out
what *the* piece is for me, you know? The point-of-view piece. The
thing that sums up everything I'm trying to say as an artist."

August glances across the room at marshmallow Judy.

"Yeah," Myla says. "I have no idea what the point of view of
that thing is."

"Um," August attempts. "It's, uh. A commentary on . . . re-
fined sugars and addiction."

Myla whistles through her teeth. "A generous interpreta-
tion."

"I'm a scholar."

"You're a bullshitter."

"That's . . . true."

"Here," she says, "I'll show you what I'm working on."

She turns on her heel, hair swishing after her like the cartoon smoke of a fast getaway.

Myla and Niko's room is like August's—long and narrow, a
single window at the end. Like her, they haven't bothered with
a bedframe, only a double-sized pallet on the floor beneath
the window, a mess of linens and shabby throw pillows shot
through with late afternoon sunlight.

Myla belly flops onto it and reaches for a crate overflowing
with records. As she digs around, August waffles at the door,

eyeing the desk covered in paint tubes and epoxy cans, the round table loaded with crystals and dripping candles.

"Oh, you can come in," Myla says over her shoulder. "Sorry it's such a mess."

It is, admittedly, a mess, and the clutter makes August's skin prick with memories of magazine stacks and file boxes. But the walls are covered only sparingly with sketches and Polaroids, and August only has to step around one abandoned sweater and a tin of charcoals to get through the door.

On a dropcloth in the center of the floor, there's a sculpture slowly coming together. It looks almost like the bottom half of a person, nearly life-sized, and made up of crushed glass and computer parts and a million other fragments. Wires overflow between the cracks like vines eating it from the inside.

"I have absolutely no idea what this is going to be," Myla says as August circles it slowly. Up close, she can see the bits of embedded bone, painted gold. "I'm trying to wire it to move and light up, but, like, what does it mean? Fuck if I know."

"The detail is incredible," August says. This close she can see all its tiny parts, but from across the room, it looked like an elaborate, shimmering work of delicate beading. "It's more than the sum of its parts."

Myla squints at it. "I guess so. You wanna listen to something?"

Most of her records look secondhand and well-loved with no discernible organization. It's a level of comfortable chaos that has Myla written all over it.

"The collection," she says, "used to belong to my parents—they KonMari'd all their vinyl a few years ago, but I saved them."

"I have, like, the most boring taste in music," August tells her. "All I listen to are podcasts about murder. I don't know who half these people are."

"We can change that," Myla says. "What're you in the mood for? Funk? Punk? Post-punk? Pop punk? Pop? Old-school pop? New-school pop? New-school old-school—"

August thinks about yesterday, about Jane sliding into the subway seat next to her, talking breathlessly about the Clash and holding out her headphones. She'd seemed so disappointed when August awkwardly confessed she didn't know the band.

"Do you have any '70s punk?"

"Ooh, yes," Myla says. She whips a record out and rolls onto her back like a lizard sunning itself. "This is an easy one. You probably already know it."

She flashes the cover, black and covered in jagged, thin white lines. August thinks she recognizes it from a T-shirt but can't place it.

"Come on," Myla says. "Joy Division? Everyone who's ever been within sniffing distance of a clove cigarette knows Joy Division."

"I told you," August says. "You're gonna have to remediate me."

"Okay, well." Myla sets the record on the turntable in the corner. "We'll start here. Come on." She fluffs a pillow beside her.

August stares. She's adjusting to having friends like Winfield adjusts to days when he has to pick up a breakfast shift: cranky and bewildered. But she sinks down onto the bed anyway.

They stay there for hours, flipping the record over and over as Myla explains how Joy Division is technically not punk but post-punk, and what the difference between the two is, and how it's possible for there to have been post-punk in the '70s when there was also punk in the '80s and '90s. Myla pulls up the Wikipedia page on her phone and starts reading it out loud, which is new to August: someone else doing the research for her.

She listens to the bass lines spilling over one another, and it starts to make sense. The music, and why it might mean so much to someone.

She can picture Jane somewhere in the city, kicked back in her bed, listening to this too. Maybe she puts on "She's Lost Control" while she drifts around the kitchen making dinner, doing the easy waltz of routine, touching pans and knives she's moved from one apartment to another, a whole life full of things. August bets she has way more than five boxes. She's probably fully realized. She's probably got a daisy chain of past loves, and kisses aren't a big deal to her anymore because she's got socks from an old girlfriend mixed up in her laundry and another one's earring lost beneath her dresser.

Crazy how August can imagine a whole life for this girl she doesn't even know, but she can't begin to picture what her own is supposed to look like.

At some point, Myla rolls over and looks at her as the music plays on.

"We'll figure it out, right?" she says.

August snorts. "Why are you asking *me*?"

"Because you have, like, the energy of someone who knows things."

"You're thinking of your boyfriend."

"Nah," she says. "You know stuff."

"I don't even know how to, like, make human connections."

"That's not true. Niko and I love you."

August blinks up at the ceiling, trying to absorb her words.

"That's—that's nice and all, but you two are . . . you know. Different."

"Different how?"

"Like, you're both your own planets. You have gravitational fields. You pull people into them and that's it. It's, like, inevitable. I'm not half as warm or hospitable. No support for life."

Myla groans. "Jesus, I didn't know you could be so fucking dire." August scowls and Myla laughs. "Do you ever hear yourself talk, though? You're cool. You're smart. Maybe people at your stupid Catholic school were just dicks, man. You've got a brighter glow than you realize."

"I—I mean, I guess. That's nice of you to say."

"It's not nice, it's true."

They're both quiet, the record spinning on.

"You do too," August says to the ceiling at last. It's hard for her to say stuff like this straight-on. "Glow."

"Oh, I know."

Classes exit the drop period, and it's August and her packs of scantrons and lecture after lecture five days a week. This lands her with the latest shifts, and she finds herself audience to the weirdest characters and most bizarre events that descend upon Billy's under the cloak of night.

Her first week, she spent twenty minutes explaining to a drunk man why he couldn't order a bratwurst and, failing that, why he couldn't do pelvic floor exercises on top of the bar. Part of being a Brooklyn institution, August has learned, is collecting all the New York strangeness at the end of the night like a pool filter full of june bugs.

Tonight, it's a table of men in leather dusters loudly discussing the social scandals of the local vampire fetish community. They sent back their first order of pancakes with a demand for more chocolate chips and did not take kindly to the Count Chocula joke August attempted. They're not leaving a tip.

At the bar, there's a drag queen fresh from a gig, sipping a milkshake, all skintight catsuit and heels, her press-on nails arranged in two neat rows of five on the counter. She watches August at the register, smoothing the ends of her pink lace front. There's something familiar about her that August can't seem to pin down.

"Can I get you anything else?" August asks.

The queen laughs. "A frontal lobotomy to forget the night I had?"

August cringes, commiserative. "Rough one?"

"Walked in on one of the girls experiencing the very graphic aftermath of a vegan tuna melt in the dressing room. That's why I'm—" She gestures widely to herself. "Usually I de-drag before I take the subway, but it was fucked up in there."

"Yikes," August says. "I thought I had it bad with the Lost Boys over there."

The queen glances at the leather-clad disciples of darkness, who are patiently passing around the butter pecan syrup from one gloved hand to the next. "Never thought I'd see a vampire I absolutely didn't want to fuck."

August laughs and leans into the bar. This close, she can catch the sticky-sweet smell of hairspray and body glitter. It smells like Mardi Gras—amazing.

"Hold up, I know you," the queen says. "You live above the Popeyes, right? Parkside and Flatbush?"

August blinks, observing the way her gold highlight gleams on top of her dark brown cheekbone. "Yeah?"

"I've seen you around a couple of times. I live there too. Sixth floor."

"Oh," August says. "Oh! You must be the drag queen who lives across the hall!"

"I'm an accountant," she deadpans. "Nah, I'm playing with you. I mean, that *is* my day job. But yeah, that's me, Annie."

She makes an expansive gesture to mimic a marquee, milkshake in one hand.

"Annie Depressant. Pride of Brooklyn." She thinks about it for a second. "Or at least Flatbush. Northeast Flatbush. Kind of." She shrugs and returns the straw to her mouth. "Anyway, I'm very prolific."

"I'm August," August says, pointing to her nametag. "I'm, uh, not famous, by Flatbush standards, or any at all."

"That's cool," Annie says. "Welcome to the building. Amenities include luxurious World War II–era plumbing and a vegetarian drag queen who can do your taxes."

"Thanks," August says. Her building must have the highest concentration of aggressively friendly people per square foot in the entire city. "Yeah, I kind of . . . like it?"

"Oh, it's the best," Annie says readily. "You moved in across the hall? So you live with Wes?"

"Yeah, you know him?"

Annie takes a noisy slurp from her shake and says, "I've been in love with Wes for, like, five hundred years."

August nearly drops the rag she's been using to wipe down the bar. "What? Are y'all . . . a thing?"

"Oh, no," Annie says. "I'm just in love with him."

August opens and closes her mouth a couple of times. "Does he know?"

"Oh, yeah, I've told him," Annie says with a dismissive wave of her hand. "We've kissed, like, three times, but he has that thing where he's terrified of being loved and refuses to believe he deserves it. It's *so* tedious." She sees the look on August's face and laughs. "I'm joking. I mean, that *is* his deal. But I've never found that boy tedious."

Annie's signing her bill when she clocks out, and August finds herself walking back to their building with a drag queen towering a foot over her, the clacking of her six-inch platforms cutting the soft thumps of August's sneakers.

In the orange glow of the Popeyes, August reaches to unlock the door to the shabby little entrance of their building, but Annie heads for the Popeyes.

"Are you actually taking the stairs?" Annie asks her.

"Are you . . . not?"

Annie laughs and heads inside, and August's curiosity wins out. She follows. The guy at the register takes a furtive look around before sliding into the hallway that leads to the bathrooms, where he unlocks a door marked EMPLOYEES ONLY.

Annie gives him a kiss on the cheek as she passes, and August waves awkwardly, buoyed along by the current of Annie's energy. They take a left and there, behind Popeyes boxes and jugs of soybean oil, is something August never imagined she'd find in this wonderful shithole of a building: an elevator.

"Service elevator," Annie explains as she jams the button with her thumb. "Nobody uses it anymore, but the busted old bitch works."

On the ride up, August unties her apron, and Annie starts pulling off all six pairs of her false eyelashes, depositing them in a retainer case alongside her nails. She's got a confident meticulousness to her chaos, a perfectly contained party with champagne. August can picture her sitting in her apartment in the middle of the night, all the spare shitty bedrooms an accountant's salary can buy, humming along to Patti LaBelle as she diligently returns each nail and lash to their places in her vanity.

The elevator dings six floors up, and the doors slide open.

"Everybody says New Yorkers are so unfriendly, but you just have to know how to win them over," Annie says as she steps out. She's holding her heels, leading the way down the hall on fishnet-covered feet, yet she seems like she could go all night. "Me and that guy go way back, ever since I broke up a fight between some drunk assholes over a chicken tender meal."

"Over chicken that doesn't even have the *bones?*"

Annie hums in agreement. "Right? I haven't even eaten meat in nine years, but fuck."

They reach their doors—August's, 6F, Annie's, 6E.

"Come to a show sometime," Annie says. "And if you see me around and I'm a boy, you can call me Isaiah."

"Isaiah. Okay." August reaches into her purse and fishes her keys out. "Thank you for the elevator thing."

"It's all good," Annie says. In the soft light of the hallway, August sees the way her face transforms, Annie and Isaiah blurring together. "Tell Wes hi for me. And that he still owes me a slice of pizza and thirty bucks."

August nods, and then. Well. She's not sure what makes her ask. Maybe it's that she's starting to feel like an extra in an extremely low-budget *Love Actually,* surrounded by people loving and being loved in all their messy, unpredictable ways, and she doesn't trust or understand it. Or maybe it's that she wants to.

"Does it ever, like . . . I don't know. Make you lonely? To love somebody who can't meet you there?"

She regrets it immediately, but Annie laughs.

"Sometimes. But, you know, that feeling? When you wake up

in the morning and you have somebody to think about? Somewhere for hope to go? It's good. Even when it's bad, it's good."

And August—well, August finds herself without a single damn thing to say to that.

There are two things coiled in August's chest these days.

The first is her usual: anxiety meets full-on dread. The part of her that says, trust nobody, even and especially anyone that pushes softly into the chambers of your heart. Do not engage. Carry a knife. Don't *stab* them, but also, maybe stab them if you have to.

The other, though, is the one that really freaks her out.

It's hope.

August finished her final semester at U of M last fall in a haze of final exams and half-packed cardboard boxes. Her Craigslist roommate was always at her boyfriend's, so August spent most days alone, to campus and back in her shitty second-hand Corolla, rolling past Catfish Cabin and people spilling out of juke joints, wondering what everyone else got that she didn't. Memphis was warm, its humid afternoons and the way its people treated one another. Except August. For two years, August was a cactus in a field of Tennessee irises.

She'd moved to get some space—some *healthy* space—from her mom and the case and all the New Orleans ghosts she doesn't believe in. But Memphis wasn't her place either, so she filed the transfer papers.

She picked New York because she thought it would be every bit as cynical as her, just as comfortable killing time. She thought, honestly, she'd finally land somewhere that felt like her.

And it does, a lot of the time. The gray streets, people with their shoulders braced against the weight of another day, all sharp elbows and tired eyes. August can get into that.

But, dangerously, there are people like Niko and Myla and Wes, and like Lucie and Winfield and Jerry. There's a kindness she doesn't understand and evidence of things she convinced herself weren't real. And worst of all, for the first time since she was a kid, she wants to trust in something.

And, there's Jane.

Her mom can tell something's up.

"You sound all dreamy," she says on one of their nightly calls.

"Um, yeah," August stammers. "Just thinking about a pizza."

Her mom hums approvingly. "You're really my kid, huh?"

August has had crushes before. Girls who sat two seats over in freshman geometry, boys who touched the back of her hand at hazy UNO parties, people who passed through her classes and part-time jobs. The older she's gotten, the more she prefers thinking of love as a hobby for other people, like rock climbing or knitting. Fine, enviable even, but she doesn't feel like investing in the equipment.

But Jane is different.

A girl who gets on the train at some blurry point and off at an unknown destination, who totes around a backpack full of useful items like a cheerful video game protagonist, whose nose scrunches hard when she laughs, like, *really* laughs. She's a beam of warmth on cold mornings, and August wants to curl up in her the way Noodles curls up in patches of sunlight that haunt the apartment.

It's like touching a hot stove and laying her hand on the burner instead of icing it. It's insane. It's irrational. It's the antithesis of every wary, thousand-yard distance she's ever kept. August believes in nothing except caution and a pocketknife.

But Jane's there, on the train and in her head, pacing the floorboards of August's room in her red sneakers, reciting Annie's words back to her, *Even when it's bad, it's good.*

And August has to admit, it's good.

Wednesday morning, she steps onto the train with dangerous optimism.

It's a pretty typical crowd—a half-dozen teenage boys huddled around someone's phone, a professional-looking couple toting briefcases, an enormously pregnant woman and her daughter hunched over a picture book, tourists buried in Google Maps.

And Jane.

Jane's leaning against a pole, leather jacket shrugged down to her elbows and backpack slouching off one shoulder, headphones on, black hair falling in her eyes as she nods to the beat. And it's just . . . hope. August looks at her, and hope blooms like crepe myrtle blossoms between her ribs. Like fucking *flowers.* How absolutely mortifying.

Jane looks up and says, "Hey, Coffee Girl."

"Hey, Subway Girl," August says, grabbing the pole and pulling herself up to all her five feet four inches. Jane's still taller. "Listening to anything good?"

She pushes one headphone back. "New York Dolls."

August huffs out a laugh. "Do you ever listen to anything released later than '75?"

Jane laughs too, and there it goes again, desperate and cloying hope in August's chest. It's gross. It's new. August wants to study it under a microscope and also never think about it for the rest of her idiot life.

"Why would I?" Jane asks.

"Well, you're missing out on Joy Division," August says, referring to the talking points she may or may not have written down after Myla's punk lesson. "Though they do owe a lot to the Clash."

She quirks an eyebrow. "Joy Division?"

"Yeah, I know they're technically post-punk and all, but. You know."

"I don't think I've heard of them. Are they new?"

Jane's fucking with her. August puts on her sarcastic voice and tries to be smooth. "Yeah, brand-new. I'll make you a mixtape."

"Maybe," Jane says. "Or maybe if you're nice, I'll let you go through *my* collection."

The light shifts as they pass into a tunnel, and there's a jerk in the train's momentum. August, who has been subconsciously leaning into Jane's space like one of Niko's most desperate houseplants reaching for the sun, loses her balance and stumbles right into her chest.

Jane catches her easily, one hand on August's shoulder, the other at her waist, and August can't stop the gasp that escapes at her touch. It's lost in the grind of the train against the tracks when it shudders to a halt.

The lights black out.

There's a low murmur, a few swears from the group of boys.

"Shit," August says into the darkness. She can feel the palm of Jane's hand burning into her waist.

"Stay still," Jane says, and she's so close that August can feel her breath ruffling her hair in the dark. She smells like leather and sugar. Her hand slides from August's waist to the small of her back, sturdy, holding her in place. "I got you."

Physically, August doesn't react, but spiritually, she's fully on fire.

"The emergency lights are gonna come on . . ." Jane says confidently. "Now."

The emergency lights flick on, washing the whole car in sickly yellow light, and August blinks at Jane suddenly right there, a breath's space between their faces. She can feel the soft juts of Jane's hip bones against her, see the buzzed hairs on the nape of her neck and the soft amusement tugging at one side of her mouth.

August has never wanted to be kissed so badly in her life.

A garbled voice crackles over the intercom for thirty indecipherable seconds.

"Anybody catch that?" says the guy in the business suit.

"We're delayed on account of electrical problems," Jane says. Her hand is still settled on the small of August's back. "Indefinitely."

A collective groan goes up. Jane offers a commiserative smile.

"You speak MTA?" August says.

"I've been taking this train for a long-ass time," Jane says. She removes her hand and strides to an empty seat, slumping into it. She looks at August and nods next to her. "Might as well make yourself comfortable."

So, there they are. The two of them and a train full of strangers, trapped.

August shuffles over and takes her spot, and Jane smoothly stretches an arm across the back of the seat, behind her shoulders. She has this way of moving through the world like she owns every place she walks into, like she's never once been told she can't do something. She carries it well, because she probably *has* been told what she can't do—plenty of times—and doesn't care.

A sideways glance: Jane in profile, chin tilted up to the emergency lights. Her nose is rounded at the tip, kissable. August *cannot* keep thinking about kissing if she wants to make it out of this alive.

"So, you've never mentioned where you're from," Jane says toward the ceiling. She's still got her head back, like she's sunbathing in the dark.

"New Orleans, originally," August tells her. "Well, right outside it. What about you?"

"New Orleans, huh?" she says. She lowers her eyes finally, and when she cuts them over, August forgets she ever asked a question. Or what questions are. Or the entire process of speech. "What brought you here?"

"Um, school," August says. The lighting is already unflattering, so it can't be helping the shade of red she turns when confronted with significant eye contact from butch girls in leather jackets. "I transferred. I've tried a few schools in different cities, but I've never really fallen in love with any of them."

"You're hoping you fall in love here?"

"Um—"

"Hey, maybe you will," Jane says, and she honest-to-God winks. August is going to take out a full-page ad in the *Times* to scream about it. The city needs to know.

"Maybe so."

Jane laughs. "How's Billy's?"

"It's all right. I'm starting to get the hang of it. I kind of scammed them on my references, so I had to fake it until I figured out what I was doing."

She raises her eyebrows. "I hadn't pegged you for a scammer."

"Well," August says. "Maybe you're underestimating me."

It surprises a laugh out of her, a good laugh, deep in her chest.

Jane nudges her shoulder and leans in, close enough that the creases of her leather sleeve brush August's arm. "So, what do you think's their story?"

She jerks her chin toward the professional-looking pair a few seats down. He's in a razor-sharp suit and she's in a deep blue dress, her heels practical and pointed at the toe, and he's laughing at whatever story she's telling him.

"Those two?" August examines them. "Well, I've never seen them before, so maybe they don't usually take our train. They're both wearing wedding bands, and she's got their bags under her feet, so I'm guessing they're married. They commute together, so maybe they work at the same place. Maybe they met there." She squints through the low light. "Oh, the cuffs of his shirtsleeves are damp—someone forgot to put the laundry in the dryer last night. That's why they're not on their usual train; they're running late."

Jane lets out a low whistle.

"Damn. That was . . . detailed."

August cringes. She did the thing—the stupid detective thing—without even realizing.

"Sorry, bad habit. I grew up on true crime so I, like . . . notice stuff." She twists her hands in her lap. "I know, it's creepy."

"I think it's cool," Jane says. August turns to check her expression, but she's watching the couple. "I was imagining them as Soviet spies in deep cover."

August bites the inside of her cheek. "Oh. Yeah, okay, I can see that."

"Okay, Nancy Drew. What about that kid over there? The one in the red jacket."

And August, who was pretty convinced this was the most unattractive side of her, sits back and lets Jane have it.

"Taller than his friends, more facial hair. Had to repeat a grade, but it made everyone think he's cooler because he's older— look how they're all facing him, he's the gravitational center of the group."

"Interesting. I think he's Spider-Man."

"Yeah?"

"Yeah, he's got the build for it."

August snorts. "He does look aerodynamic."

Jane laughs, which is rocketing straight up August's list of favorite sounds in the universe. She's gonna trap it in a shell like a sea witch. It's fine.

"Okay," August says. "The pregnant lady. What's her story?"

"Not pregnant. Smuggling a big bag of pierogies."

"A bold suggestion."

"Yep. She reminds me of this Polish lady in my building who makes the worst pierogies ever." August laughs, and Jane pulls a face like she's tasting them all over again. "I mean it! Oh man, they're so bad! But she's nice so I eat them anyway."

"Well, *I* think she's a seamstress."

"How could you possibly know that?"

"Magnifying glasses sticking out of her purse," August points out. "Way too young to need those unless she does fine detail work. And look, the bottom of her right shoe is more worn off than the left. Sewing machine pedal."

"Holy shit," Jane says, sounding genuinely impressed. "Okay. A seamstress *and* a pierogi smuggler."

"Every woman a universe."

She hums under her breath, letting a comfortable lull swell

between them, until she turns to August and says, "What about me?"

August blinks at her. "What about you?"

"Come on, what's your guess? If you have one for them, you must have one for me."

And of course August has a mental file on her. August has spent weeks ticking off a list of clues about Jane, trying to parse the buttons on her jacket and the patches on her backpack to figure out how she'd kiss August if she got her alone. But Jane doesn't need to know that part.

"Um," August says. "You—you have a super regular commute—every morning, every afternoon, but you're not a student, because you don't get off with me at the BC stop. Almost the same outfit every day, so you know exactly who you are and what you're about, and you don't work anywhere formal. Past of working in food service. And everyone you meet seems to love you, so—um, so. You work the breakfast-to-lunch shift at a restaurant off this line, and you're good at it. You make good tips because people like you. And you're probably only doing it to fund some kind of passion project, which is what you really want to do."

Jane looks at her like she's assessing everything about August too. August can't tell if that's good or bad. She just knows Jane's cheekbones look really nice from this angle.

"Hm. That's a good guess."

August raises her eyebrows. "Close?"

"You got the job part wrong."

"Then what do you do?"

She sucks her teeth, shaking her head. "Uh-uh. Where's the fun in that? You gotta guess."

"That's not fair! You're being mysterious on purpose."

"I'm mysterious by nature, August."

August rolls her eyes. "Fuck off."

"It's the truth!" She chuckles, nudging her elbow into August's side. "You gotta put in a little more work to crack this egg, baby."

Baby. It's just the way Jane talks—she probably calls everyone *baby*—but it still goes down like sweet tea.

"Fine," August says. "Give me some more clues."

Jane thinks, and says, "All right, how 'bout this?"

She scoots down one seat, unzips her backpack, and upends it in the space between them.

On top of her scarf and cassette player and orange headphones are a dozen cassette tapes, a paperback with the cover torn off, and a battered hardback. Two packs of gum, one almost empty, from a brand August doesn't recognize. A few Band-Aids, a Swiss army knife, a GREETINGS FROM CALIFORNIA postcard, a jar of Tiger Balm, a set of keys, a lighter, a tube of Lip Smackers chapstick August hasn't seen since she was a kid, three notebooks, five pencils, a sharpener. She must keep her phone in her jacket, because it's not in the mix.

"They're kind of just whatever I've found," Jane says as August starts picking through the cassettes. "They can be hard to come across, so I take what I can get, mostly. Sometimes if I sweet-talk someone who has a lot, I get lucky and find something I want."

They're from different eras—first editions from the '70s, a mixed bag of '80s and '90s. There's a Diana Ross, a Michael Bolton, a Jackson Five, a New York Dolls. Each one well-loved, kept safe from scuffs and cracks. It looks like she treats them like the most valuable things she owns. Since most have to be out of production, August imagines that might be true.

"Why cassettes?"

Jane shrugs. "It's like vinyl, but portable."

August picks up the boxy player, turning it in her hands. "I haven't seen one of these in forever. Where'd you even get it?"

It takes Jane a second to answer, carefully reeling in a cassette's tape with her fingertip. "I don't remember. Between you and me, I have no idea how this thing works."

"Me neither," August says. "It looks ancient."

"This one," Jane says, pulling a cassette from the bottom of the pile, "is one of my favorites."

Its case is a photo washed out in blue, the words RAISING HELL in lime green letters.

"Run-DMC. You know 'em?"

"Yeah," August says. "'It's Tricky,' right?"

Jane takes the player and pops open the compartment. "You know . . . I have this theory that Run-DMC can start a party anywhere."

She snaps the tape into place and unplugs her headphones. August's stomach drops.

"Oh God, you're not—"

"Oh, but I am," she says, rising to her feet. "Don't you think these nice stranded commuters deserve some entertainment?"

"Oh no, no no no, please don't—"

"Watch this," she says, and to August's extreme distress, starts to undo her belt. August's brain cues up a Magic Mike number set to Run-DMC in terrifying and erotic detail, before Jane threads her belt through the handle of the player and fastens it back up.

Oh. Oh no.

"I'm gonna kill you," August says.

"Too late," Jane says, and she punches the play button.

The cymbals start up short and sharp, and when the first

line hits, August watches in muted horror as Jane grabs a pole and swings herself out, toward the rest of the train, her mouth lining up with the words about how this speech is her recital.

And, God, that tiny, ancient speaker has got pipes. It's loud enough to cut through the car, but it's New York, so barely anyone looks up.

Unswayed by the lack of response, Jane jumps onto a seat, sneakers squeaking on the plastic, and August buries her face in her hands as Jane shouts the lyrics.

And, against all odds, Spider-Man kid shouts down the car, "It's tricky!"

"Jesus lord," August mutters.

And the thing is, in New York, everyone ends up worn down by the MTA and tourists and rent prices. Everybody's seen it all. But that also means, sometimes, everyone is the smallest nudge away from delirium—from being trapped on the subway on a Wednesday morning and turning it into a '90s hip-hop dance party. Because the bass line comes in, and Jane lunges down the aisle, and the high school boys start whooping at the tops of their lungs, and that's it. It is well and truly *on*.

It's possible, August thinks, that it's not only New York catastrophe delirium making this happen. It's possible it's Jane, irresistible and blazing, her shoulders narrow but sturdy under her leather jacket, cassette player swinging from her belt as she rocks her hips. Even the emergency lights seem to glow brighter. Jane is lightning on long legs—the dark never stood a chance.

Suddenly the song tumbles out of the first chorus, and Jane is in front of her.

She throws one foot up on August's seat, leaning in on her knee, the rips in her jeans spreading open, and her expression absolutely wicked.

"I met this little girly." She reaches out to skim a hand past August's jaw, tucking her hair behind her ear. The pad of her thumb grazes August's earlobe. August feels like she's astral projecting. *"Her hair was kinda curly."*

Jane winks, gone as fast as she came, stomping down the aisle, instigating the riot, leaving August's mouth hanging open.

As the song pounds on, the couple across the way starts getting into it, her hitting the smoothest Milly Rock August has ever seen, him holding onto the pole in front of her to shake his ass. The woman throws her head back and cackles when he drops it down to the subway floor, and the kid in the red jacket and his friends scream with laughter. Even Pierogi Mom is chuckling.

The next song is "My Adidas," and then "Walk This Way," and Jane manages to keep the party going for the entire side of the cassette. She finds her way back to August, grinning with that crooked front tooth, and she jumps up onto a seat and starts loudly reciting the cassettes she has.

"Phil Collins?"

"No!" Suit Guy shouts back.

"Britney Spears?"

The teenage boys boo.

"Jackson 5?"

A mumble of assent, and she fishes a *Greatest Hits* tape out and puts it in. "I Want You Back" erupts from her speakers, and it starts again.

August is leaning on a pole now, bobbing her head along, and it's impossible not to watch Jane. She's always charming, always coaxing surly commuters into happy conversation, but she's something else today. A smirking shot of dopamine.

Even if she's sworn off solving mysteries, August needs to know Jane's story. She has to know how someone like this exists.

After the Jackson 5, the teens take over with a Bluetooth speaker from a backpack. The adults shout down Post Malone when they attempt it, but they find a compromise in Beyoncé and crank the volume up on "Countdown."

Jane's laughing so hard, tears get caught in the crinkled corners of her eyes, and she peels her jacket off and throws it down atop her pile of cassettes.

"Hey," she says, turning to August, and then she has August by the hand. "Dance with me."

August freezes. "Oh, uh, no, I can't dance."

"Can't or don't?"

"Both? It's, like, better for the world if I don't dance."

"Come on," she says, "you're from New Orleans. People got rhythm there."

"Yes, none of which was absorbed by me."

The music keeps grooving, Beyoncé wailing through a key change in "Love On Top." People keep shouting and laughing and gyrating in the aisle, and there's Jane's hand on the small of August's back, pulling her closer until they're almost chest to chest.

"Coffee Girl, don't break my heart," Jane says.

So, August dances.

And something happens when she starts dancing.

Jane's face lights up—really lights up, like Rockefeller Center's Christmas tree, Frenchmen Street at two in the morning, full-scale sunshine. She lifts August's hand above their heads; August does a clumsy spin. It should be embarrassing. But Jane looks at her like she's never been more delighted in her entire life, and August can't do anything but laugh.

It's like slow motion. Like somebody came into August's room and threw all her textbooks out the window and said, *learn this instead.* Jane pulls her back in, fingers brushing through her hair, just behind her ear, and for a second, Jane is the whole point of being in the city in the first place.

August is opening her mouth to say something when the fluorescents come back on. The train shudders back into tentative motion to a round of cheers, and Jane sways with it, away from August. She looks flushed and thoroughly pleased with herself.

August checks her phone—nearly noon. Classes are a bust. The seedy little bar where Niko works is squirreled away a few blocks from here. It should be opening soon.

She looks at Jane, a step away but still close, and she thinks about the way Jane's hand trailed through her hair, her gasp of laughter in August's ear. Just because Jane didn't come to Billy's doesn't mean it's hopeless.

"I don't know about you," August says, "but I could use a drink. There's a pretty cool dive bar right by my stop, if, uh, you're not doing anything?"

And Jane . . . stares at her, like she's trying to work out if August really asked what she thinks she did.

"Oh," she says finally. August can hear the wince in her tone before she even says the next part. "I don't think I can."

"Oh, I—"

"I mean, that sounds nice, but I can't."

"No, it's totally okay, I was, um—I didn't mean—uh. Don't worry about it."

"I'm sorry," Jane says. She looks like she means it.

August is saved by the creak of the brakes as they pull into a station. Before Jane can say anything else, she's gone.

4

Posted November 3, 2007

Cute girl on Q train between Church Av & King's Highway (Brooklyn)

Hi, if you're reading this. We were both on the
Q headed toward Manhattan. I was across from
you. You were wearing a leather jacket and red
hi-top Converse and listening to something on
your headphones. I was wearing a red skirt and
reading a paperback copy of *Sputnik Sweetheart*.
Last night, November 2nd, around 8:30 p.m.
You smiled at me, I dropped my book, and you
laughed, but not in a mean way. I got off at King's
Highway. Please, please read this. I can't stop
thinking about you.

August can never take the Q again.

She can't believe she asked Jane out. *Jane.* Jane of the effort-
less smiles and subway dance parties, who is probably a fucking
poet or, like, a motorcycle mechanic. She probably went home

that night and sat at a bar with her equally hot motorcycle poet friends and talked about how funny it was that this weird girl on her train asked her out, and then went to bed with her even hotter girlfriend and had nice, satisfying, un-clumsy sex with someone who isn't a depressed twenty-three-year-old virgin. They'll get up in the morning and make their cool and sexy sex-haver toast and drink their well-adjusted coffee and move on with their lives, and eventually, after enough weeks of August avoiding the Q, Jane will forget all about her.

August's professor pulls up another PowerPoint slide, and August pulls up Google Maps and starts planning her new commute.

Great. Fine. She'll never see Jane again. Or ask anyone out for the rest of her life. She was on a solid streak of belligerent solitude. She can pick it back up.

Cool.

Today's lecture is on correlational research, and August is taking notes. She is. Measuring two variables to find the statistical relationship between them without any influence from other variables. Got it.

Like the correlation between August's ability to focus on this lecture and the amount of athletic, mutually gratifying sex Jane is having with her hypothetical super hot and probably French girlfriend, like, right now. Not taking into consideration the extraneous variables of August's empty stomach, her aching lower back from doubles at work, or her phone buzzing in her pocket as Myla and Wes argue in the group chat over tonight's stir-fry. She's pushed through those to take notes before. None were half as distracting as Jane.

It's annoying, because Jane is just a person on a train. Simply a very beautiful woman with a nice-smelling leather jacket and a way of becoming the absolute shimmering focal point of every space she occupies. Only marginally the reason August hasn't altered her commute once all semester.

It's chill. August is, as she has been her entire life, very deeply chill.

She gives up and checks her phone.

august my lil bb i know you hate broc but we're doing broc i'm sorry, Myla's texted.

I don't mind broccoli, August sends back.

I'm the one who hates broccoli, Wes sends with a pouty emoji.

ooo in that case i'm not sorry :), Myla replies.

This should be enough, she thinks. August has, however dubiously, stumbled into this tangle of people that want her to be a part of them. She's lived for a long-ass time on less love than this. She's been alone in every way. Now she's only alone in *some* ways.

She texts back, Fun fact: broccoli is an excellent source of vitamin C. No scurvy for this bitch.

Within seconds, Myla has sent back AYYYYYYY and changed the name of the chat to SCURVY FLIRTY & THRIVING.

When August opens the door that night, Wes is sitting on the kitchen counter with an ice pack on his face, blood spattered down his chin.

"Jesus," August says, dropping her bag next to Myla's skateboard by the door, "what'd y'all do this time?"

"Rolly Bangs," Wes says miserably. Myla is a few feet down the counter, chopping vegetables, while Niko dumps the remains of a planter into the trash. "They convinced me to do a round before I left for work, and now I have to call in on account of a busted lip and emotional distress because *someone* pushed the chair too hard."

"You said you wanted to go for the record," Myla says impartially.

"I could have lost a *tooth*," Wes says.

Myla wipes her hands on her overalls and leans over. "You're fine."

"I've been *maimed*."

"You knew the risks of the game."

"It's a game you came up with when you were fried off a pot cookie and Niko's shady kombucha, not *Game of* fucking *Thrones*."

"This is why you're supposed to wait for the line judge to get home," August says. "When y'all kill one another, I'm inheriting the apartment."

Wes slumps off to the couch with a book, and Myla continues her work on dinner while Niko tends to the plants that weren't casualties. August spreads her notes on research methods out on the living room floor and tries to catch up on what she missed in class.

"Anyway," Myla is saying, telling Niko about work. "I told her I don't care who her dead husband is, we don't buy used jock straps, not even from members of the 1975 Super Bowl–winning Pittsburgh Steelers, because we sell *nice things* that *aren't* covered in ball sweat."

"More things are covered in ball sweat than you might imagine," Niko says thoughtfully. "Ball sweat, actually, is all around us."

"Okay, then, soaked in ball sweat," Myla counters. "Brined like a Thanksgiving turkey in ball sweat. That was the situation we were dealing with."

"Can we maybe not talk about ball sweat right before dinner?" August asks.

"Good point," Myla concedes.

Niko looks up from a tomato plant at August, quizzical. "Hey, what's up with you? Who hurt your feelings?"

Living with a psychic is a pain in the ass.

"It's—ugh, it's so stupid."

Myla frowns. "Who do we need to frame for murder?"

"Nobody!" August says. "It's—did you hear how the Q shut down for a few hours the other day? Well, I was on it, and there was this girl, and I thought we had, like, a *moment.*"

"Oh shit, really?" Myla says. She's switched to peppers and is slicing them with a reckless enthusiasm that suggests she doesn't care if a finger has to be reattached later. "Oh, that's a Kate Winslet movie. Trapped in a survival scenario. Did you have to huddle naked for warmth? Are you bonded for life by trauma now?"

"It was like seventy degrees," August says, "and no, actually, I *thought* we were having a moment, so I asked her out for a drink, and she turned me down, so I'm just gonna figure out a new commute and hopefully never see her again and forget this ever happened."

"Turned you down, as in?" Myla asks.

"As in, she said no."

"But in what way?" Niko asks.

"She said, 'Sorry, but I can't.'"

Myla tuts. "So, not that she's not interested, but like . . . she can't? That could mean anything."

"Maybe she's sober," Niko suggests.

"Maybe she was busy," Myla adds.

"Maybe she was on her way to dump her current girlfriend to be with you."

"Maybe she's, like, in some kind of complicated entanglement with an ex and she has to sort it out before she gets involved with someone."

"Maybe she's been cursed by a malevolent witch to never leave the subway, not even for dates with super cute girls who smell like lemons."

"You told me that kind of thing can't happen," Wes says to Niko.

"Sure, no, it can't," Niko hedges.

"Thanks for noticing my lemon soap," August mumbles.

"I bet your subway babe noticed it," Myla says, waggling her eyebrows suggestively.

"Jesus," August says. "No, there was definitely, like, a note of finality. It wasn't 'not right now.' It was 'not ever.'"

Myla sighs. "I don't know. Maybe you wait and try again if you see her."

It's easy for Myla to say, with her perfectly highlighted cupid's bow and self-satisfied confidence and hot boyfriend, but August has the sexual prowess of a goldfish and the emotional vocabulary to match. This *was* the second try. There's no third.

"Babe, can you grab me those green onions out of the fridge?" Myla asks.

Niko, who has moved on to eyeballing his homemade Alcoholado collection with extreme scrutiny, says, "One second."

"I got it," August says, and she pulls herself up and pads over to the fridge.

The green onions are on an overcrowded shelf between a to-go box of pad thai and something Niko has been fermenting in a jar since August moved in. She hovers once she's passed them off, examining the photos on the fridge door.

At the top: Myla with faded purple hair, orangey at ends, beaming in front of a mural. A blurry polaroid of Wes allowing

Myla to smear cupcake icing down his nose. Niko, his hair a little longer, making faces at a display of radishes at an outdoor market.

Below, some older ones. A tiny Myla and her brother swaddled in towels next to a sign announcing the beach in Chinese, two parents draped in shawls and sunhats. And a photo of a child August can't quite place: long hair topped with a pink bow, pouting in a Cinderella dress as Disney World glows in the background.

"Who's this?" August asks.

Niko follows her finger and smiles softly. "Oh, that's me."

August looks at him, his sharp eyebrows and steady presence and slim cut jeans, and, well, she did wonder. She's habitually observant, though she does try to never assume with things like this. But an aggressive kind of warmth rushes into her, and she smiles back. "*Oh.* Cool."

That makes him laugh, hoarse and warm, and he pats August on the shoulder before wandering off to poke at the plant in the corner next to Judy. August swears that thing has grown a foot since she moved in. Sometimes she thinks it hums to itself at night.

It's funny. That's one big thing out of the way between the four of them, but it's also a small thing. It makes a difference, but it also makes no difference at all.

Myla hands out bowls, and Wes shuts his book, and they sit on the floor around the steamer trunk and divvy up chopsticks and pass around a dish of rice.

Niko turns up the volume on *House Hunters,* which they've been hate-watching with the cable Myla stole from the apartment next door. The wife of this couple sells lactation cookies, the husband designs custom stained-glass windows, and they have a budget of $750,000 and a powerful need for an open-concept kitchen and a backyard for their child, Calliope.

"Why do rich people always have the worst possible taste?" Wes says, feeding a piece of broccoli to Noodles. "Those countertops are a hate crime."

August snorts into her dinner, and Niko chooses that moment to whip the Polaroid camera off the bookshelf. He snaps a photo of August in an unflattering laugh, a baby corn halfway lodged in her windpipe.

"Goddammit, Niko!" she chokes out. He crows with laughter and strides off in his socks.

She hears the snap of a magnet—he's added August to the fridge.

It doesn't feel like a Friday that should change everything.

It's the same as every Friday. Fight the shower for hot water (she's finally getting the hang of it), cram cold leftovers into her mouth, make her way to campus. Return a book to the library. Sidestep a handsy stranger next to the falafel cart and trade tips for street meat. Hike back up the stairs because her name's not Annie Depressant and she doesn't have the nerve to ask about the service elevator inside Popeyes.

Change into her Pancake Billy's T-shirt. Scrub at the circles under her eyes. Tuck her knife into her back pocket and make her way to work.

At least, she thinks, there will always be Billy's. There's Winfield, gently explaining the daily specials to a new hire who looks as scared shitless as August probably did on her first day. There's Jerry, grumbling over the griddle, and Lucie, perched on a countertop, monitoring it all. Like the subway, Billy's has been here for her every day, a constant at the center of her confusing New York universe—a dingy, grease-soaked little star.

Halfway into her shift, she sees it.

She's ducking into the back hallway, checking her phone: a text from her mom, a dozen notifications in the household group chat, a reminder to refill her MetroCard. She stares at the wall, trying to remember if the MetroCard machine at her new station works, wishing she hadn't had to change her whole commute—

And, *oh.*

There are hundreds of photos cluttering the walls of Billy's, mismatched frames bumping together like bony shoulders. August has passed a lot of odd hours between rushes counting celebrities who've dined here, the vintage Dodgers photos wedged between Ray Liotta and Judith Light. But there's this one photo, a foot to the left of the men's room door, a sepia-toned four-by-six in a blue pearl frame. August must have looked past it a thousand times.

There's a yellowed notecard stuck to it with four layers of tape, reinforced again and again over the years. In handwritten black ink: *Pancake Billy's House of Pancakes Grand Opening—June 7, 1976.*

It's Billy's at its most pristine, not a scorched bit of Formica in sight, shot from above like the photographer climbed proudly up onto a barstool. There are customers with blown-out hair and shorts so short, their thighs must've stuck to the vinyl. On the left side of the frame, Jerry—no more than twenty-five—pouring a cup of coffee. August has to admit: he *was* a babe.

But what makes her rip the photo off the wall, frame and all, and fake a bout of puking so she can clock out early with it shoved down the front of her shirt—is the person in the bottom right corner.

The girl is leaning up against the corner of a booth, apron suggesting she wandered out of the kitchen to talk to some customers, the short sleeves of her T-shirt rolled up above the subtle curve of her biceps. Her hair's chin-length and spiky, swept back from her face. A little longer than August is used to.

Below the cuff of her sleeve, an anchor tattoo. Above that, the tail feathers of a bird. At her elbow, the neat line of Chinese characters.

1976. Jane. A single dimple at one side of her mouth.

Barely a day younger than she looks every morning on the train.

August runs the twelve blocks home without stopping.

August's first word was "case."

It wasn't a cute word for the baby book like "mama" (she called her mother Suzette as a toddler) or "dada" (never had one, just a sperm donor a week after her mom's thirty-seventh birthday). It wasn't something that would magically make her judgmental grandparents and their old New Orleans money decide they cared to speak to her mom or know August, like maybe "tax evasion" or "Huey P. Long." It wasn't even something cool.

No, it was simply the word she heard most while her mother taped episodes of *Dateline* and read crime novels out loud to her squishy baby form and worked the one great missing persons case of their lives.

Case.

She took developmental psych her sophomore year, so she

knows crucial developmental phases. Age three, learning how to read, so she could hand her mom the file that starts with M instead of N. Age five, able to carry on a conversation independently, like explaining tearfully to the man at the front desk of a French Quarter apartment building how she'd gotten lost, so her mom could scavenge his files while he was distracted. It's hardwired.

It's too easy, now, to dig it all back out.

She's sitting on her bedroom floor, photo on one side, notebook on the other filled with five front-and-back pages of notes and questions and half-formed theories like *hot zombie?* and *marty mcfly???* Her bedspread is burritoed around her like a foil shock blanket on a plane crash survivor. She's gone full *True Detective.* It's been four hours.

She's unearthed her mother's LexisNexis password, filed three public records requests online, put holds on five different books at the library. She's shaking down double-digit pages of Google search results, trying to find some kind of answer that isn't completely batshit fucking insane. "Immortal hottie" has no relevant returns, only people in goth bands who look like Kylo Ren.

She's taken the photo out of the frame, looked at it under natural light, LED light, yellow light, held it inches from her face, walked down to the pawn shop next to Niko's work and bought a fucking magnifying glass to examine it. No evidence that it's been doctored. Only the faded shape of Jane, tattoos and dimple and cocky set of her hips, the continuing, impossible fact that she's there. Forty-five years ago, she's there.

She said it, that day she told August her name. She worked at Billy's.

She never mentioned when.

August paces her room, trying to make sense of what she knows. Jane worked at Pancake Billy's when it opened in 1976, long enough for an off-menu item to be named after her. She's intimately familiar with the workings of the Q, and presumably lives in either Brooklyn or Manhattan.

The scraps of Craigslist posts and articles and police reports and one 2015 People of the City Instagram post with Jane blurry in the background are all August has to go on. She's searched every possible permutation of Jane Su she can think of, alternate spellings and romanizations—Sou, Soo, So, Soh. No luck.

But there's something else, a pattern she's starting to piece together, one she probably would have figured out if she weren't always so determined to reason things away.

How Jane never had a heavier coat than her leather jacket, even when it was punishingly cold back in January. How she didn't know who Joy Division was, the mess of her cassette collection, that she has a cassette player in the first place. It shouldn't have been easy to always catch her train. They should have missed each other, just once. But they never have, not since the first week.

She . . . God. What if . . .

August pulls her laptop into her lap. Her hands hover indecisively over the keys.

Jane doesn't age. She's magnetic and charming and gorgeous. She . . . kind of lives underground.

The cursor on the Google search bar blinks expectantly. August blinks back.

Through a slight fog of hysteria, she remembers those weird dudes from Billy's talking about the vampire community. She was pretty sure that was some kind of BDSM role-play thing. But what if—

August snaps her laptop shut.

Jesus Christ. What is she thinking? That Jane is some thousand-year-old succubus who's really into punk music but can't keep her references straight? That she spends her nights haunting the tunnels, eating rats and getting horned up over O-positive and using her supernatural charm to maneuver SPF 75 out of strangers' Duane Reade bags? She's Jane. She's just *Jane.*

Really, sincerely, from the very bottom of August's heart: What the fuck?

Somewhere beneath it all, a voice that sounds like August's mom says she needs a primary source. An interview. Someone who can tell her exactly what she's dealing with.

She thinks about Jerry, or even Billy, the owner of the restaurant. They must have known Jane. Jerry could tell her how long he's been cooking the Su Special. If she shows them the picture, they might remember whether they ever caught her hissing at the jugs of minced garlic in the walk-in. But August's job is hanging by a thin enough thread without barging into the kitchen demanding to know if any former employees displayed signs of bloodlust.

No, there's someone else to talk to first.

5

Classifieds

Niko's described the bar where he works enough times for August to have it filed away under Pertinent Brooklyn Locations: beneath a bookstore and down a flight of creaky metal stairs that threaten to drop her into the murky bowels of the city. She's got a coffee in hand for a bribe, and thankfully the girl checking IDs doesn't say anything about it.

She can't believe she's working a case. And she *really* can't believe she's about to do the thing her mom swore she'd die before doing again: consulting a psychic.

Slinky's is exactly the type of place where she would expect Niko to work. The whole room is washed in a bloody red glow, multicolored string lights strung up over a bar that looks sticky even from here. Most of the floor is taken up with round tea tables surrounded by curved and overstuffed booths, battered purple leather patched in every fabric pattern from starry galaxy to picnic gingham. The finishing touch is the ceiling, lined with hundreds of pairs of underoos and boxers and frilly panties, the odd bra or piece of lingerie dangling from a rafter.

Niko's behind the bar in a denim vest, both arms of tattoos on full display. He grins around a chicken wing when he sees August.

"August!" He finishes his chicken wing and casually slides the bones into the pocket of his vest. August decides not to ask. "This is awesome! Hi!"

She sidles up to a sparkly bar stool, wavering between a dozen openings—*It was a two-for-one special. The barista accidentally gave me a double order. Are vampires real?*—before giving up and plunking the coffee down.

"I got you a coffee," August says. "I know how night shifts are."

He blinks owlishly through glasses, round and tinted yellow. "A gift from August? What god have I pleased?"

"I'm not that withholding."

He smiles enigmatically. "Of course not."

"You like lavender, right?" August says. "They have a lavender honey latte at Bean & Burn and—I don't know, I thought of you. I can, um, toss it if you hate it."

"No, no!" Niko says. He picks up the cup and sniffs it. "Although we *are* going to discuss your bougie choice of coffee shop later. There is a perfectly good combination jerk chicken and donut joint across the street that does cups for fifty cents."

"Okay," August pushes on. "Can I ask you a question?"

"If it's about the underwear on the ceiling," Niko says, turning away and reaching for a couple of bottles, "it started when one guy left his underwear in the bathroom and now people just keep bringing them and the owner thinks it's hilarious."

August looks up at a pair of briefs—cartoon teeth on the crotch and UNLEASH THE BEAST across the back—and back to Niko. He's lined up three bottles on his workstation and is muddling a handful of herbs and berries.

"Not what I was going to ask, but good to know."

"Ah," Niko says with a wink, and August realizes he already knew. Stupid psychics. She's still not even sure she *believes* he knows anything, but she doesn't have any other option but to trust him.

"So, um . . ." she goes on. "Your line of work . . . you know about, like, uh. Supernatural stuff?"

The enigmatic smile is back. "Yes?"

"Like . . ." August resolves not to do anything with her facial expression. "Creatures?"

"Oh, I'm loving this already," Niko says readily. "What kind of creatures?"

"You know what?" she says, hopping down from her stool. "This is insane. Forget it."

"*August*," he says, and it's not teasing or apologetic or even like he's trying to get her to stay. It's the way he always says August's name, soft and sympathetic, like he knows something about her that she doesn't. She settles back down and buries her face in the sleeves of her sweater.

"Okay, fine," she says. "So, like. You know the girl I told y'all about? The one I asked out?"

Niko doesn't say anything. When she looks up, he keeps measuring out liquors.

"Her name's Jane. She takes the same train as me. The Q,

every single morning and afternoon. At first I thought, like, wow, okay, crazy coincidence, but tons of people probably have the same commutes, and . . . I definitely went out of my way to catch the same train as her, which I realize sounds a lot like stalking, but I promise I wasn't weird about it—*anyway*, today at work, I found this."

She slides the photo across the bar, and Niko nudges his sunglasses up onto his forehead to examine it.

"That's her," August says, pointing. "I'm a thousand percent sure it's her. She has the same tattoos." She looks up at him. "Niko, this photo is from opening day at Billy's. Summer '76. She hasn't aged in forty-five years. I think she's—"

The rattle of Niko's cocktail shaker cuts through her sentence, drowning her out, and he wiggles his eyebrows until his glasses fall back down to his nose.

August is going to kick his ass one day.

She has to wait thirty whole seconds for him to pop the top off the shaker and pour the drink into a glass so she can finish. "I think she's not . . . human."

Niko slides the drink over. "Blackberry mint mule. On the house. What do you think she is?"

She's going to have to say this out loud, isn't she? Bella Swan, eat your horny little Mormon heart out.

"I think she might be . . . a vampire?" Niko raises an eyebrow, and she buries her face in her arms again. "I told you it was insane!"

"It's not insane!" he says, a laugh in his voice, but not a mean one. It never is with Niko. "Once you're tapped into the other side, it's really easy to start seeing stuff beyond this one. Like, when I was eight I spent the summer with my cousins in Bayamón, and they totally had me convinced their neighbor's dog was a werewolf. But, as far as I know, werewolves aren't real, and neither are vampires."

August picks her head up. "Right. Of course. I'm an idiot."

"Well," Niko says. "She's not a vampire. But she might be dead."

August freezes. "What do you mean?"

"It sounds like she might be an apparition," he explains. "A particularly . . . strong one. She might not even know she's—"

"A ghost?" August offers helplessly. Niko pulls a sympathetic grimace. "Oh my God, so she's *dead*? And she doesn't know she's dead? I can't even ask her on a date; how am I supposed to tell her she's *dead*?"

"Okay, hold on. You can't just tell somebody they're dead. We have to make *sure* she's dead first."

"Right. Okay. How do we do that?" She's got her phone out, already googling *how to tell if someone is a ghost*. Apparently, there's a Groupon for this. "Wait. Holy shit. She *is* always wearing the exact same thing."

"You only just noticed she has *one* outfit?"

"I don't know! It's ripped jeans and a leather jacket! Every lesbian I've ever met has that outfit!"

"Huh. Good point," Niko says thoughtfully. "Have you ever touched her?"

"Um. Yes?"

"And how did it feel? Cold?"

"No, the opposite. Like . . . really warm. Sometimes staticky. Like a shock."

"Hmm. Interesting. Are you the only one who can see her?"

"No, she talks to people on the train all the time."

"Okay, have you ever seen her touch anything or anyone?"

"Yeah, she has this, like, backpack full of stuff, and she's given me things from it, gum, a scarf. One time she put a Band-Aid on this kid who skinned his knee on the stairs."

He rests his chin on his hand. "Cute. Maybe a poltergeist. A cute poltergeist. Can I meet her?"

August snaps her eyes up from her phone. "What?"

"Well, if I met her, I could get a better sense of what exactly she is, if she's on this side or not, or somewhere in between. It'd only take a few questions. Maybe some light physical contact."

She tries to picture it, Niko in all his Niko-ness, putting his hand on Jane's shoulder: *Hello, how are you, I think you may be an unmoored spirit trapped in some kind of MTA purgatory.*

"You said you didn't want to freak her out."

"I never said that. I said you shouldn't tell somebody they're dead unless you're sure they're dead. Very bad energy."

"What would you even ask her?"

"I don't know. It would depend on how things feel. Sounds like a fun experiment."

August grinds her teeth. "Isn't there something else we could do first? Like—can I pour a ring of salt around her or splash her with holy water or something? But like, in a subtle way?"

"You and I come at subtlety from very different directions," Niko observes. "But we could do a séance."

August can practically hear her mother scoffing into her Lean Cuisine from the next time zone.

"A . . . séance?"

"Yeah," he says casually. "To talk to her. If she's a ghost, she should be able to visit, and boom, we'd know."

"And if nothing happens, we can rule out ghost?"

"Yep."

And so, August Landry, world's leading skeptic, opens her mouth and says, "Okay, let's do a séance."

"Love it," Niko says. He's produced a toothpick from his pocket and starts chewing on it as he wipes down the bar. "Yeah, we'll need numbers, so we should ask Myla and Wes. We can do it at the shop after close. I don't like where the moon is right now, though, so let's do it night after tomorrow. Do you have anything that belongs to her?"

"I, um," August says, "I do, actually. She gave me her scarf."

"That'll do."

She leans down to take a sip of her drink and promptly chokes on it.

"Good lord, that is disgusting. You're terrible at this."

Niko laughs. "Myla tried to tell you."

"So," Wes says. He's watching August douse her fries in Cholula with an extremely New England expression on his face. "You've gathered us here today to tell us you're boned up for a ghost."

"Jesus, can you keep your voice down?" August hisses, eyeing Winfield as he passes their table. She should have known better than to slide into the booth with this information after her shift and think this particular group of delinquents would be discreet. "I *work* here."

"Wait, so—" Myla cuts in. "She really used to work here? When it first opened? And now she's on the subway looking *exactly the same*?"

"Yes."

She leans back in the booth, eyes alight. "I can't believe you've been in New York for, like, a *month* and already found the coolest person in the entire city. *Back to the Future* ass."

"We're more at the intersection of *Ghost* and *Quantum Leap*," August points out. "But that's not the point."

"The point is," Niko says, "we're doing a séance to get a feel for the situation. And considering this whole thing is low-key a psychic's wet dream, we'd love if you would help."

And so, on Sunday night, the four of them are huddled together on Church Street, trying to look small and inconspicuous outside the locked door of Miss Ivy's.

"Do you want me to pick it?" August asks, glancing nervously down the street.

"What? Pick the lock?" Wes says. "What kind of feral child are you? Are you Jessica Jones?"

"We're not breaking and entering," Niko says. "I have a key. *Somewhere.*"

August turns to sniff in Myla's direction. "You smell like a McRib."

"What?"

"You know, like, smoky."

Myla jabs an elbow into Wes's ribs. "*Someone* forgot their lunch in the toaster oven today and I had to put out a kitchen fire," she says. "We're, like, *one* fire away from losing our security deposit."

"We lost our security deposit when you took it upon yourself to rewire the entire apartment," Wes replies.

Niko chuckles under his breath. He's fingering through a ring of keys in the dim glow of the streetlights. August wonders what all the keys are for—knowing Niko, he's probably talked his way into having a key to half the plant supply stores and dive bars in Brooklyn.

"How our apartment ever had a security deposit to begin with is a joke," August says. "The oven doesn't even go over three-fifty."

"And it didn't go over *one*-fifty before I rewired it," Myla says.

"Wes?"

The four of them jolt like Scooby Doo and the gang, caught in the act. Niko is not *technically* allowed to use his key for after-hours communications with the dead. No personal calls, basically— they can't get caught.

But it's only Isaiah, fresh from a gig going by the duffel bag thrown over his shoulder and the smudged eyeliner. It's the first time August has properly seen him out of drag. In his T-shirt and jeans, it's all very superhero secret identity.

"Isaiah," Wes says. Niko returns to searching for the right key. "Hey."

Even in the washed-out darkness of the street, it's obvious Wes is blushing under his freckles. As Niko would say, that's interesting.

"Hey, uh . . . what are y'all doing?" Isaiah asks.

"Uh—" Wes stammers.

Niko glances over his shoulder and says flatly, "A séance."

Wes looks mortified, but Isaiah is intrigued. "Oh, no shit?"

"You wanna join?" Niko says. "I feel good about the number five tonight."

"Sure, uh—" He turns, addressing the guy who's been waiting for him. "You good to get home?"

"No worries, babe," the guy says. He waves and heads off toward the nearest subway stop.

"Who was that?" Wes says, very obviously trying to sound like he doesn't care at all.

Isaiah grins. "That's my new drag daughter. Freshly hatched little baby. Goes by Sara Tonin."

Myla laughs. "Genius."

"Aha!" Niko crows, victorious, and the door to the shop swings open.

Niko leaves the overhead lights off and moves purposefully around the shop, lighting velones de santos like the ones he's shown her at home until the glow mixes with the moonlight and the muddy flood of the streetlights. The space is wall-to-wall shelves, full of stones and bundles of herbs and animal skulls, bottles of Niko's home-brewed Alcoholado. One rickety bookshelf sags under hundreds of bottles and jars, most filled with murky oil and labeled things like FAST LUCK and DRAGON'S BLOOD. There's a collection of pillar candles too, with cards explaining their uses. The one closest to August is either for reuniting past loves or penis enlargement. She should probably get the prescription on her glasses updated.

"So . . . is this a . . . general séance?" Isaiah says. He's on the other side of the room, examining a jar of teeth. "Or are we trying to talk to someone in particular?"

And now August is in Wes's position, stammering and hoping Niko doesn't come through with the truth.

"We're doing a séance to reach a woman August has a crush on," Niko says, coming through with the truth.

"Please, sir," Myla says in an absolutely terrible Southern accent. "It's my girlfriend, she's very dead."

August considers pulling the shelf of potions over on herself and ending it all. "Thank you both for making me sound like a necrophiliac."

"You know, I thought you were a little spicy when I met you," says Isaiah, taking it remarkably in stride.

"We don't *know* if she's *dead*," August says. "She just happens to have not aged since 1976."

"That's basically what we said," Niko says. "Follow me."

In the back is a tiny room with a round table draped in the same heavy black cloth as the walls around it. Little poufs surround it, and a shimmery, sheer scarf rests on top, purple and glistening in the low light, spirals of gold and silver stars winking up at them.

Niko's already lit a bundle of sage and set it to smolder in an abalone bowl. He's at the table, carefully arranging incense and a ring of crystals around tall white candles, the kind you see in a Catholic church when you're leaving a prayer for the Virgin Mary, except August is definitely the only virgin here and she doesn't think praying to her would accomplish anything.

"Grab a seat," Niko says. He's holding a spent match between his teeth and a lit one between his thumb and forefinger. August has never seen him so fully in his element. Myla looks turned on.

"How is this going to work?" August asks.

"We're going to try calling Jane's spirit," Niko says. "If she's dead, she should be able to project herself here and talk to us, and then we'll know for sure. If she's not, well. Probably nothing will happen."

"Probably?"

"Something else might come forward," he says, lighting another match with total nonchalance as if he has not just suggested some unknown force from the great beyond could Beetlejuice into the room and rub its little demon hands all over them. "It happens. If you open a door, anything can come through it. But it'll be fine."

"I swear to God, if a ghost kills me, I'll haunt the shower," Wes says. "You guys will never have hot water again."

"We don't have hot water now," August points out.

"Fine, I'll haunt the toilet."

"Why do you want to haunt a bathroom, man?" Isaiah asks.

"It's where people are most vulnerable," Wes says, like it's obvious. Isaiah frowns thoughtfully and nods.

"Ghosts can't kill you," Niko says mildly. "Everyone hush."

He lights the remaining candles, speaking quiet Spanish to someone no one can see. Wes tenses at August's side as the last flame goes up.

"August?" Niko says. He's looking at her expectantly, and she realizes: the scarf. She unwinds it from her neck and lays it on the table, the image of her uncle's pocketknife laid across a gauzy cloth flashing through her brain.

"Okay," he says. "Take one anothers' hands."

Myla's callused palm slots neatly into August's. Wes hesitates, looking unwilling to release his iron grip on his sweatshirt sleeves, but he finally gives in and laces his fingers through August's. They're clammy and as bony as they look, but comforting. He tentatively picks up Isaiah's on his other side.

Across the table, Niko closes his eyes and releases a long, steady breath before speaking.

"This works better if everyone is open to what's happening," he says. "Even if you don't know that you believe, or you're afraid, try to open your mind and focus on radiating a sense of welcoming and warmth. We're asking for a favor. Be kind about it."

August bites her lip. Isaiah's usual bright glow has dimmed to a reverent smolder as he brushes his thumb across Wes's hand. It's pretty late on a weeknight for a post-drag séance, especially considering he works a desk job, but he looks unbothered by the time.

"August," Niko says, and she snaps her eyes to him. "Are you ready?"

Focus. Welcoming and warmth. Open mind. She releases a breath and nods.

"Spirit guides," Niko says, "we come to you tonight in search of understanding, in the hopes we'll receive a sign of your presence. Please feel welcome in our circle and join us when you're ready."

Should August close her eyes? Leave them open? Myla slides her eyes shut, totally at peace; August guesses she's had a lot of time to get used to this kind of thing. Niko's signature look of mild constipation is taking over his face, and August chews on the inside of her cheek, fighting a wave of nervous laughter.

"Jane," Niko says. "Jane, if you're there. August is here. I'd love for you to come forward. She'd love to talk to you."

And suddenly, August couldn't laugh if she tried.

It was one thing to talk in hypotheticals—*if* Jane isn't what she seems, *if* they can reach her, *if* she's dead. It's something else to be here, breathing in smoke, face-to-face with whatever the answer might be. This girl August has spent almost every morning and afternoon with since she moved to the city, who's made her feel things she hasn't felt since she was a kid, like reckless hope—

Niko's eyelids flicker open.

"It's gonna be okay, August."

August gulps down a breath.

"Jane," he says, louder and clearer this time. "Maybe you're lost, or you're not sure where you are, or who you can trust. But you can trust me."

They wait. The second hand on Myla's watch ticks on. Isaiah's fingers twitch. Wes exhales a shaky breath. August can't look away from Niko's face, from the set of his mouth, from his lashes twitching and fanning out on his cheeks. Minutes go by in silence.

Maybe she's imagining it—maybe it's the fear, the uncertainty, the atmosphere creeping under her skin—but she swears she feels it. Something cold brushing against the back of her neck. A hoarse whisper into the creak of the old building. A charge in the air, like someone's dropped a toaster in a bathtub down the block, a surge of power just before the lights go out. The flames on the candles list to one side, but August can't tell if it's from her sharp inhale or something she can't see.

"Hm," Niko grunts suddenly, his lips pulling into a frown. Myla's knuckles go white, gripping Niko's hand tighter, and August wonders fleetingly how many times she must have done this—grounding Niko to this side while he drags his fingers through the other.

Niko mumbles under his breath, his brow furrowed, and somehow, the air settles. Something that's been unfolded tucks itself back in and ties itself off. August's ears start ringing.

Niko opens his eyes.

"Yeah, fuck, she's not there," he says, shattering the mood, and Wes deflates with relief. Niko looks at August almost apologetically. "She's not a ghost, August. She's not dead."

"You're sure?" August asks. "Like, totally sure?"

"The spirit guides are telling me wrong number, so," he says with a small shrug.

He leads them through a closing prayer and thanks the spirits politely and promises to talk again soon like they're a grandparent he calls on major holidays—which, August realizes, they might be. He blows out the candles and starts bundling the herbs back up. The others pull themselves to their feet, tucking shirts back in, rolling sleeves back down. Like nothing happened.

August is sitting there, frozen in her seat.

"What does it mean?" she asks Niko. "If she's not a ghost? If she's not dead, and she's not alive, what is she?"

Niko dumps the crystals into a bowl of coarse salt and turns back to her. "I don't know, honestly. I've never seen anything like her before."

Maybe there are more clues, something she missed. Maybe she needs to go back over all the information she has. Maybe she can break into the employment records at Billy's. Maybe—

Shit. She sounds like her mother.

"Okay," August says, standing and dusting off her jeans. She's across the shop in seconds, dodging a table of pendulums and tarot cards, whipping her jacket off the back of a chair. She jabs a finger at Niko. "You. Let's go."

When the doors of the train hiss open, there are a few terrible seconds in which August glances at Niko and wonders if she's about to make a complete ass of herself.

It's the middle of the night. What if Jane's not on the train? What if she never was? What if she's a loneliness hallucination brought on by too little sleep and too many years of not getting laid? Or worse—what if she's some nice, normal, unsuspecting woman just trying to get through her commute without being harassed by freaks who think she's a sexy poltergeist?

But Jane's there. In the middle of an empty bench, reading a book, as matter-of-fact as the scuffs on the tunnel walls.

Jane's there, and the world tips.

The skeptic in August wanted to believe it wasn't real. But Jane's here, on the same train, at the same time as August, again.

Niko nudges her on, and Jane keeps being there, long legs stretched out loosely in front of her, battered hardback open in her lap. Niko steps on behind her, and Jane looks up and sees them.

"Coffee Girl," she says, tucking a finger between the pages.

It's the first time August has seen Jane since she was rejected by her. And despite the whole undead mystery of her—whether Jane is a vampire or a ghost or a fucking teen wolf—that remains humiliating. And Jane remains distressingly hot, all kind brown eyes and ripped jeans and a soft, conspiratorial smile. It would be really helpful if Jane would stop being confusing and gorgeous while they're trying to figure out whether or not she's human.

The train jerks into motion, and Niko has to grab August's waist to keep her from tripping over her feet. Jane eyes them, Niko's fingers clenched in the fabric of August's jacket.

"You're out late," she observes.

"Yeah, we're meeting my girlfriend in Soho," Niko lies smoothly. It's a trick of the light, August thinks, when a muscle in Jane's jaw twitches and relaxes.

Niko nudges August toward a seat, and she focuses on not letting their impending interrogation of Jane's corporeality telegraph across her face.

"Neat," Jane says, a little sarcastically. "This book sucks anyway." She flashes the cover—it's an early edition of *Watership Down,* the orangey-red print rubbed halfway off. "I feel like I've read it a dozen times trying to figure out what people like about it. It's a depressing book about bunnies. I don't get it."

"Isn't it supposed to be an allegory?" Niko offers.

"A lot of people think that," August says automatically. Her voice clips up into daughter-of-a-librarian mode, and she's powerless to stop it. She's too nervous. "Like, a lot of people think it's religious symbolism, but Richard Adams said it was just some bunny adventures he made up for his daughters as a bedtime story."

"Lot of carnage for a bedtime story," Jane says.

"Yeah."

"So, where have you been?" Jane asks her. "I feel like I haven't seen you around."

"Oh," August says. She can't tell her that she changed her entire commute in mourning of the joint Netflix account they'll never share. "I—uh, I mean, we must keep missing each other. Odds are we were gonna get on different trains one of these days, right?"

Jane leans her chin on her hand. "Yeah, you would think."

Niko crosses his legs and chimes in, "You two have really always been on the same train until now?"

"The same car, even," Jane says. "It's nuts."

"Yeah," he says. "The odds of that . . . wow."

"I'm just lucky, I guess," Jane says with a grin. And August is too busy trying to figure out everything else to figure out what that means. "I'm Jane, by the way."

She leans forward and extends her hand to Niko, and excited curiosity sparks in his eyes like Myla presented him with an antique alarm clock. He takes it gingerly, folding his other hand on top, which would be weird or creepy if it was anyone but Niko. Jane's smile softens, and August watches the faintest expression flitter across Niko's face before he lets go.

"You're not from around here, are you?" he asks her.

"Are you?" she says.

"I'm from Long Island," Niko tells her. "But I spent a lot of time in the city before I moved here."

"You came for college too?" Jane asks, gesturing between Niko and August.

"Nah. My girlfriend. College wasn't really for me." He runs a thumb along the edge of his seat, contemplative. "These trains always have the most interesting smells."

"What, like piss?"

"No, like . . . you ever smell, like, petrichor? Or sulfur?"

Jane eyes him, tongue in the corner of her mouth. "I don't think so? Piss, mostly. Sometimes someone spills their takeout and it's piss and pork lo mein."

"Uh-huh," Niko says. "Interesting."

"Your friend is weird," Jane says to August, not unkindly. She doesn't look annoyed, only mildly entertained, like she's enjoying the turn her night has taken.

"He's, uh," August attempts, "really into smells?"

"Super into smells," Niko says vaguely. "Love an aroma. You live in Brooklyn? Or Manhattan?"

She pauses before answering.

"Brooklyn."

"Us too," he says. "We live in Flatbush. What neighborhood are you in?"

"Um, I'm in Flatbush too," she says.

That one surprises August. Jane's never mentioned living in Flatbush. She's also never looked quite this shifty. Niko adjusts his shoulders. They both know Jane is lying, but that doesn't mean anything—maybe she doesn't want this guy she just met to know where she lives.

"That's interesting," he says. "Maybe we'll see you around sometime."

"Yeah, maybe so," she says with a small chuckle.

August doesn't know how long Niko needs, or what exactly he's reading off of Jane, but he watches her return to her book with his hands palm-up on his knees, fingers relaxed, holding up the weight of the air.

August keeps waiting for him to bust out another question. *Hey, ever walked through a wall?* Or, *Do you have any unfinished business in the realm of the living, like maybe a tragic unsolved murder, or a loved one who needs to give all the workers at the factory Christmas off?* Or, *Do you happen to see horned creatures when you close your eyes?* But he sits there, and Jane sits there, both of them incomprehensible.

Finally, as they're pulling into the first Manhattan station, Niko announces, "This is our stop."

August looks at him. "It is?"

He nods decisively. "Yep. You ready?"

She glances over at Jane, like she might have disappeared in the last few seconds.

"If you are."

They have to pass by Jane to exit, and August feels a gentle hand close around her elbow.

"Hey," Jane says.

When August turns, that muscle's twitching in her jaw.

"Don't be a stranger."

Niko pauses on the platform to look back at them.

"Okay," August says. "Maybe I'll—I'll see you on Monday."

She turns to Niko as soon as the train pulls away, but he's eyeing the ceiling thoughtfully. She waits like she's one of the nuns at her Catholic middle school waiting to hear if they picked a new pope.

"Yep," he says finally. "Okay." He uncrosses his arms and turns, striding off down the platform. August has to jog to catch up.

"Okay, what?"

"Hmm?"

"What's the verdict?"

"Oh, tacos," he says. "I decided tacos. There's a stand that's open late a few blocks from here; we can pick some up and take the 5 home."

"I meant about whether or not *Jane* is *dead!*"

"Oh!" he says, sounding genuinely surprised. Sometimes August wishes she could know for even a second what goes on in Niko's head. "Yeah, no, I don't think so."

Her heart does an uncomfortable sort of parkour maneuver. "You—you don't? You're sure?"

"Mostly," he says. "She's really, like, present. Solid. She's not a ghost. She's corporeal. Do you think I should try the seitan this time?"

August blows straight past his question. "So, she's an *alive* person?"

"Oh, I wouldn't say that," he says. The crystals around his neck bounce against his chest as he walks. "Yeah, I'm gonna do the seitan."

"Then what is she?"

"She's alive," he says. "But . . . also not? I don't think she's dead. She's sort of . . . in between. Not here, not on the other side. She feels really . . . distant, like not totally rooted here and now. Except when she touched you, then she felt *super* here. Which is interesting."

"Is—is there any other way to test this?"

"Not that I know of," Niko says. "Sorry, babe, it's not really an exact science. Ooh. Maybe I should do the shrimp instead."

Right. Not an exact science. This is why August has never consulted a psychic before. Her mom always said, you can't start with guesses. The first thing she learned from her: start with what you absolutely know.

She knows . . . Jane was in 1976, and Jane is here. Always here, on the Q, so maybe . . .

The first time August met Jane, she fell in love with her for a few minutes, and then stepped off the train. That's the way it happens on the subway—you lock eyes with someone, you imagine a life from one stop to the next, and you go back to your day as if the person you loved in between doesn't exist anywhere but on that train. As if they never could be anywhere else.

Maybe, with Jane on the Q, it's actually true.

Maybe the Q is the answer.

Maybe the Q is where August should start.

She glances over to the opposite platform, and she can just make out the arrival board. Brooklyn-bound Q, incoming in two minutes.

"Oh," August says. It's punched out of her, involuntary. "Oh, fuck, why didn't I think of it before?"

"I know," Niko says, "shrimp, right?"

"No, I—" She spins around, lunging for the stairs, shouting over her shoulder. "Go get your taco, I'll meet you at home, I—I have an idea!"

She loses sight of Niko as she throws herself downstairs, skittering into a trash can and sending a pizza box flying. There's one way she can prove totally, definitively, that Jane is more than she seems. That this isn't in her head.

August knows this route. She memorized it before she started taking it, determined to understand. It's a two-minute ride between Canal and Prince, and Jane left in the opposite direction.

There's no physical way Jane can be on the next train to pull up, even if she ran for it. She should still be on her way through Manhattan. If she's on this train, then August knows.

One minute.

August is alone. It's nearly four in the morning.

The rush of the train comes, headlights spilling onto the toes of her sneakers.

The brakes grind, and August pictures the night fifty feet above, the universe watching as she tries to piece together one tiny corner of its mystery. She stares down at her shoes, at the yellow paint and chewed-up gum on the concrete, and tries to think about nothing but the place where her feet touch the ground, the absolute certainty of it. That's real.

She feels unbelievably small. She feels like this is the biggest thing that's ever happened in her entire life.

She lets the train cruise past until it coasts to a stop. It doesn't matter if she chases down a particular car. The outcome will be the same.

August steps through the doors.

And there she is.

Jane looks exactly the same—jacket slouched, backpack at her side, one shoe coming untied. But the train is different. The last one was newer, with long, smooth blue benches and a ticker of stops along the top next to the advertisements. This one is older, the floors dustier, the seats a mixture of faded orange and yellow. It doesn't make any sense, but here she is. She looks as confused to see August as August is to see her.

"When I said not to be a stranger," Jane says, "I didn't think you'd be back quite so soon."

They're the only two people in the car. Maybe they're the only two people alive.

Maybe one of them isn't alive at all.

This is it, then. Jane did the impossible. She is, whatever she is, impossible.

August crosses over to her and sits down as the train sways back into motion, carrying them toward Coney Island. She wonders if Jane has ever, even once, gotten out at the end of the line and sunk her feet into the water.

August turns to her, and Jane's looking back.

There's always been a schematic in August's head of how things are supposed to be. Her whole life, she managed the noise and buzz and creeping dread in her brain by mapping things out, telling herself that if she looked hard enough, she'd find an explanation for everything. But here they are, looking at each other across the steady delineation of things August understands, watching the line blur.

"Can I ask you something?" August says. Her hand fidgets up to her ear, tucking her hair back. "It's—uh. It might sound weird."

Jane eyes her. Maybe she thinks August is going to ask her out again. Jane's beautiful, always improbably beautiful under the subway fluorescents, but a date is the last thing on August's mind.

"Yeah," Jane says. "Of course."

August curls her hands into fists in her lap. "How old are you?"

Jane laughs softly, relief flashing in her eyes. "Easy. Twenty-four."

Okay. August can work with that.

"Do you . . ." She takes a breath. "So what year were you born, then?"

And—

It takes only a second, a breath, but something passes over Jane's face like the headlights of a passing car over a bedroom wall at night, gone as soon as it was there. Jane settles into her usual sly smile. August never considered how much of a deflection that smile was.

"Why're you asking?"

"Well," August says carefully. She's watching Jane, and Jane is watching her, and she can feel this moment opening up like a manhole beneath them, waiting for them to drop. "I'm twenty-three. You should have been born about a year before me."

Jane stiffens, unreadable. "Right."

"So," August says. She braces herself. "So that's . . . that's 1995."

Jane's smile flickers out, and August swears a fluorescent light above them dims too.

"What?"

"I was born in 1996, so you should have been born in 1995," August tells her. "But you weren't, were you?"

The sleeve of Jane's jacket has ridden up on one side, and she's tracing the characters above her elbow, digging her fingertips in so the color flows out of her skin under the ink.

"Okay," she says, trying on a different smile, her eyes dropping to the floor. "You're fucking with me. I get it. You're very cute and funny."

"Jane, what year were you born?"

"I said I got it, August."

"Jane—"

"Look," she says, and when her eyes flash up, it's there, the thing August glimpsed before—anger, fear. She was half-expecting

Jane to laugh it off, like she does her cassette player and her back-pack full of years. She doesn't. "I know something's . . . wrong with me. But you don't have to fuck with me, okay?"

She doesn't know. How can she not know?

It's the first time Jane's let it show, her uncertainty, and the lines of her are filled in a little more. She was this dream girl, too good to be true, but she's real, finally, as real as August's sneakers on the subway platform. Lost. *That* August can understand.

"Jane," August says carefully. "I'm not fucking with you."

She pulls out the photo, unfolds it, smooths out the crease down the middle. She shows it to Jane—the washed-out, yellow-tinted booths, the faded neon of the sign above the to-go counter. Jane's smile, frozen in time.

"That's you, right?"

It comes over Jane in a breathless rush, like the train blow-ing August's hair back as it hurtles into the station.

"Yeah . . . yeah, that's me," Jane says. Her hands only shake a little when she takes the photo. "I told you. I got a job there right after it opened."

"Jane." The train trundles on. The word is almost too quiet to be heard over the noise. "This photo was taken in 1976."

"That sounds right," she says distantly. She's stopped tracing the tattoo on her arm—instead tracing the shape of her chin in the photo. August wonders what the distance is between the person in front of her and the one in the photo. Decades. No time at all. "I moved here a couple of years ago."

"Do you know what year?"

"God, probably. . . .'75?"

August concentrates on keeping her face and voice calm, like she's talking to someone on a ledge. "Okay. I'm gonna ask you something. I swear to God, I am not fucking with you. Try to hear me out. Do you remember the last time you weren't on this train?"

"August . . ."

"Please. Just try to remember."

She looks up at August. Her eyes are shining, wet.

"I—" she starts. "I don't know. *I don't know.* It's—it's blurry. It's all blurry. As far back as I can remember. I know I—I worked at Billy's. 1976. That's the last thing I remember, and I only know because you reminded me. You—you brought that back, I guess." Her usual confidence is gone, a shaky, panicked girl in its place. "I told you, I think, um. Something's wrong with me."

August settles a hand over Jane's wrist, bringing the photo down into her lap. She's never touched her like this before. She's never had the nerve before. She's never ruined somebody's life before.

"Okay," August says. "It's okay. There's nothing wrong with you. But I think something happened to you. And I think you've been stuck on this train for a long time. Like, a really long time."

"How long?"

"Um. About forty-five years."

August waits for her to laugh, cry, cuss her out, have some kind of meltdown. Instead, she reaches for a pole and pulls herself to her feet, her balance practiced and sure even as the train takes a curve.

When she turns to August, her jaw is set, her gaze steady and dark. She's heartbreakingly gorgeous, even now. Especially now: squared up to the universe.

"That's a long fucking time, huh?" she says flatly.

"What, um," August attempts. "What *can* you remember?"

"I remember . . ." she says. "I remember moments. Sometimes days, or only hours. I knew I was stuck here, somehow. I know I've tried to get off and blinked and opened my eyes in a different car. I remember some people I've met. That half the things in my bag are something I traded for, stole, or found. But it's— it's all fuzzy. You know when you drink too much and black out except for random pieces? It's like that. If I had to guess, I would've said I've been on here for . . . maybe a few months."

"And before? What do you remember before you were on the train?"

She fixes August with a flat gaze. "Nothing."

"Nothing?"

"Nothing but a flash of Billy's."

August bites down on her lip. "You remember your name."

Jane looks at her like she feels sorry for her, one side of her mouth pulling into a joyless approximation of her smile. She takes her jacket off and flips it around, inside-out. The worn fabric tag sticks out from the inside of the collar, block letters embroidered in careful red thread.

JANE SU

"I know my name because this jacket says it's my name," she says. "I have no fucking idea who I am."

6

JULY 25, 1976

Bunch of Punks

*Jayne County, New York Dolls, and
the teeming life inside Max's Kansas
City, a punk haven in Gramercy*

***"I left a bloodstain on that booth
over there. I kissed that bartender.
That one slept on my couch last
week. Anybody who says punk isn't
queer doesn't know what punk is."***

—Jane Su

"Okay, now!"

Jane jumps, and—

She's gone, again.

August sighs and steps onto the train before the doors close, making a note on the miniature steno she's started keeping in her jacket pocket. *Bergen Ave.: nope.*

"This is getting repetitive," says Jane's voice, her chin suddenly on August's shoulder. August yelps and stumbles back into her.

"I know," August says, letting Jane right her, "but what if one of these stops is the one you can get off at? We have to know what we're dealing with."

They try it at every stop, starting at the shiny Ninety-sixth Street Station on the Manhattan end. Every time the door opens, August steps out and says, "Now!" And Jane tries to get off.

It's not like she sees Jane physically disappear or reappear. Jane will take a step or a hop or—once in a moment of delirious frustration—a running leap through the open doors, and nothing happens. She doesn't smack into an invisible barrier or vanish with a pop. She's just there, and then she's not.

Sometimes she resets to the place where she was standing when she started. Sometimes August blinks and Jane's on the other end of the same car. Sometimes she's gone completely, and August has to wait for the next train to find her waiting against a pole. Not a single passenger notices her sudden presence; they continue their audiobooks and mascara applications like she was there all along. Like reality bends around her.

"So, you really can't get off the train," August finally admits under the glass and steel arches of Coney Island, the very last stop on the line. Jane can't get off there either.

That's the first step, figuring out how trapped Jane is. The answer is: very completely trapped. The next question is, how?

August has absolutely no fucking clue.

She's only ever dealt with hard facts. Concrete and quantifiable evidence. She can reason her way through this right up to the point of understanding how it is happening, and then: dead end. A wall made of things that aren't supposed to be possible.

Jane, ultimately, is a good sport. She's adjusting remarkably well to being forty-five years from home and doomed to take the same subway ride every minute of every day—she grins and says, "Honestly, it's nicer than my first apartment, according to the 0.5 seconds I remember of it." She eyes August with some unreadable significance. "Better company too."

But Jane still doesn't know who she is, or *why* she is, or what happened to get her stuck.

August looks at her as the train reverses past Gravesend rooftops, this girl out of time, the same face and body and hair and smile that took August's life by the shoulders in January and shook. And she can't believe Jane had the nerve, the *audacity*, to become the one thing August can't resist: a mystery.

"Okay," August says. "Time to figure out who you are."

The afternoon sun falls in Jane's brown eyes, and August thinks she's going to need more notebooks. It'll take a million to hold this girl.

When August was eight, her mom took her to the levee.

It was right after the Fourth of July. She was turning nine soon and really into her age that year. She'd tell everyone that she wasn't eight but eight and a half, eight and three-quarters. Going to the levee was one of the few things they ever did without a case file between them—just a gallon-size bag of watermelon slices and a beach towel and a perfect spot to sit.

She remembers her mother's hair, how the coppery brown would glow under the summer sun like the wet planks of the docks. She always liked how it was the same as hers, how they shared so many things. It was in those moments that August sometimes pictured how her mom looked when she was younger, before she had August, and at the same time, she couldn't begin to imagine a time when they didn't have each other. August had her and she had August, and they had secret codes they spoke in, and that was it. That was enough.

She remembers her mom explaining what levees were for. They weren't made for beach towel picnics, she said—they were made to protect them. To keep water out when storms came.

It wasn't long afterward that a storm too big for the levees came. 2005. Their apartment in Belle Chasse, the Idlewild place, got eight feet of water. All the files, maps, photos, all the years of handwritten notes, a wet pulp shoveled out the window of a condemned building. August's mom saved one tupperware tub of files on her brother and not a single one of August's baby pictures. August lost everything and thought that maybe, if she could become someone who didn't have anything to lose, she'd never have to feel that way again.

She turned nine in a Red Cross shelter, and something started to sour in her heart, and she couldn't stop it.

August sits on the edge of an air mattress in Brooklyn and tries to imagine how it would feel if she didn't have any of those memories to understand what made her who she is. If she woke up one day and just *was* and didn't know why.

Nobody tells you how those nights that stand out in your memory—levee sunset nights, hurricane nights, first kiss nights, homesick sleepover nights, nights when you stood at your bedroom window and looked at the lilies one porch over and thought they would stand out, singular and crystallized, in your memory forever—they aren't really anything. They're everything, and they're nothing. They make you who you are, and they happen at the same time a twenty-three-year-old a million miles away is warming up some leftovers, turning in early, switching off the lamp. They're so easy to lose.

You don't learn until you're older how to zoom out of that extreme proximity and make it fit into the bigger picture of your life. August didn't learn until she sat knee-to-knee with a girl who couldn't remember who she was, and tried to help her piece everything back together.

The next few days go like this:

August's alarm goes off for class. Her shifts come up at Billy's. Her essays and projects and exams stay looming over her like a cave full of bats. She ignores all of it.

She goes back in to work exactly one time, to hang the opening day photo back up on the wall and waylay Jerry as he passes it on his way out of the bathroom.

"Hey," she says, "I never noticed how cool this picture was. The seventies seem like a hell of a time."

"That's what I've been told," Jerry says. "I barely remember 'em."

"I mean, you must remember this, though, right? Opening day? All the original Billy's crew?"

She holds her breath as he leans in to squint at the photo. "Buttercup, any one of these sons of bitches could walk in here and sock me in the face and I wouldn't even know it was them."

She pushes it. "Not even the one who invented the Su Special?"

"I was what you might call an alcoholic at the time," Jerry says. "I'm lucky I can remember what goes in the sandwich at all."

"Are you sure?"

Jerry raises a bushy eyebrow at her. "Y'know people in New York mind their business, right?"

He trudges back to the kitchen, August frowning after him. How can he have forgotten Jane?

She flags down Lucie on her way out, asking about the last time Billy himself visited the restaurant, thinking maybe she could ask him—but, no. He's mostly retired, lives in Jersey now with his family and almost never comes in, just signs the paychecks. He's put Lucie and Winfield in charge and doesn't seem to be welcoming phone calls from rookie servers new to the city.

So, she leaves. She skips class. She calls in sick to work. She listens to Lucie tut at her over the phone, like she knows August is faking. She doesn't care.

Instead, she shoves her legs into jeans and her feet into Vans and her heart deep, deep down into her chest where it can't do anything stupid, and she swipes her way into her station.

Every morning, Jane's there. Usually the seats are a cool, clean blue, the lights shiny and bright, but occasionally, it's an old train, burnt orange seats with FUCK REAGAN scrawled down the side in faded marker. Sometimes there are only a few sleepy commuters, and sometimes it's packed with finance guys barking down their phones and huskers singing into the morning rush.

But Jane's always there. So August is too.

"I still don't understand," Wes says, when August finally manages to wrangle everyone into the same room. He's just stumbled home from the tattoo shop, bagel in hand, while Niko blearily pours himself coffee and Myla brushes her teeth over the kitchen sink. The bathroom plumbing must be acting up again.

"She's stuck on the train," August explains for what feels like the five hundredth time. "She's lost in time from the '70s, and she can't leave the Q train, and she doesn't remember anything before she got there."

"And you, like," Wes says, "*definitely* ruled out the possibility that she's making it up?"

"She's honest," Niko mumbles. He looks perturbed at having to open his third eye before eight in the morning. He's barely opened his two regular ones. "I met her. I could tell. Honest and sane."

"No offense, but you said the same thing about the guy who moved in downstairs, and he stole all my weed and ghosted me and moved to Long Beach to be stoned all the time. Less honest and sane and more comatose in California."

Myla spits in the sink. "*Comatose in California* is my favorite Lana Del Rey album."

"He's right," August cuts in. "I believe her. She's never not on the train when I get on, even if it's a different train a minute later. I don't see how she can do that unless she's not living by the laws of reality."

"So, what are you gonna do? *50 First Dates*? Girlfriend with no memories?"

"*First* of all," August says, gathering up her bag and sweater, "that movie was about short-term memory loss, not long-term memory loss—she remembers who I am. *Second* of all, she's not my girlfriend."

"You're wearing that red lipstick for her, though," Myla points out.

"I—that is a style choice." August maneuvers her sweater over her head so nobody can see what color her face is and talks through the wool. "Even if she wanted me to be her girlfriend,

I can't. We don't even know who she *is*. Figuring that out is way more important."

"So altruistic of you," Wes says, unwrapping his bagel. "I— Oh goddammit, they got my order wrong. How absolutely dare they."

"Criminal," Myla says.

"I go there every single morning and order the exact same thing, and they still can't get my order right. The *disrespect*. We live in a *society*."

"Good luck with that," August says, shouldering her bag. "I gotta go un-amnesia a ghost."

"She's not a ghost," Niko says, but she's already out the door.

Wes did give her an idea, though. She doesn't know how to fix Jane, but rule one is start with what you know. She knows Jane was a New Yorker. So they start there: with her coffee and bagel order.

"I don't remember," she says when August asks. "That's how it is with a lot of stuff. I remember I got here. I know there was stuff before it. But I don't remember what it was or how I felt, until something *sparks*. Like when I saw that lady who reminded me of my neighbor with the pierogies."

"It's okay," August says, and she hands over a coffee with one sugar and a plain bagel with cream cheese. "You lived in New York for at least a couple of years. There's no way you don't have a coffee and bagel order. We'll do process of elimination."

Jane takes one bite and wrinkles her nose. "I don't think this is it."

For the next four days, August brings her a different coffee and bagel. Black and an everything with lox. Cappuccino with cinnamon and a toasted parmesan with garlic herb. It's not until day five (chocolate chip and peanut butter) that she opens the paper bag and sniffs and says, "Oh my God. *Choc-olate.*"

"Jesus," August says, as Jane downs half of it in one bite like a boa constrictor. "Every New Yorker in a thirty-mile radius just became irate and they don't know why."

"Yeah. The guy at the deli always looked so disgusted."

"Like, at that point, why not eat a donut?"

"Less filling," she says through a mouthful. And then she grabs August's hand and says, "Wait. Five sugars!" And that's how they discover Jane's incorrigible sweet tooth. She takes her coffee with two creams and five sugars like some kind of maniac. August starts bringing her a chocolate chip bagel with peanut butter and a coffee full of sugar and cream every morning.

She rides the line up and down and back up again. On a Tuesday afternoon, across the East River and over the Manhattan Bridge, alongside all the landmarks she grew up pressing into the corners of envelopes in the shape of postage stamps. On a Saturday morning, down to Coney Island and the arching rafters of the station, jostled by toddlers with floppy hats and sunscreen streaks and resigned parents with beach bags.

"Who goes to the beach in March?" August mumbles as they wait for the train to pull back out of Coney Island, the end of the line. It's the longest the train is ever stationary. Jane likes to claim you can hear the ocean if you try hard enough.

"Come on, end of winter picnics near the shore?" Jane says, waving her bagel in the air. "*I* happen to think they're romantic as hell."

She glances at August like she expects a response, like there was a joke and August missed the punchline. August pulls a face and keeps eating.

They sit and eat their bagels and talk. That's all there is to do—August has hit a dead end. Without clues about her family or her life before New York, Jane is the primary source.

Her primary source, and her friend, now.

That's all. Nothing more than that. That's all it can be.

August glances at the peanut butter left behind on Jane's lip.

It's fine.

On a Wednesday, Jane's on her third bite of bagel when she remembers her elementary school.

The city's vague, but she remembers a tiny classroom, and other kids from her neighborhood sitting in tiny desks and tiny chairs, and a poster of a hot-air balloon on the wall. She remembers the smell of pencil shavings and her first best friend, a girl named Jia who loved peanut butter sandwiches, and the foggy walk between their homes, the smell of wet pavement from shopkeepers hosing down their sidewalks at the end of the night.

Another day, she's just finished her coffee when her eyes light up, and she tells August about the day she got to New York. She talks about a Greyhound bus, and a friendly old man at the station who explained how to get to Brooklyn, winked, and slid a button into her pocket, the little pink triangle pinned below her shoulder. She tells August about paying cash for her first ever ride on the subway, about climbing up from underground into a gray morning and turning in a slow circle, taking it all in, and then buying her first cup of New York coffee.

"You see the pattern, right?" August says when she's done writing everything down.

Jane turns the empty cup over in her hands. "What do you mean?"

"It's sensory stuff," August says. "You smell coffee, it brings back something associated with the smell. You taste peanut butter, same thing. That's how we can do this. We just have to experiment."

Jane's quiet, studying the board mapping out stops. "What about a song? Could that work too?"

"Probably," August says. "Actually, knowing you and music, I bet it could help a lot."

"Okay," Jane says, sitting up suddenly, attention rapt. The look on her face is one August has come to recognize as readiness to learn something she doesn't understand: head cocked slightly, one eyebrow ticked up, part confusion, part eagerness. Sometimes Jane exudes the same energy as a golden retriever. "There's this one song I halfway remember. I don't know who it was by, but it goes like, *ohhhh, giiiiirl . . .*"

"That could describe a lot of songs," August says, untucking her phone from her pocket. "Do you remember any of the other lyrics?"

Jane bites her lip and frowns. She sings under her breath, warm and off-key and a little crackly, like the air around her feels. *"How I depend on youuu, to give me love how I need it."*

August tries very hard to think only of scientific curiosity as she consults Google. "Oh, okay. *When.* It's *give me love* when I *need it.* The title of the song is 'Oh, Girl.' It's by a band called the Chi-Lites. Came out in 1972."

"Yeah! That's right! I had it on a seven-inch single." Jane closes her eyes, and August thinks they're picturing the same thing: Jane, cross-legged on a bedroom floor somewhere, letting the record spin. "God, I wish I could listen to it right now."

"You can," August says, swiping through apps. "Hang on."

It takes her all of three seconds to pull it up, and she un-winds her earbuds from her pocket and hands one to Jane.

The song fades in soulful and longing, strings and harmon-ica, and the first words come exactly how Jane sang them: *Ohhhh giiiiiirl . . .*

"Oh my God," Jane says, sitting back in her seat. "That's really it. Shit."

"Yeah," August says. "Shit."

The song plays on for another minute before Jane sits up and says, "I heard this song for the first time on a radio in a semitruck Which is weird, because I definitely don't think I ever drove semitrucks. But I think I rode in some. There are a few—like, flashes, you know?"

August jots it down. "Hitchhiking, maybe? That was a big thing back then."

"Oh yeah, it was," she says. "I bet that's it. Yeah . . . yeah, in a truck from California, heading east. But I can't remember where we were going."

August sucks on the bud of the pencil eraser, and Jane looks at her. At her mouth, specifically.

She pulls the pencil out of her mouth, self-conscious. "That's okay, this is a great start. If you remember any other songs, I can help you figure them out."

"So you can . . . listen to any song you want?" Jane says, eye-ing August's phone. "Whenever you want to?"

August nods. They've been through some pretty rudimen-tary explanations of how smartphones and the internet work, and Jane has picked up a lot from observation, but she still gets all wide-eyed and awed.

"Would you want me to get you a phone like this?" August asks.

Jane thinks about it. "I mean . . . yes and no? It's impressive, but there's something about having to work for it when you want to listen to a song. I used to love my record collection. That was the most money I ever spent in one place, shipping it to a new address whenever I landed in a new city. I wanted to see the world but still have one thing that was mine."

August's pencil flies across the paper. "Okay, so you were a drifter. A drifter and a hitchhiker. That's so . . ."

"Cool?" Jane suggests, raising an eyebrow. "Daring? Adventurous? Sexy?"

"Unbelievable that you weren't strangled by one of the dozens of serial killers murdering hitchhikers up and down the West Coast in the '70s, is what I was gonna say."

"Well," Jane says. She kicks one foot up, crossing her ankle over her knee, and peers at August, hands behind her head. "What's the point of life without a little danger?"

"Not *dying*," August suggests. She can feel color flaring inconveniently in her cheeks.

"Yeah, I didn't die my whole life, and look where it got me," Jane says.

"Okay. Point." August shuts her steno. "That was a big memory, though. We got ourselves a lead."

August gives Jane her burner phone and teaches her how to use it and they experiment, like some kind of amnesiac scavenger hunt. Jane texts her snippets of lyrics or images from movies she snuck into dollar theaters to watch, and August tears through thrift stores for records familiar to Jane's hands and a vintage *Jaws* lunchbox. August brings every food she can think of to the Q: sticky buns, challah, slices of pizza, falafel sweating through its paper wrapper, steamed sponge cakes, ice cream melting down her wrist.

"You know, this train used to be called the QB," Jane remembers casually one day. "I guess it's just the Q now. Weird."

Things start coming back slowly, in pieces, one moment at a time. A box of greasy pepperoni split with a friend on a patio in Philly. Walking down the block in her sandals on a hot July afternoon to buy soft green tea cakes with nickels from the couch. A girl she loved briefly who drank three Arnold Palmers a day. A girl she loved briefly who snuck a bottle of wine out of her family's Seudat Purim because they were both too poor to buy one. A girl she loved briefly who worked at a movie theater.

There are, August notices, a lot of girls that Jane loved briefly. There's a secret set of tally marks in the back of one of her notebooks. It's up to seven. (She's completely fine with it.)

They go through Jane's backpack for clues—the notebooks, mostly filled with journal entries and recipes in messy shorthand, the postcard from California, which has a phone number that's disconnected. August takes pictures of Jane's buttons and pins so she can research them and discovers Jane was something of a radical in the '70s, which opens up a whole new line of research.

August digs through library archives until she finds copies of pamphlets, zines, flyers, anything that might have been pinned up or pasted or crammed under a door into a seedy bar when Jane was stomping through the streets of New York. She digs up an issue of I Wor Kuen's newspaper, pages in Chinese and

English on Marxism and self-determination and escaping the draft. She finds a flyer for a Redstockings street theater performance about abortion rights. She prints out an entire issue of the Gay Liberation Front's magazine and brings it to Jane, a bright pink sticky tab marking an essay by Martha Shelley titled "Gay Is Good."

"'Your friendly smile of acceptance—from the safe position of heterosexuality,'" Jane reads aloud, "'isn't enough. As long as you cherish that secret belief that you are a little bit better because you sleep with the opposite sex, you are still asleep in your cradle . . . and we will be the nightmare that awakens you.'"

She folds the page down and licks her bottom lip.

"Yeah," she says, smirking. "Yeah, I remember this one."

To say that the papers unlock new parts of Jane would be a lie, because they've always been there. They don't reveal anything not already spelled out by the set of her chin and the way she plants her feet in the space she takes up. But they color in the lines, pin down the edges—she thumbs through and remembers protests, riots, curls her hands into fists and talks about what made the muscle memory in her knuckles, hand-painted signs and black eyes and a bandana tied over her mouth and nose.

August takes note after note and finds it almost funny—that all the fighting only conspired to make Jane gentle. Fearsome and flirty and full of bad jokes, an incorrigible sweet tooth and a steel-toe boot as a last resort. That, August is learning, is Jane.

It would be easier, August thinks, if the real Jane weren't someone August liked so much. In fact, it'd be extremely convenient if Jane was boring or selfish or an asshole. She'd love to do one piece of casework without the whole halfway-in-love-with-her-subject thing getting in the way.

In between, when Jane needs a break, August does the thing she's done her best to avoid most of her life: she talks.

"I don't understand," August says when Jane asks about her mom, "what does that have to do with your memories?"

Jane shrugs, touching the toes of her sneakers together. "I just want to know."

Jane asks about school, and August tells her about her transfers and extra semesters and her freshman roommate from Texas who loved Takis Fuego, and it reminds Jane of this student she dated when she was twenty and couch-surfing through the Midwest (tally mark number eight). She asks about August's apartment, and August tells her about Myla's sculptures and Noodles barrelling through the halls, and it brings back Jane's neighbor's dog in her Brooklyn apartment, one door down from the Polish lady.

(They almost never talk about 2020 and what it's like above ground. Not yet. August can't tell if she wants to know. Jane doesn't ask.)

August sits next to her or across from her or, sometimes, on the seat beneath her, when Jane gets worked up and paces the car. They huddle by the map of the city posted near the subway doors and try to trace Jane's old paths through Brooklyn.

Two weeks in, August has three notebooks filled with Jane's stories, her memories. She takes them home at night and spreads them out on her air mattress and take notes of her notes, looking up every name Jane can recall, searching the city for old phone books. She takes the California postcard home and reads it over and over: *Jane—Miss you. Catch me up?* It's signed only with the words *Muscadine Dreams* and a phone number with an Oakland area code, but none of the Jane Sus in 1970s San Francisco lead anywhere.

She buys two maps: one of the United States and one of New York, all five boroughs spread out in pastels. She tapes them on her bedroom wall and tucks her tongue between her teeth and presses push pins into every place Jane mentions.

They're going to find Jane. She must have left things behind, places and people that remember her. August watches her light up over the steady shake of the train every day and can't imagine how anyone could ever forget.

August asks her one afternoon, when she's blowing off an exam review to make quiet jokes about the people who get on and off the train, "When did you realize you were stuck?"

"Honestly?" Jane says. She reaches over and gently swipes frosting from that morning's donut off August's bottom lip. The eye contact is so terribly close that August has to look down before her face says something she can't take back. "The day I met you."

"Really?"

"I mean, it wasn't clear right away. But it was kind of ... foggy before. That was the first time I was really aware of staying in one time and place for a few days. After a week or so, I realized I hadn't moved. At first, I could only tell by counting when I saw you and when I didn't. The week you didn't come? Everything started getting blurry again. So . . ."

It drops quietly into the space between them: maybe it's them. Maybe it's August. Maybe she's the reason.

Myla bribes August with a bag of Zapp's from a bodega four blocks over to introduce her to Jane.

After Niko, she's held off on introducing anyone. It's not like Jane doesn't have enough to deal with, recently being informed that she's a scientific anomaly trapped forty-five years in the future with no memory of how she got there and all. She's still getting used to the idea that she's not going to get arrested for being gay in public, which was a whole three-day emotional roller coaster. August is trying to take it easy on her.

"You could just take the Q yourself," August tells Myla, tucking the chips onto her shelf in the pantry. After a moment of consideration, she attaches a Post-it note that says TOUCH THESE AND DIE. "She's always on it."

"I tried," Myla says. "I didn't see her."

August frowns, sliding a packet of strawberry Pop-Tarts out of the pantry. No time for a bagel. "Really? That's weird."

"Yeah, guess I don't have the whole *magical soul mate* bond you have with her," she says. It's a rainy Friday afternoon, and she's got a bright yellow rain jacket on like the Morton Salt girl with 4A hair.

"We do *not* have a magical soul mate bond. Why are you so invested in our relationship anyway?"

"August, I love you very much, and I want you to be happy, and I'm very confident that you and this girl are, like, fated by the universe to fingerblast each other until you both die," she says. "But honestly? I am in this for the sci-fi of it all. I'm living a real life episode of *The X-Files*, okay? This is the most interesting thing that's ever happened to me, and my life has *not* been boring. So, can we *go*, Scully?"

On the watery platform, Myla launches herself at the train so fast, she nearly shoves August into an old woman tottering out.

"Bye, Mrs. Caldera!" Jane calls after her. "Tell Paco I said hi and that he better study for his algebra test!" She sees August, and her smile shifts from friendly into something August still can't name. "Oh, hey, August!"

Myla nudges ahead, extending a hand to Jane. "Hi, wow, I'm Myla, huge fan. Love your work."

Jane bemusedly takes her hand, and August can see Myla making a whole catalog of scientific observations as they shake. She really should have pushed her onto the tracks when she had the chance.

"*Can you please sit down?*" August hisses, nudging her toward a seat. She pulls the Pop-Tarts out of her pocket and hands them over, and Jane immediately rips into them. "Um, Jane, this is one of my roommates I told you about."

"I've been dying to meet you," Myla says. "I had to bribe August with chips. Zapp's. Sweet Creole Onion."

Jane looks up from the Pop-Tarts wrapper she's brutalizing. "Zapp's?"

"It's a Louisiana chip brand," August tells her. "They're amazing. I'll bring you some."

"Whoa," Myla interjects, "you can eat?"

"*Myla!*"

"What? It's a fair question!"

Jane laughs. "It's okay. Yeah, I can eat. And drink, though I don't think I can get drunk. I found a flask of whiskey once, and it didn't really do anything."

"Maybe your first mistake was drinking out of a flask you found on the subway," August suggests.

Jane rolls her eyes, still grinning.

"Look," she says through a mouthful, "if I turned my nose up at everything that's left on the subway, I would have nothing to do."

"Wait, so," Myla says, leaning forward, elbows on her knees, "do you get hungry?"

"No," Jane says. She thinks for a second. "I *can* eat, but I don't think I have to."

"And . . . digestion?"

"Myla, I swear to God—"

"Nothing happens," Jane says with a shrug. "It's like . . ."

"Suspended animation," Myla supplies.

"Yeah, I guess."

"Wow, that is fascinating!" Myla says, and August is mortified, but she can't pretend she's not taking mental notes to be recorded later. "And you really don't remember anything?"

Jane frowns thoughtfully around another bite. "I remember more now. It's sort of like . . . muscle memory? Pop culture stuff is easier than personal stuff for some reason. And for a lot of stuff, I have a sense that I've done it before, even if I can't remember it specifically. Like, I know how to speak Cantonese and English, even though I can't remember learning either. More stuff comes back every day."

"Wow. And—"

"Myla," August says, "can we maybe not treat her like a creature of the week?"

"Ah, sorry," Myla says with a wince. "Sorry! I'm just—this is so cool. I mean, obviously, it's not cool for you, but it's fascinating. I've never heard of anything like you."

"Is that a compliment?" Jane asks.

"It can be."

"*Anyway,*" August says. "Myla's a genius and very into science fiction and multiverse theory and, like, smart-people stuff, so she's gonna help figure out what exactly happened to you and how we can fix it."

Jane, who has moved on to the second Pop-Tart and is plowing through it like she's trying to beat a land speed record, squints at August and says, "Are you assembling a task force, Landry?"

"Not a task force," August says, heart skipping at the sound of her last name in Jane's mouth. "Just a . . . ragtag band of misfits."

The corners of Jane's mouth press in a sly grin. "Love it."

"Very *Goonies,*" Myla chimes in.

"What're goonies?" Jane asks.

"Only one of the greatest adventure movies of 1985," Myla says. "Wait, oh man, you missed Spielberg completely, didn't you?"

"She would have caught Jaws in '75," August automatically supplies.

"Thank you, Encyclopedia Brown," Myla says. She leans in and tells Jane, "August knows everything about everything. It's her superpower. She should be teaching you all the '80s movies."

"I do *not* know everything."

"That's true, you didn't know about '70s punk. I had to teach you that."

Jane looks at her, smirking slightly. August swallows.

"You're the one who taught her that?"

"Oh yeah," Myla chirps happily, "I think she wanted something to talk to y—"

"*Anyway!*" August interrupts. They're pulling into a station, and she yanks Myla up by her sleeve. "Billy's isn't far from this stop, and I'm hungry. Aren't you hungry? Let's go, bye, Jane!"

Myla and Jane both seem visibly put out, but August is one embarrassing non sequitur away from throwing herself out the emergency exit. Those two are a dangerous combination.

"Wait, what's your sign?" Myla shouts over August's shoulder.

Jane scrunches her face up like she's trying to remember where she left her keys, not her own birthday. "Don't remember. Summer, though? I'm pretty sure I was born in the summer."

"I can work with that!" Myla says, and August is smiling apologetically back at Jane and whisking Myla away, and Jane is lost in the crowd of commuters.

"I'm gonna kill you," August says as they pick their way toward the stairs.

"The most interesting thing that's ever happened to me!" Myla yells over her shoulder.

"What did you think of her?"

Myla hops up on the landing, tugging her miniskirt down. "I mean, honestly? That's wife material. Like, three kids and a dog material. If she looked at me the way she looks at you, my IUD would have shot out like a party popper."

"Jesus *Christ*," August says. And, involuntarily, "How do you think she looks at me?"

"Like you're her Pop-Tart angel. Like you shit sunshine. Like you invented love as a concept."

August stares at her, trying to take that in, then turns on her heel and heads off toward the exit. "No, she doesn't."

"Like she wants to eat you alive," Myla adds, jogging to catch up.

"You don't have to lie to make me feel better," August says.

"I'm not lying! She—oh, *fuck*."

Myla has screeched to a halt—literally, the rubber of her boots squeaking on the damp tile floor—in front of a sign posted on the station wall. August backtracks to read it.

SERVICE ALERT, the sign declares.

Below, there's the yellow bubble of the Q. Commuters keep

walking right past it, just another inconvenience in their day, but August freezes and stares and feels all her rides on the Q spin out around her in a film reel until a breaker flips and they all go black.

"They're shutting the line down for maintenance at the end of the summer," Myla reads.

"Shutting it *down*?" The dates indicate September 1 through October 31. "Two *months*? I won't be able to see her for *two months*?"

Myla turns to her, eyes wide. "Didn't you say—if she doesn't see you—?"

"Yeah," August says. "When I stopped riding the Q, everything got blurry again for her. Do you . . . do you think she would . . . ?"

August pictures Jane trapped for months, alone and confused and staticky and forgetting, or worse—tripping back out of this precise moment in time just like she tripped into it, lost again, gone further than August's research could ever uncover. They have no idea how firmly she's planted here and now.

August *just* found her. It's too soon to lose her.

At Billy's, Lucie does not look happy to see August, considering she's been faking mono for weeks. But she shoves two menus and two rolls of silverware at her and wordlessly seats them at the bar.

Winfield drops off a plate of fries, and once he's gone, August leans over and asks, "What the hell do we do?"

"Okay," Myla says. "I have a theory."

August opens her mouth before snapping it shut when Winfield drops off the ketchup. As soon as he's gone, she asks, "What?"

Myla leans in. "Do you know anything about time slips?"

August blinks. "No."

"Okay," Myla says. She seizes the ketchup, dumping it over the fries. August pulls a face, and Myla waves it off. "It's this sci-fi trope where somebody gets lost in time. So, like, *A Connecticut Yankee in King Arthur's Court.* Mark Twain book. Guy gets hit in the head and wakes up in Camelot. Maybe something happened to her on the train that threw her out of time."

August frowns. "Like, she time traveled?"

"Sort of," Myla says thoughtfully. "But you found proof she was around in the '80s and '90s, right?" August nods. "So it's not only then to now. Maybe she's been, like . . . flickering through time. Maybe she's stuck on the subway because some big event, some big anomaly, tethered her there. She's, like, trapped in the in-between."

"In between what?"

"Dead and alive, maybe," she says. "Real and not real."

"So the train is like . . . purgatory?" How very Catholic.

"Yeah, but . . . not. Like, okay. You and me, we're real. We're stuck to reality, in this timeline. Linear. We started at point A, and we move forward through points B, C, D, et cetera. This is because nothing has ever interfered with our reality. There's never been an event that could have disrupted our timeline. So our points A, B, C, D, correspond to the same order of points in linear time. But say there was an event like—like on *Lost,* when they detonate the H bomb and get thrown forward in time. Something just big enough to make a crack that one person could slip through, and it knocked her loose from the timeline of reality. Her point B could be our point D, her point E could be our point C. It's not linear for her. She can be in 1980 one moment and 2005 the next and 1996 after that, because she came unstuck."

August scrunches her hands up in her hair, trying to wrap her brain around it.

"Okay, so like . . . like music on the radio," she attempts. "Like, the radio waves start in one place and they're picked up by whatever receiver catches them. She's the transmission, and her receivers are—"

"All at different moments in time, right," Myla says. "So, if we look at it that way, she's the music, and we're the receiver picking her up."

"And the other people that have seen her and interacted with her on the train over the years, those were—"

"Like antennas on cars catching a radio station as they pass through town. She's—she's always broadcasting out of the same tower."

August feels like her brain is going to melt out of her nose. "The Q. She's broadcasting out of the line."

"Right. So . . . whatever it was must have happened while she was on the train," Myla says slowly. The fries are going soggy. "We just need to figure what."

"How do we do that?"

"No idea."

August straightens, shoving her glasses up her nose. She can do this. Her brain is wired to solve things. "I mean, a big enough event to throw a person out of time—there would be a record of that, right?"

Myla looks at her. "Girl, I don't know. This is all hypothetical." She must see the frustration flash across August's face, because she picks up a fry and points it at her. It flops over pathetically, dripping ketchup onto the table. "Look, you might be right. But it could have been totally localized. People could have missed it completely."

August sighs. Props her elbows up on the table. Tries to avoid the ketchup. "What about her memories? Why are those gone?"

"Like I said, I don't know. Could be because she's not rooted to anything. She's not fully real, so her memories aren't either. The important thing is, they're not gone for good."

"So . . ." August says, "so we have to get her to remember what happened. And . . ."

"And then maybe we can find a way to fix it before the end of summer."

August lets that settle in the air between them: the idea that they could get Jane out. She's been so focused on helping Jane figure out her past, she hasn't thought about what comes after.

"And then wh-what?" August asks, wincing at the way her voice goes shaky. "If we figure out what happened and how to fix it, what happens when we do? She goes back to the '70s? She stays here? She . . . she's gone?"

"I don't know. But . . ."

August puts down her French fry. She's lost her appetite. "But what?"

"Well, she said it's only felt like a few months for her, until now? I think she's gotten anchored here and now. And from what you've told me, this is the first time that's happened."

"So, we might be her only chance? Okay," August says. She folds her arms across her chest and tucks her chin down, jaw set. "No matter what, we try."

So, that's it. August kind of knew, but now she *knows*. She can't do this and have a crush on Jane at the same time.

It's fine. It's only that August used to love *Say Anything* before life intervened to make her hate everything, and Jane is the first person to ever make her feel all John-Cusack-and-Ione-Skye. It's not a big deal that Jane's hand is the perfect size to brace against August's waist, or that when Jane looks at her, she can't look back because her heart starts doing things so big and loud that the rest of her can barely hold the size and sound. She'll live.

The bottom line: there's no chance. Even if somehow Jane feels the same, August has a deadline. She has to help Jane figure out who she is, how she got stuck, and how to get her out.

And if she manages to pull that off, Jane's not exactly here permanently. She's not exactly *here* at all. And, well, August has never truly had her heart broken before, but she's pretty sure that falling in love with someone only to send them back to the 1970s would, as first heartbreaks go, win the Fuck You Up Olympics.

Anyway, she can compartmentalize. She spent her childhood getting paid in Happy Meals to break into people's personal archives and pretending that was normal. She can pretend she's never thought about Jane holding her hand in a cute East Village brownstone with a West Elm sofa and a wine fridge. This crush, she decides, is just *not* going to work for her.

Which means, of course, the next time August steps on the Q, Jane says, "I think I should kiss you."

It doesn't start that way. It starts with August, too busy thinking about not thinking about Jane to check the weather for the morning's freak thunderstorm, slipping in her own puddle of rainwater.

"*Whoa,*" Jane says, catching her under the elbow before she hits the subway floor. "Who tried to drown you?"

"The fucking MTA," August says, letting Jane help her to

her feet. She pushes her sopping hair out of her eyes, blinking through the raindrops on her glasses. "Twenty-minute delay on an outdoor platform. They want me dead."

August takes off her glasses and desperately checks herself for a single dry inch of fabric to wipe them on.

"Here," Jane says, pulling up the tail of her shirt. August sees the smooth skin of her stomach, hints of a secret tattoo spilling up over her waistband on one hip, and forgets to breathe. Jane takes her glasses to wipe off the lenses. "You didn't have to come today."

"I wanted to," August says. She adds quickly, "We've been making good progress."

Jane looks up, halfway grinning, and stops, August's glasses still in her hand.

"Oh, wow," she says softly.

August blinks. "What?"

"It's—without your glasses, the wet hair." She hands them back, but her eyes, distant and a little dazed, don't leave August's face. "I got a flash of something."

"A memory?"

"Sort of," Jane says. "Like a half memory. You reminded me."

"Oh," August says. "What is it?"

"A kiss," Jane says. "I don't—I can't remember exactly where I was, or who *she* was, but when you looked at me, I could remember the rain."

"Okay," August says. She'd take a note if her notebook wasn't completely soaked. Also if she thought she was steady enough to hold a pen. "What, uh, what else can you remember?"

Jane chews on her bottom lip. "She had long hair, like yours, but maybe blond? It's weird, like—like a movie I saw, except I know it happened to me, because I remember her wet hair stuck to the side of her neck and how I had to peel it off so I could kiss her there."

Jesus Christ.

Life-ruining descriptions of things Jane can do with her mouth aside, it does present a . . . possibility. The fastest way to recover Jane's memories has been to make her smell or hear or touch something from her past.

"You know how we did the thing with the bagels," Jane says, apparently thinking the same thing, "and the music, the sensory stuff? If I—if we—can re-create how that moment *felt,* maybe I can remember the rest."

Jane looks around—it's a slow day for the Q, only a few people at the other end of the car.

"Do you want to—you could try, um, touching my neck?" August offers lamely, hating herself. "For, like, research."

"Maybe," Jane says. "But it was . . . it was in an alley. We had ducked out of the rain into an alley, and we were laughing, and I hadn't kissed her yet, but I'd been thinking about it for weeks. So—" She turns distractedly toward the empty back wall of the car, next to the emergency exit.

"Oh." August follows, wet sneakers squelching unattractively.

Jane turns to her, drags two fingers across the back of her hand. The look on her face is intent, like she's holding the memory tight in her head, transposing it over the present. She grabs August by the wrist, backing her into the wall of the car, and, oh *shit.*

"She was leaning against the wall," Jane explains simply.

August feels her shoulders hit smooth metal, and in a panic, she imagines bricks scraping against her back instead, a sky instead of handrails and flickering fixtures, herself with any kind of grace to survive this.

"Okay," August says. She and Jane have been pressed closer than this during commuter rushes, but it's never, not once, felt like *this*. She tips her chin up. "Like this?"

"Yeah," Jane says. Her voice hushed. She must be concentrating. "Just like that."

August swallows. It's almost funny, how much she's absolutely going to die.

"And," Jane says, "I put my hand here." She leans in and braces one hand against the wall next to August's head. Her body heat crackles between them. "Like this."

"Uh-huh."

It's research. It's only *research. Lie back and think of the fucking Dewey Decimal System.*

"And I leaned in," Jane says. "And I—"

Her other hand ghosts over August's throat before sliding backward, her thumb grazing August's pulse, and August's eyes close on instinct. She touches August's hair with her fingertips and pulls it gently away from the side of her neck. The cool air is a shock to her skin.

"Is—is it helping?"

"Hang on," Jane says. "Can I—?"

"Yeah," August says. It doesn't matter what the question is.

Jane makes a small sound, ducks her head, and there's breath against August's bare skin, close enough to mimic the gesture but only just not making contact, which is somehow worse than a kiss would be. It's more intimate, the silent promise that she could if she wanted to, and August would let her, if they both wanted the same thing in the same way.

Jane's lips skim August's skin when she says, "Jenny."

August opens her eyes. "What?"

"Jenny," Jane says, drawing back. "Her name was Jenny. We were a block from my apartment."

"Where?"

"I can't remember," Jane says. She frowns and adds, "I think I should kiss you."

August's mind goes searingly blank.

"You—what?"

"I'm almost there," Jane says, and fuck if August can't suppress a shiver at those words in that voice from that soft mouth. "I think—"

"That if you—" August clears her throat and tries again. "You think that if you—if you kiss me—"

"I'll remember, yeah." She's looking at August with a precise kind of interest. Not like she's thinking about a kiss, but more like she's focusing hard on an objective. It happens to be a disastrously good look on her. Her jaw goes all jutty and angular, and August wants to give her anything she wants and then change her own name and skip the continent.

Jane's watching her face, tracking a raindrop that rolls from her hairline to her chin, and August knows, she *knows,* if she does this, she's never going to stop thinking about it for the rest of her life. You can't un-kiss the most impossible person you've ever met. She's never going to forget what that tastes like.

But Jane looks hopeful, and August wants to help. And, well. She believes in in-depth, hands-on evidence gathering. That's all.

Compartmentalize, August tells herself. *For the love of God, Landry. Compartmentalize.*

"Okay," August says. "It's not a bad idea."

"You sure?" Jane says gently. "You don't have to if you don't want to."

"That's not—" That's not the issue, but if Jane doesn't know that by now, she probably never will. "I don't mind."

"Okay," Jane says, visibly relieved. God, she has no idea.

"Okay," August says. "For research."

"For research," Jane agrees.

August squares her shoulders. For research.

"What should I do?"

"Can you touch me?" Jane takes one of August's hands and holds it to her chest, right below the hard line of her collarbone. "Right here?"

"Okay," August says, more of a shaky exhale than a word. "Then what?"

Jane's leaning in, taking advantage of her height to bracket August in, burning so hot that August can't make sense of the chill sweeping up her spine. So steady and beautiful and close, too close, never close enough, and August is so completely, irreversibly, spectacularly screwed.

"And," Jane says, "I kissed her."

The train plunges out of a tunnel and back into the deafening rain.

"Did she kiss you back?"

Jane's other hand finds its way to August's waist, to the place that feels designed by the profound unfairness of the universe to fit it so exactly.

"Yeah," Jane says. "Yeah, she did."

And Jane kisses her.

The truth about wanting someone to kiss you for ages is, it rarely lives up to whatever you've imagined. Real kisses are messy, awkward, too dry, too wet, imperfect. August learned years ago that movie kisses don't happen. The best you can hope for in a first kiss is to be kissed back.

But then, there's this kiss.

There's Jane's hand on her waist, and the rain rushing down onto the roof of the train, and a half-remembered moment pinned against a brick wall, and this kiss, and August couldn't have imagined it would feel like this.

Jane's mouth is soft but insistent, and August feels the press of it in her body, in a place much too close to her heart. If looking at Jane feels like flowers opening, being kissed by her feels heavier, the weight of a body that'll be gone by morning settling into bed beside her. It reminds her of being homesick for months and tasting something familiar and realizing it's even better than you remember, because it comes with the sweet gut punch of knowing and being known. It melts in her mouth like ice cream at the corner store when she was eight. It aches like a brick to the shin.

Jane kisses her and kisses her, and August has completely lost track of what this was even supposed to be about, because she's kissing Jane back, swiping her thumb into the dip of Jane's collarbone, and Jane's tongue is tracing the soft seam of her lips, and August's mouth is falling open. Jane's hand drops from the wall to brace against August's face, tangled up in her wet hair, and she's everywhere and nowhere—in her mouth, at her waist, against her hips, touching too much for August to pretend this isn't real to her but not enough to know if it's real to Jane too.

And then Jane pulls back and says, "Oh, *fuck.*"

August has to blink five times before her eyes remember how to focus. What the fuck was she doing? Kissing her way to self-destruction, that's what.

"What?" she asks. Her voice comes out strangled. Jane's hand is still in her hair.

"New Orleans," she says. "The Bywater. That's where I was."

"*What?*"

"I lived there," she says. August is staring at her mouth, dark pink and swollen, and trying desperately to drag her brain in the opposite direction. "I lived in New Orleans. A year, at least. I had an apartment, and a roommate, and—oh, holy shit, I *remember.*"

"Are you sure?" August asks. "Are you sure you're not getting it mixed up because *I'm* from there?"

"No," Jane says, "no, I remember now." She moves suddenly, the way she does when she's feeling something big, and scoops August up in her arms and spins her around. "Oh my God, you're fucking *magic.*"

August thinks, as her feet lift off the ground, that nobody has ever called her magic in her entire life.

They slide right back into their normal places: August perched on the edge of a seat with her notebook open to the dryest page she can find, and Jane pacing the aisle reciting everything she can recall. She talks about a burger joint in the Quarter where she worked, about Jenny (tally mark eleven), about a shotgun apartment on the second floor of an old house and a sweet-faced roommate whose name she can't remember. August writes it all down and doesn't think about how Jane kissed her—Jane *kissed her*—Jane put her hand on August's face and *kissed her,* and August knows how her lips feel, and she can't ever stop knowing, and—

"Did you get that?" Jane says, pausing her pacing, apparently completely unaffected. "The snowball place in the Marigny? You look like you spaced out for a second."

"Oh, yeah," August says. "Definitely got it."

When she stumbles back into the apartment that night, Niko takes one look at her and says, "Oh, you fucked up."

"It's fine!" August says, shouldering past him toward the fridge.

"You are projecting so many feelings right now, I can't believe your skin's still on."

"I'm repressing it!" She yanks a carton of leftover sesame chicken out and pops the top, shoveling it into her mouth cold. "Let me repress it!"

"I can see how you would think that is what you're doing," he says, sounding genuinely sorry for her.

7

POLICE DEPARTMENT
CITY OF NEW YORK

Filed April 17, 1992

Incident: At 1715 hours on 17 April 1992, I,
Officer Jacob Haley #739, was dispatched to
Times Square-42nd Street subway station.
Mark Edelstein (DOB 8-7-1954) reported
middle-aged white male approx. 5'9 struck
him in eye with closed fist in dispute
over seat on Brooklyn-bound Q train. He
states man shouted anti-semitic slur at
him before assault. Suspect absent from
scene. Victim states another passenger,
mid-twenties Asian female approx. 5'7,
forced attacker off train at 49th Street
Station. Passenger also absent from scene.

August's phone chimes at six on a Thursday morning with a
text from Jane.

She rolls onto her side, elbow digging into her air mattress, which has halfway deflated during the night—she *needs* to get a real bed. Three texts from her mom. One missed call and voicemail from Billy's. A red bubble announcing seventeen unread messages in her school email. One notification from her bank: her account is at $23.02.

Normally, any two of those overlapping would send her into an hour-long anxiety-fueled tear of aggressive productivity until everything was squared away, even if she had to lie and cheat to do it.

Her mom's texts say: Hey, wanted to check in on that file I sent you. and Are you screening my calls, turd? and Miss you always but especially when I have a new file shipment. You were always so much better at sorting these.

She'll deal with it. She *will*. Just . . . tomorrow.

She opens Jane's text.

Hey August, got a new one: a
restaurant on Mott where I got
dumplings. I may have gotten
in a fight with a cook there. Can't
place the year. Any ideas?
Thanks, Jane Su

Jane has not yet figured out she doesn't have to include a greeting and a sign-off, and August hasn't had the heart to correct her.

P.S. I'm still thinking about that joke
you made the other day about JFK.
Hilarious. You're a genius.

August has decided, in what she believes is a show of extreme maturity and dedication to helping Jane, to pretend the kiss was completely unimportant. Did it get the information they needed? Yes. Did she lie awake that night thinking about it for three and a half hours? Yes. Did it mean anything? No. So, no, she's not sitting around, picturing Jane dropping her jacket on August's bedroom floor and pushing her down onto the bed, breaking the bed, putting the bed back together—*God, not the stupid bed-assembly fantasy again.*

No, that would be extremely impractical. And August thinks, as she spends seven of her last dollars on a container of to-go dumplings for Jane, that she's very practical, and everything is under complete control.

"My hero," Jane swoons when August boards the Q and hands the bag over.

She's looking particularly bright today, soaking in the sun that pours through the windows. She told August last week how thankful she is to at least be stuck on a train that spends a lot of its route above ground, and it shows. Her skin glows a golden brown that reminds August of humid summer afternoons in the Bywater—which, August realizes, is something they've both felt. What are the odds?

"Anything coming back to you?" August asks, climbing into the seat next to her. She perches her sneakers on the edge, tucking her knees up to her chest.

"Gimme a second," Jane says, chewing thoughtfully. "God, these are good."

"Can I—?" August stomach growls to finish the sentence.

"Yeah, here," Jane says, holding a dumpling up on the end of a plastic fork and opening her mouth, indicating August do the same. She does, and Jane shoves the entire overstuffed dumpling in and laughs as August struggles to chew, reaching over to wipe sauce off her chin. "You gotta eat it all in one."

"You're so mean to me," August says when she manages to swallow.

"I'm showing you how to eat dumplings the right way!" Jane says. "I'm being *so* nice!"

August laughs, and— God. She has to stop picturing what they look like to every other commuter: a couple laughing over takeout, ribbing each other on the ride to Manhattan. There's a couple down the car, a man and woman, wrapped around each other like they're trying to fuse by osmosis, and August hates that part of her wants to be them. It'd be so easy to slide her hand into Jane's.

Instead, she pulls a notebook from her bag and a pencil from her hair, where it's been holding a frizzy, half-assed updo in place all morning.

"Let me know if anything comes to you," August says, shaking her hair out. It falls down her shoulders, her back, everywhere. Jane watches her try to contend with it with a bemused expression.

"What?" Jane says vaguely.

"Like, if you remember anything."

"Oh," she says, blinking. "Yeah. . . . It was this tiny place on Mott, my favorite dumplings in the city—I went there once or twice a week, at least. I think I was in Chinatown a lot, even though I lived in Brooklyn. It was easy to just take the Q to Canal."

"Okay," August says, taking a note.

"But I fucked up. I slept with a cook's ex-girlfriend, and she found out and let me *have it* next time I came in, and I couldn't go back after that. But, shit, it was *worth it*."

The detective side of August contemplates a follow-up

question, but the side of her that wants to live to see tomorrow decides against it.

"All right," August says, not looking up from her notepad. "A restaurant in Chinatown that serves dumplings. There are only, like . . . five million of those."

"Sorry," Jane says, returning to her to-go box. "You can narrow it down to the ones that were open in the '70s?"

"Sure, assuming they're still operating, and have employment records going back that far, I could *maybe* get a name for that employee and *maybe* track her down and *maybe* she'll know something." August puts her pencil down, looks at Jane finally—who is staring at her with cheeks stuffed full of dumpling and a startled expression—and prays she survives this. "Or, we could get you to remember this girl's name."

"How'll we do that?" Jane says through a mouthful of pork and dough.

August looks at her puffy cheeks and swoopy hair and blows right through every piece of mental caution tape to say, "Kiss me."

Jane chokes.

"You—" Jane coughs, forcing it down. "You want me to kiss you again?"

"Here's the thing," August says. She's calm. She's totally calm, just doing casework. It doesn't mean anything. "It's April. The Q shuts down in September. We're running out of time. And the other day—when we kissed—that *worked.* It brought back something big. So, I think—"

"You think if you kiss me, it'll bring this girl back like it brought back Jenny?"

"Yeah. So. Let's . . ." August thinks back to what they said last time. "Do it for research."

"Okay," Jane says, expression unreadable. "For research."

She bundles her takeout back into its bag, and August stands and throws her hair over her shoulder. She can do this. Start with what you know and work from there. August knows this can work.

"So," August says, "tell me what to do."

A beat. Jane looks up at her, brow furrowed. Then her face smooths out, and a smile plays at the corner of her mouth, the one with the dimple.

"Okay," she says, and she spreads her legs apart a few inches, gesturing loosely for August to sit. "Get down here."

Shit. August supposes she did ask for it.

August settles herself on one of Jane's thighs and tucks her legs between them, her feet skimming the floor between Jane's sneakers. If she's being honest, she's imagined more than once, more than a few times, what Jane's thighs feel like. They're strong and firm, sturdier than they look, but August doesn't have a chance to feel anything about it before Jane's fingertips are nudging her chin up to look at her.

"Is this okay?" Jane asks. Her hand squeezes the curve of August's hip, holding her in place.

August looks at her, letting her gaze drop to Jane's lips. That's the whole point of this. It's mechanics. "Yeah. Is this how you remember it?"

"Kind of," she says. And, "Pull my hair."

For a few ringing seconds, August imagines herself melting onto the floor of the train like the ghosts of a million spilled subway slushies and dropped ice cream cones.

Completely under control.

She pushes her fingers into Jane's short hair, scraping her nails across the scalp before she closes them on a fistful and tugs.

"Like that?"

Jane releases a short breath. "Harder."

August does as she's told, and Jane makes another sound, one deep in her throat, which August assumes is a good sign.

"Now . . ." Jane says. She's looking at August's mouth, eyes dark as the pit at a punk show. "When I kiss you, bite."

And before August can ask what she means, Jane closes the space between them.

The kiss is . . . different this time. Hotter, somehow, even though it's not real. *It's not real,* August recites in her head as she tries to pretend there's absolutely anything academic about the way her mouth drops open at the press of Jane's lips, anything scientifically impartial about the way she pulls harder at Jane's hair and sinks into it, letting Jane drink her in.

Jane's words come back to her, syrupy sweet and slow, *bite,* and so she sucks Jane's bottom lip between hers and digs her teeth in. She hears her sharp inhale, feels Jane's hand tighten in the fabric of her shirt, and thinks of it as progress. Results. She moves the way she imagines the girl Jane remembers would have moved, tries to give her the memory with her mouth— bites harder, tugs at her lip, runs her tongue over it.

It lasts only a minute or two, but it feels like a year lost in Jane's hair and Jane's lips and Jane's past, Jane's hands fisting in her curls, Jane's thigh warm and steady under her, Jane for hours, Jane for days. It pulls like an undertow, and the case is up on the surface, and August is trying to stay there too.

When they break apart, August's glasses are crooked and smudged, and an old woman is staring disapprovingly at them from across the aisle.

"You got a problem?" Jane says, arm slinging protectively across August's shoulders.

The woman says nothing and returns to her newspaper.

"Mingxia," Jane says, turning to August. "That was her name.

Mingxia. I took her back to my place in Prospect Heights on . . . Underhill Avenue. It was a brownstone. I had the second floor. That was the first place I lived in New York."

August writes down the street name and the playground across the street and the nearest intersection and spends an afternoon pulling ownership records on every brownstone on the block, calling landlords until she finds the son of one who remembers a Chinese American woman renting the second floor when he was a kid.

The kiss reveals: Jane moved to New York in February 1975.

And so, it becomes another thing they do. The food and the songs and the old articles and, now, the kisses.

There are certain crucial bits of information they still don't have—like Jane's childhood, or her infuriatingly elusive birth certificate, or the event that got Jane stuck in the first place— but there's no way to predict what memory might cause a chain reaction leading to something important.

The kisses are strictly for evidence gathering. August knows this. August is absolutely, 100 percent clear on this. She's kissing Jane, but Jane is kissing Jenny, Molly, April, Niama, Maria, Beth, Mary Frances, Mingxia. It's not about her and Jane, at all.

"Kiss me slow," Jane says, grinning on a Tuesday afternoon, her sleeves rolled up enticingly, and it's still not about them.

They kiss under the dappled sunlight of the Brighton Beach Station, strawberry ice cream on their tongues, and Jane remembers summer 1974, a month crashing with an old friend named Simone who'd moved to Virginia Beach, whose cat absolutely refused to leave them alone in bed. They kiss with August's earbuds split between them playing Patti Smith, and Jane remembers autumn 1975, a bass player named Alice who left lipstick stains on her neck in the bathroom of CBGB. They kiss at midnight in a dark tunnel, and Jane remembers New Year's Eve 1977, and Mina, who tattooed the vermilion bird on her shoulder.

August learns all this, but she also learns that Jane likes to be kissed every kind of way: like a secret, like a fistfight, like candy, like a house fire. She learns Jane can make her sigh and forget her own name until it all blurs together, past and present, the two of them on Manhattan balconies and in damp New Orleans barrooms and the candy aisle of a convenience store in Los Angeles. Jane's kissed a girl in every corner of the country, and pretty soon, August feels like she has too.

For research.

It's not like kissing is all August does—the time she spends thinking about the kisses and chasing down leads from the kisses when she's not actually *having* the kisses notwithstanding. It's been three weeks since she worked a single shift. She does have to pay rent, eventually, and so to stave off absolute bankruptcy, she finally calls Billy's and, with some coughing and begging, convinces Lucie to put her on the schedule.

"Sweet Jesus, she lives," Winfield says, pretending to faint dramatically over the counter when August returns to the bar.

"You literally saw me last week." August brushes past him to clock in.

"Was that you?" Winfield asks, gathering himself back up and beginning to change the coffee filter. "Or was that some girl who looked like you but has *not* been bedridden for weeks like you told Lucie you were?"

"I was feeling better that day," August says. She turns to see Winfield's skeptical look. "What? Did you want me to get Billy's shut down for giving mono to all the customers in tables fifteen through twenty-two?"

"Mm-hmm. Okay. Well. Speaking of. You missed the big news last week."

"Is Jerry's old ass finally retiring?"

"No, but he might have to now."

August whips her head around. "What? Why?"

Winfield turns wordlessly, humming a few notes of a funeral dirge as he heads toward the kitchen and Lucie fills his place behind the bar.

She looks . . . rough. One of her typically flawless acrylics is broken, and her hair is falling out of its scraped-back ponytail. She shoots August a fleeting glare before setting a small jar down on the counter.

"If you're not sick, I don't care," she says. She jabs a finger toward the jar. "If you are, take this. Three spoonfuls. You'll feel better."

August eyes the jar. "Is that—?"

"Onion and honey. Old recipe. Just take it."

Even from three feet down the bar, it smells lethal, but August is not in a position to talk back to Lucie, so she tucks the jar into her apron and asks, "What's going on? What'd I miss?"

Lucie sniffs, picking up a rag and descending upon a spot of syrup on the counter, and says, "Billy's is closing."

August, who was in the process of sliding a handful of straws into her pocket, misses and scatters them all over the floor.

"*What? When? Why?*"

"So many questions for someone who does not come to work," Lucie tuts.

"I—"

"Landlord is doubling rent at the end of the year," she says. She's still scrubbing away at the counter like she doesn't care, but her eyeliner is smudged and there's a slight shake in her hands. She's not taking this well. August feels like a dick for missing it. "Billy can't afford it. We close in December."

"That's—Billy's can't close." The idea of Billy's boarded up— or worse, gone the way of so many po'boy joints and corner stores August frequented growing up in New Orleans, made over into IHOPs and overpriced boutique gyms—is sacrilege. Not here, not a place that has been open since 1976, not somewhere Jane loved too. "What if he—has he asked if the landlord will sell it to him?"

"Yeah," Winfield says, popping up in the kitchen window, "but unless you got a hundred grand to make up the loan the bank won't give Billy, this shit is about to become an organic juice bar in six to eight months."

"So that's it?" August asks. "It's just over?"

"That *is* how gentrification works, yeah." Winfield shoves a massive plate of pancakes into the window. "Lucie, these are yours. August, table sixteen looks ready to pop off, you better get in there."

When August clocks out eight hours later, she finds herself back on the Q, looking at Jane, who's curled up reading a book. She traded the old *Watership* a couple of weeks ago to some fan of first editions and is now reading a battered Judy Blume. She loves it earnestly. For a punk who knows how to fight, she seems to love everything earnestly.

"Hey, Coffee Girl," Jane says when she sees her. "Anything new today?"

August thinks of Billy's. Jane deserves to know. But she's

smiling, and August doesn't want her to stop smiling, so she decides not to tell her. Not today.

Maybe it's selfish, or maybe it's for Jane. It's getting harder to tell which is which.

Instead, she folds herself into the seat beside her and hands over a sandwich wrapped twice in aluminum foil so the yolk and syrup and sauce can't leak out.

"A Su Special," August says.

"God," Jane groans. "I'm so jealous you get to have these all the time."

August nudges an elbow into her ribs. "Did you kiss any girls who worked at Billy's?"

Jane rips off a bit of foil, eyes sparkling.

"You know what?" she says. "I sure did."

"I'm sorry, what are you saying?"

The BC offices are small, crammed up against the side of a lecture hall. A woman files her nails at reception. The sludgy rain half-heartedly tests the limits of the old windows, looking the way August's insides feel: sloshy and apprehensive of what's happening.

The counselor keeps clacking away on her keyboard.

Stop two on August's apology tour: figuring out if she's screwed for this semester. She's not, it turns out, since she was able to make up the two midterms she missed. She expected to have to grovel, fake a dead relative or something, anything but this: a printed-out transcript on the desk in front of her, almost every little box of requirements checked off.

"I'm surprised you didn't know," she says. "Your GPA is great. Slipping a little lately, obviously, but now that you're back on track, you'll be fine. More than fine. Most students who perform this well—especially ones who have been enrolled for as many years as you have—" At this, she glances over her cat-eye glasses at August. "Well, you're usually the ones banging down my damn door all semester asking when you can complete your degree."

"So my degree is . . . complete?"

"Almost," the counselor says. "You've got your capstone and a couple of electives left. But you can finish those in the fall." She finishes typing and turns toward August. "Pull it together for this next month, and you can graduate after one more semester."

August blinks at her a few times.

"Graduate, like . . . be done. With college."

She eyes August dubiously. "Most people are happier to hear this."

Ten minutes later, August is standing outside under a shabby overhang, watching her transcript slowly wilt in the humidity.

She's been deliberately not doing the math on her credits, caught in anxiety limbo between another student loan and the inevitable push off the ledge into adulthood. This is the ledge, she guesses. And the push. She feels like a cartoon character in midair, looking down to see the desert floor and a jacuzzi full of TNT five hundred feet below her.

What the fuck is she supposed to do?

She could call her mom, but her mother has only lived in one place, only ever wanted one thing. It's easy to know who you are when you chose once and never changed your mind.

There's this feeling August has had everywhere she's ever lived, like she's not really there. Like it's all happening in a dream. She walks down the street, and it's like she's floating a few inches off the pavement, never rooted down. She touches things, a canister of sugar at a coffee shop, or the post of a street sign warm from the afternoon sun, and it feels like she hasn't touched anything at all, like it's all a place she lives in concept. She's just out here, shoes untied, hair a mess, no idea where she's going, scraping her knees and not bleeding.

So maybe that's why, instead of calling her mom, or crawling home to some blunt truth from Myla or cryptic encouragement from Niko, she finds herself stepping onto the Q. At least here she knows where she is. Time, place, person.

"You look like you saw a ghost," Jane says. She shimmies her shoulders, jabbing a finger gun in August's direction. She scored a baseball cap from a seventh grader last week, and she's wearing it backward today. August pencils in thirty minutes between homework and public records to scream about it. "Get it?"

"You're hilarious."

Jane pulls a face. "Okay, but really. What's up with you?"

"I found out I, uh." She thinks of her transcript, inevitable, soggy, and folded up in the pocket of her raincoat. "I can graduate next semester, if I want."

"Oh, hey, that's great!" she says. "You've been in school forever!"

"Yeah, exactly," August says. "Forever. As in, it's the only thing I know how to do."

"That's not true," Jane says. "You know how to do tons of things."

"I know *logistically* how to perform *some tasks*," August tells her, squeezing her eyes shut. That dynamite hot tub is starting to sound very appealing. "I don't know how to have something that I *do*, every day, like as an adult who does a thing. It's nuts that we all start out having these vague ideas of what we like to do, hobbies, interests, and then one day everybody has their *thing,* you know? They used to just be a person and now they're a—an architect, or a banker, or a lawyer, or—or a serial killer who makes jewelry out of human teeth. Like, *things.* That they *do.* That they *are.* What if there's not that *thing* for me, Jane, I mean, what if I've never wanted to be anything other than just an August? What if that's all there is for me? What if Billy's closes and nobody else will hire me? What if I get out there and end up realizing there's not a dream for me, or a purpose, or anything—"

"*Okay,*" Jane says, cutting her off. "Okay, come on."

When August opens her eyes, Jane's standing in front of her, hand outstretched.

"Let's go."

"Go where?" August says, even as she grabs on. Immediately, she's pulled toward the back of the car, tripping over her feet. "I'm trying to have a nervous breakdown here."

"Yeah, exactly," Jane says. They're at the emergency exit, and Jane reaches for the door handle.

"Oh my God, what are you *doing?*"

"I'm gonna show you my favorite thing to do when I feel like I'm gonna lose it down here," Jane says. "All you gotta do is keep up."

"Why do I feel like I'm about to take my life into my own hands?"

"Because you should," Jane says easily. She winks as if she's sealing August's fate in an envelope with a kiss. "But I promise you'll be okay. Do you trust me?"

"What? What kind of question is that?"

"Can you turn that brain of yours off for a second and trust?"

August opens and shuts her mouth.

"I—I guess I can try."

"Good enough for me," Jane says, and she wrenches the door open.

There's barely time to panic about the noise and wind and motion exploding through the open door before Jane's stepping onto the tiny platform between trains, pulling August with her by one sweaty hand.

It's chaos—the darkness of the tunnel, the blue and yellow flashes of train lights and flickering wall fixtures, the deafening rattle of the tracks flying past, dirt and concrete rushing out from underneath them. August makes the absolutely terrible mistake of looking down and feels like she's going to throw up.

"*Oh my God, what the fuck,*" she says, but she can't hear her own voice.

The tracks are *right* there. One wrong step and a few inches of air between staying alive and being scraped off the rails. This is the worst possible idea anyone could ever have, and it's what Jane does for *fun.*

"It makes you feel alive, right?" Jane shouts, and before August can yank them both back into the car, Jane steps across the gap to the platform of the next car.

"It makes me feel like I'm gonna die!" August yells back.

"That's the same thing!"

August is clinging to the car, back pressed against the door, nails scrabbling. Jane grabs the handle of the next door with one hand and reaches out the other to her. "Come on! You can do this!"

"I really can't!"

"August, you can!"

"I can't!"

"Don't look at the tracks!" she yells. "Eyes up, Landry!"

Everything in August's brain is screaming at her not to, but she drags her eyes up from the rails and to the car in front of her, the tiny platform, Jane standing there with one hand out, the wind whipping her hair around her face.

August realizes, suddenly, it's the first time she's ever seen Jane outside of the train.

That's what makes her do it. Because August doesn't *do* this type of thing, but *Jane is outside.*

"Oh fuck," August mutters, and she grabs Jane's hand.

She clears the gap from one car to the next in a breath, a scream caught high in the back of her throat, and then her feet are on metal.

She did it. She made it across.

August crashes into Jane's chest, and Jane catches her around the waist like she did the day the lights went out, the day August thought she'd blown it for good. Jane laughs, and on a hysterical burst of adrenaline, August laughs too, her raincoat flying around them.

Here they are. Two sets of sneakers on a scrap of metal. Two girls in the middle of a hurricane, tearing down the line. She's looking up at Jane, and Jane's looking down at her, and August feels her everywhere, even the places she's not touching, pressed close as the world roars on.

"See?" she says. But she's looking at August's mouth when she says it. "You did it."

And August thinks, as she tips her chin up, that here, in the space between subway cars, right on the edge of where Jane exists, is where Jane's finally going to kiss her for real. No pretense. No memories. But because she wants to. Her fingers are spreading on August's waist, digging into the fabric of her jacket, and—

"Come on," Jane says, yanking the door open, and they tumble into the next car.

Jane pulls her half-running past unbothered commuters, dodging poles and standing passengers until they reach the next door. They jump from one car to the next, out one door and in another, until it stops being so terrifying to step off, until August barely even hesitates before taking her hand.

"Okay," Jane says, when they get to their seventh changeover. "You first."

August turns, eyes wide. That isn't what she signed up for. "What?"

"You trusted me, right?" August nods. "Now trust yourself."

August turns to the next train car. Her brain chooses this moment to remind her that forty-eight people died in subway accidents in 2016. She doesn't think she can do this without Jane standing there to catch her if she slips, and she's really not interested in going down in history as a delay on the Q while someone calls the medical examiner.

She trusted *Jane,* though. She trusted Jane and her time on this train and that cocky grin to get her there safely. Why can't she do the same for herself? She's learned this train backward and forward. The Q is home, and August is the girl with the knife picking its stops apart one by one. She doesn't believe in things. But she can believe in that.

She steps off.

"Hell yeah!" Jane crows from behind when she makes it. She doesn't wait for August's hand, hopping across and onto the platform. "That's my girl!"

Jane slides the door open, and on the other side, August collapses into the nearest seat.

"Holy shit," August says, panting. "Holy shit, I can't believe I did that."

Jane leans on a pole to catch her breath. "You did. And *that* is what you need to trust in. Because you got what you need. And sometimes, the universe has your back."

August inhales once, exhales. She looks at Jane, forty-five years away from where she's supposed to be, and yeah, she guesses in some ways, the universe does have her back.

"So," Jane says, "let's take it down to one thing. What scares you the most?"

August thinks about it as her lungs level back out.

"I—" she attempts. "I don't know who I am."

Jane snorts, raising an eyebrow. "Well, that makes fuckin' two of us."

"Yeah, but—"

"Stop, okay? For five minutes, let's pretend everything else doesn't matter, and I'm me, and you're you, and we're sitting on this train, and we're figuring it out. Can you do that?"

August grits her teeth. "Yeah."

"Okay," Jane says. "Now, listen to me."

She crouches in front of August, bracing her hands on August's knees, forcing her to look into her eyes.

"None of us know exactly who we are, and guess what? It doesn't fucking matter. God knows *I* don't, but I'll find my way to it." She rubs her thumb over August's kneecap, poking gently into the soft part below her thigh. "Like—okay, I dated this girl who was an artist, right? And she'd do figure drawing, where she'd draw the negative space around a person first, and then fill in the person. And that's how I'm trying to look at it. Maybe I don't know what fills it in yet, but I can look at the space around where I sit in the world, what creates that shape, and I can care about what it's made of, if it's good, if it hurts anyone, it makes people happy, if it makes *me* happy. And that can be enough for now."

Jane's looking up at her like she means it, like she's been riding these rails all this time on that hope. She's a fighter, a runner, a riot girl, and she can't be any of that down here, so she runs between trains to feel something. If she can be here and live with that and have enough left over for this, she must know what she's talking about.

"Shit," August says. "You're good at this."

Jane smiles wide. "Look, I was gay in the '70s. I can handle an emergency."

"God," August groans as Jane clambers into her own seat. "I can't believe I made *you* talk *me* down from an existential crisis."

Jane tilts her head to look at her. She's got this ability to move between pretty and handsome from moment to moment, a subtle difference in the way she holds her chin or the set of her mouth. Right now, she's the prettiest girl August has ever seen.

"Shut up," Jane says. "You're spending your life riding the subway to help a stranger with no evidence she can be helped, okay? Let me do one thing for you."

August releases a breath, and she's surprised at the proximity when it ruffles the ends of Jane's hair.

Jane keeps looking at her, and August swears she sees something move behind her eyes, like a memory does when she's thinking about Mingxia or Jenny or one of the other girls, but new, different. Something delicate as a spark, and only for August. It's the same feeling from the platform: maybe this time, for real.

August isn't supposed to care. She's not supposed to want that. But the way her heart kicks up into a fever frequency says that she still goddamn does.

"You're not a stranger," August says into the few inches between them.

"No, you're right," Jane agrees. "We're definitely not strangers." She leans back and stretches her arms over her head, turning her face away from August, and says, "I guess you're my best friend, huh?"

The train eases into another station, and something clenches in the vicinity of August's jaw.

Friend.

"Yeah," August says. "Yeah, I guess so."

"And you're gonna get me back to where I'm supposed to be," Jane goes on, smiling. Smiling at the idea of going back to 1970-something and never seeing August again. "Because you're a genius."

The train rattles and groans to a stop.

"Yeah," August says, and she forces a smile.

"You've been doing *what* for research?" Myla asks. It's hard to catch the question when she's got a screwdriver between her teeth, but August gets the gist.

Myla has her own office in the back of Rewind, complete with shelves full of typewriters and old radios and a workstation strewn with parts. She told August she got the job after wandering in halfway through her final semester at Columbia and pulling a pair of pliers out of the owner's hands to rewire a 1940s record player. She's a nerd for the oldies, she always says, and it came in handy. She's clearly good enough at what she does that her boss doesn't mind her decorating her workstation with a homemade cross-stitch that says BIG DICK ENERGY IS GENDER NEUTRAL.

She's looking at August through the giant magnifying lens mounted over her station, so her mouth and nose are normal sized, but her eyes are the size of dinner plates. August tries not to laugh.

"Kissing, okay, we've been making out—"

"On the *train?*"

"Don't think Niko hasn't told me about the time under the pizza box after Thanksgiving last year."

"Okay, that was a *holiday.*"

"*Anyway,*" August goes on, "*as I was saying,* remembering kisses and girls that she, you know, felt something for, brings back a lot for her, and the best way to do that is to re-create them." The grimace Myla pulls is magnified about ten times by the lens, distorted like a disapproving Dalí. "*Stop making that face,* okay, I *know* it's a bad idea."

"I mean, it's as if you like to be emotionally tortured," Myla says, finally sitting back so her facial proportions return to normal. "Wait, *is* that what it is? Because like, damn, but okay."

"No, that's the whole thing," August says. "I have to stop. I can't keep doing it. It's—it's fucking me up. So that's why I came here—I have an idea for something that could work instead."

"And what's that?"

"A radio," August says. "Another big thing for her is music. She told me she doesn't want Spotify or anything, but maybe random songs from the radio might help her remember things. I wondered if y'all had any portable radios in stock."

Myla pushes back from her station, folding her arms and surveying her domain of deconstructed cash registers and juke-box parts like a steampunk Tony Stark in a leather skirt. "We might have something in the back."

"And," August says, following her toward the storage room in the rear of the store, "I saw Jane step outside of the train."

Myla whips her head around. "She got off the train, and you led with the *kissing*? God, you are the most useless bisexual I've ever met in my entire goddamn life."

"She wasn't *off* the train, she was *outside* of it," August clari-fies. "She can walk between the cars."

"So it's not the train that's got her trapped, it's the line," Myla concludes simply, unlocking the storage room door. "Good to know."

August leaves fifteen minutes later with a portable radio and a reminder from Myla to pick up batteries, and when she hands it to Jane, she gets to watch her face light up like Christmas came early. Which, she has to admit, is part of why she bought it. The other reason quickly presents itself.

"There's this thing I'm trying to remember," Jane says. "From LA. There's a taco truck, and Coke with lime, and this song by Sly and the Family Stone . . . and a girl." She looks at August. And August could—she could get off the train and return with a wedge of lime and a kiss, *wants* to even, but she thinks about what Jane said about getting out of here, the way she smiled at the thought of leaving.

"Oh, man," August says. "That, uh—that sounds like a good lead, but I'm—I gotta clock in. I got a double today, you know, need the money so—anyway." She gathers up her bag, eyeing the board for the next stop. Not even close to work. "Try the radio. See if you can find a funk station. I bet it helps."

"Oh," Jane says, spinning the dial, "okay. Yeah, good idea."

And August dips out of the train with a wave as soon as the doors slide open.

She thinks—she is pretty sure, actually, that she's figured out a solution to her problem. A radio. That should be fine.

It starts on a Saturday morning when Jane texts, August, Put your radio on 90.9 FM. Thanks, Jane

Obviously, August doesn't own a radio. And it would never occur to Jane that August doesn't own a radio. Even if she did, she's outside for once, sitting by the water in Prospect Park, watching ducks squabble over pizza crusts and stoners pass a joint under a gazebo. She'd be on the train with Jane except Niko personally packed her a sandwich and insisted she take advantage of her Saturday morning off to "recenter" and "absorb different energies" and "try this havarti I got at the farmer's market last week, it's got a lot of character."

But it only takes a minute to download an FM tuner app, and August thumbs through the dial to the station. A guy with a dry voice is reading a list of programming for the next six hours, so she texts back, Okay, what next?

Just wait, Jane replies. I remembered another song, so I called in and requested it.

The guy on the mic switches gears and says, "And now, a request from a girl in Brooklyn who wants to hear some old-school punk, here's 'Lovers' by the Runaways."

August leans back on the bench, and the harsh guitar and pounding drums start up. Her phone buzzes.

Today I remembered that I dated a
girl in Spanish Harlem who liked to
get head to this album! XOXO Jane

August chokes on her sandwich.

It becomes the new ritual: Jane texts August day and night,
Hey! Turn on the radio! Love, Jane. And within minutes, there'll
be a song she requested. Thankfully, after the first, they're almost never songs that she used to eat girls out to.

Sometimes it's one Jane just remembered and wants to hear.
One day it's "War" by Edwin Starr, and she giddily tells August
about a Vietnam protest in '75 where she broke a finger in a fight
with some old racist while the song blasted over the speakers,
how a bunch of the guys who hung out on Mott Street passed
around a coffee can to collect the money to get it set correctly.

But sometimes, it's a song that she likes, or wants August to
hear, a song from the back of her mind or her menagerie of cassettes. Michael Bolton rasping his way through "Soul Provider"
or Jam Master Jay spitting out "You Be Illin'." It doesn't matter.
90.9 will play it, and August will listen just to feel that under-
the-same-moon feeling of Jane listening to the same thing at
the same time as she glides across the Manhattan Bridge.

And suddenly August is as handcuffed to the radio as Jane
used to be. It's extremely fucking inconvenient, honestly. She's
busy worrying about what's going to happen to Lucie and Winfield and Jerry once Billy's gets shut down. She has trains to
catch and shifts to work and classes to catch up on and, on one
particular Sunday, a Craigslist ad to answer across Brooklyn.

"Please, Wes," August begs. He has the night off, so he's actually awake before sunset, and he's using his daylight hours to
sketch on the couch and shoot deeply put-upon looks at August

across the apartment. For someone so determined to never express emotion, he can be incredibly dramatic.

"I'm sorry, how exactly do you expect us to get a desk and an entire bed home from fucking Gravesend?"

"It's a writing desk and a twin mattress," August tells him. "We can do it on the subway."

"I am not going to be the asshole who takes a mattress on the subway."

"People take obnoxious things on the subway all the time! I was on the Q last week and someone had an entire recliner! It had *cupholders*, Wes."

"Yeah, and that person was an asshole. You haven't been in New York long enough to earn the right to be an asshole with impunity. You're still in the tourist zone."

"I am *not a tourist*. A rat climbed up my shoe yesterday, and I just let it happen. Could a tourist do *that*?"

Wes rolls his eyes, sitting up and batting a dangling vine out of his face. "I thought you were into minimalism, anyway."

"I was," August says. She takes off her glasses to clean them, hoping the blurry shape of Wes doesn't recognize it for what it is: not having to see someone's face when she says something vulnerable. "But that was . . . before I found somewhere worth putting stuff in."

Wes is quiet, then sighs, putting his sketchbook down on the trunk.

He grits his teeth. "Isaiah has a car."

Two hours later, they're picking their way back to Flatbush, August Tetris'd into the back seat with her rickety new writing desk and a twin-size mattress strapped to the roof of Isaiah's Volkswagen Golf.

Isaiah is saying something about his day job, about Instagram influencers asking if they can write off handcrafted orchid crowns on their taxes, and Wes is laughing—eyes closed, head thrown back, nose scrunched up *laughing*. August knows she's staring. She's never, not once since she moved in, seen Wes crack more than a sarcastic chuckle.

"You good back there?" Isaiah asks, glancing in the rearview mirror. August whips her phone out, pretending she's not monitoring their conversation. "You got enough legroom?"

"I'll survive," August says. "Thanks again. You saved my life."

"No problem," he says. "It's not as bad as when I did this for Wes. His bed's a queen. That was a bitch to move."

"You helped Wes move a bed?"

"I—" Wes starts.

"It's very tasteful," Isaiah continues. "Birch headboard, matches his dresser. He may not be a rich kid anymore, but he still got bougie taste."

"That's not—"

"You've seen the inside of Wes's bedroom?" August interrupts. "*I* haven't even seen the inside of Wes's bedroom, and I share a wall with him."

"Yeah, it's cute! You expect it to look like a hobbit hole, but it's really nice."

"A *hobbit hole*?" Wes hisses. He's aiming for indignant, but his mouth splits into a begrudging smile.

Oh, man. He is in *love*.

August's phone chimes. Jane, telling her to put on the radio again.

"Hey," she says. "Do you mind if we put the radio on?"

"God, please," Isaiah says, pulling the AUX cord out of Wes's phone. "If I have to listen to Bon Iver for another block, I'm gonna drive into a telephone pole."

Wes grumbles but doesn't protest when August reaches forward, tuning to 90.9. The song that comes on is one she recognizes—gentle piano, a little theatrical.

"Love of My Life" by Queen.

Oh, no.

There was, she realizes, a major flaw in her plan. She may not be kissing Jane anymore, but this is worse. How is she supposed to know if, when Jane requests "I've Got Love On My Mind," August is supposed to read into the lyrics? Dear Natalie Cole, when you sang the line *When you touch me I can't resist, and you've touched me a thousand times,* were you thinking about a confused queer with a terrible crush? Dear Freddie Mercury, when you wrote "Love of My Life," did you mean for it to reach across space and time in a platonic way or a real-deal, break-your-heart, throw-you-up-against-a-wall type of way?

"You sure you got enough room?" Isaiah asks. "You kind of look like you're dying."

"I'm fine," August croaks, sliding her phone back into her pocket. If she absolutely has to have feelings, she can at least do it in private.

They unload Isaiah's car and carry everything up six flights and into August's bedroom, and Isaiah blows them both a kiss on his way out. Wes sits next to August on her deflating air mattress, each wiggling their asses to force the air out.

"So . . ." August says.

"Don't."

"I'm just . . . curious. I don't get it. You like him. He likes you."

"It's complicated."

"Is it, though? Like, my crush lives on the *subway*. You have it so much easier."

Wes grunts, abruptly getting to his feet, and the sudden lack of counterbalance sends August's ass thumping onto the floor.

"I'd disappoint him," he says, maintaining stubborn eye contact as he dusts his jeans off. "He doesn't deserve to be disappointed."

Wes leaves her on the floor. She guesses she kind of deserved that.

Later, when she's managed to assemble the cheap bedframe she ordered and tuck the sheets onto her new bed, she opens her texts.

> What's the story behind the song?

Jane texts back a minute later. She addresses and signs it the way she usually does. August is so used to it that her eyes have started skipping right over the introduction and sign off.

> I don't remember much. I listened
> to it in an apartment I had when I
> was 20. I used to think it was one
> of the most romantic songs I ever
> heard.

> Really? The lyrics are kind of
> depressing.

> No, you gotta listen to the bridge.
> It's all about loving someone so
> much you can't stand the idea of
> losing them, even if it hurts, that all

the hard stuff is worth it if you can
get through together.

August pulls it up, lets it spin past the first two verses, into the line: *You will remember, when this is blown over . . .*

Okay, she types, thinking of Wes and how determined he is not to let Isaiah hand him his heart, of Myla holding Niko's hand as he talks to things she can't see, of her mom and a whole life spent searching, of herself, of Jane, of hours on the train—all the things they put themselves through for love. Okay, I get it.

8

Posted June 8, 1999

Girl with leather jacket on Q train at 14th Street-Union Square (Manhattan)

Dear Beautiful Stranger, you'll probably never see this, but I had to try. I only saw you for about thirty seconds, but I can't forget them. I was standing on the platform waiting for the Q on Friday morning when it pulled up and you were standing there. You looked at me, and I looked at you. You smiled, and I smiled. Then the doors closed. I was so busy looking at you, I forgot to get on the train. I had to wait ten minutes for another one and was late for work. I was wearing a purple dress and platform Skechers. I think I'm in love with you.

Isaiah opens the door wearing a top hat, leather leggings, and a violently ugly button-down.

"You look like a member of Toto," Wes says.

"And what better day than this holy Sunday to bless the rains down in Africa," he says, waving them into his apartment with a flourish.

The inside of Isaiah's place *feels* like him: a sleek leather sectional, stuffed and meticulously organized bookshelves, splashes of color in rugs and paintings and a silk robe slung over the back of a kitchen chair. Tasteful, stylish, well-organized, with a spare bedroom full of drag tucked beside the kitchen. His polished walnut dining table is decorated with dozens of Jesus figurines dressed in homemade drag, and the faint sounds of the *Jesus Christ Superstar* soundtrack underscore the sloshing of the punch he's making at the counter.

So this is the event announced via handwritten flyer shoved under their door: Isaiah's annual drag family Easter brunch.

"Loving the sacrilege," Niko says, unloading a pan of vegetarian pasteles. He picks up one of the figurines, which is wrapped in a bedazzled sock. "White Jesus looks great in puce."

August hauls her contribution—an aluminum dish full of Billy's biscuits—over the threshold and contemplates if she's the reason these two households are finally merging. It's technically the first time the gang has been invited to the brunch, unless you count last year when the party spilled into the hall and Myla ended up getting a lap dance from a Bronx queen on her way to the mailbox. But last week, August rode the Popeyes service elevator with Isaiah and made a point to mention Wes's sulking fit after his sister Instagrammed a Wes-less Passover seder.

"Are we the first ones?" August asks.

Isaiah shoots her a look over his shoulder. "You ever met a punctual drag queen? Why do you think we're having brunch at seven o'clock at night?"

"Point," she says. "Wes made scones."

"It's nothing special," Wes grumbles as he shoulders past her to the kitchen.

"Tell him what kind."

There's a heavy pause in which she can practically hear Wes's teeth grinding.

"Orange cardamom with a maple chai drizzle," he bites out with all the fury in his tiny body.

"Oh shit, that's what my sister's bringing," Isaiah says.

Wes looks stricken. "Really?"

"No, dumbass, she's gonna show up with a bunch of Doritos and a ziplock bag of weed like she always does," Isaiah says with a happy laugh, and Wes turns delightfully pink.

"Praise it and blaze it," Myla comments, flopping onto the couch.

When the first members of Isaiah's drag family start to show—Sara Tonin in dewy daytime drag and a handful of twenty-somethings with flashy manicures and thick-framed glasses to hide their shaved-off brows—the music cranks up and the lights crank down. August is quickly realizing that it's only a brunch in the absolute loosest definition of the word: there is brunch food, yes, and Isaiah introduces her to a Montreal queen hot off a touring gig with a fistful of cash and a Nalgene full of mimosas. But, mostly, it's a party.

Apartment 6F isn't the the only group outside of Isaiah's drag family to warrant an invitation. There's the morning shift guy from the bodega, the owner of one of the jerk chicken joints, stoners from the park. There's Isaiah's sister, fresh off the train from Philly with purple box braids down to her waist and a Wawa bag over her shoulder. Every employee from the Popeyes downstairs ends up there the second they've clocked out, passing around boxes of spicy dark. August recognizes the guy who always lets them on the service elevator, still wearing a nametag that says GREGORY, half the letters rubbed off so it reads REG RY.

The party fills and fills, and August huddles in the kitchen between Isaiah and Wes, the former trying to greet every person who stumbles through the door while the latter pretends he's not watching him do it.

"Wait, oh my God," Isaiah says suddenly, goggling at the door. "Is that—Jade, *Jade,* is that Vera Harry? Oh my God, I've never seen her out of drag, you were *right,* bitch!" He turns to them, gesturing across the room at an incredibly hot and stubbly guy who's walked in. He looks like he fell out of a CW show and into Isaiah's living room. Wes is instantly glaring. "*That* is a new queen, moved from LA last month, everybody's been talking about her. She's this crazy stunt queen, but then, out of drag? *Trade.* Best thing to ever happen to Thursday nights."

"Sucks for Thursday nights," Wes mutters, but Isaiah has already vanished into the crowd.

"Oof," August says, "you're jealous."

"Wow, holy shit, you figured it out. You're gonna win a Peabody Award for reporting," Wes deadpans. "Where's the keg? I was told there would be a keg."

Noisy minutes lurch by in a mess of shiny eyelids and Isaiah's curated playlist—it's just shifted from "Your Own Personal Jesus" to "Faith" by George Michael—and August is snatching a biscuit from the tray she brought when someone sets a platter of bun-and-cheese down beside it and says, "Shit, I almost brought the same thing. That would have been awkward."

August looks up, and there's Winfield in a silk shirt covered in cartoon fish, his braids bundled up on top of his head. Beside him is Lucie who, when she's not in her Billy's uniform, apparently favors extremely tiny black dresses and lace-up boots. She looks more like a girl in an assassin movie than the manager of a pancake joint. August stares.

"You— What are you doing here? Y'all know Isaiah?"

"I know Annie," Winfield says. "She didn't put me in drag my first time, but she sat at my counter enough to convince me I should try it."

What?

"You're—you do drag? But you've never mentioned—and you're not—" August fumbles with half a dozen ways to end that sentence before landing eloquently on, "You have a beard?"

"What, you never met a bearded pansexual drag queen?" He laughs, and it's then that August notices: Winfield and Lucie are holding hands. What in the world goes on at drag family Easter brunch?

"I—you—y'all are—?"

"Mm-hmm," Winfield hums happily.

"As fun as it is to break your brain," Lucie says, "nobody at work knows. Tell them and I break your arm."

"Oh my God. Okay. You're . . ." August's head is going to explode. She looks at Winfield and gasps, "Oh fuck, *that's* why you know so much Czech."

Winfield laughs, and they disappear as quickly as they appeared, and it is . . . nice, August thinks. The two of them together. Like Isaiah and Wes or Myla and Niko, it makes a strange sense. And Lucie—she looked *happy,* affectionate even, which is incredible, since August kind of assumed she was made from what they use at Billy's to scrub out the floor drains. Emotional steel wool.

By the punch bowl, the conversation has shifted to every-one's Easter family traditions. August refills her cup as Isaiah asks Myla, "What about you?"

"My parents are, like, hippie agnostics, so we never cele-brated. I'm pretty sure that's the only thing Niko's parents don't like about me, my heathen upbringing," she says, rolling her eyes as Niko laughs and throws an arm over her shoulders. "Our big April holiday growing up was Tomb Sweeping Day, but my grandparents and great-grandparents keep refusing to die, so we just burn a paper Ferrari every year for my great-uncle who was in love with his car."

"My parents always made us go to Sábado de Gloria," Niko chimes in. "The Catholic church taught me everything I know about drama. And candles."

"Oh, no shit?" Isaiah says appreciatively. "My pops is a pas-tor. Mom leads the choir. Our parents should get together with the blood of Christ sometime. Except mine are Methodist, so it's grape juice."

Wes, who is perched on the countertop observing the con-versation with the vaguest of interest, says, "August, didn't you go to Catholic school for a million years? Is your family horny for Jesus too?"

"Only the extended family," she says. "Didn't go for Jesus reasons. Louisiana public schools are crazy underfunded and my mom wanted me to go private, so I went and we were broke my whole life. *Super* great time. One of the nuns got fired for selling cocaine to students."

"Damn," Wes says. He never did find the keg, but there's a thirty-rack of PBR beside him, and he's fishing one out. "Wanna shotgun a beer?"

"I absolutely don't," August says, and takes the beer Wes holds out anyway. She untucks her pocketknife from her jean jacket and hands it over, then follows Wes's lead and jams it into the side of her can.

"I still think that knife is cool," Wes says, and they pop the tops and chug.

When people start having to do shots in the hallway, Myla flings open the door to 6F and yells, "Shoes off and nobody touch the plants!" And everything overflows into both apartments, drag queens perched on the steamer trunk, Popeyes aprons dropped in the hall, Wes reclined across Isaiah's kitchen table like a Renaissance painting, Vera Harry cradling Noodles in his beefy arms. Myla busts out the grocery bag of Lunar New Year candy her mom sent and starts passing it around the room. Isaiah's Canadian friend tromps by with a box of wine on her shoulder, singing "moooore Fraaanziaaaa" to the tune of "O Canada."

At some point, August realizes her phone's been chiming insistently from her pocket. When she pulls it out, all the messages have collected to fill the screen. She swallows down an embarrassingly pleased sound and tries to play it off as a burp.

"Who's blowing up your phone, Baby Smurf?" Myla says, as if she doesn't know. August tilts her phone so Myla can see, bearing her weight when she leans in so close that August can smell the orangey lotion she puts on after showers.

Hello, I'm very bored.—Jane

Hi August!—Jane

Are you getting these?—Jane

Hellooooo?—Jane Su, Q Train,
Brooklyn, NY

"Aw, she's already learned how to double text," Myla says. "Does she think she has to sign it like a letter?"

"I guess I left that part out when I was showing her how to use her phone."

"It's so cute," Myla says. "*You're* so cute."

"I'm not cute," August says, frowning. "I'm—I'm tough. Like a cactus."

"Oh, August," Myla says. Her voice is so loud. She's very drunk. *August* is very drunk, she realizes, because she keeps looking at Myla and thinking how cool her eyeshadow is and how pretty she is and how nuts it is that she even wants to be August's friend. Myla grabs her chin in one hand, squeezing until her lips poke out like a fish. "You're a cream puff. You're a cupcake. You're a yarn ball. You're—you're a little sugar pumpkin."

"I'm a garlic clove," August says. "Pungent. Fifty layers."

"*And* the best part of every dish."

"Gross."

"We should call her."

"What?"

"Yeah, come on, let's call her!"

How it happens is a blur—August doesn't know if she agrees, or why, but her phone is in her hand and a call connecting, and—

"August?"

"Jane?"

"Did you call me from a concert?" Jane shouts over the sound of Patti LaBelle wailing "New Attitude" on someone's Bluetooth speaker. "Where are you?"

"Easter brunch!" August yells back.

"Look, I know I don't have the firmest grasp on time, but I'm pretty sure it's really late for brunch."

"What, are you into rules now?"

"Hell no," Jane says, instantly affronted. "If you care what time brunch happens, you're a cop."

That's something she's picked up from Myla, who August eventually allowed to visit Jane again, and who loves to say that all kinds of things—paying rent on time, ordering a cinnamon raisin bagel—make you a cop. August smiles at the idea of her friends rubbing off on Jane, at having friends, at having someone for her friends to rub off on. She wants Jane to be there so badly that she tucks her phone into the pocket by her heart and starts carrying Jane around the party.

It's one of those nights. Not that August has experienced a night like this—not firsthand, at least. She's been to parties, but she's not much of a drinker or a smoker, even less of a dazzling conversationalist. She's mostly observed them like some kind of house party anthropologist, never understanding how people could fall in and out of connections and conversations, flipping switches of moods and patterns of speech so easily.

But she finds herself embroiled in a mostly Spanish debate about grilled cheese sandwiches between Niko and the bodega guy ("Once you put any protein other than bacon on there, that shit is officially a melt," Jane weighs in from her pocket) and a mostly lawless drinking game in the next ("Never have I ever thrown a molotov cocktail," Jane says. "Didn't you hear the rules? When you say it like that, you're saying that you *have*," August says. "Yeah," Jane agrees, "I know."). For once, she's not thinking about staying alert to fend off danger. It's all people Isaiah knows and trusts, and August knows and trusts Isaiah.

And she's got Jane with her, which she fucking loves. It

makes everything easier, makes her braver. A Jane in her pocket. Pocket Jane.

She finds herself wedged between Lucie and Winfield, shouting over the music about customers at Billy's. Then she's trading jokes with Vera Harry, and she's laughing so hard she spills her drink down her chin, and Isaiah's sister calls out, "Not saying shit's gone off the rails, but I just saw someone mix schnapps with a Capri Sun and someone else is in the bathtub handing out shrooms."

And then somehow, she's next to Niko, as he goes on and on about the existential dread of being a young person under climate change, twirling the thread of the conversation around his finger like a magician. It hits her like things do sometimes when you're buzzed enough to forget the context your brain has built to understand something: Niko is a *psychic*. She's friends with a whole psychic, and she *believes* him.

"Can I ask you a personal question?" August says to him once the group dissolves, hearing her voice come out sloppy.

"Should I go?" Jane says from her pocket.

"Noooo," August says to her phone.

Niko eyes her over his drink. "Ask away."

"When did you know?"

"That I was trans?"

August blinks at him. "No. That you were a psychic."

"Oh," Niko says. He shakes his head, the fang dangling from his ear swinging. "Whenever someone asks me personal questions, it's always about being trans. That's, like, so low on the list of the most interesting things about me. But it's funny because the answer's the same. I just always knew."

"Really?" August thinks distantly about her gradual stumble into knowing she was bisexual, the years of confusing crushes she tried to rationalize away. She can't imagine always knowing something huge about herself and never questioning it.

"Yeah. I knew I was a boy and I knew my sister was a girl and I knew that the people who lived in our house before us had gotten a divorce because the wife was having an affair, and that was it," he explains. "I don't even remember coming out to my parents or telling them I could see things they couldn't. It was just always . . . what it was."

"And your family, they're—?"

"Catholic?" Niko says. "Yeah, they are. Kinda. More when I was a kid. The whole psychic thing—my mom always called it my gift from God. So they believed me about being a boy. Our church wasn't so chill about it when I wanted to transition though. My mom kinda got into it with the priest, so none of the Riveras have been to mass in a while. Not that my abuelo knows that."

"That's cool," Jane's voice says.

"Very cool," August agrees. Suddenly she knows where Niko gets his confidence from. She pulls on his arm. "Come on."

"Where?"

"You have to be on my team for Rolly Bangs."

The battered office chair appears out of nowhere, and Wes tapes off the floor of the hallway while Myla stands on a table and shouts the rules. An assortment of protective gear manifests on the kitchen counter: two bicycle helmets, Myla's welding goggles, some ski gear that must belong to Wes, one lonely kneepad. August posts a sheet of paper on the wall and gets Isaiah to help her devise a tournament bracket—two drunk brains make one smart brain—and it's on, the kitchen cleared and cheering crowds gathered on either side of the apartment as the games start.

August puts on a helmet, and when Niko flings her chair toward the hallway and she goes flying and screaming through the air, Jane warm in her pocket and no care for whether she breaks something, the only thought in her head is that she's twenty-three years old. She's twenty-three years old, and she's doing something absolutely stupid, and she's allowed to do absolutely stupid things whenever she wants, and the rest doesn't have to matter right now. How had she not realized it sooner?

As it turns out, letting herself have fun is *fun*.

"Where does that disembodied voice keep coming from?" says Isaiah between rounds, sidling up beside August. He's wearing a fur muff as a helmet.

"That's August's girlfriend," Wes supplies, slurring slightly. "She's a ghost."

"Oh my God, I knew this place was haunted," Isaiah says. "Wait, the one from the séance? She's—?"

Someone else leans into the conversation. "Séance?"

"Ghost?" Sara Tonin chimes in from atop the refrigerator.

"Is she hot?" Isaiah's sister asks.

"She's not my girlfriend," August says, waving them off. She points to the phone sticking out of her front pocket. "And she's not a ghost, she's just on speaker."

"Boo," says Jane's voice.

"She's always wearing the exact same thing," Wes says as he hauls the office chair back, one of the wheels listing pathetically. "That's ghost behavior if you ask me."

"If I'm ever a ghost, I hope I get a choice in what I'm cursed to wear for the rest of eternity," Isaiah says. "Like, do you think it's just whatever you're wearing when you die? Or is there an afterlife greatest hits mood board where you get to assemble your own ghost drag?"

"If I get to pick, I want to be wearing, like . . ." Myla thinks about it for a long second. Her drink sloshes down her arm. "One of those jumpsuits from the end of *Mamma Mia*. I go to haunt people but it always turns into a musical number. That's the energy I want to bring to the hereafter."

"Brocade suit, open jacket, no shirt," Niko says confidently.

"Wes," Myla shouts at him as he climbs into the rolling chair, "what would your ghost wear?"

He straps on a pair of ski goggles. "A slanket covered in shrimp chip crumbs."

"Very Tiny Tim," Isaiah notes.

"Shut up and throw me across the room, you big bitch."

Isaiah obliges, and the tournament continues, but he comes back three rounds later, smiling a broad smile, the gap between his two front teeth unfairly charming.

He points at August's phone. "What's her name?"

"Jane," August says.

"Jane," Isaiah repeats, leaning into August's boobs to shout at the phone. "*Jane!* Why aren't you *here* at my *party*?"

"Because she's a blip in reality from the 1970s bound to the Q and she can't leave," Niko supplies.

"What he said," Jane agrees.

Isaiah ignores them and continues to yell at August's tits. "Jane! The party's not over yet! You should come!"

"Man, I'd love to," Jane says, "I haven't been to a good party in forever. And I'm pretty sure my birthday is coming up."

"Your birthday?" Isaiah says. "You're having a party for that, right? I wanna come."

"Probably not," Jane tells him. "I'm sort of—well, my friends are kind of unavailable."

"That's such bullshit. Oh my God. You can't have a birthday

and not celebrate it." Isaiah leans back and addresses the party. "Hey! Hey everybody! Since this is my party, I get to decide what kind of party it is, and I am deciding it's Jane's birthday party!"

"I don't know who Jane is, but okay!" someone yells.

"How soon can you get here, Jane?"

"I—"

And maybe Isaiah remembers the séance, and maybe he believes what's happening here, and maybe he sees the panicked look August and Niko exchange, or maybe he's just drunk. But his grin spreads impossibly wider, and he says, "Actually. Hang on. Everybody, please transfer your drink to an unmarked container, we're taking it to the subway!"

Isaiah's friends are nothing if not game—and, in many cases, crossed—so they flow down the stairs and out onto the street like a dam breaking, drinks in the air, caftans and capes and aprons trailing behind them. August is between Lucie and Sara Tonin, carried by the current toward her usual station.

"Which one is he?" Sara is asking Lucie.

Lucie points at Winfield, who's throwing his head back to laugh, glitter glinting in his beard, looking like the life of the party. She tamps down a smile and says, "That's him," and August laughs and wants so badly to know what it feels like to show off the person who's yours from across the crowd.

Then they all pile onto the train, August up front, pointing to Jane and telling Isaiah, "That's her," and she guesses she *does* know. Maybe what she really wants is to be the person across the crowd who belongs to someone.

"You brought me a *party*?" Jane asks as the car fills. Niko has already started blasting "Suavamente."

"Technically, *Isaiah* brought you a party," August points out.

But Jane looks around at the dozens of people on the train,

painted nails and shrieks of laughter up and down her quiet night, and it's August, not Isaiah, she looks at when she grins and says, "*Thank you.*"

Someone places a plastic crown on Jane's head, and someone else presses a cup into her hand, and she rides on into the night, beaming and proud as a war hero.

Myla's bag of candy starts making the rounds again—August can't be sure, but she thinks someone has slipped in some edibles—and at some point, maybe after Isaiah and the Canadian Franzia enthusiast have a dance-off, August gets an idea. She convinces one of Isaiah's drag daughters to give her the safety pin stuck through their earlobe, and she returns to Jane with it, grabbing her shoulders to catch her balance.

"Hi again," Jane says, watching as August sticks the pin through the collar of her leather jacket. "What's this?"

"Something we do in New Orleans," August says, pulling a dollar out of her pocket and pinning it to Jane's chest. "Thought you might remember."

"Oh . . . oh yeah!" Jane says. "You pin a dollar to somebody's shirt on their birthday, and when they go out—"

"—everyone who sees it is supposed to add a dollar," August finishes, and the light of happy recognition in Jane's eyes is so bright that August surprises herself with her own volume when she yells to the crowd. "Hey! Hey, new party rule! Pin the cash on the birthday girl! Keep it going, tell your friends!"

By the time the train loops back into Brooklyn, there are people swinging from subway poles and a stack of bills stuck through Jane's safety pin, and August wants to do things she never wants to do. She wants to talk to people, shout through conversations. She wants to dance. She watches Wes as he slowly, warily lets himself slip against Isaiah's side, and she turns to Jane and does the same. Niko bobs by with his Polaroid camera and snaps a photo of them, and August doesn't even want to duck away.

Jane looks at her through a dusting of confetti that's appeared out of nowhere and smiles, and August can't control her body. She wants to climb up onto a seat, so she does.

"I like being taller than you," she says to Jane, chewing on a piece of peanut and sesame brittle from Myla's bag of candy.

"I don't know," Jane ribs her. "I don't think it suits you."

August swallows. She wants to do something stupid. She's twenty-three years old, and she's allowed to do something stupid. She touches the side of Jane's neck and says, "Did you ever kiss any girls who were taller than you?"

Jane eyes her. "I don't think so."

"Too bad," August says. She leans down so Jane has to tip her chin up to maintain eye contact, and she finds that she likes that angle quite a lot. "No memories to bring back."

"Yeah," Jane says. "It'd just be kissing to kiss."

August is warm, and Jane is beautiful. Steady and improbable and unlike anyone August's ever met in her life. "Sure would."

"Uh-huh." Jane covers August's hand with hers, their fingers tangling. "And you're drunk. I don't think—"

"I'm not that drunk," August says. "I'm happy."

She sways forward, and she lets herself kiss Jane on the mouth.

For half a second, the train and the party and everything else exist on the other side of a pocket of air. They're underground, underwater, sharing a breath. August brushes her thumb behind Jane's ear, and Jane's mouth parts, and—

Jane breaks off abruptly.

"What is that?" she asks.

August blinks at her. "Um. It was supposed to be a kiss."

"No, that . . . the—your lips. They taste like peanuts. And . . . sesame paste? They taste like—"

She touches a hand to her mouth and staggers back, eyes wide, and August's stomach drops. She's remembering something. Someone. Another girl who's not August.

"Oh," Jane says finally. Someone crashes into her shoulder as they dance by, and she doesn't even notice. "*Oh, it's—Biyu.*"

"Who's Biyu?"

Jane lowers her hand slowly and says, "I am."

August's feet hit the floor.

"I'm Biyu," Jane goes on. August reaches out blindly and gets a handful of Jane's jacket, watching her face, holding on to her as she trips backward into memories. "That's my name—what my parents named me. Su Biyu. I was the oldest, and my sisters and me, we used to—we used to eat all the fah sung tong before the New Year party was even over, so my dad would hide them on top of the fridge in a sewing tin, but I always knew where it was, and he always knew when I stole some because he'd catch me smelling like—like peanuts."

August tightens her grip. The music keeps playing. She thinks of storm surges, of rushes and walls of water, and holds on tighter, feels it coming and plants her feet.

"His name, Jane," she says, suddenly and startlingly sober. "Tell me his name."

"Biming," she says. "My mom's is Margaret. They own a—a restaurant. In Chinatown."

"Here?"

"No—no. San Francisco. That's where I'm from. We lived above the restaurant in a little apartment, and the wallpaper in the kitchen was green and gold, and my sisters and I shared a room and we—we had a cat. We had a cat and a pot of flowers by the front door and a picture of my po po next to the phone."

"Okay," August says. "What else do you remember?"

"I think . . ." A smile spreads across her face, awestruck and distant. "I think I remember everything."

9

The party's gone. August has been on the train for five hours straight, glitter in her hair, dollar bills on Jane's collar, riding the line and listening to the flow of Jane's memories. They watched the sun rise over the East River with the first commuters of the day, recorded a slew of voice notes on August's phone, waited for Niko to return with an encouraging smile, two coffees, and a stack of blank stenos.

August writes and Jane talks and—wedged between half-asleep rastas and mothers of three—they rebuild a whole life from the beginning. And more than ever, more than when she asked Jane out, more than the first time they kissed, August wishes Jane could leave the goddamn subway.

"Barbara," Jane says. "I was two when my sister Barbara was

born. Betty came the next year. My parents gave me the only Chinese name because I was the oldest, but they didn't want any trouble for my sisters. They always told me, 'Biyu, look after the girls.' And I left them. That's . . . fuck. I forgot how that felt. I left them."

She swallows, and they both wait for her voice to even out before she explains that she left when she was eighteen.

"My—my parents—they wanted me to take over the restaurant. My dad taught me to cook, and I loved it, but I didn't want to be tied down. I mean, I was sneaking out at night to see girls, and my parents wanted me to care about balancing the books. I—I don't even think I fully knew I was gay yet? I was just different, and my dad and I would fight, and my mom would cry, and I felt like shit all the time. I couldn't make them happy. I thought running away would be better than letting them down."

Leaving, she says, was the hardest thing she ever did. Her family had been in San Francisco for generations. It never felt like the right choice. But it felt like the only choice.

"Summer '71, I was eighteen, and this band—some no-name band, total proto-punk trash playing the absolute worst shit— asked my dad if they could play at the restaurant. And he let them. And I fell in love—with the music, the way they dressed, the way they carried themselves. I went upstairs, cut off all my hair, and packed my backpack."

In the van, they asked her name, and she said, "Biyu."

"It was LA first," she goes on. "Three months working for a fishmonger because my uncle back home owned a fish market— that's this tattoo, right here." She points to the anchor. Her first one. "I had a friend who'd moved there, so he put me up, then he took a job in Pittsburgh and I left. That was when I started hitching rides wherever people were going and seeing how I liked it. I did Cleveland for a couple of weeks, that was a nightmare. Des Moines, Philly, Houston. And in '72, I ended up in New Orleans."

She remembers stray details about every city she passed through. An apartment with bars on the windows. Reciting her parents' phone number to the rafters of an attic in the Houston Heights, wondering if she should call. Almost breaking her arm at a Vietnam protest in Philadelphia.

New Orleans is blurry, but August thinks that's because it meant more. For Jane, the most important memories are either razor-sharp Technicolor or pixelated and muted, like they're too much to hold in her head. She remembers two years, an apartment with a sweet-faced roommate whose name still won't come, a basket of clothes in the kitchen between their rooms that they'd both pull from.

She remembers meeting other lesbians in grungy bars—she learned to cook burgers and fries in the kitchen of one called Drunk Jane's. The girls spent her first month watching her across the bar, daring one another to talk to her, until one asked her on a date and confessed they'd been calling her Drunk Jane because no one had the nerve to ask her name. Every lesbian in the neighborhood had a nickname—Birdy, Noochie, T-Bev, Natty Light, a million hilarious names born from a million messy stories. She used to joke they sounded like a band of pirates. She considered herself lucky, really, that the name that stuck on her was Drunk Jane, and that over the months it became one word. Jane.

New Orleans was the first place she felt at home since the Bay, but the specifics are hard, and the reason she left is gone.

Something happened there, something that sent her running

again. The first time someone asked her name afterward—a bus driver in Biloxi—she swallowed and gave her nickname, because it was the one thing from that part of her life she chose to keep: Jane. It stuck.

After New Orleans, a year of hitchhiking from city to city on the East Coast, falling halfway in love with a girl in every one and then cutting and running. She says she loved every girl like summer: bright and warm and fleeting, never too deep because she'd be gone soon.

"There were people in the punk scene and the anti-war crowd who hated gays, and people in the lesbian crowd who hated Asians," Jane explains. "Some of the girls wanted me to wear a dress like it'd make straight people take us seriously. Everywhere I went, someone loved me. But everywhere I went, someone hated me. And then there were other girls who were like me, who . . . I don't know, they were stronger than me, or more patient. They'd stay and build bridges. Or at least try. I wasn't a builder. I wasn't a leader. I was a fighter. I cooked people dinner. I took them to the hospital. I stitched them up. But I only stayed long enough to take the good, and I always left when the bad got bad."

(Jane says she's not a hero. August disagrees, but she doesn't want to interrupt, so she puts a pin in it for later.)

She read about San Francisco, about the movements happening there, about Asian lesbians riding on the backs of cable cars just to show the city they existed, about leather bars on Fulton Street and basement meetings in Castro, but she couldn't go back.

She didn't stop until New York.

Back in New Orleans, her friends would talk about a butch they used to know named Stormé, who'd moved to New York and patrolled outside lesbian bars with a bat, who threw a punch at cops outside the Stonewall Inn and instigated a riot back in '69. That sounded like the kind of person she wanted to know and the kind of fight she wanted to be in. So she went to New York.

She remembers finding friends in a different Chinatown, in Greenwich Village, in Prospect Heights, in Flatbush. She remembers curling up on twin mattresses with girls who were working nights to save up for the big operation, pushing their curls behind their ears and cooking them congee for breakfast. She remembers fights in the streets, raids on bars, the police dragging her out in cuffs for wearing men's jeans, spitting blood on the floor of a packed cell. It was early—too early for anyone to have any idea what was happening—but she remembers friends getting sick, taking a guy from the floor above to the hospital in the back of a cab and being told she wasn't allowed to see him, and later, watching his boyfriend get told the same thing. Sterile whites, skinny ankles, hunched in waiting room chairs with bruises from cops still mottling her skin.

(August goes home and does her own research later: nobody was calling it AIDS until '81, but it was there, creeping silently through New York.)

But she also remembers bright lights on her face at clubs full of feathers and thrift store evening gowns and glittering turbans perched atop ginger wigs, bare shoulders smudged with lipstick, bottom shelf gin. She lists off the names of guys with heavy eyeliner who threw punches at CBGB and recites the summer '75 concert calendar, which she'd pinned to her bedroom wall. She remembers getting in a fight with her upstairs neighbor, before he got sick, and settling it over a pack of cigarettes and a game of bridge, laughing until they cried. She remembers steaming dumplings in a kitchen the size of a closet and inviting a small crowd of girls from Chinatown to eat around her coffee table and talk about things they were just beginning to suspect about themselves. She remembers Billy's, jabbing an elbow into Jerry's ribs at the grill, hot sauce and syrup dribbling down her wrists as she bit into her sandwich and declared it the best idea she ever had, the exact look on Jerry's face when he tasted it and agreed.

She remembers the phone, always the phone looking back at her, always the same nine digits repeating in her head. Her parents. She knew she should call. She *wanted* to. She never did.

August can see it pull at her—around her eyes, her mouth. Sometimes she laughs, remembering making herself sick on too much fried chicken from the shop down the block and her mom mumbling "yeet hay" at her disapprovingly even as she patted her forehead and brought her chrysanthemum tea. Sometimes she stares at the ceiling when she talks about her sisters and the way they used to whisper to one another in their room at night, giggling into the darkness. She's found and lost everything, all in the span of a few hours.

It all makes sense, though. It fills in most of the gaps in August's research—the lack of official documents using her name, the confusing timelines, the impossibility of pinning down exactly where Jane was for most of the '70s. And it makes sense of Jane too. She ran away because she didn't think she could make her family happy, and she never went back because she thought she did them a favor. She kept running, because she never quite learned what home was supposed to feel like. That, especially, August can understand.

It's hard, to picture Jane's life forty-five years ago and understand how close it feels for her—a matter of months, she said once. It's always soaked in sepia for August, grainy and worn at the edges. But Jane tells it in full color, and August sees it in her eyes, in the shake of her hands. She wants to go back. To her, it's only a short summer away.

But how New York ended for Jane is still missing. She took the Q to and from her apartment often, but she can't remember how she ended up stuck there.

"That's okay," August says. She leans her shoulder into Jane's. Jane leans back, and August pushes away the knowledge that she kissed her a few hours ago, lets it be buried under everything else. Jane watches another station slide away with a soft expression on her face, freedom unreachable on the other side of a sliding door. "That's what I'm here for."

When August clocks in at Billy's on Thursday afternoon, Lucie is on the phone, staring blankly at a Mets clipping on the wall.

"We can only sell three," she says in a monotone, sounding absolutely bored. "$100 each, $250 for the set. It's a historic New York landmark. No, not on the registry." A pause. "I see." A much longer pause. "Yes, thank you. I invite you to eat a dick. Goodbye."

She slams down the phone hard enough that the coffee in the pot behind the counter trembles.

"Who was that?" August asks.

"Billy wants to raise money to buy the building by selling things we can spare," Lucie explains tersely. "Put some of the barstools on Craigslist. People are cheap. And idiots. Cheap idiots."

She storms off into the kitchen, and August can hear her swearing up a storm in Czech. She thinks of the jar of onion and honey and the way Lucie concealed a smile under the streetlights, and she turns to Winfield, who's puttering around the counter.

"There's more to it than she lets on," August says, "isn't there?"

Winfield sighs, throwing a towel over his shoulder.

"You know, I'm from Brooklyn," he says after a pause. "Seems like nobody who lives here is from here, but I am—grew up in East Flatbush, big-ass Jamaican family. But Lucie—she emigrated when she was seventeen, was on her own longer. Came here hungry one night and couldn't pay the bill, and Billy came out the back and offered her a job instead."

He hops up onto the bar, narrowly avoiding putting his ass in a pecan pie.

"I'd just started working here the year before. I was only a kid. *She* was only a kid. She was so skinny, mean as shit, dishwater blond, learning English on the job, and she started telling people what to do, and then one day she showed up with red hair and black nails like she had some kinda Wonder Woman level up. This place made her who she is. It's the first home she ever had. Shit, I *had* a home, and even I feel that sometimes."

"There's gotta be a way we can save Billy's," August says.

Winfield shrugs. "That's Brooklyn, man. Places get bought up and shut down all the time."

She glances over her shoulder through the kitchen window, to where Jerry is busy with an omelette. She asked him a week ago if he remembers the person who came up with the Su Special. He doesn't.

August passes her shift thinking about Jane and ghosts, things that disappear from the city but can't ever really be erased. That afternoon, August finds her on the Q, sitting cross-legged across three seats.

"Mmm," Jane hums when August sits down next to her. "You smell good."

August pulls a face. "I smell like the inside of a deep fryer."

"Yeah, like I said." She buries her nose in August's shoulder, inhaling the greasy ghost of Billy's. August's face flashes warm. "You smell good."

"You're weird."

"Maybe," Jane says, drawing back. "Maybe I just miss Billy's. It smells exactly the same. It's nice to know some things'll never change."

God, it sucks. Places like Billy's, they're never just places. They're homes, central points of memories, first loves. To Jane, it's as much of an anchor as the one on her bicep.

"Jane, I, uh," August starts. "I have to tell you something."

And she breaks the news.

Jane leans forward, elbows on her knees, tonguing her bottom lip. "God, I—I never imagined it'd ever not be there, not even now."

"I know."

"Maybe . . ." she says, turning to August, "maybe if you get me back to where I'm supposed to be, I could do something. Maybe I could fix this."

"I mean, maybe. I don't really know how any of this works. Myla's pretty sure whatever's happening now is happening because whatever happened in the past is already done."

Jane frowns, deflating slightly. "I think I understood some of those words. So, you're saying . . . if there's anything I could do about it, it'd already be done."

"Maybe," August says. "But we don't know."

There's long beat of quiet, and Jane says, "Have you . . . have you ever found anything about me now? Like, if I make it back, and I stay there . . . there should be another me out there, right? Back on the right track? All old and wise and shit?"

August folds her hands in her lap, looking down at Jane's red sneakers. She's been wondering when Jane would ask this; it's something that's bugged August since the beginning.

"No," she admits. "I'm sure she's out there, but I haven't found her yet."

Jane sighs. "Damn."

"Hey." She looks up, attempting a small smile. "That doesn't necessarily mean anything. We don't *know* that things can't change. Maybe they can. Or maybe you'll change your name again, and that's why I can't find you."

"Yeah," Jane says, quiet and heavy. "Maybe."

August feels it hanging around Jane, the same thing that pulled at her the other morning as she told her stories.

"Anything you want to talk about?" August asks.

Jane releases a long breath and closes her eyes. "I just . . . miss it."

"Billy's?"

"Yeah, but also . . . life," she says. She folds her arms and shifts, sliding down until she's lying across the bench, her head on August's lap. "My dim sum place. The cat in my bodega. Banging on the ceiling because the neighbor was practicing his trombone too loud, you know? Dumb shit. I miss figuring out scams with my friends. Having a beer. Going to the movies. Dumb, small life things."

"Yeah," August says, because she doesn't know what else to say. "I know what you mean."

"It just—it sucks." Jane's eyes are closed, her face turned up toward August, mouth soft, jaw clenched. August wants to smooth her thumb across her strong, straight brows and pull the tension out of her, but she settles for pushing a hand into her hair. Jane leans into the touch. "I can remember it now, how I felt my whole life—I wanted to go places, see the world. Always hated staying in one place for too long. Fuckin' ironic, huh?"

She falls silent, tracing her fingertips over her side, where a tattoo is peeking around the hem of her T-shirt.

August wishes she were better at this. She's great at taking notes and picking apart facts, but she's never been good at navigating the rivers of feelings that run beneath. Jane's cheekbone is pressed into the knob of her knee through her jeans, and August wants to touch it, hold her closer, make it better, but she doesn't know how.

"If it helps . . ." August says finally. Jane's hair is sleek and thick between her fingers, and she shivers when August scratches her scalp. "I've never found anywhere I wanted to stay either, until now. And I still feel trapped sometimes, in my head. Like, even when I'm with my friends, and I'm having fun, and I'm doing all the dumb, small life things, sometimes it still feels like something's wrong. Like something's wrong with *me*. Even people who aren't stuck on a train feel that way. Which I realize sounds . . . bleak. But what I've figured out is, I'm never as alone as I think I am."

Jane's quiet, considering. "That does help," she says.

"Cool," August says. She bumps her knee gently, nudging Jane's head. "You said you missed going to the movies, right?"

Jane opens her eyes finally, looking up into August's. "Yeah."

"Okay, so, my favorite movie of all time," August says, fishing her phone out. "It's from the '80s. It's called *Say Anything.* How 'bout this—we listen to the soundtrack, and I'll tell you about it, and it'll be almost as good."

August extends an earbud to her. She eyes it.

"Myla *did* say you should be teaching me this stuff."

"She's a smart woman," August says. "Come on."

Jane takes it, and August cues up the music. August tells her about Lloyd and Diane and the party and the keys, the dinner, the diatribes about capitalism and the back seat of the car. She talks about the boom box and the pen and the payphone. She talks about the plane at the end, about how Diane says nobody believes it'll work out, how Lloyd says that every success story starts out that way too.

Jane hums and taps the toe of her sneaker, and August keeps touching her hair, and she tries to make her feelings small and quiet enough to focus on getting it right, the quote about not knowing what you're supposed to be doing or who you're supposed to be when everyone else around you seems so sure: *I don't know, but I know that I don't know.* That one feels important.

It's embarrassing to the August who likes to play tough, for this stupid movie to mean so much to her, but "In Your Eyes" comes on, and Jane breathes out like she's been punched in the gut. She gets it.

August doesn't want to think about kissing Jane when the music fades out or when the doors slide open at Parkside Ave. or when she tucks her apron under her arm and waves good night. But she does, and she does, and she does.

When she gets home, Myla's sprawled out on the couch and Niko is puttering around the kitchen, finishing up the last few days' worth of dishes.

"We decided to finish a season of *Lost*," Niko says as he

towels off a cereal bowl. "I can't believe they moved the island. I am, as Isaiah would say, gooped."

"Yeah, wait until you get to the part with Claire's creepy *Blair Witch* baby."

"Don't spoil him!" Myla says. She's cradling an enormous bag of jelly beans like it's a baby. August thinks she might be stoned.

"He's literally a psychic."

"Still."

August holds up her hands in surrender.

"How's our girl tonight?" Niko asks.

"She's all right," August tells him. "Kinda sad. It's hard on her, being stuck down there."

"I didn't mean Jane," he says. "I meant you."

"Oh," August says. "I'm . . . I'm okay."

Niko narrows his eyes. "You're not. But you don't have to talk about it."

"I just . . ." August paces over to one of the Eames chairs and drops into it bonelessly. *"Ugh."*

"What's wrong, little swamp frog?" Myla says, shoving a handful of jelly beans into her mouth.

August buries her face in her hands. "How do you know if a girl likes you?"

"Oh, this again," Myla says. "I already told you."

August groans. "It's just . . . it's all gotten so complicated, and I never know what's real and what's not and what's because she needs somebody and what's because I need somebody, and it's—*ugh*. It's just *ugh*."

"You have to actually *say something* to her, August."

"But what if she doesn't feel the same? We're stuck with each other. I'm the only one who can help her. I'll make the whole thing weird, and she'll end up hating me because it's always awkward, and I can't do that to either of us."

"Okay, but—"

"But what if she *does* like me, and she goes back to the '70s and I never see her again and I could have told her and I didn't? And she never knows? If someone felt this way about me, I'd want to know. So does she *deserve* to know? Or—"

Myla starts laughing.

August pulls her face out of her hands. "What are you *laughing* about?"

Myla burrows the side of her face into the armrest, still giggling. A few jelly beans spill onto the floor. "It's just that, you're in love with a ghost from the 1970s who lives on the subway, and it's still the *exact* same as always."

"She's not a ghost, and I'm not in love with her," August says with an eye roll. Then, "What do you mean?"

"I *mean*," Myla says, "you have fallen into the homoerotic queer girl friendship. It's all cute at first, and then you catch feelings, and it's impossible to tell if the joke flirting is actual flirting and if the platonic cuddling is romantic cuddling, and next thing you know, three years have gone by, and you're obsessed with her, and you haven't done anything about it because you're too terrified to fuck up the friendship by guessing it wrong, so instead you send each other horny plausible deniability love letters until you're both dead. Except she's *already* dead." She laughs. "That's wild, bruh."

Niko drifts into the room, setting a few handleless teacups and a teapot down on the steamer trunk with a tinkling of chipped porcelain.

"Myla, Jane is our friend," he says. "You have to stop making jokes about her being dead. It *would* be cooler if she was, though."

August groans. *"Y'all."*

"Sorry." Myla sighs, accepting a teacup. "Just text her like, 'Hey Jane, you got a rockin' bod, would love to consensually smash. XOXO, August.'"

"Sounds exactly like something I would say."

Myla laughs. "Well, say it in an August way."

August exhales. "It's the worst possible timing, though. She *just* remembered who she is. And it hasn't exactly been easy on her."

"There's no good timing in this situation," Myla says.

"Maybe no good timing means there's no bad timing either," Niko says simply. "And maybe you can make her happy while she's here. Maybe it's selfish to keep that from her. Maybe it's selfish to keep it from *you.*"

An hour goes by, and Myla falls asleep on the couch while Niko's cleaning up the tea. August watches him gently tug the bag of jelly beans out of her arms and wonders if he's going to wake her and move her to their room. It feels strange and private to watch indecision flicker across his face when she's used to his certain, confident lines, but eventually it softens into something quiet and fond.

He pulls a blanket off the back of the couch and spreads it over her, taking special care to tuck it around her shoulders and feet. He brushes her hair off her forehead and ghosts the faintest of unintrusive kisses over it.

He switches off the lamp, and when he turns toward their room, August sees the soft melt of his smile, the gentle crease at one side of his mouth, a secret thing. They'll sleep separately tonight, and somehow this hurts her heart more, the easy tether between them that doesn't need a constant touch. The assurance that the other person is right there in your orbit, always, waiting to be tugged back in. Niko and Myla could be on opposite sides of an ocean and they'd breathe in sync.

A phantom feeling burns into the back of her throat, like at Isaiah's party, on the walk to the station: of what it would be like to have someone bite down a smile when they point and say, "Yeah, her. She's mine." To live alongside someone, to kiss and be kissed, to be wanted.

"Night," Niko says.

"Night," August says, her voice thick in her ears.

That night in her room, Jane's there. She smiles warm and slow, until it's so big it scrunches her nose up. She leans against the window and talks about the people she met on the train that day. She stands in her socks at the foot of the bed and says she's not going anywhere. She touches the pad of her thumb to a freckle on August's shoulder and looks at her like she's something to look at. Like she doesn't ever want to stop looking.

August rolls onto her back and levels her palms against the mattress, and Jane's on either side of her hips, knees digging into the sheets. In the dark, it's harder to stop herself from painting soft oranges filtered in from the street. She can see them threaded into Jane's hair, tucked behind her ears, brushed along the gentle cant of her jaw. There she is. This girl, and a want so bad, it burrows into August's bones until they feel like they'll crack.

She wonders if things were different, if maybe they could fall into the kind of love that doesn't need to announce itself. Something that settles into the bricks as easily as every other true thing that's ever unfolded its legs and walked up these stairs.

Her phone buzzes from within the sheets.

Radio, it says. Hope you're not asleep yet.

August pulls up the station, and the next song comes up. By request. "In Your Eyes."

The moonlight moves, a cool slash across the foot of the bed, and August squeezes her eyes shut. There's no point to it, loving a girl who can't touch the ground. August knows this.

But to kiss and be kissed. To be wanted. That's a different thing from love. And maybe, maybe if she tried, they could have something. Not everything, but something.

August has a plan.

Myla told her to say it in an August way. The August way is having a plan.

It's contingent on a few things. It has to be the right day and time. But she's ridden the Q from one end to the other enough to have the data she needs, carefully tallied in the back of a notebook right below all of Jane's girls.

Definitely not during peak work commute hours, or midnight, which brings a rush of people getting off hospital night shifts, or weekends when shitfaced commuters will be barfing along the line. The slowest time, when the train is most likely to be almost completely empty, is 3:30 a.m. on a Tuesday morning.

So she gathers up what she needs and stuffs it into the reusable grocery bags Niko's guilted her into using religiously. She sets her alarm for 2:00 a.m. to give herself time to tame her hair and apply a lipstick that won't smudge. It takes twenty minutes to figure out what to wear—she ends up with a button-down tucked into a skirt, a pair of gray thigh-high socks she bought last month, her ankle boots with heels. She tugs on the socks in the mirror, fussing over the fit, but there's no time to second-guess. She has a train to catch.

She sits on the bench and waits. And waits some more. Jane will be on whichever train she gets on, and she wants it to be a good one. A new one, with shiny seats and pretty lights that count down the stops—and an empty car. She's trying to make the subway romantic. She needs all the help she can get.

Finally, a train with a well-maintained, cool blue interior pulls up, and August gathers her bags and stands at the yellow line like a nervous teenager picking up their prom date. (She assumes. She never went to prom.)

The doors open.

Jane is in the far corner of the train, sprawled on her back, jacket bunched up under her head, tape player balanced on her stomach, eyes closed, one foot tapping along to the beat. Her mouth is quirked up in the corner like she's really enjoying it, the lines of her loose and languid and overflowing. August's heart goes unforgivably soft in her chest.

That's her girl.

Jane is, at the moment, blissfully unaware of her surroundings, and August can't resist. She edges up to her silently, leans close to her ear, and says, "Hey, Subway Girl."

Jane yelps, flails sideways, and punches August in the nose.

"Agh, what the fuck, Jane?" August yells, dropping her bags to clutch her face. "Are you Jason Bourne?"

"Don't sneak up on me like that!" Jane yells back, pulling herself upright. "I don't know who Jason Bourne is."

August pulls one hand away from her nose to examine it: no blood, at least. Off to an auspicious start. "He's an action movie character, a secret agent who had his memories erased and finds out he's a badass because he knows how to, like, shoot people and do computer stuff he can't remember learning." She thinks about it for a second. "Hang on. Maybe you *are* Jason Bourne."

"I'm sorry," Jane says, but she's laughing. She leans forward, tugging August's hands down. "Are you okay?"

"I'm fine, I'm fine," August tells her. Her eyes are watering, but it really doesn't hurt much. It was more of a glancing, half-asleep blow than the riot girl punch she knows Jane is capable of.

"What are you even doing here?" Jane asks. "It's the middle of the night."

"Exactly," August says. She scoops her bags up and deposits them on the seat next to Jane, yanking out the first item: a blanket. She throws it down over the bench. "We almost never get to hang out just the two of us."

"So we're . . . having a sleepover?"

"No, we're having food," August says. Her face feels hot and red, and not because it was recently punched, so she focuses on unpacking. A bottle of wine. A corkscrew. Two plastic cups. "All the stuff you want to try. I thought we could do, like, a taste test."

August pulls out one of Myla's cutting boards next, scorched on one side from a saucepan. Then the Takis, the sweet creole onion Zapp's, box after box of Pop-Tarts. Five different flavors.

"A feast," Jane says, reaching for a packet of chips. She sounds a little dubious, a little awed. "You got me a feast."

"That's a generous use of the word. I'm pretty sure the guy at the bodega thought I was stoned."

August finally looks up to find Jane turning the Takis over in her hands like she's not sure what to do with them.

"I brought this too," August says, pulling a cassette tape out of her pocket. It took her three different thrift stores, but it finally turned up: the Chi-Lites' greatest hits. She holds it out to Jane, who blinks at her a few times before popping open the deck on her cassette player and sliding the tape in.

"This is . . . nice," Jane says. "Like I'm a normal person. That's nice."

"You are a normal person," August says, sitting on the other side of their makeshift junk food charcuterie board. "Under un-normal circumstances."

"Pretty sure the word for that is abnormal."

"Hush and open the wine," August says, handing the bottle over.

She does, and then she rips the bag of Takis open with her teeth, and August's brain rapidly runs through a whole 3D View-Master reel of other things she'd like Jane to do with her teeth, but *that* is getting ahead of herself. She doesn't even know if Jane *wants* to do anything with her teeth. This isn't even about that. This is about making Jane happy. It's about *trying*.

They eat, and they toast their little plastic cups of wine, and Jane ranks the Pop-Tart flavors from worst to best, with the sweetest (strawberry milkshake) predictably at the top. The Chi-Lites croon, and they go round and round the city in their well-traveled loop. August can't believe how comfortable this has gotten. She can almost forget where they are.

August thinks, all things considered, for a 3:00 a.m. date on the subway with a girl untethered from reality, it's going pretty well. They do what they've always done: they talk. That's what August likes best, the way they eat up each other's thoughts and feelings and stories just as hungrily as the bagels or dumplings or Pop-Tarts. Jane tells August about the time she kicked in a door to rescue a distressed child that turned out to be an especially vocal house cat, August tells Jane about how her mom led a bartender on for two months so she could access the bar employment records. They laugh. August wants. It's good.

"I think this wine is actually doing something," Jane says, inspecting her plastic cup. She keeps peering at August over her chips for a second too long, and there's a faint flush over the top of her cheeks. Sometimes August thinks Jane looks like a watercolor painting, fluid and lovely, darker in places, bleeding through the page. Right now, the warm shadows of her eyes look like a heavy downstroke. The jut of her chin is a careful flick of the wrist.

"Yeah?" August says. She's comparing Jane to a Van Gogh in her head, so obviously the wine is working on *her*. "That's new for you, huh? Being able to get drunk?"

"Yeah," Jane says. "Huh. How 'bout that?"

The cassette runs out, and the rush and rattle of the train feels too quiet stretched out between them.

This is it, August thinks.

"Flip the tape," she says, and she pushes herself to her feet.

"Where're you going?" Jane asks.

"We're about to be on the bridge," August says. "We cross this bridge every single day, and we never enjoy the view."

She turns to look at Jane, who's sitting on their blanket, watching August with careful eyes. August wants to say something lovely and profound and sexy and cool, something that'll make Jane want her just as much, but when she opens her mouth, all that comes out is, "Come here."

Jane stands, and August hovers on the edge of the moment and tries to imagine what they look like, watching each other from ten feet apart on a speeding train, the Statue of Liberty gliding past over her shoulder, the Brooklyn Bridge, the glittering skyline and its shivering reflection on the water, the lights flickering over them through the beams of the bridge. John Cusack and Ione Skye could never.

And then, Jane looks August straight on, folds her arms across her chest, and says, "What the fuck, August?"

August mentally flips through the plan for tonight—nope, definitely not part of it.

"What?"

"I can't do this anymore," Jane says. She paces toward August, sneakers thumping hard on the floor of the car. She's pissed off. Brow furrowed, eyes vivid and angry. August scrambles to figure out how she screwed this up so fast.

"You—you can't do what?"

"August," she says, and she's right in front of her. "Is this a date? Am I on a date right now?"

Fuck. August leans against the door, equivocating. "Do you want it to be a date?"

"No," Jane says, "*you* tell *me,* because I have been putting every move I know on you for *months* and I can't figure you out, and you kept saying you were only kissing me for *research,* and then you stopped kissing me, but then you kissed me *again,* and you're standing there looking like *that* in fucking *thigh highs* and bringing me *wine* and making me feel things I didn't even know I could remember how to feel, and I'm going *out of my goddamn mind—*"

"Wait." August holds both hands up. Jane's breaths are coming high and short, and August suddenly feels close to hysterical. "You *like* me?"

Jane's hands clench into fists. "Are you *kidding* me?"

"But I asked you on a date!"

"*When?*"

"That time I asked you out to drinks!"

"*That* was a date?"

"I—but—and you—all those other girls you told me about, you were always—you just *went* for it, I thought if you wanted me like that, you would have gone for it by now—"

"Yeah," Jane says flatly, "but none of those girls were you."

August stares.

"What do you mean?"

"Jesus, August, what do you think I mean?" Jane says, voice cracking, arms thrown out at her sides. "None of them were *you*. Not a single one of them was this girl who dropped out of the fucking future to save me with her ridiculous hair and her pretty hands and her big, sexy brain, okay, is that what you want me to say? Because it's the truth. Everything else about my life is fucked, so, can you—can you *please* just tell me, am I on a fucking date right now?"

She makes a helpless gesture, and August is breathless at the pure frustration in it, the way it looks so broken in, like Jane's been living with it for months. And her hands are shaking. She's nervous. August makes her *nervous*.

It sinks in and rearranges in August's brain—the borrowed kisses, the times Jane's bit her lip or slid her hand across August's waist or asked her to dance, all the ways she's tried to say it without saying it. They're both hopeless at saying it, August realizes.

So August opens her mouth and says, "It was never just research."

"Of course it fucking wasn't," Jane says, and she hauls August in by the sway of her waist and finally, *finally* kisses her.

It starts hard, but quickly dissolves into something softer. Tentative. Gentler than August expected, gentler than she's been in any of the stories she's told August. It's nice. It's sweet. It's what August has been waiting for, a soft slide of lips, the loose presence of her mouth, but August breaks off.

"What are you doing?" August asks.

Jane stares back, gaze flickering between her eyes and mouth. "I'm kissing you."

"Yeah," August says, "but that's not how you kiss."

"It is sometimes."

"Not when you really want something."

"Look, I—this isn't fair," Jane says, and the fluorescents illuminate the blush on her cheeks. August has to bite down a smile. "You know how I like to be kissed, but I don't know what you like. You've—you've been pretending. You have a head start."

"Jane," August says. "Any way you want to kiss me is the way I wanna be kissed, okay?"

A pause.

"Oh," Jane says. She studies August's face, and August can practically see that confidence meter of hers filling up, right to Smug Bastard, where it usually sits. August would roll her eyes if it weren't so endearing. "It's like that?"

"Shut up and kiss me," August says. "Like you mean it."

"Here?" She leans up and teases at the hinge of August's jaw.

"You know that's not what I meant."

"Oh, here?" Another kiss, her earlobe this time.

"Don't make me—"

Before August can get the threat out, Jane twists her around, backing her into the doors of the train. She pins August at the hips, shoulders braced against hers, hand wrapped around her racing pulse at the wrist, and August can feel Jane like lightning in her veins. Her knees part on an answering instinct, and Jane doesn't waste time getting a leg between them, leaning in so August's own weight grinds her down into Jane's thigh.

"So pretty for me," she murmurs into the corner of August's mouth when she gasps, and they're kissing again.

Jane Su kisses like she talks—with leisure and indulgent confidence, like she's got all the time in the world and she knows exactly what she wants to do with it. Like a girl who's never been unsure of a single thing in her life.

She kisses like she wants you to picture what else she could do given the chance: the swing of her hips if you passed her on the street, every beer bottle she's ever had her mouth around. Like she wants you to know, down to your guts, the sound her boots make on the concrete floor of a punk show, the split lips and the way her skin smells sweet at the end of the night, all the things she's capable of. She kisses like she's making a reputation.

And August . . . August cheats.

Because she *does* have a head start. She spent weeks learning what Jane likes. So she grabs at her hair and tugs, nips at her bottom lip, tilts her chin up and bares her neck for Jane's lips, just to hear the soft little moans that fall out of her mouth, high on the feeling of giving Jane exactly what she wants. It's better than any of their first kisses, any memory, red hot and real under her hands. The city glides past through the window, framing them in, and August's skin is on fire. Her skin is on fire, and Jane's dragging her fingers through the embers.

"These fuckin' thigh highs," Jane mutters. Her hand grazes over the top of one, short fingernails skimming the place where elastic cuts into August's thigh. She was nervous when she put them on, afraid of looking like she was trying too hard, worried about the way they dig into her soft fat. "What the fuck, August?"

"What—ah—about them?"

"They're criminal, that's what," Jane says, pressing her thumb hard enough into the flesh there that August hisses, knowing it'll leave a mark.

Jane snaps the elastic over the same spot, and the sharp pain goes straight through her and out her mouth in a breathless "*fuck*."

"August," Jane says. She dips into her shoulder, nosing at her collarbone through her shirt, and August's brain slowly surfaces. "August, what do you want?"

"I wanna . . . kiss you."

"You are kissing me," Jane says. "What else do you want?"

"It's embarrassing."

"It's not embarrassing."

"It is when you've never done it before," August blurts out, and Jane stills.

"Is that it?" she says. "You've never had sex with a girl before?"

August feels her face flush. "I've never had sex with anyone before."

"Oh," Jane says. "*Oh.*"

"Yeah, I know, it's—"

"It's okay," Jane says easily. "I don't care. I mean—I *care,* it just doesn't bother me." She traces a thumb up the inside of August's thigh, and her mouth melts into a loose smirk when August gasps quietly. "But you have to tell me what you want."

August watches Jane lick her bottom lip, and a thousand images flash through her mind so fast, she feels like she might black out—Jane's short hair between her fingers, her teeth digging into the ink lines on Jane's bicep, wet fingers, wet mouths, wet everywhere, Jane's low voice pitched up an octave, Jane's eyes burning up at her from the end of the bed, the insides of Jane's knees, miles of skin shining with sweat and the light through her bedroom window. She wants Jane's hands fisted in her bed sheets. She wants the impossible.

"I want you to touch me," she finally makes herself say. "But we can't."

And the train stops. The lights go off.

For a second, August thinks she *did* black out, until her eyes pick out the shape of Jane squinting back at her in the dark.

"Shit," August says. "Did it just—?"

"Yeah."

August blinks, waiting for her vision to adjust. She's suddenly painfully aware of herself, of Jane's fingers wrapped around her wrist. "Emergency lights?"

Jane closes her eyes, mouthing along as she counts the seconds in her head. She opens them.

"I don't think they're coming on."

August looks at her. Jane looks back.

"So we're . . . trapped on a dark train," August says.

"Yeah."

"Alone."

"Yes."

"With no chance for anyone else to get on."

"Correct."

"On the bridge," August says, more slowly. "Where no one can see us."

She shifts, adjusting her weight on Jane's thigh, and closes her mouth on the sound that tries to slip out at the friction.

"August."

"No, you're right," August says, moving to slide Jane's hand off her, "it's a bad idea—"

Jane's grip tightens.

"That is literally the opposite of what I was about to say."

August blinks once, twice. "Really?"

"I mean . . . what if it's the only chance we get?"

"Yeah," August agrees. It really is a good point, pragmatically. They have finite resources of time and privacy. Also, August will die if Jane doesn't touch her within the next thirty seconds. Which is another logistical consideration. "You—yeah."

"Yeah? You sure?"

"Yeah. Yes. Please."

It happens fast—August inhales, exhales, and suddenly Jane's jacket is gone, thrown blindly at the nearest seat, and they're kissing, hands everywhere, messy and wet and full of small sounds. August's hair keeps getting in the way, and when she breaks off to rip a ponytail holder off her wrist and haphazardly pull it back, Jane's at her neck, tongue soothing over every spot she introduces her teeth to. Everything goes fuzzy, and August realizes Jane has taken her glasses off and chucked them in the direction of her jacket.

Somehow the buttons of August's shirt are undone, and she can't think about anything but wanting more, wanting skin on skin. She wants to rip their clothes off, use her teeth and her fingernails if she has to, and can't—not here, not the way she wants. Still, she slides her fingertips under the waistband of Jane's jeans, catches the hem of her T-shirt, and she waits half a second for Jane to stop kissing her and nod before she's untucking and pushing it up, and *oh God,* there she is, this is happening.

In the moonlight, Jane's body is kinetic. She shivers and tenses and relaxes under August's hands, a nipped-in waist and sharp hip bones, a simple black bra, gentle ridges of ribs, tattoos winding up and down her skin like spilled ink. And August— August has never gotten this far before, not really, but something takes over, and she's dropping a kiss on Jane's sternum, and she's pressing her open mouth to the swell just above the cup of her bra, the devastating give of it. Every part of Jane is spartan, practical, made into what it is by years of survival, and yet, somehow, it gives. She always gives.

It occurs to August that Jane is thinner than her, and maybe she should care that her own hips are wider and her stomach is softer, but Jane's hands are on her, pushing her shirt open, everywhere she's afraid to be touched—the shape of her waist, the dimples of her thighs, the fullness of her chest. And Jane groans and says, for the third time of the night, "What the fuck, August?"

August has to choke down a sigh to say, "What?"

"Look at you," she says, dragging her thumbs out from the center of August's stomach to her hips, skimming over the waistband of her skirt. She leans in and tucks her face under August's collar, bites her shoulder, presses a kiss there, then pulls back and just looks at her. Looks at her like she doesn't ever want to stop looking. "You're like—like a fucking painting or something stupid like that, what the fuck. You just walk around like this all the time."

"I—" August's mouth tries to form several words, maybe even some that make sense, but Jane's hands are spanning her waist, brushing the delicate lace edges of her bra, and her mouth is trailing lower, and all that comes out is, "I didn't know. You—I didn't know you thought that."

Jane's eyes flash up to her, glinting wicked in the low light.

"You have no fuckin' idea, girl," Jane says, and then she's pushing the lace out of the way.

There are hands, and mouths, and fingertips, and tongues, and a sound coming out of August somewhere between a hiss and a sigh, and there's Jane's breath hot on her skin. There are, objectively, a lot of things going on, August understands vaguely, but all she can think is want—how much, how hard, how deep she's been wanting it, *Jane's* been wanting it, all of it held between Jane's lips now, pressing and blooming through her, so keen that it hurts. Jane bites down, and August sucks in a breath through her teeth.

The hand on August's thigh is inching up her skirt, fabric gathering at Jane's wrist. When Jane leans into August's ear, the cotton of Jane's bra is against her, the insistent heat of her body, the unbearable slide of skin against hers.

"I wanna go down on you," Jane murmurs. "Is that cool?"

August's eyes snap open.

"Wha-what the fuck kind of question is that?"

Jane's head drops back with a bark of laughter, eyes shut and lips swollen, the line of her throat obscene and gorgeous.

"I need a yes or no."

"Yes, okay, Jesus."

"They call me Jane, actually," Jane says, and August rolls her eyes as Jane sinks down to one knee.

"That's the worst line I've ever heard," August says, fighting to keep her breath steady as Jane tugs on the top of one of her thigh highs with her teeth. The elastic snaps back, and Jane grins against the inside of August's thigh at the little yelp it earns her. "Did that shit really work on girls in the '70s?"

"It seems," Jane says, kissing her way up, and August knows her hand is shaking when she pushes it into the hair at the crown of Jane's head, but she'll be goddamned if she'll act like it, "to be working just fine now."

"I don't know." Jane's fingers catch on the waistband of August's underwear. August stares across the car at a Brooklinen ad, of all ridiculous things, because if she confronts the reality of Jane kneeling between her legs and tugging her underwear down her thighs, she's going to have a full-scale mental collapse. "Don't get too cocky."

"You might wanna use the door," Jane says, "for balance."

"Why?"

"Because in a minute you're not gonna be able to feel your legs," Jane says, and when August finally looks down at her, mouth open in shock, she's smiling innocently. She pushes the hem of August's skirt up and says, "Hold this for me, yeah? I'm busy."

"Absolutely fuck you." August laughs, and she does as she's asked.

Truthfully: Jane has never once made a promise she couldn't back up.

August turns her head to the side, trying to ground herself to the sturdiness of the door against her back, the way her shirt bunches up between her shoulder blades when she shivers, how her breath clouds the glass in a steady, too-fast rhythm. Through the glass, the city is shining—the bridges and buildings, the carousel on the edge of the water, the pinpricks of boats in the distance, and she's trying to take stock of it all, of how it feels to have someone so impossibly close to her for the first time. She can't believe she gets to have all this, this view and this girl on her knees.

August has stepped inside a million other moments with Jane and a million other girls, but nobody else can have this one.

If this were one of Jane's memories, she can almost imagine how Jane would tell it: a girl with long hair twisted up messily, her shirt thrown open, moonlight turning the lace on her chest to gossamer, her mouth slipping open around a broken sound, underwear around her knees and looking absolutely wrecked. She looks up at August, a strand of dark hair falling across her eyes, mouth busy, and August knows she'd tell it herself in five words: girl, tongue, subway, saw God.

August never knew—she never worked it out in her head, exactly, what would qualify as sex with someone who has the same type of body as hers, no matter how much she wanted it, pictured it with one hand beneath the sheets. She didn't think she'd know, since she's never done any of it, where the line is. But this, *this*—Jane's mouth on her, wet fingers, every hum and hitch of Jane's breath getting her off as much as a touch, the give and take of how good it feels to make someone else feel good—is sex. It's sex, and August is drowning in it. She wants more. She wants to fill her lungs up.

"Jane," she says, and it comes out weak from the back of her throat. Her knuckles are white in Jane's hair, so she makes herself relax them, drags her fingers down to Jane's sharp cheekbone. "Jane."

"Hm?"

"*Fuck*, I—come back," she grinds out. "Up here. Please."

When August pulls her into another kiss, she can taste herself on Jane's tongue, and that, more than anything, the fierce wave of possessiveness it pulls over her, is what has her fumbling at the fastenings of Jane's jeans.

It's a blur—August doesn't know how she senses what to do. There's supposed to be an awkward learning curve with someone you've never fucked before, but there's not. There's this flow between them that's never made any goddamn sense since that static shock the day they met, and it's like she's found her way into this girl's jeans a thousand times, like Jane's had her figured out for years. She thinks dazedly that maybe it's time to start believing in something. The fucking divine construction of Jane's fingers when they press into her, maybe—that's a higher power for sure.

It's over in a gasp, a trip over some edge August doesn't see until they're suddenly there, an open-mouthed kiss that's more a hot exchange of breath than anything else, teeth and skin, a low swear. Jane slumps forward, her shoulder digging into August's chest, one hand still tucked neatly beneath the lace of August's bra, and August feels alive. She feels *present,* somehow, *here.* Exactly, really here. She smears a messy kiss across the top of Jane's cheek and feels like Jane is the first thing she's ever touched in her life.

"You were right," August says.

"About what?"

"I can't feel my legs."

Jane laughs, and the lights come back on.

Jane moves first, picking her head up to glare at the lights. And it's so ridiculous, so funny and unbelievable and Jane, perturbed at the world for daring to defy her instead of the other way around, that August has to laugh.

"Get your hand off my boob. We're in public," she says as the train eases back into motion.

"Shut the fuck up," Jane snorts, and she stumbles back half a step to let August button her shirt. She watches August shimmy her underwear back up her thighs with devilish interest, looking pleased with herself, and August would blush if she weren't already pink from everything else.

Jane buttons her jeans and tucks her shirt in and disentangles August's glasses from her jacket, and then she's crowding back into August's space, gently sliding her glasses on.

"I can't believe you threw them," August says. "They could have fallen on the floor and picked up a bacterial infection. You could have given me conjunctivitis."

"Mmm, yeah, say more big words."

"It's not sexy!" August says, even as her smile gets so big it hurts, even as she lets Jane press her into the door. "I could have lost an eye!"

"I was in a hurry," Jane says. "I haven't gotten laid in forty-five years."

"Technicality," August says.

"Let me have this," Jane says, trailing her smiling mouth over August's pulse.

"Okay." August laughs, and she does.

They kiss again, and again, melting kisses that barely hold the weight of what just happened, and August keeps waiting. August keeps waiting for one of them to say something that will change everything, but they don't. They just kiss until they pull into a station in Brooklyn, and a bleary commuter climbs on with a coffee and an unamused expression, and Jane muffles a laugh in her neck.

It's good, August thinks, that they don't say anything. Jane loves like summer for a reason—she doesn't stick around. August knows it. Jane knows it. There's nothing either of them can do about it.

It's enough, August decides. To have her like this, here, for now. Time, place, person.

10

New Restaurant Lucille's Burgers Opens in French Quarter

PUBLISHED AUGUST 17, 1972

[Photo: An older woman in an apron stands in front of a bar, arms crossed, while a young woman in the background carries a tray of burgers]

Lucille Clement remembers growing up in her mother's kitchen while waitress Biyu Su delivers orders to customers.

Robert Gautreaux for *The Times-Picayune*

"So you're sleeping with Jane?"

August turns, toothbrush in mouth. Niko's looking at her from the end of the hallway, holding a golden barrel cactus the size of a basketball between two tattooed hands.

She managed to dodge him when she stumbled back into the apartment at five in the morning with her shirt buttoned wrong and the shape of Jane's mouth bruised onto the side of her neck. But she should have known she could only avoid the resident psychic for so long.

She spits and rinses. "Can you not do that?"

"Sorry, was I skulking? Sometimes I skulk without realizing."

"No, the thing where you know things about my personal life just by looking at me." She racks her toothbrush. "But also the skulking."

He pulls a face. "I don't mean to, it's just, like . . . the energy you put out about Jane. It's burning a new hole in the ozone layer."

"You know, the old hole in the ozone layer closed up."

"I feel that you are deflecting."

"I can send you a *National Geographic* article about it."

"We don't have to talk about it," Niko says. "But I'm happy for you. You care so much about her, and she cares so much about you."

August stares into the mirror, getting the rare chance to watch herself turn pink. It happens in big, unattractive splotches. This is what Jane sees. It's a miracle she wants to have sex with her.

Sex. She and Jane had sex. She and Jane are, if they can figure out the logistics, possibly going to have more sex. August isn't a virgin anymore.

She wonders if she should be having some kind of mental journey about that. She doesn't feel different. She doesn't look any different, just round-faced and splotchy, like a hard-boiled egg with a sunburn.

"Virginity is a social construct," Niko says mildly, and August glares at him. He does a vague sorry-for-reading-your-mind gesture. August is going to dropkick his cactus out the window.

"It's true," Myla says, head popping out of their bedroom, eyes wide behind her welding goggles, still wearing her satin bonnet from the night before. "The whole idea is based on cis-sexist and heteronormative and quite frankly colonial-ass bullshit from a time when getting a dick in you was the only definition of sex. If that's true, me and Niko have never had sex at all."

"And we both know that's absolutely not the case," Niko says.

"Yeah, our walls are thin and I have ears," August says, heading toward her bedroom in search of something to tie her hair up. "What kind of safeword is 'waffle cone,' anyway?"

"Speaking of overhearing things," Myla presses on, "did I hear Niko say you're sleeping with Jane?"

"I—" August shoots a perturbed glance at Niko, who has the decency to look as sheepish as he ever does, which is mostly just a slightly less jovial jut of his hips. "You can't really call it 'sleeping.' There's not really a bed involved."

"Fucking finally! Like, literally!"

"*Lord.*"

"Did you make sure she was clean? Can you catch an STI from a ghost?"

"She's not a ghost," August and Niko say in unison.

"Okay, still, let me be a mom for a second."

"Look, yeah, she's—it's fine." August would love for their creaky floorboards to finally open up and drop her out of this conversation. "It's come up before. I have to keep track of everything she remembers, okay?"

"Oh, yeah, classic getting-to-know-you conversation," Myla says from across the hall. "What kind of music do you like? Where are you from? Do you now or have you ever had crabs?"

"You just described our first date, verbatim," Niko points out.

August, still searching for a ponytail holder, picks up her bag and upends it on the bed.

Her blue ponytail holder from last night falls out, and she

tries not to think about tying her hair up while Jane's teeth worried at her skin. With Niko on the other side of the wall, she might as well project a PowerPoint presentation of herself getting railed on the subway for the whole apartment.

She frowns down at the mess from her bag. A pack of batteries? Where did those come from?

"Oh," she says, realizing. *"Ohhhh, bitch."*

God, she can't believe it took her so long to notice. This is why you aren't supposed to kiss your case. She fumbles her phone off her desk so fast, she nearly flings it out the open window.

Weird question, she texts Jane, fingers trembling. Distantly, she hears Niko and Myla in the hallway discussing soil brands. Can you open the battery compartment on your radio and tell me what you see?

Nothing? There's nothing in there.
Why?

There are no batteries in your
radio?

Nope.

Didn't you ever wonder how it
works?

I figured it was like my cassette
player? It doesn't have batteries
either. I'm a sci-fi freak show, I just
assumed that was part of it.

You've had a magical cassette
player all this time and you never
thought to investigate?????? Or
mention it???????

I don't know! I told you when I
showed it to you that I didn't know
how it worked! I thought you knew!

I thought you meant you didn't
know how it worked because it was
so old???

Wow, that's calling ME old.

asldfjasf if I thought you could die I
would strangle you

She slams back out of her room and into the hall, almost
getting a faceful of Niko's cactus.

"Careful! Cecil is sensitive!"

She ignores him, throwing the package down on the floor in
front of the alarm clocks Myla has been blowtorching together
all afternoon. "Batteries!"

"What?"

"*Batteries,*" August repeats. "When you sold me that radio,
you told me to make sure I put batteries in it. So I bought those,
but—but that was in the middle of the whole kissing-induced
horniness fog, so I forgot to give them to her."

"Uh-huh."

"But it *still works.* Her radio, her cassette player—shit, her *phone,* I gave her a portable battery for it weeks ago but I've never seen her use it. None of her electronics need batteries to work. So that means—"

"—whatever is keeping her on the train has to do with electricity," Myla finishes. She shoves her goggles up onto her forehead. "Whoa."

"Yeah."

"Wait. Wow. Yeah, that would make sense. It's not the train, it's the line. Maybe she's bound to—"

"The current. The electrical current of the tracks."

"So—so whatever event threw her out of time—it might have been electrical. A shock, maybe." She sits back on her heels, sending LaCroix cans rattling across the floor. It's impossible to tell if they're for Myla's project or hydration. "But something like that, the voltage of the line—I don't understand how it wouldn't just kill her."

"And she's definitely not dead," Niko helpfully reminds them.

"I don't know either," August says. "There must be more to it. But this is something, right? This is big."

"It could be," Myla says.

It's a conversation that goes on for days. August jots down thoughts on her arm in the middle of finals, takes notes during shifts in her guest check pad, meets Myla at Miss Ivy's to talk it through for the hundredth time.

"You remember the first time I tried to meet her on my own?" Myla says. She's unpacking a to-go bag full of vegan curry and patties, Niko's lunch. He's in the back with a client, and Miss Ivy is on the other side of the shop, watching them warily. "And I couldn't find her? But when you brought Niko with you, she was there."

"Yeah," August says. She glances at Miss Ivy. It's probably not the weirdest topic ever discussed here. She lowers her voice anyway. "But we've all gone down alone and seen her at some point."

"But not until after *you* introduced us. You're the most important point of contact. We can find her because she recognizes us through you."

"What do you mean?"

"August, you said it yourself—if she doesn't see you for a while, she starts to come unstuck. It's not like she's on every train all the time—she's flickering to the one you're on. *You're* what's keeping her here. You've watched *Lost*—you're her constant."

August drops down onto a rickety stool, rattling the shelf of crystals behind it. Her *constant*.

"But . . . why?" August asks. "How? Why me?"

"Think about it. What are feelings? How does your body communicate to your brain?"

"Electrical impulses?"

"And how do you feel when you look at Jane? When you talk to her? When you touch her?"

"I don't know. Like my heart is gonna come out of my ass and suplex me into the mantle of the earth, I guess."

"Exactly," she says, jabbing a plastic fork in August's direction. She's started in on Niko's curry. If he doesn't finish communing with the beyond soon, he's not going to have a lunch. "That's chemistry. That's attraction. That's, like, boner city. And that comes with all these super powerful electrical impulses between your nerve endings, all throughout that big beautiful brain of yours. If we're right and her existence is tethered to the electricity of the line, then every time you make her feel something, every time you touch her or kiss her, every interaction you have is generating more electrical impulses, which means you're making her more . . . real."

"When we—" August realizes out loud. "The other day, when we—you know—"

"August, we're adults, just say you got your back blown out."

Across the room, Miss Ivy unfurls a paper fan like she does when she's having a hot flash.

"Can you *please*," August begs. "Anyway, before, right when I said I wanted to—the train broke down. So, are you saying—?"

A dirty smile dawns on Myla's face.

"Oh my God. She literally shorted out the train because she was *horny*," she says, eyes sparkling with absolute awestruck admiration. "She's an icon."

"Myla."

"She's my *hero*."

"God, so—so that's . . . that's why," August says. "It's a feedback loop between her and the line. That's how she knows when the emergency lights are gonna come on and when they aren't. That's why the lights go crazy when she's upset. It's all interconnected."

"And why your insane kissing-for-research plan worked," Myla says. "The attraction between you two is literally a spark, and it's the same spark that's bringing her back into reality. She feels something, the line feels it, electrical impulses in her brain start firing, it pieces her back together. It's you, August. You're the reason she's staying in one place. You're what's keeping her here."

That's . . . a lot, August thinks.

Jane texts her that night, Missed you today, and August thinks about her warm mouth and collarbones in the moonlight and *wants,* but the next day is an exam straight into a late shift.

So she takes a different train, and Myla meets her at Billy's and sits at the counter with a burger, picking up right where they left off.

"Okay, but why *me*?" August says.

"I thought we had gotten past your denial that she wants to eat chocolate fondue off your ass and then cosign a mortgage."

"No, I mean, I can believe that she—she *likes* me," August says in a tone that sounds like she cannot believe it at all. "But she's been on that train so long. I've found Craigslist posts and personal ads—people have been falling in love with her for years. She really never had a crush on anyone before now? Why was meeting *me* the first time she locked into a moment in time?"

Myla swallows an enormous bite of beef. It's not that Niko enforces a vegetarian household, it's just that Myla enjoys meat more when Niko's not there to look distantly sad about the environment.

"Maybe you're meant to be. Love at first sight. It happened to me."

"I don't accept that as a hypothesis."

"That's because you're a Virgo."

"I thought you said virginity was a construct."

"A *Virgo*, you fucking Virgo nightmare. All this, and you still don't believe in things. Typical Virgo bullshit." Myla puts her burger down. "But maybe there was, like, an extra spark when you met, that pulled the trigger. What do you remember about it?"

God, what does she remember? Besides the smile and kind eyes and general aura of punk rock guardian angel?

She tries to think past that—to the skinned knee, the way she had tugged the sleeves of her jacket over her hands to hide the scrapes, trying not to cry.

"I had spilled coffee all over my tits," August says.

"Very sexy," Myla notes, nodding. "I get what she sees in you."

"And she gave me her scarf to cover it up."

"Dream girl status."

"I do remember there was, like, a static shock, when I reached for the scarf and our hands brushed, but I was wearing wool and the scarf was wool and I just never thought anything of it. Do you think that was it?"

Myla considers. "Maybe. Or maybe that was a side effect. Energy going nuts. Anything else?"

"I had just come from work, and she told me I smelled like pancakes."

"Oh. Hm." She uncrosses her legs, leaning forward across the counter. "She used to work here, right?"

"Right."

"And this place does have a . . . very particular smell, right?"

"Right . . ." August says. "Oh. Oh! So you think it was a sense memory? Like she recognized Billy's?"

"Smell is the strongest memory trigger. Could have done it. Maybe it was the first time she encountered something she really recognized on the train."

"Seriously?" August lifts the collar of her T-shirt to her nose. "Wow, I'm never gonna bitch about smelling like pancakes again."

"You know," Myla says, "if we can figure out what happened, exactly how her energy got tied into the energy of the line, and we can re-create the event . . ."

August drops her shirt collar. "We could undo it? That's how we get her out?"

"Yeah," Myla says. "Yeah, I think it could work."

"And—and she snaps back to the '70s for good?"

Myla thinks. "Probably. But there's a chance . . . I mean, there aren't really any rules in this. So who knows? Maybe there's a chance she could lock into right here, right now."

August stares at her. "Like . . . permanently?"

"Yeah," Myla says.

August allows herself five seconds to picture it: Jane's jeans tangled up in August's laundry, late nights and split bills, kisses on the sidewalk, oversweet coffee in bed.

She shakes the idea out, turning back to the register. "She probably won't, though."

That afternoon, August finally makes her way to the Q. She didn't mean to go three days without seeing Jane after they had sex, honestly—she just got caught up in the case. It has absolutely nothing to do with how Jane kissed her for real inside a perfect moment in the middle of the night and August doesn't know how to approach this inside a normal Thursday afternoon.

On her way to the platform, she sees the sign. Same warning, same deadline: September. The Q is closing in September. She could lose Jane forever in September. And even if she figures things out, she'll probably lose Jane anyway—to the '70s, her own time.

So, there's that, and there's the very fresh memory of gasping into oblivion on the Manhattan Bridge, and there's the idea that whatever they are to each other is what makes Jane real, and there's August, standing on a platform, trying to file each thing neatly away into different file drawers in her brain.

It's crowded today, but Jane's sitting, tucked at the end of a bench between the back wall of the car and someone's towering Ikea haul.

"Hey, Coffee Girl," Jane says when August manages to wedge her way between commuters. August tries to read her face, but her features assemble into her usual expression: gentle amusement, like she's thinking of a half-remembered joke at nobody's expense.

August wants to kiss her mouth again. August, inconveniently, wants to do a lot of things again.

"Where've you been?" Jane asks.

"Sorry, I didn't mean to—I had this big breakthrough with your case, and finals, everything was nuts, but—anyway, I have a lot to catch you up on."

"Okay," Jane says placidly. "But can you come down here and tell me?"

"What—" August starts, before Jane grabs her and pulls her down. She thumps gently into Jane's lap. "Oof. Hello."

Jane grins back. "Hi."

"Oh, it's nicer down here," August says.

"Yeah, I made reservations."

There's a certain threshold at which a packed subway car goes from too personal to completely impersonal, so many people that they blend together and nobody takes notice of anyone else. In Jane's little pocket of bench, surrounded by backpacks and turned backs and boxed-up Björksnäs units, it almost feels private.

August settles in, bundling her jean jacket into her lap. Her skirt has fanned out behind her, draping over them both, and she's acutely aware of the way Jane's denim feels against her bare thighs, the rips that allow skin to touch skin.

"What?" Jane says, studying her face. August imagines the look on it: a combination of uptight and turned on, which pretty much sums her up.

"I need to tell you about the case," August says.

"Uh-huh," Jane says. "But what?"

"You know what."

One of Jane's hands travels up, spanning the top of August's thigh. August looks at her, and something tugs in her chest, and she wonders if that's it—the electricity. Desire and chemistry coiled up inside something bigger, something deeper and softer.

"Listen," Jane says. "You can't look at me like that and not tell me what you're thinking."

"I'm thinking—" August starts, and the thing in her chest tugs harder, and she can't. She can't say that whatever is between them is the reason this is happening at all. If she says it, she'll break it. "I'm thinking about you."

Jane narrows her eyes. "What about me?"

"About . . . the other night." Not a complete lie.

"Yeah," Jane says. "I guess we haven't talked about it."

"Do we have to?"

"I guess not," she replies, her thumb stroking a curved line up the inside of August's leg. "But we should talk about what you want."

And it's . . . God. August can feel it: the way things have shifted, the intent that sparks off of Jane like flint, the way she rakes her eyes down from August's mouth to her throat like she's thinking about the mark she left there. August came down here to debrief, but she might as well be unbuttoning her shirt for how present her brain is.

Is this what it's always like? To want someone and know they want you back? How in the world does anyone get anything done?

"I want to talk about the case." August wants to scream. Spiritually, she is screaming.

Jane's hand pauses. "Okay."

"It's—it's super important. Really big stuff."

"Sounds like it."

"But."

"Yeah," Jane says. Their eyes meet. God, it's hopeless.

"This whole thing we have going on is . . . it's very bad for my productivity," August says.

"What exactly do we have going on?" Jane asks her. "You still haven't told me."

"The thing where I wanted you for months, and then I had you, and now I want you all the time," August says before she can stop herself. She feels her face go pink. "We're on a *deadline*, and it's *distracting*."

Jane's smiling, her eyes whiskey brown and full of trouble.

"All the time?" Jane says. "Like . . . right now?"

Yeah, definitely trouble.

"I mean," August says, "not necessarily *right* now." Yes, right now. Right now all the time always. "I have to tell you about the case."

"Sure," Jane says. But her fingertips slide under the hem of August's skirt. It startles a soft gasp out of her, and Jane says quietly, "I'll stop any time you tell me to stop."

She moves as if to pull her hand away, and August holds her wrist down on reflex.

"Don't stop."

"Okay, then," Jane says. "You tell me about the case, and I'll . . ." Her hand disappears beneath the fabric pooled in August's lap. "Listen."

August swallows. "Right."

She talks about the electricity and the tracks, holding just enough back—the parts about the connection between the two of them—and Jane listens quietly as she unravels their ideas about feedback loops and feelings and memories.

"So," August goes on, "if you can remember what exactly

happened that got you stuck here, maybe there'll be a way to re-create the event and undo it. Like a manual reboot."

"Knock me back into place," Jane says.

"Yeah," August agrees. "And then . . . then, theoretically, we could get you back to the '70s. Where you're supposed to be. Unless we can't figure it out, then . . . well, it doesn't matter. I'll figure it out."

"Okay," Jane says. Her eyes have gone a little distant.

"So, we have to get you to remember what happened the day you got stuck here."

"Uh-huh."

"Any ideas how we might do that?"

Jane hums, her hand sliding higher, hidden completely under August's skirt and the jacket in her lap. "I have a lot of ideas, actually."

"I—" August stutters. "I don't understand how you're so laid-back about this. It's *your* existence on the mortal plane."

"Look," Jane says, fingers spreading to grip right below her ass. August's hand tightens on Jane's collar. "If you're right, I'm here for a good time, not a long time. So, maybe I want to have a little fun. It doesn't always have to be so serious."

August thinks about the tally marks, the girls Jane kissed in every city, and she wonders if this is all Jane really wants from her. Maybe August is different from the other girls, but Jane is still Jane, loving with firecracker quickness, using her hands and her mouth and half of her heart. A good time. Nothing serious.

And August, who has spent most of her life taking everything seriously with the occasional detour into cynical jokes for survival, has to admit—Jane has a point.

"Okay," August says. "You got me."

"I know I got you," Jane says, and there it is: the dull scrape of short nails against the cotton of August's underwear.

Fuck.

"Jane," she says, even though nobody around is remotely paying attention.

Jane's hand stills carefully, but she leans up, into August's neck, lips brushing her earlobe when she says, "Tell me to stop."

And August should. August should tell her to stop.

She should really *want* to tell her to stop.

But Jane's fingertips are brushing against her, teasing out her nerve endings and making her hips ache, and she thinks about all the months of wanting honed down to an exquisitely fine point, sharp against her skin until it feels like it could draw blood.

Caution and a knife. She used to swear by it. But this is sharper, and she doesn't want it to stop.

So when Jane's thumb swipes up under the cotton, and Jane looks into her eyes for an answer, August nods.

The thing about Jane is, she's exactly what August isn't, and it works. Where she's soft, Jane is hard. Where she's harsh and prickly and resistant, Jane is all generous smiles and ease. August is lost in something dangerously like love, and Jane is laughing. And here, between stops, between her legs, she's anxious and tense and Jane is confident and smooth, dragging her fingers, finding her way, slick and maddening.

Her mind is softening at the edges, sinking into the feeling of not having to be in control, letting Jane push her right to the edge of her limits.

"Keep talking, angel," Jane whispers in her ear.

"Uh—" August stammers, struggling to keep a blank face. Jane's middle finger does a tight circle and August wants to push into it, press down, but she can't move. She's never been so thankful for people who bring Ikea furniture on the subway. *"Shit."*

She feels the warm burst of Jane's quiet laugh against the side of her neck.

"We could—" August attempts. It takes everything to keep her voice level. "We could try rebuilding everything from summer of '76 on. I can break—*fuck*—um, into the office at Billy's and see if there's—*oh*—uh, if they have any records that would be helpful."

"Breaking and entering," Jane says. The car sways into daylight, and August has to dig her fingernails into Jane's knee to keep her composure. "Do you know how hot that is?"

"I'm, uh—" A short gasp. She can't believe this is happening. She can't believe she's doing this. She can't believe she ever has to stop doing this. "I guess criminal behavior isn't as much of a turn-on for me."

"That's interesting," Jane says conversationally. "Because it seems like doing things you're not supposed to do kind of gets you off."

"I don't know if you have enough—*ah*—evidence to support that theory."

Jane leans in and says, "Try not to come, then."

And August thinks, she has to find a way to get Jane out of here, just so she can kill her.

It goes slow at first—from the tension in Jane's shoulder, it's obvious she can't move like she wants to, so she settles for working short and precise and deadly—until it doesn't, until it's quick and shallow and August is talking, trying to make words happen from her mouth, to swallow down sighs, trying not to look at Jane looking at her. It's the stupidest thing she's done since she jumped between train cars, but somehow it feels like her body finally makes sense. She bites her lip through the build, the whiteout, her eyes screwed shut and her hips burning from the effort not to move. Jane kisses the side of her neck, beneath her hair.

"Well," Jane says casually. August's cheeks are burning a furious pink, and Jane looks coolly unfazed, except for her pupils, which are blown wide. "It sounds like you have a pretty good plan."

So that's how things will be, August deduces as she walks home, goodbye kiss lingering on her lips. She works the case, and Jane kisses her, and they talk about the first thing but not the second.

Sometimes it feels like there are three Augusts—one born hopeful, one who learned how to pick locks, and one who moved to New York alone—all sticking out knife blades and tripping one another to get to the front of the line. But every time the doors open and she spots Jane at the far end of the car, listening to music that shouldn't even be playing, she knows it doesn't make a difference. Every possible version of August is completely stupid for this girl, no matter the deadline. She'll take what she can get and figure out the rest.

She gets to be an adult who has sex, sex with *Jane,* and Jane gets to feel something that's not boredom or waiting, and it's fun. It's *good,* so good that August's mouth will start watering in the middle of a graveyard shift at Billy's just thinking about it. Jane seems happier, which was the point, she reminds herself.

They're friends. Cross-timeline friends with semi-public benefits, because they're attracted to each other and lonely and there, and August has learned to like feeling a little reckless. She never thought she was meant for any kind of danger until she met Jane.

Not that she's meant for Jane.

She tells herself very seriously that if anyone is meant for anything, it's Jane meant for the '70s. That's the job. That's the case.

That's all.

August starts a sex notebook.

It's not that they're having *that* much sex. When one person lives on the subway and the other is busting their ass to get them *off* the subway, there are only so many opportunities.

But she's used to taking notes on Jane, and, well, it never hurts to have a reference guide. So, she starts a notebook to catalogue everything she discovers that Jane likes.

She starts with the things she already knew. *Hair pulling (giving and receiving)*, August writes at the top of the first page. Below it, *lip biting*, followed by *thigh highs*, and, *leaving marks*. She pauses, sucks on the end of her pen, and adds, *semi-public sex** and notes at the bottom of the page, **unsure if always into this or simply making best of situation.*

She keeps it in her bag alongside the other notebooks for geographic locations (the green one), biographical anecdotes (blue), and dates and figures (red), and she updates it meticulously. If she doesn't have it on her, she'll write on her hand, which is how she ends up having to explain to Winfield in the middle of a shift why she has the words *neck biting* scrawled from her first to third knuckles.

Sometimes she adds things that aren't sex but turn Jane

on anyway. *Long hair* makes the list the third time she catches
Jane watching her tie her hair up. One afternoon, she goes on
a five-minute tangent about UV light and document facsimiles
only to find Jane staring at her with her mouth halfway open
and her tongue resting wetly between her teeth, and she pulls
out the notebook and writes, *niche technical expertise + competence.*

Most of the items, though, are pretty straightforward. She
boards the Q in the middle of the night wearing a pair of fish-
nets to test a theory, and when she stumbles off an hour later
kiss-drunk with the thin strings of nylon ripped in two places,
she adds, *lingerie.*

"We'd meet at Max's," Jane's saying over the phone as August stuffs a load of darks in the coin-operated washer. They've
been embroiled in a conversation for a day and a half about how
they would have met if August had lived in Jane's 1970s New
York. August keeps insisting they'd have a longstanding feud
over the library's last copy of *The Second Sex.* Jane disagrees.

"You think I'd be at one of your satanic punk shows?" August asks, closing the door and sitting on a dryer.

"Yeah, you'd wander in all lost and confused. Short skirt,
long hair, hugging the wall, and I'd come stumbling out of the
pit with a bloody nose, see you, and that'd be it."

August huffs a laugh, but she can picture it: Jane swagger-
ing out of the crush of bodies like a shooting star, snarling and
wiping blood on the back of her hand, eyes rimmed with kohl
and the collar of her shirt smeared with someone else's lipstick.

"What'd be your line?" she asks.

Jane makes a considering noise. "Keep it simple. Ask you for
a smoke."

"But you don't smoke," August points out.

"And you don't have a smoke," Jane says. "I never thought

you would. But I had to get real close for you to hear me over the music, and now you're looking at me, and when I kiss you, it tastes a little like blood."

"Uh-huh," August says, heat flaring up the back of her neck. She crosses her legs, squeezing her thighs together. "Keep talking."

By the time the buzzer announces the end of the wash cycle, Jane's described in quiet detail just how she'd get August into the bathroom at Max's, the black leather dog collar she used to wear at shows, and the way she'd let August slip her fingers under it when she got on her knees. August pulls her skirt back down, takes the notebook out, and writes, *blood & bruises.* Then *light bondage.* She goes back up several lines and underlines *semi-public sex.*

June moves through New York like one of Miss Ivy's hot flashes, steaming up windows and slowing traffic to a tempermental crawl. It's a decidedly unsexy time, and yet—

"I can't believe you don't sweat," August says, neck-deep in a heatwave at one in the morning, her hands braced against the wall of an empty train car. Jane kisses her hair, slips her thumb under the hem of August's Billy's T-shirt. "I'm out here dying, and you look like something out of a movie."

Jane laughs and swipes her tongue against the side of August's neck. "It tastes nice on you, though."

"You know, if you're going to go around being a whole metaphysical anomaly, you should have, like, control over your magical powers." She opens her eyes as Jane turns her around and pulls her in. "You should be able to stop the train whenever you want. Or conjure things. Like a couch. That would be nice."

"Are you saying subway seats aren't good enough for you?" Jane teases. "This is my *house.*"

"You're right, I'm sorry. I really love what you've done with the place. And the view, well." She looks at Jane's kiss-swollen lips. Outside the window: nothing but brown tunnel walls. "You can't beat it."

"Hmm," Jane says. "Nice try."

She stomps home forty-five sweaty, delirious minutes later, Jane still laughing in her ear, and she whips her shorts across her bedroom and furiously adds to the list, *orgasm denial.*

(Jane makes it up to her eventually.)

August guesses it's predictable that this is how a person like her would handle entry into the mythical ranks of sex-havers—itemized lists, shorthand, the occasional unhelpful diagram. But it's not her usual compulsive need to organize. It's the way Jane kisses her like she's trying to know everything about her, the revelation of what her own body can do, the way Jane's willing to *work* for it in five stolen minutes between stops. August wants to give that back to her, and the August way is having a plan of exactly how.

So, she scrapes together tips to buy Jane a new phone, one that can send and receive grainy photos, and she plucks up the courage to take one in her bedroom mirror. She stares at it on her phone, at the hair falling down her shoulders, the lips painted red, the lace, the fading mark on her neck turned up to the light from the window, and she almost can't believe it's her. She didn't know she had it in herself to be this until Jane pulled it out of her. She likes it. She likes it a *lot.*

She hits send, and Jane texts back a string of swears, and August bites a smile into her pillow and writes, *red lipstick.*

In between, she picks the lock on the back office of Billy's and discovers it hasn't been used since 2008. It's no more than an ancient filing cabinet of yellowing paystubs and an empty desk, prime real estate for a secondary caseworking outpost. So that's exactly what she turns it into, deep in the back of the restaurant where nobody notices if she spends her breaks on science fiction storytime. She pins copies of her maps to the walls and thumbs through the files until she finds Jane's application from 1976. She spends a long minute with that one, running her fingers over the letters, but pins it up too.

She uses Jane's real name to finally find her birth certificate—May 28, 1953—and since Jane knows she's twenty-four, they narrow down the timeframe of the event that got her stuck to between summer 1977 and summer 1978.

She makes two copies of a timeline and posts one in her room and the other in the office. Summer 1971: Jane leaves San Francisco. January 1972: Jane moves to New Orleans. 1974: Jane leaves New Orleans. February 1975: Jane moves to New York. Summer 1976: Jane starts working at Billy's. Everything after: question mark, question mark, question mark.

She scores a boom box from Myla's shop, a silver '80s-era *Say Anything*–style thing. She hides it in the office and tunes it to their station. When she's too busy for the Q, Jane sends her songs.

August starts sending songs back. It's a game they play, and August pretends not to look up every lyric of every song and agonize over the meanings. Jane requests "I Want to Be Your Boyfriend," and August answers with "The Obvious Child." August calls in "I'm on Fire," and Jane replies with "Gloria," and August thumps her head back against the brick wall of the office and tries not to sink through the floor.

"What, exactly," Wes asks, sitting at the counter with a plate of French toast and watching August doodle a cartoon subway train in the margin of the Sex Notebook, "are you doing?"

"Working," August says. She ducks automatically as Lucie passes with a tray over her head.

"I meant with Jane," he says.

"Just having fun," August says.

"You've never *just had fun* in your life," Wes points out.

August puts her pen down. "What are you doing with Isaiah?"

Wes shovels an enormous bite into his mouth instead of answering.

Something keeps bothering her about Jane's name. Her first one, Biyu. Biyu Su. Su Biyu.

She's repeated it over and over in her head, run it through every database, stared at the cracks in her ceiling trying to pry it out of the filing cabinets of her brain. Where the hell has she heard that name before?

She flips through her notes, returning to the timeline she's sketched out.

Why does Biyu Su sound so familiar?

If this weren't so insane, and if she thought her mom wouldn't drag her back into the black hole of the Uncle Augie investigation, she'd ask her for help. Suzette Landry may not have found what she's looking for, but she's good. She's solved two unrelated cold cases in the course of her work. She plays dirty, she knows her shit, and she never lets things go. It's the best and worst thing about her.

So when she answers her mom's nightly phone call—the one she's been sending to voicemail for a couple of hazy weeks—she doesn't plan on bringing Jane up. At all.

But her mom knows.

"Why do I get the feeling there is something you're not telling me?" August can hear the shredder in the background. She must have gotten her hands on some files she's not supposed to have. "Or someone?"

"I—"

"Oh, it's a someone."

"I literally said one syllable."

"I know my kid. You sound like you did when Dylan Chowdhury accidentally put his promposal note in your locker junior year and then asked for it back so he could give it to the girl two lockers down."

"Oh my God, *Mom*—"

"So who is he?"

"The—"

"Or she! It could be a she! Or a . . . they?"

August doesn't even have it in her to be moved at how hard she's trying to be inclusive. "It's *nobody*."

"Cut the shit, kid."

"Okay, fine," August says. Once her mother wants an answer, she won't stop until she gets it. "There's a girl I met, um, on the subway. That I've kind of been seeing. But I don't think she wants anything serious. She's not exactly . . . available."

"I see," her mom says. "Well, you know what my policy is."

"Never go to a second location with someone unless you've checked their trunk for weapons first," August monotones.

"You can mock it all you want, but I've never been murdered."

August could explain that Jane can't even leave the subway, but instead, she shifts and asks, "What about Detective Primeaux? Is he still a shit?"

"Oh, let me tell you what that smarmy fuck said to me last time I called," she says, and she's off.

August switches her phone to speaker, letting her mom's voice blur into white noise. She goes over the timeline as her mom talks about a lead she's tracked down, that Augie could have passed through Little Rock in 1974, and she thinks about Jane's name. Su Biyu. Biyu Su.

"Anyway," her mom says, "there's an answer out there somewhere. I've been thinking about him so much lately, you know?"

August looks at her bedroom wall, at the photos pinned up with the exact brand of pushpin her mom once used to poke holes in their living room. She thinks about her mom, consumed by this person who can't ever come back, living and dying by this mystery that doesn't have a solution. Orienting her entire life around a ghost.

"Yeah," August says.

Thank God she's nothing like that.

"Does my lipstick look okay?" Myla says, turning sideways to blink at August. Her elbow knocks Wes's phone out of his hands, and he grumbles as he retrieves it from the subway floor.

"Hang on," Jane says, leaning across to fix a smudge of bright blue lipstick with the edge of her thumb. "There. Now you're perfect."

"She's always perfect," Niko says.

"Gross," Wes groans. "You're lucky it's your birthday."

"It's my birthdaaaay," Niko singsongs happily.

"The ripe old age of twenty-five," Myla says. She kisses him on the cheek, effectively smudging her lipstick again.

Niko straightens the red bandana around his neck like a cowboy sauntering out of a saloon. He's wearing denim on denim, a thrifted jean jacket from which he ripped an American flag patch to stitch on a Puerto Rican flag in its place. A Boricua Spring-steen on the Fourth of July. It is, in fact, the Fourth of July.

"So what exactly is Christmas in July?" August asks, tug-ging at the hideous Valentine's Day T-shirt she picked up from Goodwill. It has a picture of Garfield surrounded by cartoon hearts and says I'LL BE YOUR LASAGNA. It took two tries to ex-plain it to Jane. "And why is it Niko's birthday tradition?"

"Christmas in July," Myla says grandly, with a broad gesture that knocks Wes's phone back to the floor, "is an annual Fourth of July tradition at Delilah's in which we celebrate the birth-day of this great nation"—she does a jerk-off gesture and Niko boos—"with themed beverages and an all-star lineup of drag royalty doing holiday-themed performances."

"It's not just Christmas, though," Niko notes.

"Right," Myla adds. "They still *call* it Christmas in July, but it's evolved to include all holidays. Last year, Isaiah did a Thanksgiving dessert burlesque number to 'My Goodies' and wore sweet potato titty tassels and an apple pie g-string. It was amazing. Wes just, like, walked out of the building and sprinted ten blocks."

"That is *not* what happened," Wes says. "I went out for a *smoke*."

"Sure."

"It's also how Myla and I met," Niko adds.

"Really?" Jane asks.

"You never mentioned that," August says.

"Yeah, I used go to Delilah's all the time when I was still living with my parents," Niko says. "Everyone there has always been really cool about whatever you are or want to be or think you might be. Good energy."

"And I was dating one of the bartenders," Myla finishes.

"Whoa, wait." August turns to Myla. "You were with some-one else when y'all met?"

"Yep," Myla says, cheerfully adjusting her sweater, a hideous Hanukkah relic from Wes's childhood. "I don't want to say I dumped the guy on the spot when I saw Niko, but . . . I mean, we *did* have to wait for him to quit bartending before we could show our faces there again."

"The path of the universe," Niko says sagely.

"The path of my boner," Myla echoes.

"Yeah, I'm gonna tuck and roll," Wes says, maneuvering for the emergency exit.

"That's so nuts," Jane says, deftly catching him by the collar of his shirt. "I can't picture either of you with anyone else."

"I don't think we ever really *were* with anyone else," Niko says. "Not all the way. I don't think we could have been."

"Let go of me. I deserve to be free," Wes says to Jane, who boops him on the nose.

"*Anyway*," Myla says. "We met on Niko's birthday, at Christmas in July. And we met Isaiah a couple of Christmas in Julys later, and he helped us get the apartment. And so, it's the birth-day tradition."

"And what a tradition it is," Niko says.

"God," Jane says, her smile going soft around the edges. "I wish I could go."

August touches the back of her hand. "Me too."

They pull up to their stop and elbow their way toward the doors, and when August is stepping off, she hears Jane say, "Hey, Landry. Forgot something."

August turns, and Jane's standing there under the fluores-cents with her jacket falling off one shoulder and her eyes bright, looking like something August made up, like a long night and sore legs in the morning. She leans out of the car, just barely, just enough to piss off the universe, and she hauls August in by the front of her idiot T-shirt and kisses her so hard that, for a second, she feels sparks down her spine.

"Have fun," she says.

The doors shut, and Myla lets out a low whistle. "Goddamn, August."

"Shut up," August says, cheeks burning, but she floats up the stairs like she's on the moon.

Like Slinky's, Delilah's is underground, but where Slinky's has only a grease-stained C from the health department marking the entrance, Delilah's is all neon, radiant cursive. A flashing pink arrow points down, and the bouncer looks like Jason Momoa with Easter bunny ears. He waves them toward the beaded curtain, and the world explodes into Technicolor.

Floor to ceiling, wall to wall, Delilah's is decked out in rainbows of Christmas lights, shining Valentine's hearts, shimmering streamers in red, white, and blue, rows of enormous jack-o'-lanterns stuffed with green and purple string lights, blazing Eid lanterns along the rafters. There's an oversized menorah on the bar, star-shaped pinatas dangling over the tables, and—startling a loud laugh out of August—Mardi Gras beads flung on nearly every available surface. And not the dollar-store plastic ones, the good ones, the ones you'd shoulder check a child on Canal Street for.

But it's not the decor that has the room lit up with life. It's the people. August can see what Niko meant: it has good energy.

You could throw an eggnog—one of the festive shots being passed around on trays—in any direction and hit a different kind of person. Butches, femmes, six-foot beefcakes, Pratt students with terrible haircuts, the type of petite tattooed twenty-somethings

Wes refers to as "Bushwick twinks," women with Adam's apples, men without them. People who don't fit into any category but look as happy and wanted here as anyone else, bobbing their heads to the house music and gripping drinks with painted nails. It smells like sweat, like spilled whiskey, like a million sweet perfumes applied in tight three-bedroom apartments like August's in giddy anticipation of being here, somewhere people love you.

Jane would love this, August thinks.

The bar staff apparently has no grudge against Myla, because one of them nearly vaults the bar when they see her, reindeer onesie and all. Within seconds, there are four glasses of a suspiciously piss-colored concoction on the bar.

"Apple cider margaritas," the bartender says cheerfully. They spin around and produce four shots like some kind of liquor magician. "And a round of our world famous Oh Shit shot, on the house, for my favorite babes."

"Thanks, Luz," Myla coos. "This is our new kid. August. We adopted her in January."

"Welcome to the family," Luz tells her, and a drink and a shot are in her hands, and she's whisked away toward a booth just vacated by a herd of surly goths in perfunctory Halloween headwear.

"To Niko," Myla says, raising her shot. "Born on the Fourth of July with both fingers in the air, pissing middle America off by living their dream: looks great in jeans and has a hot girlfriend."

"To family," Niko says. "And viva Puerto Rico libre."

"To alcohol," Wes adds.

"To Hanukkah sweaters," August finishes, and they all throw it back.

The shot is awful, but the drink, it turns out, isn't half bad, and the company is great. Niko is in rare form, long limbs stretched out and head cocked, exuding honey-smooth blue-collar boyishness. Molten moonshine. He looks like he could jumpstart a jet engine with his heart.

Beside him, Myla is glowing, the piercing in her nose sparkling. Niko's usually clean-shaven, but tonight there's stubble on his chin, and Myla scrapes her nails across it, looking wicked. August makes a mental note to find her headphones before bed.

"They're like," Wes says to her in a low voice, "gonna get married, probably."

"They basically already are."

"Yeah, except they live with us," he says.

August glances over. Wes is sitting cross-legged in his usual skinny jeans and baggy T-shirt, topped off with an angel halo Myla shoved onto his head on the way out the door. He looks like a pissed-off cherub.

"They're not gonna leave us if they get married, Wes," August tells him.

"Maybe," he says. "Maybe not."

"What are you making that face about?" Myla half-shouts across the table.

"Wes thinks we're gonna get married and move out, and he'll never see us again," Niko says. Wes glowers. August can't help laughing.

"Wes. Wes, oh my God," Myla says, laughing too. "I mean, yes, we'll probably get married one day. But we would never leave you. Like we could even afford to. Like we'd even *want* to. Maybe one day we'll all move out and get our own places with our own people but, like, even then. We'll be weirdly co-dependent neighbors. We'll all move into a compound. Niko was born to be a cult leader."

"You say that now," Wes says.

"Yeah, and I'll say it then, you punk-ass bitch," Myla says.

"I'm just saying," Wes says. "I've seen, like, ten different engagement announcements on Instagram this month, okay? I know how it goes! We all age out of our parents' insurance, and all of a sudden your friends stop having time to hang out because they have a person and *that's* their best friend now, and they have a kid, and they move to the suburbs and you never see them again because you're a lonely old spinster—"

"Wes! First of all, we already have two kids." She gestures significantly across the table at him and August.

"Rude, but fair," August says.

"Second of all, we would never move to the suburbs. Maybe, like . . . Queens. But never the suburbs."

"I don't think I'm allowed back on Long Island after I dropped that jar of spiders on the LIRR," Niko says.

"*Why* did you—" August starts.

"Third of all," Myla plows on, "there's nothing wrong with being alone. A lot of people are happier that way. A lot of people are supposed to be that way. But I don't think you will be."

"You don't know that."

"Actually, despite your best efforts at this whole one-man production of *Cask of Amontillado* in which you're both Montresor *and* Fortunato, I'm pretty sure you're gonna find love. Like, good love."

"What makes you so sure?"

"Two main reasons. One, because you're a fucking prize."

He rolls his eyes. "And the second?"

"He's walking up behind you."

Wes whips around, and there is Isaiah, makeup done, wearing a vibrant fuschia scarf around his head and laughing with a couple in matching Pilgrim costumes. He glances over, and August knows the second his eyes lock on Wes's, because it's the second Wes starts trying to climb under the table.

"Absolutely not, bruh," Myla says, throwing a kick. "Stand and face love."

"I don't understand why you're doing this when he literally lives across the hall from us," August says. "You see him all the time."

"Says August of the six-month-long gay panic."

"How did this become a roast of me? Wes is the one under the table!"

"Oh," Niko says simply, "he's freaking out because they slept together after the Easter party."

The top of Wes's head pops up from under the table, along with one accusatory finger.

"Nobody asked the fucking Long Island Medium."

Niko smiles. "Lucky guess. My third eye is closed tonight, baby. But thanks for confirming."

Wes gapes at him. "I hate you."

"Apartment 6F!" says a silky voice, and there Isaiah is, one foot into Annie, painted for the gods, all devastating cheekbones and dark, glittering eyes. "Whatcha doin', Wes?"

Wes blinks for a full three seconds before loudly exclaiming, "Oh, here it is!" He waves his phone in front of his face. "Dropped my phone."

Myla snorts as Wes clambers out from under the table, but Isaiah just smiles. August doesn't know how he does it.

"Well, glad y'all came out. It's gonna be a good one!" Isaiah says. He adds ominously: "Hope you brought a poncho."

He's gone with a flourish of his robe, flashing a nice, long view of leather leggings and an ass produced by dancing in heels and doing squats to fill out catsuits. Wes makes a sound of profound suffering.

"Hate to see him go, hate to watch him leave," he mumbles. "It's all terrible."

August leans back, looking sideways at Wes as he dedicates himself to picking at the label on his beer and emanating an air of abject misery.

"Wes," August says. "Have you ever heard of a hairy frog?"

Wes eyes her with suspicion. "Is that, like . . . a sex act?"

"It's a kind of *frog*," she tells him. He shrugs. She swirls a crumpled lime around her drink and continues. "Also known as a Wolverine frog, or a horror frog. They're this weird-looking subtropical species that are super defensive of themselves. When they feel attacked or threatened, they'll break the bones in their own toes and force the fragments through their skin to use as claws."

"Metal," Wes says flatly. "Is there a reason you're telling me this?"

August waves her hands in a come-on, it's-right-there sort of gesture. He purses his lips and carries on fingering the label of his beer. He looks faintly green in the bar lights. August could strangle him.

"*You're* the horror frog."

"I—" Wes huffs. "You don't know what you're talking about."

"What, being abrasive and emotionally shut off because you're afraid of wanting something? Yeah, I have no idea what that's like."

The night goes on, a blur of cheek kisses, a bathroom with Sharpie and lipstick graffiti that says GENDER IS FAKE and JD

MONTERO REARRANGED MY GUTS, people with hairy legs jutting out of pleated skirts, a lipstick-stained joint making the rounds. August drifts into the crowd and lets it buoy her back: this way is the stage, someone flitting around the edges setting up dry ice and confetti cannons, and this way is Lucie, rare smile across her face, and that way is the bar, sticky with spilled shots, and—

Wait.

She blinks through the flashing lights. There's Lucie, hair down and smudgy eyeliner shot through with glitter that makes her eyes look crazy blue. August doesn't even realize how close she is until acrylic nails are digging into her shoulders.

"Lucie!" August shouts.

"Are you lost?" she shouts back. "Are you alone?"

"What?" Lucie's face is sliding in and out of focus, but August thinks she looks nice. Pretty. She's wearing a shimmery blue dress with a fur shrug and shiny ankle boots. August is so happy she's here. "No, my friends are over there. Somewhere. I have friends, and they're here. But oh my God, you look amazing! It's so cool you came to Isaiah's show!"

"I'm at my boyfriend's show," she says. She's released August to return her attention to the plastic cup in her hand. Even two feet away, August smells pure vodka.

"Oh shit, Winfield's performing tonight?"

"Yes," she says. Someone brushes too close, threatening to spill her drink, and she throws an elbow out hard without missing a beat.

"When's he up?"

The song switches to "Big Ole Freak," and the cheer that goes up is so loud, Lucie has to lean in when she yells, "Second to last! Show starts soon!"

"Yeah, I gotta go! See you later, though! Have fun! You look really pretty!"

She pinches down a smile. "I know!"

August's friends have elbowed their way right up to the edge of the stage, and the wave of bodies eddies her to them as the lights go down and the cheers go up.

The curtains look ancient and a little moth-eaten, but they shimmer when the first queen throws them open and strides out into the spotlight. She's tiny but towering on eight-inch platform boots, wrapped in skintight green leather and sporting a pastel green wig laced with ivy.

"Hello, hello, good evening, Delilah's!" she shouts into the mic, waving at the roaring audience. "My name is Mary Poppers, and I am here tonight representing Arbor Day, make some noise for the trees!" The crowd cheers louder. "Yes, that's right, thank you, our planet is dying! But we are *living* tonight, darlings, because it is Christmas in July and these queens are ready to stuff your stockings, light your menorahs, hide your eggs, trick your treats, and do whatever the fuck it is that people do for Labor Day. Are you ready, Brooklyn?"

It starts off fast and keeps going—a "Party in the U.S.A.," a queen named Marie Antwatnette doing a Bastille Day–themed voguing routine to "Lady Marmalade" that ends in frisbeeing French macarons into the crowd. Another queen comes out full-on New Year's Baby in a rhinestoned diaper and sash and brings the house down with "Always Be My Baby" and some well-timed sparklers.

Second to last in the lineup is a queen introduced as Bomb Bumboclaat, and she stomps out in thigh-high boots, a saxophone thrown around her neck, and a red fur-trimmed dress with a matching cape. Her beard shimmers with silver glitter.

It's not until the memory of Winfield's one-man-band business cards swims into focus that August realizes who it is, and she screams on impulse as the number starts up—that ridiculous live Springsteen version of "Santa Claus is Coming to Town."

"Hey, band!" Bomb Bumboclaat lip-syncs in Bruce Springsteen's voice.

Mary Poppers sticks her head back out from the curtain. "Yeah! Hey, babe!"

"You guys know what time of year it is?"

"Yeah!"

"What time, huh? What?"

This time, the crowd shouts: "Christmastime!"

She puts her hand up to her ear dramatically. "What?"

"Christmastime!"

"Oh, Christmastime!"

Bomb Bumboclaat is pure comedy, all subtle hand gestures that have everyone screaming with laughter and throwing bills onstage and movements of her face that look impossible. She's the first one to do a Christmas number at Christmas in July, and the crowd has been waiting. When she absolutely shreds the saxophone solo, the rafters shake.

By the time she's done, the stage is littered in ones, fives, tens, twenties. Mary Poppers comes out with a push broom to get it all off the stage before the next number.

"Delilah's! You've been amazing. We got one more for ya. Y'all ready to witness a *legend*?" Everyone screams. Myla snaps her fingers in the air. "Ladies and gentlemen, please welcome to the stage, just what the doctor ordered—Annie Depressant!"

The curtains fly apart, and there's Annie in her signature pink—pink Lucite platform heels, pink thigh highs topped with red bows, pastel pink hair cascading down the front of her pink chiffon robe and pinned up on one side with a glittering, heart-shaped fascinator. She's absolutely stunning.

She preens in the spotlight, soaking in the screams and claps and finger snaps, flourishing her rose-colored latex gloves through the air. She's never seemed anything but confident since August first watched her sip a milkshake at Billy's, but seeing her on stage, hearing the way the crowd shrieks itself hoarse for her, August thinks about what Annie said about being the pride of Brooklyn. It wasn't quite the joke she played it off as.

The music starts welling up with soft strings and twinkly synth triangle, a few drum beats, and then Annie snaps her eyes forward to the crowd and mouths, *"Give it to me."*

It's "Candy" by Mandy Moore, and the crowd has about one second to react before she throws her robe off to reveal a bra and miniskirt made entirely out of candy hearts.

"Oh my *God*," Wes says, lost in the wail of the crowd.

Annie winks and launches into her routine, writhing down the catwalk that splits the audience, leaning in to drag her gloved finger down the length of an awestruck guy's jaw on *begging you to come out and play*. August has always seen Annie and Isaiah as two sides of the same person, but the way she soaks in the light, the way her eyes drip honey—that's a different person entirely from the accountant who moved August's desk up six flights of stairs.

She spins gracefully back down the catwalk, beaming, glowing, burning at five hundred degrees—and the music drops out. Annie's own dubbed voice comes in.

"Actually," she says, "fuck this."

In an instant, the stage lights switch to pink, and when Annie throws out her right hand, a flood of rain starts pouring down from the ceiling above the stage.

The music comes back funky and loud and ballsy—Chaka Khan this time, "Like Sugar"—and two things become clear very quickly. The first, as water splatters from the stage and into their drinks: this is why Isaiah suggested they might need ponchos. The second: Annie made her outfit out of something that dissolves in water.

Within the first thirty seconds, her miniskirt and bra have melted, and with a twirl, she whips the last sugary wisps across the stage, leaving behind ornate red latex lingerie. Backup dancers come sashaying out from backstage and hoist her onto their shoulders, spinning her under the falling water, the crowd damp and transported and screaming themselves hoarse. August grew up a short drive from Bourbon Street, but she has never, ever seen anything quite like this.

She thinks of the last text Jane sent: a picture of fireworks from the Manhattan Bridge, Give the queens my love.

It's hazy, but she remembers Jane telling her about drag shows she used to go to in the '70s, the balls, how queens would go hungry for weeks to buy gowns, the shimmering nightclubs that sometimes felt like the only safe places. She lets Jane's memories transpose over here, now, like double-exposed film, two different generations of messy, loud, brave and scared and brave again people stomping their feet and waving hands with bitten nails, all the things they share and all the things they don't, the things she has that people like Jane smashed windows and spat blood for.

Annie twirls across the stage, and August can't stop thinking how much Jane would love to be here. Jane *deserves* to be here. She deserves to see it, to feel the bass in her chest and know it's the result of her work, to have a beer in her hand and a twenty between her teeth. She'd be free, lit up by stage lights, dug up from underground and dancing until she can't breathe, loving it. Living.

Jane would love this.

Jane would love this. It keeps coming back and back and back, Jane tossing her head and laughing up at the disco ball, pulling August into a dark corner and kissing her dizzy. She'd love *this,* specifically, slotted right into place in August's family of moody misfits, tucked against August's side.

The second August lets herself really picture it is the second she can't pretend any longer—she wants Jane to stay.

She wants to solve the case and get Jane out from underground because she wants Jane to stay here with her.

She'd promised herself—she'd promised Jane—she was doing this to get Jane back where she belonged. But it's as blazing and unforgiving as the spotlight on the stage, nothing left in August's sloshy drunk brain to hold it back. She wants to keep Jane. She wants to take her home and buy her a new record collection and wake up next to her every stupid morning. She wants Jane here in full-on, split-the-pizza-bill-five-ways, new-toothbrush-holder, violate-the-terms-of-the-lease permanence.

And not a single part of her is prepared to handle any other outcome.

She turns to her right, and Wes is standing there watching the show, mouth agape. The grip on his cup has gone slack, and his drink is slowly dribbling down the front of his shirt.

August gets it. He's in love. August is in love too.

11

[ariana voice] yuh @chelssss_
UMMMM on the Q this morning this little kid
was getting picked on by two older kids and
before i could do anything this hot butch girl
jumped in and the bullies SCATTERED hello
911 how am i supposed to work now that
i've seen an angel irl????
7:42 AM · 8 Nov 2018

Myla's hair smells like Cajun fries.

August's nose is buried in it, upside down behind Myla's ear, sucking curls into her nostrils.

There's something wrapped around her, something too warm and slightly itchy and, if her stomach doesn't subside soon, in imminent peril of being puked on.

She tries to pull her arm free, but Wes has a freaky death grip on her wrist as he white-knuckles through REMs. There's something lumpy with weird corners crushed between August's arm and one of Niko's shoulder blades. She cracks one eye open—a Popeyes box. Which churns up: one, a hazy memory of Niko putting on his soberest face at the Popeyes register downstairs, and two, the too-many apple cider margaritas in her stomach.

As far as August can tell, the four of them collapsed into a pile on the couch as soon as they stumbled through the door last night. Niko and Myla are on one side, tangled up in each other, Myla's jean jacket thrown over their bodies like a blanket. Wes has spilled halfway off the couch, his shoulders digging into the floor where one of the rugs should be.

The rug that's . . . wrapped around her?

Noodles trots over and starts cheerfully licking Myla's face.

"Wes," August croaks. She nudges one of Wes's knees with her foot. He must have liberated himself of his pants at some point before they passed out. *"Wes."*

"No," Wes grunts. He doesn't relinquish her wrist.

"Wes," she says. "I'm gonna throw up on you."

"No, you're not."

"I literally am," she says. "My mouth tastes like hot ass."

"Sounds like a you problem," he says. He cracks one eye halfway open, smacks his dry lips. "Where are my pants?"

"Wes—"

"I'm wearing a shirt and no pants," he says. "I'm Winnie the Pooh-ing it."

"Your pants are in the window by the TV," says a voice, much too clear and much too loud for the hangover bog. August looks up, and there's Lucie, glitter lingering around her eyes, glowering into the cabinets. "You said, 'They need to get some air.'"

"Why," August says. "Here. Why are you. Here?"

"You really don't remember inviting me to Popeyes," Lucie says flatly. "You are lucky Isaiah knows about the service elevator. Would have left you there."

"Yikes."

"Anyway," she says. "Winfield helped me get you home."

"Yes, but." August finally manages to dislodge her arm from Wes's and gingerly begins to de-crumple herself into an upright position she immediately regrets. "Why are you *here*? Why didn't you leave with him?"

"Because," she says, emerging triumphant with a skillet, "it was funny. I love to watch people with hangovers. Half the reason to stay at Billy's." She points the pan at August. "Slept in your room."

She turns to the fridge and withdraws a carton of eggs, and August remembers her first week at Billy's, when Lucie made sure she'd eaten. There's another pinched smile in the corner of her mouth, like the one she saw last night.

"Making breakfast," Lucie says. "Thankless job, being your boss, but someone has to do it."

Another memory comes back at that: Wes, three drinks deep, lipstick marks on his cheek, Isaiah in his full Annie glory, wig and all, saving him from slipping in a puddle of vodka on the bar floor, and Lucie laughing. It was supposed to be Niko's birthday thing but ended up a five-drinks-and-where's-my-pants thing. Apparently only Lucie made it through intact.

At least August's stomach has stopped threatening an *Exorcist* live show. She rolls onto the floor, and Myla and Niko start to stir.

She runs through everything she can remember: Lucie's fur shrug, eggnog, water falling from the ceiling, being in love with Jane, Myla's lipstick, Niko's bandana—

She's in love with Jane.

Shit, no, it's worse than that. She's in love with Jane, and she wants Jane to stay, and what she thought was her emergency emotional escape hatch for when Jane goes merrily back to the 1970s is just a trick door into more feelings.

Niko's voice echoes in the back of her head from the first time she kissed Jane, *Oh, you fucked up.*

She fucked up. She fucked up *bad.*

She feels around inside her chest like it's the bottom of her jeans pocket, grasping for anything less life-ruining than this. The harsh light of a sober morning should dull it, turn it back into a crush.

It doesn't.

It was never a crush, if she's being honest, not since she started planning her mornings around a girl she didn't even know. Her last shred of self-preservation was pretending it was enough to have Jane temporarily, and she shoved that like a twenty-dollar bill down Annie Depressant's tits last night.

"I wish I were never *born,*" August moans into the floor.

"Retweet," Wes says solemnly.

It takes twenty minutes, but eventually they extricate themselves from the couch. Myla, who slithered across the floor to the bathroom and threw up twice before army crawling back out, looks half-dead and altogether unlikely to partake in the scrambled eggs. Niko has already chugged a full bottle of kombucha in an impressive show of faith in his intestines to work things out on their own. And Wes has dislodged his pants from the window.

August manages to smile blearily at Lucie as she dumps eggs out of the frying pan and onto a plate before throwing a handful of forks down.

"Family style," she says, and man. Everything is a disaster, but August does love her.

"Thank you," August says. "Don't you have a morning shift?"

Lucie pulls a face. She's wearing one of August's T-shirts. "Billy is reducing my hours. Told me yesterday."

"What? He can't do that; you're basically the only person keeping that place together."

"Yes," she says with a grim nod. "Most expensive person on the payroll."

"Wait," says Myla's voice, muffled by the floor. She drags her head up and squints. "What's going on with Billy's?"

August sighs. "The landlord is doubling the rent at the end of the year, so it's probably gonna shut down and become a Cheesecake Factory or something."

With what looks like a Herculean effort, Myla pulls herself up onto her knees and says, "That is unacceptable."

"Billy needs another hundred grand to buy the unit, and he can't get the loan."

"Okay, so." She does an alarming closed-mouth burp, shakes it off, and presses on. "Let's get the money."

"We're all broke," Lucie says. "Why you think we work in food service?"

"Right," Myla counters. "But we can find it."

August tries to think, but it's hard when her brain feels like a garbage bag full of wet socks and the socks are wet because they're soaked in grain alcohol. Myla and Niko were right about Christmas in July—it's the type of night you'll never forget, *if* you can remember it. There must have been way more than the fire code max capacity in there—

Oh.

"Wait," August says. "What if we did . . . a charity drag show."

Myla perks up slightly. "Like, donate the tips?"

"No, what if we charged a cover? Sold drink tickets? We could use your pull at Delilah's and get them to let us use the space, and we donate everything we make that night to saving Billy's."

"Winfield would perform," Lucie offers.

"Isaiah too," Wes chimes in.

"Oh, we could do a whole breakfast food theme!" Myla says. "Winfield and Isaiah can get their friends on the lineup."

"I could probably get Slinky's to donate some liquor," Niko adds.

The five of them exchange unsteady eye contact, buzzing with possibility.

Lucie deigns to give them a smile. "I like this idea."

The first week of July brings the transformation of apartment 6F into the Save Billy's campaign headquarters.

Niko brings a whiteboard home from the pawn shop by Miss Ivy's, and Myla starts making double portions of stir-fry, and they spend late nights circled up in the living room: Lucie and Winfield, Myla and Niko, Wes, Isaiah, the odd handful of servers, and August. Lucie's the de facto leader, burdened with the combination of hating extracurricular activities and large groups of friendly people while also loving Billy's and knowing Billy's-related logistics. She's taken to wearing a silver whistle around her neck like a sullen camp counselor just to keep them in line while she's reading spreadsheets aloud.

"How soon are we doing this?" Niko asks, shoveling an enormous piece of tofu into his mouth. "Not to be a buzzkill, but Mercury is in retrograde for another week, which is . . . not optimal."

"That's okay," August tells him. She glances at Lucie, who is poring over permit requirements on the kitchen floor. "We're gonna need more time to set this up anyway. Plus, we have to advertise it, drum up publicity—that's at least a month, right?"

Lucie nods. "Probably."

August turns to the whiteboard and makes a note. They'll plan on mid-August. Two weeks before the Q shuts down.

"So, what you're telling me is, you're gonna rally a bunch of queers to save Billy's with pancakes and a drag show?" Jane says when August catches her up. She's sun-warmed in the window of the train. August is trying not to think, *In love, in love, I'm in terrible dumbass love.*

"Yeah," August says, "basically."

"That's so fucking hot," Jane says, and she grabs August by the chin and kisses her hard and brilliant, an openmouthed exhale, shotgunning summer sunshine.

Terrible dumbass love, August thinks.

It comes together piece by piece. Isaiah and Winfield are down to headline, and after asking around, they get three more Brooklyn queens on board. Myla sweet-talks the manager of Delilah's into donating the space, Isaiah calculates the costs, and Wes even convinces some of the artists at his shop to set up a booth for flash tattoos in exchange for donations. It helps that so many of them have an in with so many tiny Brooklyn businesses—no one wants to see Billy's turned into an overpriced gourmet juice bar when they could be next.

It takes thirty minutes on the phone for Winfield to strong-arm Billy into accepting charity, and when he caves, he passes it off to August and tells her she's in charge of figuring out food. Cut to: Jerry and August swearing up a storm, trying to average out the number of pancakes they need per person and how much it'll cost. They get there, though.

All along, it hums under the surface—that feeling August felt when she stepped inside Delilah's, when Miss Ivy calls her by name, when they paraded down to the Q behind Isaiah in his top hat, when the guy at the bodega doesn't card her, when Jane looks at her like she could be part of her mental photo album of the city. That feeling that she lives here, like, *really* lives here. Her shadow's passed through a thousand busted-up crosswalks and under a million creaking rows of scaffolding. She's been here, and here, and here.

New York takes from her, sometimes. But she takes too. She takes its muggy air in fistfuls, and she packs it into the cracks in her heart.

And now, she's gonna give it something. *They're* gonna give it something.

It's the end of the first week, a late night sitting around a pizza talking about flyers, when August's phone rings.

She slides it out from under the box: her mom.

"Helloooo," she answers.

A short pause—August sits up straight. Something's up. Her mother never allows even half a second of silence.

"Hey, August, honey," she says. "Are you alone?"

August climbs to her feet, shrugging at Myla's concerned look. "Um, not right now. Hang on." She crosses to her room and shuts the door behind her. "What happened? Are you okay?"

"I'm fine, I'm fine," she says. "It's your grandmother."

August hisses out a long breath. Her grandmother? The old broad probably called her a test-tube science project baby again or decided to bankroll another Republican congressional campaign. That, she can deal with.

"Oh. What's going on?"

"Well, she had a stroke last night, and she . . . she didn't make it."

August sits down heavily on the edge of her bed.

"Shit. Are you okay?"

"I'm all right," her mom says in the tone she gets when she's leafing through evidence, half-distracted and clipped. "She'd already made arrangements after your grandfather died, so it's all handled."

"I meant, like." August tries to speak slowly, deliberately. Her mother has always been about as emotive as a mossy boulder, but August feels like this should probably be an exception. "Are *you* okay?"

"Oh, yeah, I'm—I'm okay. I mean, she and I had said everything we were ever going to say to each other. I got closure a long time ago. It is what it is, you know?"

"Yeah. Yeah, I'm really sorry, Mom. Is there anything I can do? Do you need me to come down for the funeral?"

"Oh, no, honey, don't worry about that. I'll be fine. But I did need to talk to you about something."

"What's up?"

"Well, I got a call from the family lawyer last night. Your grandmother left you some money."

"What?" August blinks at the wall. "What do you mean? Why would she leave me something? I'm the shameful family secret."

"No. No, that's me. You're her granddaughter."

"Since when? She's barely spoken to me. She's never even sent me a birthday present."

Another pause. "August, that's not true."

"What do you mean it's not true? What are you talking about?"

"August, I . . . I need to tell you something. But I need you not to hate me."

"What?"

"Look, your grandparents . . . they were difficult people. It's always been complicated between us. And I do think they're ashamed of me because I decided to have you on my own. I never wanted to become the trophy wife with a rich husband they raised me to be. But they were never ashamed of you."

August grinds her teeth. "They didn't even know me."

"Well . . . they did, kind of. I'd—I'd keep them updated, sometimes. And they'd hear from St. Margaret's how you were doing."

"Why would St. Margaret's talk to them about me?"

Another pause. A long one.

"Because they keep the people paying a student's tuition updated on their student."

What?

"What? They—they paid my tuition? This whole time?"

"Yes."

"But you told me—you always said we were broke because you had to pay for St. Margaret's."

"I did! I paid for your lunches, I paid for your field trips, your uniforms, your extracurriculars, your—your library fines. But they were the ones who wrote the big checks. They'd send one every birthday."

August's childhood and teenage years flutter into focus— the way kids used to look at her in her Walmart tennis shoes, the things her mom said they couldn't afford to replace after the storm. "So then, why were we broke, Mom? Why were we broke?"

"Well, August, I mean . . . it's not cheap, to pay for an investigation. Sometimes there were people I had to pay for information, there was equipment to buy—"

"How long?" August asks. "How long did they send money?"

"Only until you graduated high school, honey. I—I told them to stop once you turned eighteen, so they did. I didn't want them to keep helping us forever."

"And what if I had wanted help?"

She's quiet for a few seconds. "I don't know."

"I mean, based on the will, they would have, right?"

"Maybe so."

"You're telling me, I'm sitting here on a mountain of student loans that I didn't have to take out, because you didn't want to tell me this?"

"August, they—they're not like you and me, okay? They always judged me, and they would have judged the way we lived, the way I raised you, and I didn't want that for you. I didn't want to give them a chance to treat you the way they treated me, or Augie."

"But they wanted—they wanted to see me?"

"August, you don't understand—"

"So, you just decided for me that I wouldn't have a family? That it'd be just you and me? This isn't some *Gilmore Girls* fantasy, okay? This is my life, and I've spent most of it alone, because you told me I was, that I *should* be, that I should be *happy* about it, but it was only because you didn't want anyone to come between us, wasn't it?"

Her mom's voice comes back sharp, with a bitter, defensive anger that August knows lives in her too. "You can't even imagine it, August. You can't imagine the way they treated Augie. He left because they made him miserable, and I couldn't lose you like that—"

"Can you shut up about Augie for once? It's been almost fifty years! He's gone! People leave!"

There's a terrible moment of silence, long enough for August to play back what she said, but not long enough to regret it.

"August," her mom says once, like a nail going in.

"You know what?" August says. "You never listen to me. You never care about what I want unless it's what *you* want. I told you five years ago that I didn't want to work the case with you anymore, and you didn't care. Sometimes it's like you had me just so you could have a—a fucking assistant."

"August—"

"No, I'm done. Don't call me tomorrow. In fact, don't call me at all. I'll let you know when I'm ready to talk, but I—I am gonna need you to leave me alone for a while, Mom." She squeezes her eyes shut. "I'm sorry about your mom. And I'm sorry they treated you like shit. But that didn't give you the right."

August hangs up and throws her phone onto the floorboards, flopping back on her bed. She and her mom have fought before—God knows two hardheaded people with a tendency to go icy when threatened in only seven hundred square feet of living space will go at it. But never like this.

She can hear everyone in the living room laughing. She feels as separate from it as she did the day she moved in.

Her whole life, the gnaw of anxiety has made people opaque to her. No matter how well she knows someone, no matter the logical patterns, no matter how many allowances she knows someone might make for her—that bone-deep fear of rejection has always made it impossible for her to see any of it. It frosts over the glass. She never had anyone to begin with, so she let it be unsurprising that nobody would want to have her around.

She slides her hand over the bedspread and her knuckles

brush something cool and hard: her pocketknife. It must have slid out when she threw her bag down earlier.

She scoops it up, turns it over in her palm. The fish scales, the sticker on the handle. If she wanted to, she could twirl it between her fingers, flip the blade out, and jimmy a window open. Her mom taught her. She remembers it all. She shouldn't have had to learn any of it, but she did.

And now she's using everything she learned to help Jane.

Shit.

You can try, she guesses. You can tear yourself apart and rebuild from scratch, bring yourself to every corner of the map, sew a new self from the scraps of a thousand other people and places. You can try to expand to fill a different shape. But at the end of the day, there's a place at the foot of the bed where your shoes hit the floor, and it's the same.

It's always the same.

The next day, August takes the file her mother mailed her down from the top of the fridge.

She didn't open it after the first time, didn't think about it, but she didn't dump it in the garbage either. She wants it gone, so she crams it into her bag and climbs onto the Q heading toward the post office. It feels heavy in her bag, like a relic of the family religion.

It's incredible, really, how the sight of Jane sitting there like she always is, picking at the edge of the seat with her Swiss Army knife, unspools the tension in her shoulders.

"Hey, Landry," Jane says. She smiles when August leans down to kiss her hello. "Save Billy's yet?"

"Working on it," August says, sitting beside her. "Have any epiphanies yet?"

"Working on it," Jane says. She gives August a once-over. "What's going on? You're, like . . . all staticky."

"Is that a thing you can do?" August asks. "Because of the electricity thing? Like, can you feel other people's emotional frequencies?"

"Not really," Jane says, leaning her face on her hand. "But sometimes, lately, yours have started coming through. Not totally clear, but like music from the next room, you know?"

Uh-oh. Can she feel terrible dumbass love radiating off of August?

"I wonder if that means you're becoming more present," August says, "like how the wine worked on you even though you couldn't get drunk before. Maybe that's progress."

"Sure as hell hope so," Jane says. She leans back, hooking one arm over the handrail beside her. "But you didn't answer my question. What's going on?"

August hisses out a breath and shrugs. "I got in a fight with my mom. It's stupid. I don't really want to talk about it."

Jane lets out a low whistle. "I got you." A short lull absorbs the tension before Jane speaks again. "Oh, it's probably not that helpful, but I did remember something."

She lifts the hem of her T-shirt, baring the tattoos that span her side from ribs to thigh. August has seen them all, mostly in hurried glimpses or in semidarkness.

"I remembered what these guys mean," Jane says.

August peers at the inky animals. "Yeah?"

"It's the zodiac signs for my family." She touches the tail feathers of the rooster sprawling down her rib cage. "My dad, '33." The snout of the dog on her side. "Mom, '34." The horns of a goat on her hip. "Betty, '55." Disappearing past her waistband and down her thigh, a monkey. "Barbara, '56."

"Wow," August says. "What's yours?"

She points to her opposite hip, at the serpent winding up from her thigh, separate from the others. "Year of the Snake."

The art is beautiful, and she can't imagine Jane got any of them before she ran away. Which means she sat through hours of needles for her family *after* she left them.

"Hey," August says. "Are you sure you don't want me to . . . ?"

She's asked before, if she should try to find Jane's family. Jane said no, and August hasn't pushed it.

"Yeah, no, I—I can't," Jane says, tucking her shirt back in. "I don't know what's worse—the idea that they've been looking for me and missing me and probably thinking I'm dead, or the idea that they just gave up and moved on with their lives. I don't want to know. I can't—I can't face that."

August thinks of her mom and the file in her bag. "I get it."

"When I left home," Jane says after a few seconds. She's returned to her Swiss Army knife, carving a thin line into the shiny blue of the seat. "I called from LA once, and God, my parents were furious. My dad told me not to come back. And I couldn't even blame him. That was the last time I called, and I . . . I really believed that was the best thing I could do for them. For us. To drift. But I thought about them every single day. Every minute of the day, like they were with me. I got the tattoos so they would be."

"They're beautiful."

"I like permanent marks, you know? Tattoos, scars." She crosses the letter A she's been carving and moves on to N with a soft chuckle. "Vandalism. It's like, when you spend your life running, sometimes that's the only thing you have to show for it."

She carves a small plus sign underneath her name and looks up at August, extending the knife. "Your turn."

August glances between her, the knife, and the blank space below the plus sign for a full ten seconds before she gets it. Jane wants August's name next to hers in the permanent mark she's leaving on the Q.

Reaching into her back pocket, August clears the feelings out of her throat and says, "I have my own."

She flicks the blade of her knife out and gets to work, scratching a clumsy AUGUST. When it's done, she sits back, holding the knife loosely in her palm, admiring their work. JANE + AUGUST. She likes the way they look together.

When she turns to look at Jane, she's staring down at August's hand.

"What's that?" Jane asks.

August follows her gaze. "My knife?"

"Your—where did you get that?"

"It was a gift?" August says. "My mom gave it to me; it belonged to her brother."

"August."

"Yeah?"

"No. *August*," Jane says. August frowns at her, and she goes on: "That was his name. The guy who owned that knife. Augie."

August stares. "How did you—"

"How old is he?" Jane cuts in. Her eyes are wide. "Your mom's brother—how old is he?"

"He was born in '48, but he's—he's been missing since—"

"1973," Jane finishes flatly.

August never told Jane any of the specifics. It was nice to have one thing in her life that wasn't touched by it. But Jane knows. She knows his name, the year, and she—

"Fuck," August swears.

Biyu Su. She remembers where she saw that name.

She fumbles the fastening on her bag three times, before she finally pulls out the file.

"Open it," August says.

Jane's fingers are tentative on the edge of the manila folder, and when it falls open, there's a newspaper photograph paper-clipped to the first page, yellowing black and white. Jane, missing a couple of tattoos, in the background of a restaurant that had just opened in the Quarter. In the cutline, she's listed as *Biyu Su*.

"My mom sent me this," August says. "She said she'd found someone who might have known her brother and traced them to New York."

It takes a second, but it comes: the fluorescent above their heads surges brighter and blinks out.

"Her brother—" Jane starts and stops, hand shaking when she touches the edge of the clipping. "*Landry*. That was . . . that was her *brother*. I knew—I knew there was something familiar about you."

August's voice is mostly breath when she asks, "How did you know him?"

"We lived together," Jane says. Her voice sounds muffled through decades. "The roommate—the one I couldn't remember. It was him."

August knows from the look on her face what the answer is going to be, but she has to ask.

"What happened to him?"

Jane's hand curls into a fist.

"August, he's dead."

Jane tells August about the UpStairs Lounge.

It was a bar on the second floor of a building at the corner of Chartres and Iberville, a jukebox and a tiny stage, bars on the windows like all the spots in the city used to have. One of the best places for blue-collar boys on the low. Augie was short-haired and square-jawed, shoulders filling out a white T-shirt, a towel over his shoulder behind the bar.

It was the summer of '73, Jane tells her, but August already knows. She could never forget it. She's spent years trying to picture that summer. Her mom was sure he'd left the city, but August used to wonder if he was hidden away a few neighborhoods over, if ivy climbed the wrought iron on his balcony, or power lines heavy with Mardi Gras beads dipped into the oak trees outside his window.

Her mom had theories—he got a girl pregnant and ran away, made enemies with the guys who bribed the NOPD to guard their craps games and skipped town, got lost, got married, got out of town and disappeared beyond the cypress trees.

Instead, *instead,* Jane tells August he was loved. She remembers him at the stove of their tiny kitchen, teaching her how to make pancakes. She tells August how he used to frown at the bathroom mirror and run a wet comb through his hair trying to tame it. He was happy, she says, even though he never talked about his family, even though she heard him through the walls sometimes, on the phone using a voice so gentle that he must have been talking to the round-faced, green-eyed little girl whose picture he kept in his wallet. He was happy because he had Jane, he had friends, he had the job at the UpStairs and guys with sweet eyes and broad shoulders who wanted to kiss him in the streetlamp light. He had hope. He liked to march, liked to help Jane make signs. He had dreams for a future and friends all over the city, tight-knit circles, hands that slapped his back when he walked into a room.

He was the guy you called if you needed to move a couch or someone to tell the guy across the hall that if he ever says that word to you again, he'll get his ass beat. He made people laugh. He had a pair of red shorts that he loved especially well, and she has this stark memory of him wearing them, smoking a cigarette on the porch, perched on the top step, hands spread wide across the floorboards as the first drops of a summer storm started falling.

They talked about their dreams a lot, Jane says. They wanted to travel and would pass a bottle of Muscadine wine back and forth and talk about Paris, Hong Kong, Milan, New York. She told him about her hometown, San Francisco, and the sprawling woods and winding roads to the north, and he told her he'd always, always wanted to drive the Panoramic Highway, ever since he read about it in a library book. He loved books, brought home stacks and stacks from thrift stores and secondhand shops.

The day it happened was the last day of Pride. The beer was free that night, but it was the best night of the summer for tips. For the first time, he mentioned his little sister to Jane as he was shrugging on his jacket on his way out for his shift. He was going to buy her an encyclopedia set for her birthday, he said. He was worried their parents weren't letting her read enough. The night's tips would be just enough for it.

And then, that night at the UpStairs, gasoline and smoke.

And then, the ceiling falling in. And then, fire, and bars on windows, and a door that wouldn't open. Arson. Thirty-two men gone.

Augie didn't come home.

There are a couple of unmarked graves, Jane explains in a low, hoarse voice. It wasn't uncommon for there to be people like her or Augie, queer people who ran away and didn't want to be found, who didn't have families who could or would claim them, people who kept secrets so well nobody would even have known they were there.

And that was bad enough. The empty bedroom, the rolls of socks, the milk left in the fridge, the aftershave in the bathroom, it was all bad enough. But then there were the months that came after.

The city barely tried to investigate. The news mentioned the fire but left out that it was a gay bar. The radio hosts made jokes. Not a single politician said a goddamn word. Church after church refused to hold the funerals. The one priest who did gather a handful of people for prayers was nearly excommunicated by his congregation.

It hurt, and it hurt again, this horrible thing that had happened, this ripping, unfathomable, terrible thing, and it only hurt more, spreading like the bruises on Jane's ribs when the cops would decide to make an example out of her.

New Orleans, Jane tells her, was the first place that convinced her to stay. It was the first place she was herself. She'd spent a year on the road before she ended up there, but she fell in love with the city and its Southern girls, and she began to think she might put down roots.

After the fire, she made it six months before she packed up her records and left. She moved out in January of '74, nothing of her left in New Orleans but a name scratched into a couple bar tops and a kiss on a stone with no name. She lost touch with everyone. She wanted to become a ghost, like Augie.

And then she found New York. And it finished the job.

12

Photo from the archives of <u>The Tulane Hullabaloo</u>, Tulane University's weekly student-run newspaper, dated June 23, 1973

[Photo depicts a group of young women marching down Iberville Street, carrying signs and banners as part of the third annual New Orleans Gay Pride. In the foreground, a dark-haired woman in jeans and a button-down shirt holds a poster that reads DYKES FIGHT BACK. The following day, the New Orleans gay community would be struck by the UpStairs Lounge arson attack.]

At the entrance to the Parkside Ave. Station, August's finger hovers over the call button for the tenth time in as many hours.

There was a time when Uncle Augie loomed like Clark Kent in her childhood, this mysterious hero to be chased through squares of public record forms like comic book panels. Her mother told her stories—he was twelve years older, the heir-gone-wrong to an old New Orleans family, the little sister born in his rocky adolescence an attempt at a do-over. He had hair like August's, like her mother's, wild and thick and unkempt. He intimidated schoolyard bullies, snuck dessert when their mother said little girls shouldn't eat so much, hid whiskey and a box of photographs beneath a floorboard in his room.

She told August about the big fight she overheard one night, how Augie kissed her forehead fiercely and left with a suitcase, how he wrote her every week and sometimes arranged late-night calls until the letters and calls stopped coming. She told August about a streetcar ride to the police station, an officer saying they couldn't waste time on runaways, her parents inviting the chief for dinner when he drove her home and then taking her books away as punishment.

It makes sense now that Augie left and never came back, more than it did when it was only petty family arguments. August understands why he never told his sister he was still in the city, why her grandparents preferred to act as if he'd never existed. He was like Jane, just geographically closer.

She doesn't know how to tell her mom. She doesn't even know how to *speak* to her mom right now.

It's too much to think about, too much to put into a text or a phone call, so she pushes her phone into her pocket and decides she'll figure out as much as she can before she tells anyone else.

It's not until the Q pulls up and she sees Jane that it occurs to her this might have finally been too much for Jane too.

Jane's sitting there, staring straight ahead. There's a rip in her shirt collar and a fresh cut on her lip. She's flexing her right hand over and over in her lap.

"What happened?" August says, rushing onto the car and dropping her bag to kneel in front of her. She takes Jane's face in her hands. "Hey, talk to me."

Jane shrugs, impassive.

"Some guy called me some shit I'd rather not repeat," she finally says. "That old racist-homophobic combo. Always a winner."

"Oh my God, did he hit you? I'll kill him."

She laughs darkly, eyes flat. "No, I hit him. The lip is from when someone else pulled me off him."

August tries to brush her thumb by Jane's mouth, but she jerks away.

"Jesus," August hisses. "Did they call the cops?"

"Nah. Me and some guy shoved him off at the next stop, and I doubt his ego could handle calling the cops on a skinny Chinese girl."

"I meant for you. You're hurt."

Jane knocks August's hands off of her, finally making eye contact. August flinches at the razor's edge there.

"I don't fuck with pigs. You *know* I don't fuck with pigs."

August sits back on her heels. There's something off about Jane, in the air around her. Usually, it's like August can feel the frequency she vibrates at, like she's a space heater or a live wire, but it's still. Eerily still.

"No, of course, that was stupid," August says slowly. "Hey, are you . . . okay?"

"What do you fucking think, August?" she snaps.

"I know—it's, it's fucked up," August tells her. She's thinking about the fire, the things that drove Jane from city to city. "But I promise, most people aren't like that anymore. If you could go out, you'd see."

Jane grabs a pole and heaves herself to her feet. Her eyes are slate, flint, stone. The train takes a curve. She doesn't falter.

"That's not what it's about."

"Then what, Jane?"

"God, you don't—you don't get it. You can't."

For a second, August feels like she did that night after the séance, when she put her hand on Jane's wrist and felt the pulse buzzing impossibly fast under her fingers, when she talked to Jane like she was on a ledge. Jane might as well be hanging out the emergency exit.

"Try me."

"Okay, fine, it's like—I woke up one day and half the people I ever loved were dead, and the other half had lived a whole life *without me,* and I never got a chance to see it," Jane says. "I never got a chance to be at their weddings or their art shows. I never got to see my sisters grow up. I never got to tell my parents why I left. I never got to make it right. I mean, fuck, my friend Frankie had just gotten a new boyfriend who was *so* annoying, and I was gonna tell him to dump him, and I never even got to do *that.* Do you see what I mean? Have you ever thought about what this is like for me?"

"Of course I—"

"It's like I *died,*" she cuts in. Her voice cracks in the middle. "I died, except I have to *feel it.* And on top of that, I have to feel everything else I've ever felt all over again. I have to get the bad news again every day, I have to deal with the choices I made, and I can't fix it. I can't even run from it. It's *miserable,* August."

Okay. This is it. Jane's been shockingly casual about her entire existential predicament. August wondered when something like this was coming.

"I know," August says. The seat creaks faintly as she pushes herself to her feet, and Jane watches her sway closer with wide eyes, like she could bolt at any second. August moves until she's close enough to touch her. She doesn't. But she could. "I'm sorry. But it's—it's not too late to fix some of it. We're gonna figure it out, and we'll get you back to where you're supposed to be, and—"

"I swear to fucking God, August, can you for once not act like you know everything?"

"Okay," August says, feeling something defensive prick up her spine. Jane's not the only one who's spent the last day in a fighting mood. "Jesus."

Jane's teeth work her split lip for a second, like she's thinking. She backs up another three steps, out of reach.

"God, it's—you're so sure there's an answer, but there's no reason to believe there is one. None of this makes any fucking sense."

"Is that why you've been acting like you don't care about the case? Because you don't think I can solve it?"

"I'm not a fucking *case* to be *solved*, August."

"I know that—"

"What if I'm on the line forever, huh?" Jane asks her. "It's all interesting and exciting right now, but one day you're gonna be thirty, and I'll be twenty-four and *here*, and you're gonna get bored, and I'm just gonna stay. Alone."

"I'm not gonna leave you," August says.

August sees the riot girl in the way Jane rolls her eyes and says, "You should. I would."

"Yeah, well, I'm not you," August snaps.

That stops them both. August didn't mean to say it.

"What's that supposed to mean?"

"Nothing. Forget it." August twists her hands into fists in her pockets. "Look, I'm not the one you're mad at. I didn't get you stuck here."

"No, you didn't," Jane agrees. She turns her face away, hair falling in her eyes. "But you made me realize it. You made me remember. And maybe that's worse."

August swallows. "You don't mean that."

"You don't know what I mean," she says hoarsely. "August, I'm *tired.* I want to sleep in a bed. I want my life back, I want—I want *you* and I want to go back and I can't want those things at the same time, and everything's *too much,* and I—I don't want to feel like this anymore."

"I'm trying," August says helplessly.

"What if you didn't?" Jane says. "What if you stopped?"

In the silence that follows, August remembers how it feels to hit an ice patch on a frigid morning, those few seconds of terrible suspension before you scrape all the skin off your knees, when your stomach drops out and the only thought is, *This is about to kick my ass.*

"Stopped what?"

"Stopped trying," Jane says. "Just—just let it go. Get a new train. Don't see me anymore."

"No. *No.* I can't—I can't *leave,* Jane—if I leave, you're *gone.* That's the whole reason September matters. It's me, it's us, it's whatever the hell is happening between us, that's what's keeping you here." She staggers closer, grasping at Jane's jacket. "Come on, I know you feel it. The first time you saw me, you recognized me—my name, my face, the way I smelled, it made you remember." Her hand moves gracelessly to Jane's chest, over her heart. "This is what's keeping you here. It's not just fucking dumplings and Patti Smith songs, Jane, it's us."

"I know," Jane says quietly, like it hurts to say it. "I always knew it was you. That's why I didn't—it's why I shouldn't have ever kissed you. I look at you, and it feels like I'm realer than

I've ever been, from right here." She covers August's hand with hers. "So big it burns. God, August, it's beautiful, but it hurts so bad." And, damningly, "You're the reason I feel like this."

It connects like a punch.

She's right. August knows she's right. She's been digging Jane's life back up, but Jane is the one who has to sit on the train alone and live it all over again.

Something in her recoils violently, and her fingers dig into the fabric of Jane's jacket, bunching it up in her fist.

"Just because you can't run doesn't mean you can make me do it for you."

A muscle clenches in Jane's jaw, and August wants to kiss it. She wants to kiss her and fight her and hold her down and set this storm loose on the world, but the doors open at the next stop, and for just a second, Jane glances through them. Her foot twitches toward the platform, like she'd have a chance if she tried, and that's what makes August's throat go tight.

"You want me to stay," Jane says. It's a quiet accusation, a push she doesn't have the strength to do physically. "That's what this is, isn't it? Myla said there's a chance I could stay. That's why you're doing this."

August still has a fistful of Jane's jacket. "You wouldn't be so angry if part of you didn't want that too."

"I don't—" Jane says. She squeezes her eyes shut. "I can't want that. I can't."

"We've done all this work," August says.

"No, *you've* done all this work," Jane points out. Her eyes open, and August can't tell if she's imagining the wetness there. "I never asked you to."

"Then what?" The part of her that's all blade is squaring up. "What do you want me to do?"

"I already told you," Jane says. Her eyes are flashing. A fluorescent above their heads goes out with a loud pop.

If August were different, this is the part where she'd stay and fight. Instead, she thinks viciously that Jane's idea won't work. It can't possibly be that easy to split this apart, not in just a few days. She'll be back before it's too late. She'll leave just to prove it.

They're pulling into the next stop soon, a big Manhattan one that will bring a rush of people with it.

"Fine. But this?" August hears her voice come out caustic and harsh, and she hates it. "All this? I did it for you, not me."

The doors slide open, and the last thing August sees of Jane is the stiff set of her jaw. Her split lip. The furious determination not to cry. And then people push on, and August is lost in the current of bodies, dumped out onto the platform.

The doors shut. The train pulls away.

August reaches into her heart for the sour thing that lives there and squeezes.

August slams her bag down on the bar within five seconds of stepping into Billy's for her dinner shift.

"Hey, hey, hey, watch it!" Winfield warns, snatching a pie out of range. "This is blackberry. She's a special lady."

"Sorry," she grumbles, plopping down onto a stool. "Rough week."

"Yeah, well," Winfield says, "my super has been saying he's gonna fix my toilet since last Thursday. We're all having a time."

"You're right, you're right." August sighs. "Lucie working this shift?"

"Nope," he says. "She's taking the day to yell at city officials about permits."

"Yeah, about that," August says. "Myla and I are starting to think we're gonna need a bigger venue."

Winfield turns and raises his eyebrows at her. "The capacity of Delilah's is eight hundred. You think we're getting more than that?"

"I think we're gonna get, like, double that," August tells him. "We've already sold eight hundred-something tickets, and it's not for another month."

"Holy shit," he says. "How the hell did y'all manage that?"

August shrugs. "People love Billy's. And it turns out Bomb Bumboclaat and Annie Depressant are big sellers."

He grins wide, preening in the grimy glow of the kitchen window heat lamps. "Well, I coulda told you that."

August smiles half-heartedly back at him. She wishes she could match his excitement, but the fact is, she's been throwing herself into the fundraiser to stop thinking about how she hasn't heard from Jane in two days. She wanted to be left alone, so August is leaving her alone. She hasn't set foot on the Q since Jane told her to forget about her.

"Who's on the schedule today?"

"You're looking at it, baby," Winfield says. "It feels like Satan's taint outside. Nobody's coming to get afternoon pancakes today. It's just us and Jerry."

"Oh God. Okay." August peels herself off her stool and rounds the counter to clock in. "I need to talk to Jerry anyway."

In the kitchen, Jerry's hefting a bucket of hashbrown shavings out of the fridge and toward the prep station. He gives her a quick nod.

"Hey, Jerry, you got a minute?"

He grunts. "What's up, buttercup?"

"So, it's looking like we might end up with double the people we planned for the fundraiser," she says. "We should probably talk pancake logistics again."

"Shit," he swears, "that's gonna be at least thirty gallons of batter."

"I know. But we don't have to make a pancake for every guest—I mean, there have gotta be people who are gluten-free, or low carb, or whatever—"

"So, let's say twenty gallons of batter, then. That's still a lot, and I don't even know how we'd transport that many pancakes."

"Billy said he has a spare grill in storage. He was gonna sell it, but if he could bring it to the venue, you and some of the line cooks could cook them there."

He thinks on it. "Sounds like a pain in the ass."

"But it could work. We can use the catering van to get the batter there."

"Yeah, okay, it could work."

Winfield's head pops up in the window. "Hey, can I get some bacon?"

Jerry glances at him. "For you or for a table?"

"No tables, I'm just hun—"

At that exact moment, the creaky pipe along the wall by the dishwasher finally does what it's been threatening since long before August started working there: it bursts.

Water explodes all over the floor of the kitchen, soaking through the canvas of August's sneakers and down to her socks, gushing into the tubs of biscuits under the prep table. She lunges forward and tries to wrap her hands around the split of the pipe, but all it does is redirect most of the water onto her—her shirt, her face, her hair—

"Uh," August says, kicking a tub of biscuits out of harm's way with one soggy foot. It tips and biscuits spill all over the tiles, floating away like little biscuit boats. "Can I get some help here?"

"I *told* Billy it was just a matter of time on that piece of shit," Jerry grumbles, sloshing through the water. "I gotta turn off the fuckin' main and—fuck!"

With a colossal crash, Jerry's feet fly out from under him, and down he goes, bringing a ten-gallon tub of pancake batter with him.

"Jesus titty-fucking Christ," Winfield says when he throws the door open on the scene—Jerry on his back in a growing lake of pancake batter, August soaked head to toe, hands around the spewing pipe and soggy biscuits swimming around her ankles. He takes one step into the kitchen and slips, tumbling into a stack of dishes, which shatter spectacularly.

"Where the hell is the water main, Jerry?" August asks.

"It's not in here," Jerry says, struggling to his feet. "Stupid old fucking building. It's in the back office."

The back office—

"Wait," August says, rushing to follow Jerry. He's already halfway down the hall. "Jerry, don't, I can—"

Jerry wrenches the door open and disappears into the office before August can skid into the doorway.

He straightens up in the corner, the main switched off at last, and August watches him finally see the maps and photos and notes pinned on the walls. He turns slowly, taking it all in.

"The fuck is this? We got a squatter?"

"It's—" August doesn't know how the hell to explain. "I was—"

"You did this?" Jerry asks. He leans toward the clipping August pulled out of her mom's file and added to the wall. "How come you got a picture of Jane?"

August's stomach flips.

"You said you didn't remember her," she says faintly.

Jerry looks at her for a second, before the unmistakable jingle of the front door sounds.

"Well," Jerry says. He turns away, headed for the kitchen. "Somebody's gotta feed the poor bastard."

Winfield crunches off through shards of coffee mugs to take the customer, and Jerry salvages the kitchen enough to make a plate of food. He calls Billy to let him know they're going to have to close until a plumber can come, and even from across the room August can hear Billy swearing about the costs of lost business and new pipes. Another few weeks off the Pancake Billy's prognosis.

Winfield serves their one customer a shortstack with orange juice and sends them on their merry way, and Jerry tells Winfield to go home.

August stays.

"You said," she says, cornering Jerry by the walk-in, "you didn't remember Jane."

Jerry groans, rolling his eyes and throwing a tub of butter on the shelf. "How was I supposed to know there was a waitress operating a Jane Su shrine out the back of my restaurant?"

"It's not—" August takes a squishy step back. "Look, I'm trying to figure out what happened to her."

"What do you mean what happened to her?" Jerry asks. "She left. It's New York, people leave. The end."

"She didn't," August says. She thinks about Jane, alone on the train. No matter how angry she is, she can't stop imagining Jane fading in and out of the line, untethering herself. But she doesn't really think Jane will forget, not after all this time. Maybe, if she can find proof that there's hope, she can change Jane's mind. "She never left New York."

"What?" Jerry asks.

"She's been missing since 1977," August says.

Jerry takes that in, slumping heavily against the door. "No shit?"

"No shit." August levels her gaze at him. "Why did you tell me you didn't remember her?"

Jerry huffs out another sigh. His mustache really has a life of its own.

"I'm not proud of who I was back then," Jerry says. "I'm not proud of the friend I was to her. But I'd never forget her. That girl saved my life."

"What? Like, figuratively?"

"Literally."

August's eyes widen. "How?"

"Well, y'know, we were friends," he says. "I mean, she was friends with everyone, but me and her lived on the same block. We'd give each other shit all day in the kitchen, and then we'd go to a bar after work and drink a Pabst and talk about girls. But one day she comes into work and says she's moving."

"She was?" August blurts out, and he nods. That's new. That's not on the timeline.

"Yeah," he goes on. "Said she'd heard from an old friend she never expected to hear from again, and he convinced her to go. Last time I saw her, it was her last day in town. July of '77. We went to Coney Island, said goodbye to the Atlantic, rode the Wonder Wheel, had way too many beers. And then she dragged my drunk ass to the Q, and let me tell you what a dumbass I used to be—there I was, drunk as my aunt Naomi at my cousin's bris, and I walked to the edge of the platform and puked my guts out, and when I got done, I fell clean off."

August presses a hand to her lips. "Onto the tracks?"

"*Right* onto the tracks. Biggest dumbass move of my life."

"What happened?"

He laughs. "Jane. She jumped down and got me out."

"Holy shit," August exhales. Typical Jane, throwing herself onto the tracks to save someone else like it was nothing. "And then what?"

Jerry gives her a look. "Kid, do you know what happened in New York in July of '77?"

She runs through her mental files. Son of Sam. The birth of hip-hop. The blackout.

Wait.

Myla's voice jumps into her head: *But let's say there was a big event—*

"The blackout," August says. It comes out high and tight.

"The blackout," Jerry confirms. "I passed out on a bench, and when I woke up, it was fuckin' chaos. I mean, I barely made it home. I guess I lost her in the chaos, and her bus was first thing in the morning. So that was it. I never saw her again."

"You didn't try to call her? To make sure she made it out?"

"You do know what blackout means, right? I couldn't even get down the street to see if she was at her apartment. Anyway, she lost my number after that. Can't say that I blame her, after I almost got us both killed. Whole reason I stopped drinking that year."

August gulps down a mouthful of air.

"And you never heard from her again?"

"Nope."

"Can I ask you one more question?"

Jerry grumbles but says, "Sure."

"The place she was moving . . . it was California, wasn't it?"

"You know what . . . yeah, I think it was. How'd you know?"

August throws her apron over her shoulder, already halfway out the door.

"Lucky guess," she says. On her way out, she stops in the back office and plucks the postcard off the wall.

At a tiny electronics shop a few blocks over, she buys a hand-held blacklight and ducks into an alley. She shines the light over the postmark, the way her mom used to with old documents where the ink had rubbed off, and it reveals the shadow of where the numbers used to be. She didn't think the exact date would matter, until now.

An Oakland area code at the bottom. *Muscadine Dreams.* The hometown Jane told him about, passing wine back and forth on the porch. August can picture him and his red shorts and messy hair, cruising down the Panoramic Highway in golden sunshine.

It's postmarked April 1976.

Augie didn't die that night in 1973. He went to California.

"This is like an episode of *CSI*," Wes says through a mouthful of popcorn.

"I'm taking that as a compliment," August says.

She finishes taping up the last photo, and she has to admit, it *is* a little primetime television detective. There's no yarn yet, though. August is proud of that. Yarn is the one thing separating her from a full-scale conspiracy theorist—also known as the Full Suzette.

(She hasn't integrated what she figured out about Augie into the timeline yet. There's not enough dry-erase marker in the world to work that one out, and certainly not enough space in her head. One thing at a time.)

Myla and Niko are out for dinner, but August couldn't wait, so it's just Wes and his huge bowl of popcorn watching her pace back and forth in front of the whiteboard in the kitchen. He looks deeply bored, which means he's having a great time and finding this all very entertaining.

"Okay, so," she says. She nudges her glasses up her nose with the end of her dry-erase marker. "Here's what we know."

"Tell us what we know, August."

"Thank you for your support, Wesley."

"My name is Weston."

"It's— Jesus, are you a fucking Vanderbilt or something?"

"Focus, August."

"Right. Okay. We know Jane was on the tracks during the citywide power surge that caused the 1977 blackout. So, my theory: the burst of power on the already super-powerful electrified rail created some kind of . . . crack in time that she slipped through, and now she's tethered to the electricity of the rails."

"C'mon, Doctor Who," Wes says.

"Myla thinks that if we can re-create the event, we can break her out of the time slip. All we have to do is . . . figure out a way to re-create the conditions of the '77 blackout."

"Don't you think that's kind of a dick move?" Wes asks. "I mean, even if we could somehow find a way to do it, which we can't, the blackout was like . . . universally considered a bad thing. You'd be throwing the whole city into Purge territory."

"You're right. We'd have to find a way to target only Jane's line. Which is where this comes in."

August jabs her marker at the photo stuck in the top right corner.

"The New York City Transit Power Control Center. Located in Manhattan, on West Fifty-third Street. These two blocks of buildings manage the power to the entire MTA, with several substations. If we can get access, we can figure out which substation controls the Q, and we can find a way to create a power surge . . . that might work."

"Loving this TED Talk," Wes says. "Unsure how exactly you plan to handle the *if*."

As if on cue, there's the familiar jingle of Myla's five million key chains as she unlocks the door.

"Hey, we brought leftovers if you—oh my God." Myla stops halfway into the door, Niko colliding with her back. "You started without me?"

"I—"

"You text me that you, and I quote, 'scored the clue of a lifetime' and are 'about to bust this shit wide open,'" Myla says, throwing her skateboard down in a righteous fury, "and you don't even wait for me to have a free afternoon to break out the whiteboard. Wow. I thought I could trust you."

"Look, I can't talk to Jane about it," August tells her. "I needed to do *something*."

"You're still in a fight?" Niko asks.

"I'm giving her space." August extends a dry-erase marker to

Myla, who glares as she snatches it up. "She said that was what she wanted."

"Uh-huh, and this wouldn't have anything to do with the way you reflexively ice out anyone who even appears to have rejected or wronged you?"

"Don't answer that, it's a trap," Wes calls from the couch. "He's using his powers for evil."

"That wasn't a reading," Niko says. "It was just a read."

"*Anyway,*" August presses on, "she's gonna come around. And she may not be speaking to me, but that doesn't change the fact that she's stuck in the nebulous in-between—"

"Aren't we all?" Wes adds, and August throws a stack of Post-its at his face.

"And we're the only ones who can fix it. So I'm gonna keep trying."

Niko gives her a cryptic look before curling up on the couch with his head in Wes's lap. August gives Myla a quick rundown of what she's figured out so far.

"You're missing something," Myla points out. "Just being near the Q when the blackout happened isn't enough for her to get stuck. There must have been thousands of people on trains and in stations during that surge, and none of them got stuck. There's another variable you're not accounting for."

August leans against the fridge. "Yeah . . . shit, yeah, you're right."

"You haven't talked to Jane? Told her what you learned?"

"She told me to leave her alone. But I. . . . I feel like if I could talk to her about it, she might remember the rest."

Myla pats her on the shoulder and spins back to the board.

"So, basically, when you have an event like the blackout, and an outage is caused by a power surge—a lightning strike, in this case—there are actually two surges. The first one that over-loads the line and makes the lights go out. And the second." She points at August with the marker. "You know when you were a kid and the electricity would go out during a storm, and then when it comes back, there's half a second when the lights come on too bright? That's the second surge. So, if we were . . . some-how able to do this, we'd have two chances."

August nods. They can work with that, she thinks.

"And how are we gonna access the substation?"

Myla frowns. "That, I don't know. I can ask around and see if anyone who was in the engineering program with me has connections, but . . . I don't know."

"Yeah," August says. She's already thinking through con-tingency plans. Do they know anyone skilled in espionage? Or who'd be willing to sleep with a security guard for the cause?

"You have a bigger problem, though," Myla says.

August snaps back into focus. "What?"

"If all this is right, and it's an electrical event . . . when they cut the power in September, it's not only that you won't be able to see her. She might just . . . blink out."

"What?" August says. "No, that can't—the train broke down before, when she was on it. She was fine."

"Yeah, the *train* broke down," Myla says. "But there was still power in the line. And maybe it was okay before you, when she never stayed in one time or place for long enough to be there when they cut the power to the tracks for maintenance, but if we're right about how strong your connection is, you've got her pinned, here and now. She won't be able to avoid it."

The reality of that spins out: Jane would have been fine if she wasn't stuck here and now. The Q has probably lost power or had its power cut a hundred times before, but Jane always missed it, until August. Until August fell in love with her and got greedy with kisses and turned herself into a weight holding Jane in one spot.

And now, if she doesn't pull this off, Jane might be gone forever. Not now. Not then. Nowhere.

Maybe Jane was right. This *is* her fault.

"*August,*" Myla yells through August's bedroom door. "August!"

She buries her face in her pillow and groans. It's seven in the morning, and she didn't get home from work until four hours ago. Myla is really betting on not getting stabbed.

The door flies open, and there's Myla, wild-eyed, a soldering gun in one hand and a string of lights in the other. "August, it's a *nerve.*"

August squints through a wall of her hair. "What?"

"My sculpture," she says. "The one I've been working on for, like, ever. I've—I've been looking at it all wrong. I thought I was supposed to be making something big, but it was right in front of me with all this Jane stuff—the branches, the lights, the moving parts—it's a *nerve.* It's what I *do*! Electricity of the heart! That's what the point of view is!"

August rolls over to stare at the ceiling. "Damn. That's . . . genius."

"*Right?* I can't believe I didn't think of it before! I have to thank Jane the next time I see her, she—"

August's face must fold into something tragic, because Myla stops.

"Oh, shit," Myla says. "You *still* aren't talking to her?"

August shakes her head. "Five days now."

"I thought you were gonna go back after three?"

August rolls back over and curls around her pillow. "Yeah, that was before I knew trying to save her life might get her killed. Now I feel like maybe she was right to want me to leave her alone."

Myla sighs, leaning against the doorframe. "Look, remember what we said when you first moved in and I made you listen to Joy Division? We'll figure it out. We have most of a plan now."

"I think I know everything, but I don't," August mumbles. "Maybe I started with a relationship difficulty level too far above my skill set."

"Oh, we're in self-pity mode," Myla says. "I can't help you with that. Good luck, though! Talk to Jane!"

Myla leaves August in her unwashed sheets, feeling sorry for herself, tasting strawberry milkshake on the back of her tongue.

Her phone buzzes somewhere in the tangle of her bed.

It's probably another passive-aggressive text from her mom, or Niko in the group chat checking the household rice inventory from the grocery store. She grumbles and fishes it out from beneath her ass.

Her breath hitches. It's Jane.

Put the radio on.

She catches the outro of a Beach Boys song, fading into warm quiet, before the early morning DJ's voice picks up over the waves.

"That was 'I Know There's an Answer' from the album *Pet Sounds,* and you're listening to WTKF 90.9, your one-stop shop for the new, the old, the whatever, as long as it's good," he says. "This next one's a request from a frequent caller, one with a taste for the oldies. And this one's a goodie. It goes out to August—Jane says she's sorry."

The intro comes up, drums and strings, and August knows it right away. The first song they chased a memory to, the one they played on her clumsy attempt at a first date.

Oh, girl, I'd be in trouble if you left me now. . . .

Her phone thumps down onto her chest.

The song buzzes over her little speakers and the music wells up wistful and heartsick, and she pictures that seven-inch single Jane told her about. For the first time, she really sees it: Jane, 1977, on her own and alive.

It's hard to believe colors looked the same back then, crisp and bright and present, not washed-out, grainy sepia, but there it is. Strings and faraway vocals and Jane. There's her skin glowing golden under crosswalk lights as she carries a bundle of new records home. There's the stack of books on her nightstand. There's the Indian place she used to like, the cigarettes she used to bum when she was stressed, the woman down the hall who makes the terrible pierogies, a tube of toothpaste rolled up at the end with CREST in the big block letters of a discontinued font.

There's the bright red of her sneakers, fresh out the box, and the sun that used to fall across her bedroom floor, and the mirror where she checked the swoop of her hair, and the blue sky over her head. She's there. Only leaving what she means to leave. Exactly where she's supposed to be.

Jane's been on the train thinking of home, and August has been at home thinking of Jane moving in, cooking breakfast, building a life with her. It feels like a million years ago that she sat over a plate of fries at Billy's and told Myla that they had to help her no matter what. Even if she lost her. She really did believe it.

Another text. Jane.

Come back.

Maybe that's the worst thing August can do. Maybe it's the only thing.

She rolls out of bed and reaches for her keys.

13

Radio transcript from WTKF 90.9 FM
Broadcast November 14, 1976

STEVEN STRONG, HOST: That was
"Unchained Melody" by the Righteous
Brothers, and you're listening to 90.9
The Mix, your home for everything you
want to listen to at the push of a
button. Hope you're staying warm out
there, New York—it's a cold one tonight.
Up next, I have a request from a Jane
in Brooklyn, who wanted to hear from
some of our favorite British boys. This
is "Love of My Life" by Queen.

Jane's not on the train.

August tries to pick her way through the people clogging
the aisle, but it's packed tight and she's too short to see over
their heads. She ends up jostled to the end of the car, and she
clambers up onto the one empty seat to see if the boost helps.

It doesn't.

Something lodges in her throat. Jane's not there. She's never
not been there before.

No, no, no, not possible. It's only been a few days since August saw her, less than an hour since she heard from her. That song was *just* on the radio. She doesn't completely understand this tether between them, but it can't be that fragile. Jane can't be gone. She can't be.

She drops down onto the floor, panic prickling along the bones of her fingers and wrists.

August didn't have enough time. They've spent months digging Jane up, one scoop at a time, and she's supposed to live. Jane is supposed to have a life, even if it's not with her.

The track bends, and August stumbles. Her shoulders hit the metal wall of the car.

Maybe she missed her. Maybe she can get off at the next stop and try another car. Maybe she can grab a train in the opposite direction and Jane will be there, like always, book in hand and a mischievous smile. Maybe there's still time. Maybe—

She turns her head, glancing through the window at the end of the car.

There's someone sitting in the last seat of the next car over, absently looking back at her. The collar of her jacket's flipped up around her jaw, and her dark hair is falling in her eyes. She looks miserable.

"Jane!" August shouts, even though Jane can't hear her. All she must see is the cartoonish shape of August's mouth miming her name, but it's enough. It's enough for her to jump out of her seat, and August can see Jane call her name back. It might be the best thing she's ever seen.

She watches Jane lunge sideways—the emergency exit— and she reaches for hers. It comes open easily, and there's the tiny platform she remembers so well, and Jane's on the next one, close enough to touch, beaming out the back of a speeding train, and August was wrong—*this* is the best thing she's ever seen.

There aren't perfect moments in life, not really, not when shit has gotten as weird as it can get and you're broke in a mean city and the things that hurt feel so big. But there's the wind flying and the weight of months and a girl hanging out an emergency exit, train roaring all around, tunnel lights flashing, and it feels perfect. It feels insane and impossible and perfect. Jane reels her in by the side of her neck, right there between the subway cars, and kisses her like it's the end of the world.

She lets August go as they exit the tunnel into blazing sunlight.

"I'm sorry!" Jane shouts.

"*I'm* sorry!" August shouts back.

"It's okay!"

"Do you fuckin' *mind?*" a guy yells from behind her.

Oh fuck. Right. Other people exist, somehow.

"You better get over here before someone pushes me off!"

Jane laughs and jumps over, grabbing August's shoulders on the way, the momentum carrying them through the door. August catches Jane right before she staggers into the pissed-off guy in a Yankees hat.

"You done?" he says. "It's the fuckin' subway, not the fuckin' *Notebook.* Wanna get us all fuckin' stuck here for an hour while they scrape a couple of lesbians off the fuckin' tracks—"

"You're right!" Jane says through a slightly hysterical laugh, snatching August's hand up and tugging her away. "Don't know what we were thinking!"

"I'm actually bisexual!" August adds faintly over her shoulder.

They make their way to the other side of the car, past strollers and umbrellas, past khaki-covered knees and bags of groceries, to a pocket of space near the last pole, and Jane whips around to face her.

"I was—"

"You were—"

"I didn't mean to—"

"I should have—"

Jane stops, holding in a mouthful of laughter. August has never been so happy to see her, not even those early days when she was a fever of an idea. She's not an idea anymore—she's Jane, hardheaded Jane, runaway Jane, smart-mouthed Jane, bruise-knuckled, soft-hearted agitator Jane. The girl stuck on the line with August's heart in the pocket of her ratty jeans.

"You go first," she says.

August leans her shoulder against the pole, edging closer. "You were—not totally wrong. I *was* doing this for you, or at least I think I was, but you're right. I didn't want you to go back." Her instincts say to shift her eyes anywhere but to Jane, but she doesn't. She looks Jane straight in the eyes and says, "I wanted—I want you to stay here, with me. And that's fucked up, and I'm sorry."

There's a second of quiet, Jane looking at her, and then she shrugs her backpack off and hands August something from the side pocket.

"You're not the only one who has notebooks," Jane says quietly.

It's a tiny, battered Moleskine folded open to a page covered in Jane's messy handwriting: *Overwatch. Frank Ocean. Easy Mac. Apple vs. PC. Postmates. Barack Obama. The Golden Girls. Instagram. Jurassic Park. Gogurt. Jolly Ranchers. Star Wars. What is a prequel?*

"What is this?"

"It's a list," Jane says. "Of things and people you've mentioned, or Niko or Myla or Wes, or people I've overheard on the train. There's a lot I have to catch up on."

August pulls her eyes up to search Jane's face. She looks . . . nervous.

"How long have you been making this?" August asks.

She rubs a hand over the short hairs at the back of her neck. "A few months."

"You—you want to know all this stuff? You never asked. I thought you didn't want to know."

"I didn't, at first," Jane admits. "I wanted to go back, and I was so determined to get there that I didn't care about anything else. I didn't want to know anything that might make it harder. But then there was you, and I wanted to know what made you *you*, and I—I don't know." She kicks the toe of her sneaker against the floor. "At some point I guess I decided . . . it wouldn't be the worst thing if I had to stay. It could be okay."

August clutches the Moleskine to her chest. "I—I know I said—but I didn't think you'd actually want to stay. You really mean that?"

"Part of me, yeah. You were right. There's a lot more to it than going back to where I started. I mean, I ride this train every day, and I see gay people just holding hands in public, in front of everyone, and most of the time, nobody fucks with them, and that's . . . I don't know if you realize how crazy that is to me. I know things aren't perfect, but at least if I stayed, it'd be different." She's been studying her cuticles, but she looks up. "And I could be with you."

August's mouth falls open.

"With me."

"Yeah, I—I know what it would cost me, but . . . I don't know. All this—this whole mess—it scares the shit out of me."

She swallows, sets her jaw. "But the thought of staying with *you* doesn't scare me at all."

"I didn't—I thought this was just a good time to you."

That earns her a short, quiet laugh.

"I wanted it to be, but it's not. It hasn't ever been." Her eyes have this way of swallowing up the grimy fluorescent light of the train and transforming it into something new. Right now, when she looks at August: stars. The goddamn Milky Way. "What is it to you?"

"It's—you're—God, Jane, it's . . . I want you," August says. It's not eloquent or cool, but it's true, finally. "Whatever it means, however you want me, as long as you're here, that's what it is to me, and maybe that sounds desperate, but I—"

She never gets to finish, because Jane's yanking her in and kissing her, drinking down the rest of her sentence.

August touches her face and opens her eyes, breaking off to demand, "What does *that* mean?"

"It means I—you—" Jane attempts. She leans down for another kiss, but August holds her stubbornly in place. "Okay— yeah, I want that. I want what you want."

"Okay," August says. She licks her lips. They taste like a clean room and a full house and a 4.5 GPA. Like her own specific heaven. "So, we're—we're together until we're not, if that's what it comes down to."

"Yeah," Jane says.

It's as simple as that, one syllable dropping off Jane's tongue, two pairs of sneakers tucked between each other, this long career of wanting but not having and having but not knowing folded up into a word.

"Okay," August says. "I can live with that."

"Even if I end up leaving?"

"It doesn't matter," August says, even though it does. It matters, but it doesn't make a difference. "Whatever happens, I want you."

She rises up on her toes and kisses Jane, short, soft, a flashbulb burst, and Jane says, "But in case I do end up staying . . . you have to teach me about my list."

August opens her eyes. "Really?"

"I mean, I can't just jump into the twenty-first century without knowing how the wifey works—"

"*Wi-Fi.*"

"See!" She points at August. "Tip of the iceberg, Landry. You've got so much to teach me."

August grins as the train stops at Union Square and commuters start piling off, freeing up a few spaces on the bench. "All right. Sit down. I'll tell you about the Fast and Furious franchise. That'll be a good hour."

Jane does, kicking one foot up and folding her hands behind her head.

"Man," she says, smiling up at August. "I'm having one hell of a year."

August waits until the next day to bring it up.

Sometimes, the process of bringing back Jane's memories feels mystical and profound, like they're digging around in invisible magic, pulling up wispy roots. But a lot of the time, it's this: August shoving a PBR tallboy into a brown paper bag and carrying it down to the subway at one in the afternoon like a lush, hoping the smell of shitty beer will jog something in Jane's brain.

"Okay, so," August says when she sits. "I found something out, and I—I didn't tell you because we weren't talking, but I need to tell you now, because you need to remember the rest. This might be really big."

Jane eyes her warily. "Okay . . ."

"All right, so, um, first let me give you this." August hands her the beer, shooting a glare at a tourist who looks up from his guidebook to goggle at them. "You don't have to drink it, but Jerry mentioned that the two of you used to drink them together, so I thought the smell might help."

"Okay," Jane says. She cracks the can open. The tourist makes a disapproving noise, and Jane rolls her eyes at him. "You're gonna see worse things than this on the subway, man." She turns back to August. "I'm ready."

August clears her throat. "So . . . have you ever heard of the New York blackout of 1977? Huge power outage across most of the city?"

"Um . . . no. No, I guess that was after I got down here. Sounds like hell, though."

"Yeah, so . . . you remember Jerry? The cook at Billy's?"

Jane nods, her mouth quirking in a fond smile. "Yeah."

"I talked to him about you, and he . . . um, I think he told me how you got stuck."

Jane's been holding the PBR up to her nose to sniff it, but she lowers it at that. "What?"

"Yeah, he—the last time he saw you was your last day in New York. The two of you went to Coney Island and got drunk together, and y'all were waiting for the Q when the blackout happened. He said he never saw or heard from you again. And if that was supposed to be your last day, it would explain why none of your friends looked for you when you disappeared. They basically thought you ghosted them."

"I thought you said I wasn't a ghost."

"No," August says, biting back a smile, "it's, like, an expression for when you cut contact with someone without explanation."

"Oh, so they . . . they thought I just left without saying goodbye?"

That brings August up short.

She leans in, touches Jane's knee. "Do you want to take a break?"

"No," Jane says, shrugging it off. "I'm fine. What's your question?"

"My question is if you can remember anything else that happened that night."

Jane squeezes her eyes shut. "I'm—I'm trying."

"He said he fell on the tracks, and you jumped down to help him back up."

Her eyes are closed, hand still curled around the beer. Something faint slides over her face.

"I jumped down . . ." she repeats.

The doors open at a new stop, and a tourist pushes past them, his suitcase slamming into Jane's knee. Her beer sloshes out of the can and all over the sleeve of her jacket, dripping onto her jeans.

"Hey, asshole, watch where you're going!" August yells. She reaches out to brush the beer off, but Jane's eyes have snapped open. "Jane?"

"He spilled a beer," Jane says. "Jerry. We were . . . we were drinking Pabst from my backpack on the beach. It was the middle of a heat wave, and he kept giving me shit for carrying my leather jacket around, but I told him he just didn't understand my devotion to the punk lifestyle, and we laughed. And he . . ." Her eyes slide shut, like she's lost in the memory. "Oh man, then a wave knocked him off-balance and he spilled his whole beer, and I told him it was time to get him home before I had to fish his stupid drunk ass out of the Atlantic. We went to catch the Q, and he started throwing up, then he fell on the tracks. I—I remember he was wearing a fucking CCR T-shirt. And I helped him out, but then I—oh. Oh."

She opens her eyes, looking right back at August.

"What?"

"I tripped. I dropped my backpack, and every—everything I care about is in here, so I was trying to get it, and I tripped. And I fell. On the third rail. I remember seeing the third rail right in front of my face, and I thought, 'Fuck, this is it. This is how I die. That's so fucking stupid.' And then . . . there's nothing."

She looks scared, like she just lived it all over again.

"You didn't die."

"But I should have, right?"

August pushes her glasses up into her hair, rubbing at her eyes, trying to think. "I'm not Myla, but . . . I think you touched the third rail at the exact moment of the power surge that caused the blackout. It must have been enough of a burst of energy that it did more than kill you. It threw you out of time."

Jane considers this. "That's kind of cool, actually."

August pushes her glasses back down, blinking Jane into focus and checking her face for the warning signs she didn't pay enough attention to the last time they brought back something big. She doesn't see any.

She holds a breath. There's one more thing.

From her pocket, she pulls out the postcard from California. She hands it to Jane, pointing at the signature.

"There's something else," August says. "This might sound

crazy, but I . . . I think Augie sent you this. I just don't understand how. Do you remember it at all?"

She turns it over in her hands, touching the paper like she's trying to absorb it through her skin.

"He's alive," she says slowly. It's not a recitation of a fact she already knew. It sounds fresh. August has shown this postcard to her a dozen times, but this is the first time she's looked at it with recognition.

"It came out of nowhere," Jane says. "I don't . . . I don't even know how he found me. I was fucking terrified when I got it, because I was sure he was dead and I was getting mail from a ghost. I almost didn't call the number, but I did."

"And it was him?"

"Yeah," Jane says with a gradual nod. "Something happened, on his way to work that night. I don't even remember—some neighbor needed help, someone had a flat tire or something. He missed his shift. He was supposed to be there when the fire happened, but he missed his shift. He wasn't there. He survived."

August releases a breath.

He told her, Jane says, that he couldn't bear that he lived when his friends didn't, so he left, sick and blind with grief. He borrowed a car and drove out of town and woke up three days later strung out in Beaumont and decided not to come back. Started drinking too much, started hitchhiking, lost himself for a year or two, until a truck driver dropped him off in Castro, and someone pulled him off the sidewalk and told him they'd get him some help.

"He was doing well," Jane remembers, smiling a little. "He was sober, he'd gotten his life together. He had a steady boyfriend. They were living together. He sounded happy. And he told me he thought I should come home, that San Francisco was ready for people like us now. *We'll take care of each other, Jane.*"

"Jerry said," August says, "well, he said you were supposed to be moving back to California."

"Yeah, it was . . . the way Augie talked about his family . . . that's what did it for me," she says. "He felt like he missed his chance with them, and I—I saw through the guilt for a second. I realized I didn't have to miss mine."

She swallows, palming her side, the dog inked there for her mother. August waits for her to go on.

"New York was—it was good. It was really good. It gave me a lot of stuff I hadn't had since New Orleans. It was like I finally figured out who I was. How to *be* who I was," Jane says. "And I wanted my family to know that person. So, I mailed Augie my record collection, and I was gonna call him when I got into town."

"Did they know?" August asks. "Your family, did they know you were coming back?"

"No," Jane says. "I haven't talked to them since '71. I was too nervous to call."

August nods.

"Can I ask you something else?"

Jane, still examining the handwriting, nods without looking up.

"Did he say . . . did Augie tell you why he stopped writing home?"

"Hmm?"

"He used to write my mom every week, until summer 1973. She never heard from him again after that."

"No, he—he told me he was still writing to her. He said she hadn't written back in years, and he didn't think she wanted to hear from him anymore, but he was still writing." Her eyes move from the card to August's face, studying her. "She never got them, did she?"

"No," August says. "She didn't."

"Shit." It hangs unsaid in the air: someone else must have gotten to those letters first. August has a pretty good idea who. "What a fucking mess."

"Yeah," August agrees. She slides her hand over Jane's at her side and squeezes.

They ride in quiet for a few stops, watching the sun set behind apartment blocks, until Jane stands and starts pacing the aisle in that way she does, like a tiger in captivity.

"So, if you're right about how I got stuck," she says, turning to August, "what does that mean for getting me out?"

"It means, if we can . . . somehow re-create the event, and have you touch the third rail the same way you did last time, maybe it'd reset you."

Jane nods. "Could you do that?"

She's rallying, throwing memories over her back like luggage, cracking the knuckles of one hand against the palm of the other like she's getting ready for a fight. August would kill for her. Space and time are nothing.

"I think so," August says. "We'd have to cause a surge, and we'd need access to the power controls for the substation that manages this line, but I'm close. I'm waiting to get some public records about exactly which one that is."

"Then it's only a matter of . . . breaking into city property and not electrocuting yourself."

"Yeah, basically."

"Sounds simple enough," Jane says with a wink. "Have you tried a Molotov cocktail?"

August groans. "Man, how did you avoid the FBI watch list? That would have made this whole mystery so much easier to solve."

Myla agrees with August's theory. So now, they have a plan. But when they're not trying to figure out how to take down part of New York City's power grid, they're selling out double Delilah's capacity for the Save Billy's Pancakepalooza, which means there are two weeks to find a new venue. They've been through bars, concert venues, art galleries, *bingo halls*—all booked or asking for a fee they can't begin to afford.

For August, it's nights waiting tables and days split between research on substations and every logistical snag of planning a massive fundraiser. With whatever she has leftover, she's on the Q, threading her fingers through Jane's and trying to memorize everything about her while she still can.

Her mom has given up on texting her, and August really doesn't know what to say. She can't tell her what she's found out over the phone. But she also isn't ready to see her.

It occurs to August that it's just as fucked up to keep this information to herself as it was for her mom to hide things. At least, she tells herself, she's doing it to protect her. But maybe that really is what her mom thought too.

It's a train of thought that always brings her back to Jane. She thinks about Jane's family, her parents and sisters, none of them ever knowing what happened to her. August has checked the records enough times to know that there was never a missing persons report filed for Biyu Su. As far as Jane's family knew, Jane left and didn't want to be found.

August wonders if any of them have boxes of files like her

mom. When this is over, one way or the other, she'll find them. If Jane goes back to her time, she'll probably find them on her own. But if she stays, or if—well, if she's *gone*, they deserve to know.

That's what she's thinking about when she clocks out of her late shift and takes her Su Special from the window. People who leave, people who get left behind. The Q closes in a month, Billy's in four, and it's all over unless they find a way to stop it.

"So," Myla says when August slides into the booth. She's been giving August significant eyes across the dining room since she and Niko sat down, so she must have some news. "You know how I've been, like, shaking down all my old Columbia classmates to find out if anyone has any MTA connections?"

August swallows a bite of sandwich. "Yeah."

"Well . . . I found a lead."

"Really? Who? What do they do?"

"Um," Myla says, watching her pancake slowly absorb syrup, "he actually works at the Transit Power Control Center."

"What?" August says, nearly upsetting a ketchup bottle. "Are you kidding me? That's perfect! Have you talked to him about it?"

"Yeah, so, uh . . ." She's being something she never is: cagey. "That's the thing. It's kind of . . . my ex."

August stares at her. Beside her, Niko continues serenely eating his cinnamon roll.

"Your ex," August says flatly. "As in the one you dropped the night you met *him*." She points at Niko with a fork, but he looks unbothered, chewing like a contented cow.

"Yeah, so," Myla says, wincing. "In retrospect, maybe not my finest moment. The Libra jumped out. In my defense, though, he, like, high-key sucked. Way too into himself."

"Is he still mad?"

"I mean, uh. He has me blocked on social. I found out from a friend of a friend who talks to him. So . . ."

August wants to scream. "So, we have a perfect in at the exact place we need access to, but we can't use it because of your inability to keep it in your pants."

"Says the woman getting subway head from a revenant," Myla counters.

"The heart wants what it wants, August," Niko says sincerely.

"I'm gonna murder both of you," August says. "What are we gonna do?"

"Okay, anyway," Myla says. "I have an idea. The Billy's fundraiser, right? Obviously we need a new venue. I've been looking into a lot of unconventional places, like public spaces, condemned warehouses—"

"I thought you meant an idea for the Jane thing."

"I'm getting there!" Myla chides. "Have you ever seen what the substations look like?"

She's pretty sure she's read and looked at every shred of information on substations in existence over the past couple of weeks, so, "Yeah."

"They've got a kind of old-school techno-punk industrial vibe, right?" Myla continues. "And I was thinking, what if we could convince the city to let us use the Control Center as a venue? People use decommissioned subway stops for art installations all the time. We could say we're into the aesthetic and want somewhere with a greater capacity to bring in more people. I can reach out to Gabe and see if he'll help—he used to work at Delilah's, maybe he'll be sympathetic to the cause. *Then* once we get in, we just have to keep people distracted while I fuck with the line, which should be easy with a party that size. It'll only take a couple of minutes, I think."

August stares at her across the table.

"So . . . your idea is . . . a heist. You want us to pull off a heist." August gestures helplessly at Niko, who has given up on his meal with a quarter left to go. "Niko can't even pull off that cinnamon roll."

Niko pats his stomach. "It was really filling."

"It's not a heist," Myla hisses. "It's . . . an elaborate, planned crime."

"That's a heist."

"Look, do you have any other ideas? Because if not, I think we should give this a try. And if we do it right, we can raise a shitload of money for Billy's at the same time."

August listens to the murmur of tables and the scrape of forks and maybe, if she strains, Lucie cursing out the cash register. She does love this place. And Jane loves it too.

"Okay," August says. "We can try."

It's Jane's idea, actually, that puts one of the last crucial pieces in place.

"I'm pretty sure," August says, "that if you can walk between cars, you can walk on the tracks. So, on the night of the party, when Myla does the surge, you should be able to touch the third rail. But I don't know how to prove it before then. The Q's always running, so there's not really a time to test it. We could jump out, but there's no way to make sure we'd be off the tracks safely before the next train."

Jane thinks and says, "What about the R/W?"

August frowns. "What about it?"

"Look," Jane says, jabbing her finger at the subway map posted by the doors. "Right here, at Canal Street, they split off

from the Q." She traces the yellow line down to the bottom tip
of Manhattan and across the river, to where it meets up with
the blue and orange lines at Jay Street. "Those are the only two
trains that run on this track."

"You're right," August says.

"I've only met Wes three times," Jane says, "but every single time, he's bitched about how the R wasn't running that
day. So if the R isn't running, we could have time to sneak
out the back of the train at Canal and follow the R tracks
toward city hall, and maybe, *maybe* it'd be close enough to the
Q that I could walk on them. Maybe we could even see how
far I can go."

August thinks—she's not sure, exactly, that it'll work, but
Jane's also become a lot more solidly *here* lately. Tangibly rooted
in reality. Maybe she couldn't have done it months ago, but it's
possible the line will afford her a little more slack now.

"Okay," August says. "We just have to hope the MTA fucks
up soon."

The MTA, reliably, fucks up soon. Three days later, Wes
texts her bitterly from his evening commute: As requested,
here is your notification that the R is out of service.

Hell yes!!! August texts back.

My night is fucked, Wes responds, but go off I guess.

She meets Jane on the Q's very last car, and when it stops at
Canal, they slide the door open as quietly as they can.

"Okay," August says, "just, you know, a general reminder
that the third rail carries 625 volts that will absolutely kill a
person and should have killed you before. So, you know. Uh."
She glances down at the rails and wonders how Jane Su can get
her to flirt with death so often. "Be careful."

"Sure," Jane says, and she jumps off the back of the train, and—

Like that first day when they tried every stop, she's gone.

August finds her six cars up, and they weave their way to the back and try again.

"This is annoying," Jane says when she reappears behind August like an exasperated Bloody Mary.

"We have to keep trying," August tells her. "It's—"

Before August can finish her sentence, Jane brushes past her and jumps off the platform—aiming straight for the third rail.

"Jane, don't—!"

She lands firmly on her feet, both sneakers planted on the third rail, and she grins. No shock. Not a single singed hair. August gapes.

"I knew it!" Jane crows. "I'm part of the electricity! It can't hurt me!"

"You—" The train's brakes disengage, and August has to hold her breath and jump, throwing herself hard in the opposite direction of Jane. She lands in the packed dirt to the side of the tracks, ripping one knee of her jeans, and rolls to look at Jane's smug expression. "You could have *died*!"

"I'm pretty confident I can't," Jane says, like it's nothing. "At least, not that way." She paces down the rail, one foot in front of the other, headed toward the fork in the tracks. "Come on! Next train's coming soon!"

"Un-fucking-believable," August mumbles, but she dusts herself off and follows.

When they reach the relative safety of the tunnel toward City Hall, the light from the station starts to shrink, and they're lit only by blue and yellow lights lining the tunnel. It's strange to walk alongside Jane without stopping, but when Jane shouts happily into the echoing dark, it's infectious. She starts to run, and August runs after her, hair flying and the hard floor of the tracks under her shoes. It feels like she could run forever if it's with Jane.

But Jane's footsteps stutter abruptly to a halt.

"Oh," she says.

August turns back to her, out of breath. "What?"

"I can't—I don't think I can go any farther. It's—it feels weird. Wrong." She touches a hand to the center of her chest, like she's having existential heartburn. "Oh, yikes. Yeah, this is it. This is as far as I can go."

She sits on the third rail.

"Still cool though, right?"

August nods. "Yeah, and, this is only, like, a taste. An appetizer. An amuse-bouche of freedom. We're gonna get you the real deal."

"I know. I believe you," Jane says, looking at August like she means it.

August sinks down across from her, sitting gingerly on a track. She's read that the other two rails are very lightly electrified, only enough to carry signals, so she figures she's okay. "We can sit here for a while, if you want."

"Yeah," Jane says, pulling her knees up. She stretches her arms out like she's trying to touch as much open air as she can, even in the stuffy confines of the tunnel. "Yeah, this is nice."

"I have—" August feels around the bottom of her bag. "Um, one orange, if you want to split it."

"Oh, yeah, please."

August tosses it over, and she catches it smoothly.

More and more lately, August has stopped studying Jane.

She's stopped looking for clues in every expression or offhand comment, and it feels good to just *see* her. To listen to the sound of her low voice talking about nothing, to watch her fingers effortlessly work the orange rind, to soak in her company. August feels like one of the little packets of cream she always dumps into Jane's coffee, steeping in sugar and warmth.

Jane piles bits of orange peel on her knee and splits the segments into halves. When August reaches out to take one, her fingertips brush the back of Jane's hand, and she yelps and jumps backward from a short, sharp shock.

"Whoa," Jane says. "Are you okay?"

"Yeah," August says, shaking out her hand. "You're, like, *conductive.*"

Jane holds her fingers up in front of her face, going slightly cross-eyed to examine them. *"Cool."* She glances up to see August watching her. "What?"

"You're . . ." August attempts. "I just like everything about you." She waves her hands at the smile that appears on Jane's face. "Stop! It's gross! What I said is gross!"

"Everything about me?" Jane teases.

"No, definitely not that shit-eating grin. Categorically hate that."

"Oh, I think you like that the best."

"Shut up," August says. The darkness, she hopes, hides the blushing.

Jane laughs, popping a bit of orange into her mouth. "It is crazy, though, when you think about it." She licks a drop of juice off her bottom lip. "You kind of know everything there is to know about me."

August scoffs. "There's no way that's true."

"It is! And I used to be so mysterious and sexy."

"I mean, you're literally sitting on the third rail conducting electricity right now, so, still mysterious. Now, *sexy* . . . hmm. I don't know about that."

Jane rolls her eyes. "Oh, fuck off."

August laughs and dodges the orange peel Jane throws at her. "Tell me something I don't know about you, then," she says. "Surprise me."

"Okay," Jane says, "but you have to do one too."

"You already know more about me than most people."

"That's a testament to you living like you're under deep cover and can't compromise your civilian identity, not how much you've told me."

"Fine," August relents. Jane taps her nose, and August scowls—she's a pushover for Jane. They both know it. "You go first."

"Okay . . . hmm . . . oh, I've made friends with a subway rat."

"You've *what?*"

"Look, it gets really boring down here!" Jane says defensively. "But there's this one white rat that hangs out on the Q sometimes. She's so big and so fat and so round, like a gigantic steamed bun. I named her Bao."

"That's disgusting."

"I love her. Sometimes I give her snacks."

"You're a nightmare."

"Judge all you want, but I'm the only one who'll be spared in the inevitable Great Rat Uprising. Your turn."

August thinks, and says, "I've cheated on one test my entire life. Junior year of high school. I'd been up all night going through public records with my mom, and I ran out of time to study, so I picked the lock on my teacher's room before school, found out what the essay question was, and memorized an entire page from the book by fifth period so I could answer it."

"God, you fucking *nerd*." Jane snorts. "That's not even cheating. That's . . . being unfairly prepared."

"Excuse me, I thought it was very edgy at the time. Your turn."

"My mom started going gray at, like, twenty-five," she says, "and I'm pretty sure it's gonna happen to me too. Or at least it would have if I weren't, you know." She does a vague hand gesture to express the whole ineffability of being. August shoots a finger gun back.

"In fourth grade, I memorized the entire periodic table and all of the presidents and vice presidents in chronological order, and I still remember it all."

"I saw *The Exorcist* opening weekend and didn't sleep for four days."

"I hate pickles."

"I snore."

"I can't sleep if it's too quiet."

Jane pauses, and says, "Sometimes I wonder if I fell out of time because I never really belonged where I started and the universe is trying to tell me something."

It's offhand, casual, and August watches her pull off another orange segment and eat it unceremoniously, but she knows Jane. It's not easy for her to say things like that.

She figures she can give something back.

"When I was a kid, after Katrina—you remember how I told you about the hurricane?" Jane nods. August goes on, "There was this year I got moved around to different schools until my old school reopened and we could go home. And my anxiety got . . . bad. Like, *really* bad. So, I convinced myself that, because the statistical likelihood of something happening in real life exactly the way I imagined it was so low, if I imagined the worst possible things in vivid detail, I could mathematically reduce the odds of them happening. I convinced myself that my brain had power over the probability projections of the universe. I'd lie awake at night thinking about all the worst stuff that could happen like it was my job, and I don't know if I ever really broke the habit."

Jane listens silently, nodding. One of the things August loves most about her is that she doesn't go chasing after unspoken words when August is done talking. She can let a silence settle, let a truth breathe.

Then she opens her mouth and says, "Sometimes I like to have my ass slapped during sex."

August squawks out a laugh, caught off guard. "What? You've never asked me to do that."

"Angel, there are a lot of things I'd like to do with you that can't be done on a train."

August swallows. "Point."

Jane raises her eyebrows. "Well?"

"Well what?"

"Aren't you gonna write that down in your little sex notebook?"

"My—" August's face is instantly hot. "You weren't supposed to know about that!"

"You're not that discreet, August. One time I swear you whipped it out before I even got my pants buttoned."

August moans in dismay. She knows exactly what entry Jane is talking about. Page three, section M, subheading four: *overstimulation.*

"I have to die now," August says into her hands.

"No, it's cute! You're such a nerd. It's endearing!" Jane laughs, always so amused about making August suffer. It's despicable. "Your turn."

"No way, you already exposed a thing I didn't think you knew about me," August says. "I'm feeling very vulnerable."

"Oh my God, you're impossible."

"I'm not going."

"Then we're at an impasse. Unless you wanna come over here and kiss me."

August lifts her face out of her hands. "And get electrocuted? I'm pretty sure if I kissed you right now, it would literally kill me."

"That's how it always feels, isn't it?"

"Oh my *God*," August groans, even though her heart does something humiliating at the words. "Shut up and eat your orange."

Jane sticks her tongue out but does as she's told, finishing off her half and licking her fingertips when she's done.

"I missed oranges," she says. "Really good ones, though. You gotta start grocery shopping in Chinatown."

"Yeah?"

"Yeah, back home, my mom would take me to all the markets every Sunday morning and let me pick out the fruit because I always had this sixth sense with sweet stuff. Best oranges you could find. We used to get so many, I'd have to carry some home in my pockets."

August smiles to herself as she pictures a tiny Jane, chubby cheeks and untied shoes, toddling through a fruit stand with her pockets full of produce. She imagines Jane's mom as a young woman with her hair tied up and shot through with premature gray, haggling with a butcher in Cantonese. San Francisco, Chinatown, the place that made Jane.

"What's the first thing you'll do," August asks, "when you get back to '77?"

"I don't know," Jane says. "Try to catch that bus to California, I guess."

"You should. I bet California misses you."

Jane nods. "Yeah."

"You know," August says, "if this works, by now you'll be almost seventy."

Jane pulls a face. "Oh my God, that's so weird."

"Oh yeah." August gazes up at the tunnel ceiling. "I bet you have a house, and it's filled with souvenirs from all over the world because you spent your thirties backpacking through Europe and Asia. Windchimes everywhere. Nothing matches."

"The furniture is nice and sturdy, but I never take care of the yard," Jane puts in. "It's a jungle. You can't even see the front door."

"The homeowners' association hates you."

Jane chuckles. "Good."

August lets a quiet moment go by before adding, carefully, "I bet you're married."

In the low light, she can see Jane's smile dip downward, a corner of her mouth tugging. "I don't know."

"I hope you are," August says. "Maybe some girl finally came along at the right time, and you married her."

Jane shrugs, pursing her lips. The dimple pops out on one side.

"She's gonna have to live with the fact that I'll always wish she were someone else."

"Come on," August says. "That's not fair. She's a nice lady."

Jane looks up and rolls her eyes, but her mouth relaxes. She rests her hands on the rail and cranes her head back.

"What if I stay?" she says. "What's the first thing you'll do?"

There are a thousand things August could say, a thousand

things she wants to do. Sleep next to her. Buy her lunch at the jerk chicken joint across the street. Brighton Beach. Prospect Park. Kiss her with the door shut.

But she says simply, "Take you home with me."

Before Jane can respond, a flashlight beam cuts through the darkness at the city hall end of the tunnel. Jane's head whips around.

"Hey! Who's in there?" a gruff voice shouts. "Get the fuck out of the tunnel!"

"Fuckin' *pigs*," Jane says, jumping up and scattering orange peel everywhere. "Run!"

They run back through the tunnel toward Canal Street, Jane stumbling in the rush but never losing her balance on the third rail, and at some point near the fork, they start laughing. Loud, breathless, incredulous, hysterical laughter, filling up the tracks and pulling at August's lungs as she struggles toward their line. When they reach the Q, there's a train just pulling out of the station, and Jane takes a running jump and grabs the handle on the back of the last car.

"Come on!" she yells, turning back for August's hand. August grabs on and lets Jane's strong grip pull her up.

"Is this our thing?" Jane shouts over the rattle of the train as it carries them toward Brooklyn. "Kissing between subway cars?"

"You haven't kissed me yet!" August points out.

"Oh, right," Jane says. She brushes August's windswept hair out of her face, and when their lips meet, she tastes like oranges and lightning.

August stays on the train late into the night, until the cars start to clear out and the timetable stretches longer and longer. She waits for the magic hour, and from the way Jane drags her hand along her waist, she's waiting too.

There's no convenient darkness this time, no perfectly timed stall, but there's an empty car and the Manhattan Bridge and Jane pressing into her, hips moving and short breaths and kiss-slick lips. It should feel dirty, to be with Jane like this, here, but what's crazy is, she finally understands it all. Love. The whole shape of it. What it means to touch someone like this and want to have a life with them at the same time.

Deliriously, the image of Jane with her house and her plants and her windchimes swims into view, and August is there too, wearing the shape of her body into an old bed. Jane slots between her legs and she thinks, *fifty years.* Jane bites down on her throat and she thinks of framed photos and stained recipe cards. Jane tightens against her fingertips and she thinks, *home.* Her eyes shut for Jane's mouth and a good night's sleep just the same.

I love you, she thinks. *I love you. Please stay. I don't know what I'll do if you leave.*

She thinks it, but she doesn't say it. That wouldn't be fair to either of them.

14

Posted October 12, 2004

Woman with red Converse on the Q (Brooklyn)

Apologies if this isn't the right place for this, but I'm not sure where else to post. Not looking for a romantic connection. I was riding the Q with my son on Wednesday evening when a short-haired mid-twenties woman approached us and offered my son a pin from her jacket. It was a 70s-era gay pride pin, clearly a well-loved antique. My son is 15 and hasn't had the easiest time at school since coming out earlier this year. Her act of kindness made his whole week. If you're her, or you think you might know her, please let me know. I'd love to thank her.

In the end, it takes exactly one phone call for Gabe to agree to meet Myla for coffee.

"What can I say?" Myla says, pulling on an extremely flimsy top. "I'm the one who got away."

"I'm going with you," August tells her. She slings her bag over her shoulder, double-checking the pocketknife and mace. "This could be a ploy to get you alone so he can exact a bloody revenge."

"Okay, *Dateline,* reel it in," Myla says, shaking her hair out. "Love the instinctive mistrust of cis straight white men, but Gabe is harmless. He's just boring. Like, really boring, but thinks he's really interesting."

"How did he get a job at Delilah's?"

"He's from one of those New York families, so his dad's the landlord. He's very straight."

"And you dated him because . . . ?"

"Look," Myla says, "we all make mistakes when we're young. Mine just happens to be six-foot-three and look exactly like Leonardo DiCaprio."

"*Revenant* or *Inception?*"

"You really got me fucked up if you think I'd settle for anything less than *Romeo + Juliet.*"

"Damn, okay, I guess I get it." August shrugs. "But I'm still going with you."

Gabe lives in Manhattan, so they take the Q over the river, Jane wedged between them as they catch her up the latest status of the plan.

"I have to say, I'm impressed," she says, throwing her arm over August's shoulders. "This is definitely the most organized crime I've ever been involved in."

"*When* are you going to tell me about all the other crimes?" August says.

"I *have* told you. They were mostly vandalism. Squatting.

Disrupting the peace. The occasional breaking and entering. Maybe some light petty theft. One incident of arson, but I was wearing a mask, so nobody could prove it was me."

"Those are some of the sexiest crimes," August points out. "For people who are into crimes. Very Bender from *The Breakfast Club.*"

"That's—" Myla starts.

"I know," Jane says. "August told me about *The Breakfast Club.*"

Myla nods, mollified.

August forces Myla to let her go into the coffee shop a minute ahead to maintain cover, so she's perched at the bar with an iced coffee when Myla enters. She tries to case out which of the twenty-something guys with black coffees and dogeared moleskines could be Gabe, until one with floppy hair and a pointy chin waves Myla over. He's got a flannel tied around his waist and a faded Pickle Rick button on his messenger bag. August cannot imagine what he and Myla ever had in common. He looks almost pathetically happy to see her.

August sits back and sips her coffee and swipes through the substation homework she gave herself this week. She's narrowed down which substation they need access to, so now it's just about making sure they can get into the control room. Myla will take care of the rest.

Myla and Gabe wrap up after an hour, and she hugs him goodbye and throws him a *call me!* gesture before easing out the door. August hangs back for a minute, watching him stare after her. He looks like he might cry.

"Yikes," August says under her breath as she heads for the door.

She meets Myla down the block, where she's thumbing through her phone.

"That looked like it went unexpectedly well."

Myla smiles. "Turns out he blocked me on social media because he 'couldn't stand to see how I'm doing' without him. Which, I mean, fair. A bitch is doing spectacularly." She holds up her phone. "He already texted me."

"What did he say about the event?"

"Oh, this is the best part. Get this: he got the job because his uncle is one of the managers, so he doesn't think he'll have any trouble getting them to agree to let us use the space. Good old-fashioned nepotism to the rescue."

"Holy shit," August says. She thinks about Niko pulling the ace of swords from his tarot deck, about all the jade he's been hiding around the apartment lately. Maybe it's luck, but August can't help but feel like someone has his thumb on the scale. "So now what?"

"He's gonna talk to his uncle and call me tomorrow. I'm gonna head to Billy's and talk to Lucie about moving things to the new venue."

"Cool, I'll come with you."

Myla puts a hand out. "Nope. You have something else you need to take care of."

"What?"

"You need to figure out how to talk to Jane," she says, pointing toward the Q stop down the street. "Because if we pull this off and it works, you might never see her again, and Niko says you have a lot of things left to say to each other."

August looks at her, the summer sunset gleaming off her sunglasses and sparkling against the Manhattan sidewalk. The city moves around them like they're pebbles in a creek bed.

"It's—we're gonna be fine," August says. "She knows how I feel about her. And—and if it's gonna end like this, there's nothing either of us can do. There's no point ruining whatever time we have left by being sad about it."

Myla sighs. "Sometimes the point is to be sad, August. Sometimes you just have to feel it because it deserves to be felt."

She leaves her on the corner, staring at the sharp tops of buildings heavy with pink and orange light.

How does she talk to Jane? Where does she even start? How does she explain that she used to be afraid to love anyone because there's a well at the center of her chest and she doesn't know where the bottom is? How does she tell Jane that she boarded it up years ago, and that this thing—not even love, but the *hope* for it—has pried up nails that have nothing to do with love at all?

She's standing on a New York sidewalk, nearly twenty-four years old, and she's found herself back at the first version of August, the one who hoped for things. Who wanted things. Who cried to Peter Gabriel and believed in psychics. And it all started when she met Jane.

She met Jane, and now she wants a home, one she's made for herself, one nobody can take away because it lives in her like a funny little glass terrarium filled with growing plants and shiny rocks and tiny lopsided statues, warm with penthouse views of Myla's paint-stained hands and Niko's sly smile and Wes's freckly nose. She wants somewhere to belong, things that hold the shape of her body even when she's not touching them, a place and a purpose and a happy, familiar routine. She wants to be happy. To be well.

She wants to feel it all without being afraid it'll fuck her up.

She wants Jane. She loves Jane.

And she doesn't know how to tell Jane any of that.

———

It's a week later when Gabe comes through—they secure the Control Center as a venue, and Lucie passes out personalized to-do lists like juice boxes at a little league soccer game.

"These are legit," August says, looking hers over. "We should hang out more."

"No, thank you," Lucie says.

She and Niko are assigned to meet with the manager of Slinky's to arrange the liquor, and after a back-room conversation that involves Niko promising the man a free psychic reading and his mom's empanadillas, they return to the apartment with booze donations checked off the list.

"Have you talked to Jane yet?" Niko asks as they ascend the stairs. He doesn't specify what they need to talk about. They both know.

"Why are you even asking me if you already know?" August counters.

Niko eyes her mildly. "Sometimes things that are supposed to happen still need to be nudged along."

"Niko Rivera, fate's enforcer since 1995," August says with an eye roll.

"I like that," Niko says. "Makes it sound like I carry a nail bat."

As they reach the front door, it flies open, and Wes comes marching out with both arms full of bright yellow flyers.

"Whoa, where are you going?" Niko asks.

"Lucie put flyers on my to-do list," Wes says. "Winfield just dropped them off."

"*SAVE PANCAKE BILLY'S HOUSE OF PANCAKES PANCAKEPALOOZA DRAG & ART EXTRAGANZA,*" August reads out loud. "Good lord, did we let Billy name it? Nobody in his family knows how to edit."

Wes shrugs, heading for the stairs. "All I know is I'm supposed to post them around the neighborhood."

"Running away isn't going to help!" Niko calls after him.

August raises an eyebrow. "Running away from what?"

As if on cue, Isaiah rounds the last corner of the stairs. He and Wes freeze, separated by ten steps.

Niko idly pulls a toothpick from his vest pocket and puts it in his mouth. "From that."

There are a few seconds of tense silence before Wes takes his flyers and his shell-shocked expression and darts down the stairs. August can hear his sneakers echoing at double-time all the way down.

Isaiah rolls his eyes. Niko and August exchange a look.

"I'll go," August says.

She finds Wes on the street outside of the building, cussing out a stapler as he tries to affix a flyer to a telephone pole.

"Uh-oh," August says, drawing up to him. "Did that stapler try to get emotionally intimate with you?"

Wes glares. "You're hilarious."

August reaches over and pries half the flyers out of Wes's hands. "Will you at least let me help you?"

"Fine," he grumbles.

They set off down the block, Wes attacking electrical poles and signposts while August wedges flyers into mail slots and between the bars of windows. Winfield must have dropped off something close to five hundred, because as they work their way through Flatbush, they barely make a dent in the stacks.

After an hour, Wes turns to her and says, "I need a smoke."

August shrugs. "Go ahead."

"No," he says, rolling up his leftover flyers and shoving them into the back pocket of his jeans. "I need a *smoke.*"

Back in their apartment, Wes leads her to the door to his bedroom and says, "If you tell Niko or Myla I let you in here, I will deny it, and I will wait months until you're no longer expecting my retribution and give all your stuff to that guy on the second floor whose apartment smells like onions."

August nudges Noodles away from where he's nipping at her heels. "Noted."

Wes swings the door open, and there's his bedroom, exactly how Isaiah described it: nice and neat and stylish, light woods, stone gray linens, his own artwork matted and framed on the walls. He's got the taste of someone who grew up with the finest things, and August thinks about the trust fund Myla mentioned. He pops open an ornate wooden cigar box on his nightstand and retrieves a heavy silver lighter and a joint.

August can see the benefits to Wes's slight build when he easily hops through the open window and onto the fire escape. She's wider in the hips and not half as graceful; by the time she meets him, she's out of breath and he's perched mid-roof against one of the air-conditioning units, lighting up without breaking a sweat.

August nudges next to him and turns to face the street, looking out over the lights of Brooklyn. It's not quiet, but it's that smooth, constant flow of noise she's grown used to. She likes to imagine if she listened closely enough, she could hear the Q rattling down the block, carrying Jane into the night.

She has to talk to Jane. She knows she has to.

Wes passes the joint over, and she takes it, thankful for any reason to stop thinking.

"What part of New York were you born in?" she asks him.

Wes exhales a stream of smoke. "I'm from Rhode Island."

August pauses with the joint halfway to her mouth. "Oh, I just assumed because you're such a—"

"Dick?"

She turns her head, squinting at him. It's gray and dim up here, shot through with orange and yellow and red from the street below. The freckles on his nose blur together.

"I was gonna say a New York purist."

The first hit burns on the way down, catching high in her chest. She's only done this once before—passed to her at a party, desperately trying to act like she knew what to do—but she repeats what Wes did and holds the smoke for a few long seconds before letting it out through her nose. It all seems smooth until she spends the next twenty seconds coughing into her elbow.

"I moved here when I was eighteen," Wes says once August is done, mercifully not commenting on her inability to handle her smoke. "And my parents basically pruned me off the family tree a year later once they realized I wasn't going back to architecture school. But at least I still had this shitty, smelly, overpriced, nightmare city."

He says the last part with a smile.

"Yeah," August says. "Myla and Niko kind of . . . alluded."

Wes sucks on the joint, the cherry flaring. "Yeah."

"My, um . . . my mom. Her parents were super rich. Lots of expectations. And they, uh, basically acted like she didn't exist either. But my mom is pretty fucked up too."

"How so?" Wes asks, flicking ash before passing the joint back.

August manages to hold the second hit longer. She feels it in her face, spreading across her skin, starting to soften her edges. "She told me my whole life that her family didn't want anything to do with me, so I never really had a family. And a couple of weeks ago, I found out that was all a lie, and now they're all dead, so."

She doesn't mention the son they forgot or the letters they intercepted. By now, she knows she wouldn't have wanted anything to do with her mom's family, even if she had known they cared about her. But she's Suzette Landry's daughter, which means she's bad at letting shit go.

"Is that why you haven't been talking to her?" Wes asks.

August drops her eyes back to him. "How do you know I haven't been talking to her?"

"It's pretty easy to notice when the person on the other side of your wall stops having loud phone conversations with their mom every morning at the ass-crack of dawn."

August winces. "Sorry."

Wes accepts the joint from her and holds it between his thumb and forefinger. He looks distant, a stray breeze ruffling the ends of his hair.

"Look, nobody's parents are perfect," he says finally. "I mean, Niko's parents let him transition when he was like nine, and they've always been super cool about it, but his mom still won't let him tell his grandpa. And she's constantly bugging him to move back to Long Island because she wants him to be closer to the family, but he likes it in the city, and they fight about it all the time."

"I didn't know that."

"Yeah, but at least she's trying, you know? People like my parents, though, like your mom's parents—that's another level. I mean, I wanted to go to art school, and my parents were like, great, you can sketch buildings, and then you can take over the firm one day, and no, we're not paying for therapy. And when I couldn't do what they wanted, that was just it. They cut off the money and told me not to come home. They care about how it *looks*. They care about what they can circle jerk about with their idiot fucking Ivy League friends. But the minute you need something—like, actually *need* something—they'll let you know just how much of a disappointment you are for asking."

August has never thought of it quite that way.

Every day, she watches Wes turn cold and fuck his own life up, and she never says a word, because she knows there's something big and heavy pinning him down. She's never given her mom the same understanding. She's never thought to transpose his hurt onto her mother's to make better sense of it.

One of his last words sticks in her head, a drag at the bottom of the pool, her brain sloshing around it. *Disappointment,* he said. August remembers what he said after Isaiah helped them move a mattress.

He doesn't deserve to be disappointed.

"For what it's worth, you've never disappointed me once since I've met you." August scrunches her nose at him. "In fact, I would say you have exceeded my expectations."

Wes takes a hit and laughs it back out. "Thank you."

He stubs out the joint and pulls himself to his feet.

"And . . . you know. For the record." Carefully, August rises. "I, uh, I know how it feels to spend a long time alone on purpose, just to avoid the risk of what might happen if I wasn't. And with Jane . . . I don't think I could possibly have found a more doomed first love, but it's worth it. It's probably going to break my heart, and it's still worth it."

Wes avoids her eyes. "I just . . . he's so . . . he deserves the best. And that's not me."

"You don't get to decide that for him," August points out.

Wes looks like he's working on something to say to that when there's a sound below. Someone's opened a top-floor window. They wait it out, and there it is: Donna Summer at a truly inconsiderate volume, pouring out of Isaiah's apartment.

They hold each other's gaze for a full second before they dissolve into laughter, staggering into each other's sides. Donna wails on about someone leaving a cake out in the rain, and Wes reaches into his back pocket and walks over to the edge of the roof and throws a hundred flyers into the night, raining down past the fire escape, the windows, the salty-warm smell of Popeyes, tumbling down the sidewalk and floating away on the breeze, wrapping around traffic lights, carried off toward the open tracks of the Q.

It's the afternoon before the fundraiser, the last day before they try to send Jane home, when August finally fulfills Niko's prophecy and climbs onto the Q.

She chooses a stop farther down than her usual one, Kings Highway near Gravesend, because there'll be fewer people on the train closer to the end of the line. This far down, the track is mostly elevated, running through residential neighborhoods at eye level with third-story windows. The sun is bright today, but the train is cool when she steps on.

Jane's sitting reliably at the end of the car, headphones on, eyes closed.

August stays near the door, watching her. This might be the last time she gets to see Jane in the sunset.

There's a kick in her heart—one she knows Jane feels sometimes too—that says she should run. Spare herself the heartbreak and step off this train and switch cities, switch schools, switch lives until she finds somewhere else she could maybe be happy again.

But it's too late. She could live another fifty years, love and leave a hundred cities, press her fingerprints into a thousand turnstiles and plane tickets, and Jane would still be there at the bottom of her heart. This girl in Brooklyn she just can't shake.

The train pulls out of the station, and August pushes against its momentum to walk toward Jane's seat.

She opens her eyes when August sits next to her.

"Hey," she says, sliding her headphones off to rest around her neck.

August takes a breath to look at her, committing to memory the angle at which the sun hits the round tip of her nose and the lines of her jaw and her full bottom lip.

Then she reaches into her bag and pulls out a silver packet of Pop-Tarts.

"I brought you these," August says, handing them over. "Since they won't have the strawberry milkshake ones back where you came from."

Jane takes them and slides them carefully into the front pocket of her backpack. She looks at August with her head tilted slightly, tracking the expression on her face.

"Tomorrow's the big day, huh?"

August tries to smile. "Yeah."

"Everything ready?"

"I think so," she says. She's done everything short of making her roommates run actual drills. They're as prepared as they're ever going to be. "What about you? Are you ready?"

"I mean, the way I see it, there are three possible outcomes of tomorrow. I go back, I stay, I die." She shrugs, like it's nothing. "I have to be okay with any of those."

"Are you?"

"I don't know," Jane tells her. "I don't want to die. I didn't want to die when I was *supposed* to. So, I'm choosing to believe it'll be one of the first two."

August nods. "I like that attitude."

There's a goodbye here, somewhere. There's a conclusion underneath the too-casual sprawl of Jane's legs and their too-quiet voices. But August doesn't know how to work up to what she has to say. If this was an easy case to solve, she'd find an answer and circle it in red ink and pin it to the wall: there it is, the thing she's supposed to say to the girl she loves. She figured it out.

Instead, she says, "Is there anything else you want, before tomorrow?"

Jane shifts, dropping one foot onto the floor. The sunset's making her glow, and it spreads when she smiles softly at August, one crooked tooth up front. August loves that tooth. It feels so stupid and small to love Jane's crooked tooth when she might be about to lose her forever.

"I just want to say . . ." Jane starts, and she holds it like water in her mouth until she swallows and goes on: "Thank you, I guess. You didn't have to help me, but you did."

August huffs out a laugh. "I just did it because I thought you were hot."

Jane touches her chin with the back of her knuckles. "There are worse reasons to break the laws of space and time."

Next stop: Coney Island. The station where Jane's long ride on the Q started years ago, where they're going to try to save her. Slowly, the Wonder Wheel slides into view in the distance. They've seen it a thousand times from this train, lit up on summer nights, cutting yellow and green lines through the midday sky. August told Jane once about how it stayed when half the park was swept away. She knows how Jane likes stories about surviving.

"Don't, uh . . ." Jane says, clearing her throat. "If I go back, after tomorrow. Don't waste too much more time on me. I mean, don't get me wrong—wait a respectful amount of time and all. But, you know." She tucks August's hair behind her ear, rubbing the side of her thumb once against her cheek. "Just make sure you make them nervous. They shouldn't underestimate you."

"Okay," August says thickly. "I'll write that down."

Jane's looking at her, and she's looking at Jane, and the sun's going down, and the goddamn thing is that it's right there in both of their throats, but they can't say it. They've always been hopeless at saying it.

Instead, August leans forward and kisses Jane on the lips. It's soft, shaky like the rattle of the train but so much quieter. Their knees bump together, and Jane's fingertips tangle in the ends of her hair. She feels something warm and wet on her cheek. She doesn't know if she's crying, or if Jane is.

Sometimes, when they kiss, it's like August can see it. Just for a second, she can see a life that's not here on this train. Not a distant future, not a house. An immediate present unspooling like film: shoes in a pile by the door, a bark of laughter under bar lights, passing a box of cereal over on a Saturday morning. A hand in her back pocket. Jane, walking up the subway steps and into the light.

When they break apart, August tips her head against Jane's

shoulder, pressing her cheek to the leather. It smells like years, like a lightning storm, like engine grease and smoke, like Jane.

There's so much to say, but all she has is: "I was really lonely before I met you."

Jane's silent for a few seconds. August doesn't look at her, but she knows how the shadows of telephone poles and rooftops slide over the high points of her cheekbones and the soft dips of her mouth. She's memorized it. She closes her eyes and tries to picture them again, anywhere else.

Jane's hand wraps around hers.

"So was I."

15

 peopleofcity

[Photo shows a young white man with red hair sitting on a subway train holding a bag of groceries. In the background, just out of focus, a dark-haired woman reads a book with headphones on, a leather jacket bundled under one arm.]

peopleofcity My parents split up when I was a kid, and I lost touch with my dad, but I knew he was in New York. I moved up here a year ago after my mother died. I couldn't stand the thought of having a parent who was still alive and not even trying to have a relationship with him, you know? I've been looking for him since I got here. Dad, if you see this, I forgive you. Let's have a burger.

May 14, 2015

"I swear to God, if I have to inflate one more balloon . . ." Wes says as he ties off a red balloon with his teeth.

"Get used to it," Myla says. She's tying a bundle of them together with a rainbow of ribbons. "We need about two hundred more of these to pull this off."

Wes halfheartedly gives her the finger. Myla blows him a kiss.

August checks her phone. Three hours until doors open on the most ambitious—and only—party she's ever attempted to throw in her life. Six hours until they put their plan into motion. Seven hours until Myla overloads the circuit and blacks out the line.

Seven hours until Jane might be gone for good.

And here August is, blowing up a ten-foot inflatable cat with sunglasses and an electric guitar.

The party store by Myla's work donated their least popular decorations, and they had to take what giant inflatables they could get—anything tall enough to block a security camera. The balloons will take care of the rest.

"Do you need anything?" Gabe asks, hovering around Myla like an enormous gnat with a Shawn Hunter haircut. Part of the agreement with the city was that Gabe's uncle would supervise the event, and Gabe's uncle apparently does not give a shit, because he sent Gabe instead. They keep having to switch topics when he drifts too close, so he doesn't figure out the whole thing is partially a cover for a time crime.

"Actually," Myla says, "I would love a Filet-O-Fish. Ooh, and a bubble tea."

"Oh, uh—sure, okay." And Gabe wanders off, glowering at Niko when he thinks nobody's looking.

"That should buy us an hour," Myla says when he's gone. "Do you think I should feel bad about this?"

"I overheard him explaining wage disparity to Lucie earlier," Wes says. "He said he believes he's 'undermining capitalism' by 'choosing' not to pay his own rent."

"Ew," Myla groans. "Nope, okay, sticking to the plan."

The Plan, as outlined on the whiteboard, and then thoroughly erased to destroy all evidence: One. Wait for the party to hit maximum capacity. Two. Myla seduces Gabe's security clearance badge away from him. Three. August sneaks out to meet Jane on the Q. Four. Wes stages a diversion to pull security guards away from the control room door. Five. Myla overloads the line while Jane stands on the third rail.

August ties off her last balloon and texts Jane a selfie—tongue out, peace sign, hair static from all the helium-filled latex.

sup, ugly, Jane texts back, and August almost spits out her gum. She should never have given Jane and Myla each other's numbers. Jane's going to be bringing millennial humor back to the '70s.

God, she'll miss her.

While Lucie and Jerry set up the pancake station, Myla's network of Brooklyn artists start wheeling in sculptures and paintings and wood reliefs of ugly dogs for the silent auction. There are wristbands to wrangle, drink tickets to count, lights and a stage and a sound system to set up, gendered bathroom signs to cover with pictures of breakfast foods.

"Put it on, Wes." August sighs, throwing the last remaining Pancake Billy's House of Pancakes T-shirt at him.

"This is a small," he argues. "You know I wear XL."

"Please, that is a youth medium-ass man," says a loud voice, and it's Isaiah, brows already glued down, swanning in with a clothing rack full of drag and a trail of half-done drag daughters. Winfield's bringing up the rear, and once they disappear into the back to paint, Wes pouts and puts his size small T-shirt on and trudges to the corner where his friends from the tattoo shop have set up their booth.

Six kegs and ten crates full of liquor get unloaded from someone's borrowed minivan, courtesy of Slinky's and a few other neighborhood bars, and Lucie directs a couple of Billy's busboys hanging lights from the rafters over the makeshift dance floor and the stage they've set up for the show. When Myla kills the overheads, August has to admit the place looks incredible, all brutalist lines and giant antique levers and dingy tubes of wires transformed in the glow.

Eight o'clock draws closer and closer, and August can't believe it, but they actually made this happen.

"You ready for this, old man?" August asks, tying her hair up as she takes her spot at Jerry's side, next to the griddle. He and a small army of line cooks will be slinging pancakes all night, and August and Lucie will be passing them out to the drunk and hungry.

"Born ready, buttercup," Jerry says with a wink.

She knew, mathematically, that they sold more than two thousand tickets for tonight. But it's one thing to see the number, and another entirely to see this many people in the flesh, dancing and bellying up to the makeshift bar. Jerry and the line cooks start pouring batter on the griddle, and August realizes they might save Billy's and Jane in one night after all.

The first hour passes in a riot of color and noise and maple syrup. Art school kids in Filas pick their way down the silent auction line, oohing and ahhing at Myla's enormous, glittering, twitching sculpture, which she's entitled IT DO TAKE NERVE. People line up to have Wes or someone else from his shop ink something impulsive onto their arms. The first queens take the stage, spinning under the lights and crowing crass jokes into the microphone.

It gets louder, and louder, and louder.

Lucie leans over, scrambling to fill a plate with pancakes before a shitfaced NYU student with corduroy overalls and half-pink hair can chug any more of the complimentary syrup. "Did we give out too many drink tickets?"

August watches two girls nearby go from making out to viciously arguing and back to making out in the span of four seconds. "We were trying to get them to donate more."

"Have you seen Myla?" says a voice to her right. It's Gabe, out of breath and sweaty, a rapidly separating milk tea in one hand and a crumpled McDonald's bag in the other.

August looks him over. "Man, I don't think she wants that Filet-O-Fish anymore. It's been, like, four hours."

"Shit," he says. He looks around at the pandemonium in time to see Vera Harry throw herself off the stage and start crowdsurfing. "Things got, uh, kinda crazy while I was gone."

"Yeah," August says. The tires on Gabe's Tesla may or may not have been slashed by a fish-shaped knife before his errand to keep him busy for a few hours. August isn't taking questions. "You want a drink?"

The night blares on—the guys from the post office next to Billy's having a disjointed dance-off, a person with a lip ring shotgunning two White Claws at once, bodies jumping and swaying as the queen who is sometimes Winfield takes the stage in a magenta beard and performs an elaborate socialism-themed number set to a mix of "She Works Hard for the Money" and clips from AOC speeches.

Isaiah's Easter brunch was madness. Christmas in July was chaos. But this is a full-tilt, balls-to-the-wall, someone-getting-a-tattoo-of-Chuckie-Finster, drag-king-named-Knob-Dylan-doing-a-full-gymnastics-routine shitshow. The tip jar by the pancake griddle is overflowing with cash. August feels like the entire belly of New York's weirdest and queerest has emptied out on the dance floor, smelling like syrup and weed and hairspray. If she weren't double occupied by her pancake job and the Jane plan, Myla and Niko would have her out there in a cloud of glitter.

The feeling she had at Delilah's comes back, tugging at her hair, pushing her heart against her ribs. *Jane should be here.* Not on a train waiting for this party to smuggle her out of purgatory. Here, in it, defiant by existing, in a room full of people who would love her.

"And what are we here for tonight?" Bomb Bumboclaat shouts into the mic.

"Billy's!" the crowd shouts.

"Who has held down the corner of Church and Bedford for forty-five years?"

"Billy's!"

"Who's gon' do it for forty-five more?"

"Billy's!"

"And *what* do we *say* to *landlords*?"

The crowd inhales as one, through smoke and dry ice and paint fumes, and they bellow out in one resounding voice, middle fingers raised up to the lights, *"Fuck you!"*

Bomb Bumboclaat leaves the stage, and the alarm goes off on August's phone.

It's time.

August's fingers are sweaty on her phone.

She can do this. She *can*.

She registered with one of those conference call services last week so they could keep a group call going while they try to pull this off—the bootleg version of *Mission Impossible* comms. She ducks behind a bundle of balloons and starts the call.

Myla dials in first, then Wes, Niko, and finally Jane. She knows exactly where each of them is, because they agreed on it beforehand: Wes is taking a break from the tattoo booth to smoke a cigarette dangerously close to a trash can full of alcohol-soaked paper cups. Myla is milling around the edge of the dance floor, keeping an eye on Gabe as he refills his drink. Niko is one floor up, looking over the railing of the catwalk to keep tabs on everyone.

"And I'm on the subway," Jane says. "You know, in case anyone was wondering."

August switches her phone to speaker and slides it upside down into the front pocket of her T-shirt, like she did the night of Isaiah's party. Only it's not just Jane in her pocket this time. It's a whole family.

"Y'all ready?"

"Yep," Myla says.

"As I'll ever be," Wes says.

"I like when you're in crime boss mode," Jane adds.

"These pancakes are fantastic," Niko says, muffled through a mouthful. "Tell Jerry I said he's doing great."

"Do the spirit guides have anything to say about whether or not this is gonna work?" Jane asks.

August looks up to see Niko lick a finger and stick it in the air. "Hmm. I'm feeling pretty good about it."

"Dope," Myla says. "Let's go."

August can't see her through the enormous crowd, but she can hear the noise shifting through the speaker as she moves.

"Hey, Gabe?" she says. "Can I talk to you for a second?"

Gabe's voice comes faintly across the line. "Sure, what's up?"

"No, I meant . . . *alone.*" Myla leans heavily on the last word. She's heard Myla use that voice on Niko more than she'd care to think about around the apartment, usually followed by a lot of loud music from their room and August taking a trip down-stairs for an extra-long Popeyes dinner.

"*Oh.* Okay, yeah."

She drags him off toward a storage closet they scouted ear-lier, and August finally catches a glimpse of them, Myla's hand wrapped around his elbow. The badge is where it's been all day—on the lanyard hanging around his neck. August watches Myla lean away from him and into the phone tucked under her bra strap, ducking her head down so he can't see her mouth move.

"Niko, everything I'm about to say to this guy is a complete and total lie, and I love you and will marry you and adopt a hun-dred three-eyed ravens or whatever it is your weird ass wants instead of kids," she mutters.

"I know," Niko says back. "Did you just propose to me?"

"Oh shit, I guess I did?" Myla opens the door and shoves Gabe through it.

"I'm so mad at you," Niko says. "I already have a ring at home."

"Oh my God, seriously?" says Jane.

"Mazel," Wes chimes in.

"*Y'all,*" August says.

"Right," Myla says. "Here I go. Muting you guys now."

August sees her slide a hand under her shirt to turn the volume on her phone down, but she leaves the mic on. "Hey, Gabe. Sorry to bug you. But I . . . I just really wanted to thank you for helping us."

August can practically hear him blushing. "Oh, it's no big deal. Anything for you, Myles."

"*Myles?*" Wes and August mutter in disgusted unison.

"I wanted to let you know . . . I'm so sorry about what happened between us. I was a dick. I don't know what I was thinking. You deserved better."

"I appreciate you saying that."

"And, I . . . I know you have every right to hate me. But fuck if I don't still think about you all the time."

"You do?"

"Yeah . . . when Niko's asleep, sometimes, I think about you. That one time, in the elevator of my dorm, you remember? I couldn't walk straight for two days."

"Yikes," Wes says.

"Amateur," Niko notes.

"And especially when I hear that song you used to like— you remember? Sometimes it comes on, and I'll think, wow, I wonder what Gabe's doing. I really let a good one get away." She sighs for dramatic effect. "I missed you. I didn't even know what you'd been doing for the past two years. You've been keeping yourself from me, huh?"

"I mean, honestly, it's mostly this job. Um, yeah, and I got really into intermittent fasting. And vaping. Those are, like, my two main hobbies."

"Those are hobbies?" Wes deadpans.

"Do I even want to know what that means?" Jane asks.

"Shh," Niko hisses, "it's getting good."

"Wow," Myla continues. "I'd love to hear all about that sometime—"

"It's actually really interesting. I read about how Silicon Valley programmers can go for twenty, twenty-two hours straight without eating or only supplementing with a meal replacement shake. Apparently skipping meals and restricting nutrients makes time go by more slowly, so you can get more done in your day. That's how I have time to do this job *and* start making a business plan for my line of JUULpods."

"Oh my God," August says.

"Yeah, um," Myla stammers. "Wow. You always were so . . . creative. I—"

"Yeah!" Gabe says, suddenly excited. This was not the plan. "I'm close to having my first product line developed, then I'll go into market testing. My concept is, like, savory pods. You know how you only ever see sweet ones? But what about, like, a buffalo chicken vape? Or—"

"This is transcendent," Niko says. It sounds like he's got a mouthful of pancake.

"She has to kill him," Wes says. "It's the only way."

"—pepperoni pizza vape, bacon cheeseburger vape, you know? And for the vegetarians, there's a whole line with bean burrito and nacho cheese and paneer tikka masala flavors—"

"I'm gonna barf," August says.

"Anyway, I'm still looking for investors. I'm so glad you're into the idea. It's been hard to pitch."

"Yeah, I guess some people have preconceived notions about, uh, what vapes should taste like? But anyway—"

"You know what? I have some samples in my car—did I tell you I got a Tesla last year? I mean technically, my dad got it, but anyway, let me go grab some and you can taste for yourself."

"Oh, you really don't have to do that—"

"No problem at all, Myles."

"No, Gabe—*fuck*." There's a rustling over the line as Myla pulls her phone out and unmutes the group call. "I didn't get the badge."

August spins on the spot. On the other side of the crowd is Gabe, headed for the door.

"Fuck it, I'll get it," August says into her phone, and she snatches up the nearest bowl of batter and plows straight toward him.

In the crush of bodies, it's easy to play the last few steps into a stumble—right into Gabe's chest, pancake batter splattering everywhere, up his neck and into his hair, soaking his Members Only jacket.

"Oh, fuck, I'm so sorry!" August shouts over the crowd. Gabe holds his hands out in shock, and she pulls a towel from her apron and start sopping up the batter. "I'm a disaster, oh my God."

"This jacket is *vintage*," he hisses.

And that's all it takes—concern over his stupid jacket—for him not to notice when she slides her hand under the towel and unclips the badge from his lanyard.

"I'm so sorry," August repeats. She slides the card into her back pocket. "I—I can give you my Venmo and you can charge me for the dry cleaning."

He sighs heavily. "Don't worry about it."

He storms away and August waves apologetically after him, then leans back into the phone in her front pocket. "Got it."

"That's my girl," Jane replies.

"Oh, thank God," comes Myla's voice. "I thought I was gonna have to vape some lamb vindaloo."

"No crimes against nature tonight," August says. "Except for the big one, I guess. Meet me in the bathroom, Niko?"

"Be there with bells on."

"Okay, Jane," August says. "I'm gonna end the call, but I should be there in ten. Just—just stay where you are."

"I think I can manage," Jane says, and August disconnects.

She passes the ID to Niko, and he gives her a vague salute and heads off. He'll meet Myla near the control room once everyone is in place. Just one more step—setting up the diversion.

"You ready?" August asks Wes, sidling up beside him at the trash can.

He smirks and raises an eyebrow. "Ready to commit arson at a loud party? This is what I was born to do."

"Okay," August says, untying her apron. "I'll give you the signal when we get over the bridge. I'm gonna—"

"Where have you been?" says Lucie's voice from behind her. Fuck. She sounds like she's about to start spitting curses in Czech. August spins around to find her glaring, a bottle of maple syrup clutched in her hand like a grenade. "These people. *Nightmare.* I need *help.*"

"I—" How the fuck is she going to get out of this? "I'm sorry, I—"

"She had the most genius idea," says another familiar voice, and there's Annie Depressant herself, bewigged and costumed, a stack of stuffed pancakes balanced atop her head. "I'm gonna take over for her." She points to the tip jar. "I can double that in fifteen minutes."

Lucie looks between Annie and August, eyes narrowed. August tries to look like she's in on it.

"Fine," Lucie says. "We try for half an hour." She jabs August's shoulder with one of her pointy acrylics. "Then you are back on shift."

"Sure, no problem," August says. Lucie stalks off, and August whips back to Annie, who's casually buffing her nails on her fake tits. "How did you—"

"You think I'm stupid?" she says. "Like it's not obvious to anyone who knows y'all that something's going on. Look at Wes. He's sweating like a fucking hard cheese on the A train. I don't need to know what you're *doing,* but, you know, I can help."

Wes stares at Annie for a full five seconds, and says, "Oh Jesus Christ, I'm in love with you."

Annie blinks. "Can you say that without looking like you're gonna throw up?"

"I'm—uh—" He visibly gulps down whatever else he was going to say. "Actually, yeah, I am. Yeah. In love with you."

"Look, I am very happy for both of you," August says, "but we are on a clock here—"

"Right," Annie says. She smiles. She's a supernova.

"Right," Wes says. Neither of them is even pretending to look at August.

"I'm gonna kiss you," Annie says to Wes. "And then I'm gonna go serve some pancakes to some drunks, and you can tell me why later."

"Okay," Wes says.

They kiss. And August runs.

———

Times Square is streaking, blazing, burning through August's glasses.

Like most people who live in Brooklyn, she never comes here, but it's the nearest Q stop to the Control Center. The streets are nearly empty at one in the morning, but August still has to vault over someone slumped on the sidewalk in a Hello Kitty costume and bank hard to avoid a shuttered halal cart.

She throws herself down the subway stairs, races to the platform, and there, somehow in perfect alignment with the universe, is the Q waiting for her with doors open. She lunges onto the train as they slide shut.

Momentum carries her across the aisle, and she smacks into the opposite side of the car, startling a drunk couple so much, they nearly drop their takeout.

To her right, a voice says, "Hell of an entrance, Coffee Girl."

And there's Jane. Same as always: tall and smirking and the girl of August's dreams. She's got her jacket settled carefully onto her shoulders, her things neatly tucked away inside her backpack like it's the first day of school. The way she might have looked stepping onto that bus to California if she'd ever made it. August chokes out a laugh and lets the movement of the train carry her into Jane's side.

"Incredible," Jane says as she gathers August up in her arms. "Ran all that way, and you still smell like pancakes."

They ride through Manhattan, across the Manhattan Bridge, and into Brooklyn, where August texts Wes his cue and Wes texts back fire in the hole and a photo of security guards rushing to put out a blaze in the designated trash can.

"Okay," August says, turning to Jane. She holds out a hand. "Once more for old time's sake?"

Jane laces their fingers together, and they walk from one car to the next, platform after platform, like they did all those months ago when Jane dragged her through the emergency exit for the first time. August can't even remember to be afraid.

With every car, there are fewer and fewer passengers, until they hit the very last one. It's empty.

They're easing past Parkside Ave., where it all started. It's too dark to see the painted tiles or climbing ivy, but August can picture the apartment buildings and nail salons and pawn shops standing over the tracks, turned down for the night. She imagines New York ghosts unfurling from under stairs and between shelves to stand at the windows and watch Jane skate away.

"I guess I should give you this," Jane says, pulling her phone out of her back pocket. "I don't want to accidentally cause a paradox or something by bringing that back to the '70s."

"But what if I need to—" August says automatically. "Oh. Right. Yeah, of course. Obviously not."

She takes the phone and tucks it into her pocket.

"I also, uh," Jane says.

She hesitates before tugging her backpack off and shrugging out of her jacket. She hands that over too.

"I want you to have this."

August stares at her. She's looking back softly, something pulling at the dimple on the side of her mouth, exactly and nothing at all like she did that morning they met and she held out a scarf.

"I can't—I can't take your jacket."

"I'm not asking you to," Jane says, "I'm telling you. I want you to have it. And who knows? Maybe I'll stay, and you can give it right back."

"Fine," August says, reaching into her bag. "But you have to take *this* with *you*."

It's a Polaroid, the one Niko took of them the night of Easter brunch, before August accidentally solved part of the mystery with a kiss. Inside the little square of film, Jane's screaming with laughter, a wad of cash pinned to her chest and a crown on her head, the constant backdrop of the Q behind her. She has a red lipstick print on the side of her sharp jaw. Under her arm is August, turned away from the chaos, gazing up at Jane's profile like she's the only person on the planet. Her lipstick is smudged.

It's not the only picture she has of her and Jane together, but it is her favorite. If Jane can only have one thing to remember her by, it should be this.

Jane spends a long second looking at it before tucking it into her backpack and shouldering it again.

"Deal," she says, and August takes the jacket.

She puts it on over her Pancake Billy's House of Pancakes T-shirt, turning under the fluorescents to show it off. It's surprisingly light on her shoulders. The sleeves are slightly too long.

"Well? How does it look?"

"Ridiculous," Jane says with a grin. "Awful. Perfect."

They've moved through Brooklyn swiftly, barely anyone at the final few stops.

August glances up at the board. One last stop.

"Hey," she says. "If you go back."

Jane nods. "If I do."

"Will you tell people about me?"

Jane huffs out a laugh. "Are you kidding me? Of course I will."

August curls her hands up inside the sleeves of Jane's jacket. "What'll you tell them?"

When Jane speaks again, her voice has shifted, and August imagines her on a fat ottoman in a smoky apartment in July 1977, a few sweaty girls circled around the floor to listen to her story.

"There was this girl," she says. "There was this *girl*. I met her on a train. The first time I saw her, she was covered in coffee and smelled like pancakes, and she was beautiful like a city you always wanted to go to, like how you wait years and years for the right time, and then as soon as you get there, you have to taste everything and touch everything and learn every street by name. I felt like I knew her. She reminded me who I was. She had soft lips and green eyes and a body that wouldn't quit." August elbows her, Jane smiles. "Hair like you wouldn't believe. Stubborn, sharp as a knife. And I never, ever wanted a person to save me until she did."

Hands shaking, August pulls her phone out. "I didn't save you. You're saving yourself."

Jane nods. "I've figured out you can't do that alone."

And that, August thinks, as she dials up Myla's number, has to be true.

"Y'all good to go?" August asks as Myla swears into the line. "We're almost there."

"Yeah," Myla grunts. It sounds like she's manhandling some machinery. "It was a bitch, but there's one more lever and it'll put the line over. Get her in place and I'll tell you when."

August turns to Jane as the brakes scream into the station. This is it.

"Ready?"

She courageously wrestles a smile onto her face. "Yeah."

With one hand on the emergency exit handle and the other wound up in August's hair, she kisses August long and deep, pulling at it like music, a whole creation of a kiss. Her mouth is soft and warm, and August kisses her back and touches her face to brand its shape into her palm with permanence. Above their heads, the letters announcing the stop flicker on the board.

August can't help grinning—she'll miss kisses that break things.

The doors open, and August steps onto the platform alone.

It's past two in the morning, the amusement park shut down for the night, trains coming only once or twice an hour, so they have a brief window during which there's nobody to stop them. She planned it exactly, timed it perfectly.

When she looks down, Jane's swinging herself out the emergency exit and dropping down onto the third rail. She looks so small from up here.

She picks her way down the tracks carefully, hidden behind the parked train, and August sits on the ledge of the platform, right on the yellow line, hooking her knees over.

"Okay," Jane says from below.

She takes a deep breath, holding it high in her shoulders, shaking her hands out. From here, she could be anyone. She could pull herself back up onto the platform and take the stairs two at a time up into the muggy night. She gazes off down the track, peering into freedom, and August wonders if this is the last time she'll ever get to see the set of Jane's smirk, her long legs, her soft black hair swept up off her brow.

What if it's the last time?

What if this is August's last chance?

Wes told Isaiah. Winfield probably tells Lucie every day. Niko and Myla are going to get *married*. And August? August is going to let the girl who changed her entire life disappear without ever telling her, because she's afraid of how it'll hurt.

She feels the knife in her pocket, heavy and light all at once.

Fuck caution.

"Hey, Subway Girl," August calls out.

Jane turns to her, eyebrows raised, and August reaches for her phone and mutes the mic.

"I love you."

Her voice echoes off the glass ceiling, off the silver of the trains stored on the side of the tracks, out toward the street and the moonlit beach beyond.

"I'm in absolute fuck-off, life-ruining love with you, and I can't—I can't do this and not tell you," she goes on. Jane's staring at her with her mouth popped open in soft surprise. "Maybe you already know, maybe it's obvious and saying it is just gonna make this harder, but—God, I love you."

August's mouth keeps moving, half-shouting into the empty tracks, and she barely knows what she's saying anymore, but she can't stop.

"I fell in love with you the day I met you, and then I fell in love with the person you remembered you are. I got to fall in love with you *twice*. That's—that's *magic*. You're the first thing I've believed in since—since I don't even remember, okay, you're—you're movies and destiny and every stupid, impossible thing, and it's not because of the fucking train, it's because of you. It's because you fight and you care and you're always kind but never easy, and you won't let anything take that away from you. You're my fucking hero, Jane. I don't care if you think you're not one. You are."

The last two words flutter down between the slats of the elevated tracks, past Jane's feet and onto the street below. Jane's still looking up at her, eyes bright, feet planted. Seconds to go and unforgettable.

"Of course," Jane says. Her voice comes from deep in the solid center of her chest—her protest voice, projected up to the platform. It could wake the dead. "Of course I love you. I could go back and have a whole life and get old and never see you again, and you would still be it. You were—you are the love of my life."

Myla's voice crackles out of August's pocket. "Ready?"

August's eyes don't leave Jane's as she pulls her phone out and unmutes the mic.

"I'm ready," Jane says.

August breathes in, knuckles white.

"She's ready."

"*Now.*"

And everything goes black.

Silence, nothing but the shock of darkness. The street outside the station goes dark too, eerily quiet and still. August's lungs refuse to release. She remembers what Jane said, the day they danced with strangers on a stalled train. *The emergency lights.*

They flicker on, and August half expects them to flood down onto a deserted track, but there's Jane, feet on the third rail. That kind of shock would have killed anyone else. She doesn't even look startled.

"Oh my God," August says. "Did it—are you—?"

"I—" Jane's voice is hoarse, almost staticky. "I don't know."

She makes a weird, jerky motion with one foot, trying to take a step outside of the tracks.

She can't.

"It didn't—" August has to swallow twice to get her throat to cooperate. She holds her phone closer to her mouth. "It didn't work, Myla. She's still stuck."

"Fuck," she swears. "Was anything off? Was the timing right? Are you sure she was touching the third rail?"

"Yeah, she was touching it. She's still touching it."

"She's—okay. So, it's not hurting her?"

"No. Is there something wrong with it?" August leans past the edge of the platform, trying to see better. "Should I—"

"Don't touch it, August, Jesus! There's nothing wrong with the third rail. She's just—she's still in between."

"Okay," August says. Jane looks up at her, paler somehow. Drawn. "What do I do?"

"Make sure she keeps touching it," Myla says. "If I blacked out the line and she's still there, it means residual electrification on the rail is what's keeping her here for now."

"For *now*? What—why didn't it work?"

"I don't know," Myla says. She's grunting and out of breath, like she's working on something. "We were never going to be able to produce a surge as powerful as the one that got her stuck—I mean, fuck, this station's part solar-powered now, which is a whole other factor. The hope was that something *close* would be enough."

"So—so that's it?" August says, flat. "It's not going to work?"

"There's one more chance. The second surge, remember? When I undo what I did and restore power, there'll be another surge. We can—we can hope this one will put it over. She might have some charge left over from the first one. That could help."

"Okay," August says. "Okay, when's the next surge?"

"Give me a couple of minutes. I'm passing the phone to Niko. Just—just talk to her."

August shoves her phone back into her front pocket and

looks down at Jane. Without power coursing through the line, she—well, she doesn't look good. All the color has drained from her face. No more summer glow. Even her eyes seem flat. It's the first time August has looked at her and actually seen a ghost.

"Hey," August calls down to her. "You're okay."

Jane holds a hand in front of her face, examining her own fingers. "I don't know about that."

"You heard Myla, right?" August demands. "We have another chance."

"Yeah," Jane says vaguely. "It . . . it doesn't feel good. I feel weird."

"Hey. Hey, look at me. You're getting out of here tonight, one way or another. I don't care what it takes, okay?"

"August—" she says. And August can see it in her eyes, a dullness that has nothing to do with electricity. She's losing hope.

"*Jane,*" August shouts, pulling herself to her feet. "Don't you dare fucking give up, do you hear me? You know how your emotions affect the line, right? What you feel, right now, it's holding onto that charge. It's what's keeping you alive. Don't let that go. You remember when we got in that fight, and you blew out a light? You remember when you stopped the whole train just because—because you wanted to get *laid*—" Despite herself, Jane's face splits into a smile, she laughs weakly. "Come on. Jane, that was all you. You have power here too."

"Okay," she says. She closes her eyes, and when she speaks again, it's to herself. "Okay. I'm gonna live. I *want* to live."

"Almost ready," says Niko's voice from August's pocket.

And August—August thinks about what she just said.

The nerves in Jane's body, electrical impulses, feedback

loops, a scarf, an orange, hands brushing into sparks. What Jane feels. What August makes her feel. *The love of my life.*

She pushes herself off the platform.

Jane's eyes snap open at the sound of August's feet landing on the tracks.

"Whoa, whoa, what are you doing?"

"What's the one thing that's worked?" August says. She crosses the first two rails, balancing on the tracks. One wrong step, and she'll be crashing down to the street. "This whole time, Jane. What's the one thing that made this all happen?"

She sees the moment when Jane realizes what she means— her eyes go wide, frightened, furious.

"*No,*" she says.

"Ten seconds," Niko says.

"Come on," August says. She's inches away. "I'm right. You know I'm right."

"August, don't—"

"Jane—"

"*Please*—"

"What is it, Jane? What's the one thing that could put it over?"

And here they are. August and Jane and the third rail and the thing she's prepared to do, and Jane is looking at August like she's breaking her heart.

"It's you," Jane says.

"*Now,*" says Niko's voice, and August doesn't think, doesn't breathe, doesn't hesitate. She slams her foot down on Jane's to hold it to the rail, and she grabs Jane's face in both hands, and she kisses her as hard as she can.

16

Letter from Augie Landry to Suzette Landry
Postmarked from a P.O. Box in Metairie, LA

4/28/73

Hi Suzie,

How have you been? I'm so sorry I haven't had
a chance to stop by the house. I got the birthday
card you sent—thank you so much!!! I loved the
picture you drew me. What kind of bird is that?

I'm doing really well! I have a good job and my
coworkers are like family. Not as much as you
are my family, but it's nice. Sometimes when
my customers talk about their kids, I tell them
about you. They all agree you're the smartest
kid they've ever heard of. Don't forget what I
told you: don't listen to Mom and Dad, go to the
library and read whatever books you want.

I think you'd really like my roommate. She's
smart and funny, just like you, and she doesn't
take any crap from anyone. Maybe one day I'll
introduce y'all.

I'm so proud of you, Suzie. I'm sorry I can't be home. I think about you every day, and I miss you so much. When you're older, I'll tell you everything, and I hope you'll understand. Knowing you, I think you will.

All my love,
Augie

There's a moment, in between.

August wakes up on the trash couch in the living room, surrounded by a swampy fog of burning sage and lavender, ears ringing, whole body sore. Jane's jacket is draped over her like a blanket.

She can remember the tracks, the look on Jane's face, something white-hot flashing through her. And then she wakes up.

But there's a moment in between.

Myla touches her hair gently and says that Wes and Isaiah got to the station first and found her on the platform. At the end of the couch, Wes hugs his knees to his chest. He's got a black eye—apparently August didn't want to go without Jane. Apparently, she fought.

They brought her back here, and as soon as Niko and Myla could leave the party, they caught the Q home. It was running again. They didn't see Jane.

She's gone. She was gone by the time Wes and Isaiah got to the station.

But there was a moment. Right after August kissed her.

It didn't hurt, somehow. It was a heat that blazed through her, wrapping around, like standing on wet, hot asphalt on a hundred-degree day and feeling a breeze whip the warmth from the ground around her legs. Her eyes were squeezed shut, but for a moment, before everything went black, she saw something.

She saw a street corner. Boxy brown cars parked along the road. Graffiti on buildings that aren't there anymore. She saw, for a second, like looking through the slats in the blinds before they flutter shut, Jane's time. The place where Jane belongs.

And now August is here.

"It worked," August says, half-hysterical, before she rolls over and throws up on the rug.

The thing about life without Jane is, it does go on.

There's rent to pay, shifts to pick up. The dog needs to go outside. The MetroCard needs to be refilled. School starts, and August has to register for graduation and get fitted for a cap and gown. The Q shuts down for maintenance. They count the money they managed to raise—sixty grand. Forty away from saving Billy's, but they're working on it.

The city moves, trudges on, lights up and shouts and spits steam up through the grates the same as always. August lives here. That finally feels real all the time, even when nothing else does. This is the city where she got her heart broken. Nothing anchors a person to a place quite like that.

The first week, she keeps the radio on. She convinces Lucie to let her put it on at Billy's, plays it in her headphones on her commute, takes the boom box home when she packs up the office and plays it in her room. Jane's not going to call in, but sometimes August swears she can feel her on the other side, humming at the same frequency. The station has added enough of their songs to the rotation over the past year that sometimes she'll hear one, Michael Bolton or Natalie Cole, and it's a comfort to know Jane was there. It all really happened. Here are the things she left behind: songs and a name scratched into a train and a jacket that August keeps over the chair at her desk but never wears.

On Saturday morning, the DJ's voice comes over the speakers as she's folding laundry in her room.

"All right, listeners," he says, "I've got something special for you this morning. Normally we don't take requests in advance, but this particular caller has been so loyal to us that when she called last week and asked if we'd play a song today, we decided to make an exception."

Oh. Oh, no.

"This one's for you, August. Jane says, 'Just in case.'"

"Love of My Life" starts to play, and August drops her socks on the floor and climbs into bed.

The next day, she takes a different train to Coney Island, the last place she saw her. The arched ceilings, metal and glass sprawling over her head. She gets off at the same platform but walks down the steps instead, out to the street and the shadow of the Wonder Wheel.

At the edge of the beach, she takes her shoes off, ties the laces together, and throws them over her shoulder so she can walk out into the water with bare feet. It's almost fall, but there are still hundreds of families and teenagers and sun-starved twenty-somethings sitting on beach blankets drinking nutcrackers. She walks past them all and sinks onto the wet seat of the tide in her jeans.

Water rushes over her feet, and she contemplates the horizon of the Atlantic Ocean, thinking of Jane standing there with a backpack full of contraband beer a lifetime ago.

She thinks of the Gulf Coast back home, generations of her family soaking it into their pores, storms in the streets and in the tiny two-bedroom apartment she grew up in, what it took from her, what it gave her.

She thinks of the Bay, of Jane's family. The Sus. She wonders if Jane's made it home yet, if she's tripped through the doorway of the apartment above the restaurant in Chinatown and found the candy in the tin atop the fridge, if she and her sisters have tugged each other down to the edge of the water under the Golden Gate. Maybe when Jane was a kid, she'd look out at the Pacific and wonder what got left behind when her great-great-grandparents left Hong Kong, what came with them.

August hasn't been able to bring herself to check the records yet to find out what happened to Jane after 1977. She's not ready to know. Whatever she did, wherever she's been, August hopes she was happy.

She's learned grief through her mother, and through Jane. She looked in their eyes and learned that what she's feeling right now is worth spending time with: a distance, but a fresh one, when someone who's far from you can still feel close.

It won't take long, she thinks, for the farness to feel like wrongness. It was only eight months. They only knew each other for eight months. A year and a half, and she'll have lost Jane for longer than she had her. That's the worst part. Eight months shrinking away into nothing. Never being the exact person she was with Jane again. Jane, somewhere else, but the exact person she was with August gone. Those two exact people ceasing to exist, and nobody else in the world even feeling the loss.

When she gets home that night, sand in her hair, Niko's waiting for her.

He pours her a cup of tea like he did the day they met, but he adds a splash of rum. He puts a record on, and they sit cross-legged on the living room floor, letting the incense he lit burn until it smolders out.

Niko usually lives along a y-axis, getting taller and taller the more he talks, but when he turns to her, there's nothing big or expansive about him. Only a soft sigh and the downturn of his mouth as he takes her hand.

"You remember when you came to meet me and Myla before you moved in? When I touched your hand?"

"Yeah."

"I saw this," he says. "Not—not that this would happen. But I saw that you had something in you that could reach across. That could make impossible things happen. And I saw . . . I saw a lot of pain. Behind you. In front of you. I'm sorry I didn't tell you sooner."

"It's okay," August tells him. "I wouldn't have changed anything."

He hums, rotating his teacup slowly.

The record switches to a new song, something old, strings and brassy vocals in a slow, heavy melody, like it was recorded in a smoky room.

She's not really listening, but she catches a few lines. *I like the sight and the sound and even the stink of it, I happen to like New York . . .*

"I like this song," she says, leaning her head back against the wall. Her eyes are rubbed pink and raw. She's been making a lot of exceptions to her "no crying" rule lately. "Who's it by?"

"Hmm, this?" Niko leans his head on top of hers and points to the sculpture in the corner. "This is Judy Garland."

Her mom comes to visit in October.

It's tense, at first. When she talks, it's clipped, audibly struggling to stay even, but that makes August appreciate her more. She can hear the old razor-sharp Suzette defenses trying to cut through, but she's fighting them. August can appreciate that. She's learned a lot in the past year about how much of that is in her too.

Her mom has never really traveled, and she's definitely never been to New York, so August takes her to see the sights—the Empire State Building, the Statue of Liberty. She takes her to Billy's so she can see where August works, and she immediately takes a shine to Lucie. She orders French toast and pays the ticket. Lucie brings August a Su Special without her even asking.

"I've missed you," her mom says, dragging a piece of toast through a pool of syrup. "So much. Just, like, the pictures of ugly dogs you used to text me. The way you talk too fast when you have an idea. I'm really sorry if I made you feel like I didn't love all of you. You're my baby."

It's more sentiment than she's handed August since she was a kid. And August loves her, endlessly, unconditionally, even if she likes to play at being August's friend more than her mom, even if she's difficult and stubborn and unable to let anything go. August is all three of those too. Her mom gave her that, just like she gave her everything else.

"I missed you too," August says. "The past few months . . . well. It was a lot. There were a lot of times I thought about calling you, but I—I just wasn't ready."

"It's okay," she says. "Anything you want to talk about?"

That's new too: the asking. August imagines her going to work at the library and digging through the shelves, pulling out books on how to be a more emotionally supportive parent, taking notes. She bites down on a small smile.

"I was seeing someone for a few months," August tells her. "It, uh. It's over now. But it wasn't because we wanted it to be. She . . . she had to leave the city."

Her mom chews thoughtfully and swallows before she asks, "Did you love her?"

Maybe her mom will think it's a waste of time and energy, to love somebody as hard as August does. But then she remembers the file burning a hole in her bag, the things she's going to have to tell her later. Maybe she'll get it after all.

"Yeah," August says. Her mouth tastes like hot sauce and syrup. "Yeah, I did. I do."

That afternoon, they walk through Prospect Park, under the autumn sun dappled through the changing leaves.

"You remember that file you sent me earlier this year? The one about Augie's friend who moved to New York?"

Her mom stiffens slightly. Her lips twitch in the corners, but she's physically holding herself back, trying not to look too eager or anxious. August loves her for it. It almost makes her change her mind about what she's about to do.

"I remember," she says, voice carefully neutral.

"Well, I looked into it," August says. "And I, um . . . I found her."

"You found her?" she says, abandoning pretense to stop in the middle of the path. "How? I couldn't find anything beyond, like, two utility bills."

"She was still going by her birth name sometimes when she knew Augie," August explains, "but by the time she got here, she'd started using a different name full-time."

"Wow," she says. "So, have you talked to her yet?"

August almost wants to laugh. Has she talked to Jane? "Yeah, I have."

"What'd she say?"

They've drawn up to an isolated bench perched near the water's edge, quiet and separate from the runners and the geese and the sounds of the street.

August gestures toward it. "Wanna sit?"

There on the bench, she pulls out her own file, a new one.

In the weeks since Jane left, August hasn't looked for her, but she *has* looked for Augie. Everything she's found is in the manila folder she hands to her mom. A postcard in Augie's handwriting, from California to New York. A phone number, which she finally managed to match to an old classified ad that led to a storage facility with blessedly stringent record keeping. The name of the man who shared Augie's number and apartment in Oakland, now happily married to another man but struck momentarily speechless when August told him over the phone that she was Augie's niece.

A copy of a fake driver's license with Augie's photo, a few years older than the last time her mom saw him, a different name. He'd gotten in some trouble on his way to California, and he'd stopped using his legal name. It was all behind him by 1976 when he wrote to Jane, but it meant they never could find him after '73.

The last item is a newspaper clipping about a car accident. A twenty-nine-year-old bachelor with an Oakland address wrecked his convertible in August of '77. He was driving the Panoramic Highway.

He died, but not the way Jane thought. He died happy. He died chasing a dream, loved and sober and sun-drenched in California. The man he left behind still has a box in his attic

filled with photos—Augie smiling in front of the Painted Ladies, Augie hugging a redwood, Augie getting kissed under the
mistletoe. There are copies of those in the folder too, along with
a carbon copy of a letter Augie wrote to his kid sister in 1975,
proof that he never stopped trying to reach her.

Her mom cries. Of course she does.

"Sometimes . . . sometimes you just have to feel it," August
tells her. She looks out over the water as her mom hugs the
file to her chest. It's over. It's finally over. "Because it deserves to
be felt."

Her mom sleeps on the old air mattress that night, tucked
in on August's bedroom floor, and in the dark, she talks about
what she might do with her time now that the case is solved.
August smiles faintly at the cracked ceiling, listening to her toss
around ideas.

"Maybe cooking," she says. "Maybe I'll finally learn how to
bake. Maybe I'll get into ceramics. Ooh, do you think I'd like
kickboxing?"

"Based on the number of self-defense classes you made me
take when I was thirteen, yeah, I think you would."

She reaches for August's hand where it's dangling over the
edge of her mattress, and August pictures her doing the same
when she was a kid and shaking through a nightmare. She has
always loved August. That's never not been true.

"One thing, though," her mom says. "This . . . Biyu person.
The one who lived with Augie. Could I meet her?"

And suddenly August's throat is almost too thick to answer.

"I really wish you could," she manages. "But she doesn't live
here anymore."

"Oh," her mom says. She gives August's hand a squeeze.
"That's okay."

And, somehow, it actually sounds like she's done asking questions.

August lies awake for another hour after her mom falls asleep, staring at the moonlight on the wall. If, after all these years, Suzette Landry can let the case go, maybe one day, August can let Jane go too.

There are a lot of impossibilities in August's life. A lot of things that transpire despite the odds, despite every law of this world and the next saying it shouldn't work out.

It's November, and Pancake Billy's House of Pancakes is still $14,327 dollars away from shuttering for good, when her mom calls to tell her that her grandmother's estate has been settled and she should get a check in the mail next week. She doesn't think much of it—after all, her mom said there hadn't been that much left.

She has to sign for the envelope when it arrives, and she gets so distracted arguing with Wes over what to order on tonight's pizza that she almost forgets to open it altogether.

It's light, thin. It feels inconsequential, like a tax return when you work minimum wage and you know the IRS is sending you a bullshit check for thirty-six bucks. She slides her finger down the seam anyway.

It's written out to August. Signed at the bottom. Right there, in the total box: $15,000.

"Oh," she says. "*Oh.*"

Three months after Jane vanishes, August's grandmother's money—the money from a woman August met twice, who paid her tuition for thirteen years in adherence to tradition but who couldn't be fucked to look for her own son—silently makes up the difference.

She holds the check in her hands, and she thinks of the box her mom found in her grandparents' attic, all of the unopened letters from Augie, and it feels dirty. She didn't earn it. She doesn't want it. It should go where it can be transformed into something good.

So, she digs the account numbers up from the office in the back, and she wires the money to Billy anonymously, and she clocks into work just like she does every day. She takes her table assignments, fixes herself a coffee. Slaps palms with Winfield when he clocks in. Puts in an order of pancakes for table seven. Stares at the spot on the wall by the men's room where she's returned the opening day photo she stole.

The front door flies open, and there's all six-feet-something of Billy filling the doorway, eyes wide, a sheen of sweat across his expansive, bald forehead.

Lucie freezes halfway out the kitchen door when she sees him, plates of pancakes balanced up and down each arm.

"What?" she asks flatly. "What happened?"

"God happened," he says. "We got the money. We're buying the unit."

And, for the first time in her career, Lucie spills an order on the floor.

It's a Saturday afternoon, but they finish up their tables and close the restaurant, Lucie nudging the last customer out the door with a free takeaway dessert to get them moving faster. The minute they're out, she shuts the door and flips the OPEN sign around.

"Closed for private party," she says, and she crosses to the bar and yanks Winfield into a furious kiss.

"I'll drink to that," Jerry whoops through the kitchen window.

August grins, joy swarming in her stomach. "Cheers."

The whole restaurant explodes into chaos—servers screaming over the phone to people who aren't on shift, Jerry screaming at Winfield about why he never told anyone about Lucie, Lucie screaming at Billy about where the money could have come from. Billy puts Earth, Wind & Fire on the sound system and cranks it up, and a busboy runs to the liquor store down the block and returns with a bus tub full of champagne bottles.

People start flooding in. Not customers, but longtime waiters who heard the news and wanted to celebrate, a couple of regulars close enough to Billy to get a personal call, line cooks still smelling like their second jobs at other restaurants in the neighborhood. August didn't tell anyone about the money—not even Myla or Niko or Wes—so when she sends a message to the group chat, they're there within twenty minutes, out of breath and in mismatched shoes. Isaiah shows up around the time the fifth bottle is popped, beaming and pulling Wes into his side, accepting a juice glass of champagne when it's passed to him.

August came to New York almost a year ago, alone. She didn't know a soul. She was supposed to muddle through like she always did, bury herself in the gray. Tonight, under the neon lights of the bar, under Niko's arm, Myla's fingers looped through her belt loop, she barely knows that feeling's name.

"You did good," Niko tells her. When she looks at him, there's that distant, funny smile playing around his mouth, the one he gives when he knows something he shouldn't. She ducks her head.

"I don't know what you're talking about."

Jerry drags a crate of potatoes out of the kitchen, and Billy steps up onto it, raising up an entire bottle of André.

"All I've ever wanted," Billy says, "was to keep the family business alive. And it hasn't been easy, not with the way things have been changing around here. My parents put everything they had into this place. I did my homework on that bar." He points to the bar, and everyone laughs. "I met my wife in that booth." He points to one in the back corner, where the vinyl's split across the seat and one side sinks too far down. August always wondered why it hadn't been replaced. "I had my daughter's first birthday party here—Jerry, you baked a fuckin' cake, remember? And it was *awful*." Jerry laughs and gives him the finger, and Billy bellows out a laugh so loud, the room shakes.

"But, anyway," he says, sobering. "I'm just . . . I feel so blessed to get to keep it. And to have people I trust." He inclines his head toward Lucie and Jerry and Winfield, huddled by a table. "People I love. So, I wanna make a toast." He lifts his bottle, and all over the restaurant, people raise coffee mugs and juice glasses and styrofoam to-go cups. "To Pancake Billy's House of Pancakes, serving the good people of Brooklyn for nearly forty-five years now. When my momma opened this place, she told me, 'Son, you gotta make your own place to belong.' So, to a place to belong."

Everyone cheers, loud and happy and a little misty, the sound filling the place up to the brim, rushing over the Formica table-tops and the sticky kitchen floor and the photo to the side of the men's room door of the first day Billy's fed the neighborhood.

Just as Billy takes a swig, the front door opens.

The room's too busy throwing back champagne to notice, but when August glances across the dining room, there's a young woman standing in the door.

She looks lost, a little shocked, unsteady on her feet. Her hair's inky black and short, swept back from her face, and her cheeks are flushed from the November chill outside.

White T-shirt, ripped jeans, sharp cheekbones, an armful of tattoos. A single dimple at one side of her mouth.

August thinks she throws a chair out of the way. It's possible a bottle of hot sauce hits the linoleum and shatters. The specifics blur out. All she knows is, she clears the room in seconds.

Jane.

Impossibly, here. Now. Her red Chucks planted on the black-and-white floor.

"Hi," Jane says, and her voice sounds the same.

Her voice sounds the same, and she looks the same, and when August reaches out and grasps desperately for her shoulders, they feel exactly the same as they always have under her hands.

Solid. Real. Alive.

"*How—?*"

"I don't know," she says. "One second I was—I was with you on the tracks, and you were kissing me, and then I, I opened my eyes and I was just standing on the platform, and it was *cold,* and I knew. I could tell when it was. I didn't know where else to look for you, so I came here. I had to make sure you were—you were okay."

"That *I* was okay?"

"I can't believe you did that, August, you could have *died—*"

"I—I thought you went back—"

"You got me out—"

"Wait." August can barely hear what Jane is saying. Her brain is still catching up. "It's only been a second for you?"

"Yeah," Jane says, "yeah, how long has it been for you?"

Her fingers squeeze in Jane's shirt. "Three months."

"*Oh*," she says. She looks at August like she did that night on the tracks, like it's breaking her heart. "Oh, you thought I was—"

"Yeah."

"I'm—" she says, but she doesn't get to finish the sentence, because August has thrown her arms around her waist and crashed into her chest. Her arms close around August's neck, tight and fierce, and August breathes in the smell of her, sweet and warm and faintly, under it all, something a little strange and singed.

All those months. All the trips up and down the line. All the songs on the radio. All of it, all the work, all the trying and scraping and tearing at the seams of what she can see, all for this. All for her arms wrapped around Jane in a diner on a Saturday afternoon.

Her girl. She came back.

17

Photo from the archives of <u>New York
Magazine</u>, from a photo series on Brooklyn
diners, dated August 2, 1976

[Photo depicts a plate of pancakes
with a side of bacon in the hands of a
waitress, illuminated by the blue and
pink glow of the neon lights that wrap
the underside of the bar at Pancake
Billy's House of Pancakes. Though
the waitress's face is out of frame,
several tattoos are visible on her left
arm: an anchor, Chinese characters, a
red bird.]

August takes her home.

The sky splits open the second they step out of Billy's, but
Jane just turns to her under the onslaught of rain and smiles.
Jane in the rain. That's something new.

"Which way we goin', angel?" she asks, raindrops sliding into
her mouth.

August blinks water out of her eyes. "I don't guess you wanna
take the subway?"

"Fuck you," she says, and she laughs.

August grabs her hand, and they throw themselves into the back of a cab.

As soon as the door slams shut, she's in Jane's lap, swinging a leg over to straddle her hips, and she can't stop, not when she thought she was never going to see Jane again. Jane's fingers dig into her waist, and hers twist into Jane's hair, and they kiss hard enough that the days they missed all fold together like a map, like the pages of a notebook shut, like it was no time at all.

Jane's mouth falls open, and August chases after it. She skims that soft bottom lip with her teeth and finds her tongue, and Jane makes a low, hurt sound and holds her tighter.

The first time Jane kissed her for real, it felt like a warning. This time, it's a promise. It's a sigh of relief in the back of her throat. It's a string of fate August never thought she'd believe in, pulling tight.

"You wanna give me an address or what?" the driver says from the front seat, sounding absolutely bored.

Jane laughs, wide and bright, right up against August's mouth, and August leans back to say, "Parkside and Flatbush."

On the curb outside the Popeyes, August drops her keys, and a moving truck trundles through a deep puddle of sludge on the street and drenches them both.

"Fuck," August says, taking her dirty glasses off and plucking her keys out of the gutter. "I pictured this a lot more cinematic."

She turns to Jane, dripping and soaked through and slightly blurry, covered in mud and grinning, still there. Just continuing to be there, somehow, despite every goddamn law of the universe saying she shouldn't be.

"I don't know," Jane says, reaching out to thumb at the mascara raccooning under August's eyes. "I think you look great."

August breathes out a delirious laugh, and at the top of the stairs, she pushes Jane through the front door of the apartment.

"Shower," August says, "I'm covered in street juice."

"*So* sexy," Jane teases, but she doesn't argue.

They stumble toward the bathroom, leaving a trail of shoes and wet clothes. August turns on the faucet—somehow, miraculously, for the first time since she moved in, the water is hot.

Jane pins her to the bathroom sink and kisses her, and when August is finally down to only her wet bra and underwear, she opens her eyes.

She keeps having these moments, where she has to stare at Jane, like if she looks away for too long, she'll disappear. But here she is, standing in August's bathroom, hair damp and sticking out in every direction from where August has been tugging at it, in a black bra and briefs. There are her hipbones, and her bare thighs, and the rest of her tattoos—the animals up and down her sides.

August reaches down and trails her fingers over the snake's tongue just below Jane's waist. Jane shivers.

"You're here," August says.

"I'm here," Jane confirms.

"What does it feel like?" August asks.

There's a pause as Jane's eyes sweep open and closed, her fingertips grazing over the porcelain of the sink behind August's back.

"Permanent." She says it like a complete sentence.

August's hand slides up her back, to the clasp of her bra. "We need to talk about what this means."

"Yeah," Jane says. "I know. But I . . ." She leans back down, kissing the top of August's cheekbone. She's moving again, restless, finally let off the leash. "I can think later. Right now I just want to be here, okay?"

And August, who has spent every minute of the last few months wishing she could touch Jane one more time, says *yes*.

They manage to work wet underthings off wet bodies and then, in the shower, they dissolve into each other, graceless and messy. August loses track of who washes whose hair or where the suds are coming from. The whole landscape of the world becomes golden-brown skin and fluid black lines of ink and a feeling in her chest like flowers. She kisses, and Jane kisses back, again, forever.

It's supposed to be just a shower—August swears—but everything is wet and warm and slick and it's too easy and natural for her hand to slip down between Jane's legs, and Jane's pushing back into her palm, and it's been so long. What else is she supposed to do?

"Missed you so fucking much," August breathes out. She thinks it's lost in the rush of the shower, but Jane hears it.

"I'm here," Jane says, licking water from the hollow of August's throat. August replaces her hand with her thigh, bearing down on Jane's in return, and they move together, one of Jane's hands on the wall for balance. Her breath hitches when she says it again: "I'm here."

They're kissing, and Jane's grinding against her, and she feels herself sinking into a fog of want, molten skin, a mouth on hers. It's too much, and it's not enough, and then they're stumbling out of the tub and August's back is on the bathmat, on the bathroom floor, and Jane is kissing her like she wants to disappear into her, hands roaming.

"Hang on," Jane says, moving to pull back. August grabs her wrist.

"Why—*ah*—" August gasps at the change of angle before Jane takes her fingers away completely. "For God's sake—why would you *ever* stop doing that—"

"Because," Jane says, pinching August on the hip, "I don't want to fuck you on the bathroom floor."

"We've fucked on the subway," August says. Her voice comes out pouty and petulant. She does not care. "The bathroom floor is an upgrade."

"I'm not *against* the bathroom floor," Jane says. "I mean, there are a lot of places in this apartment where I have every intention of fucking you. I just want to start with the bed."

Oh, right. The bed. They can have sex in a *bed* now.

"Hurry up, then," August says, clambering to her feet and pulling a towel with her. It's a testament to all they've been through together that she doesn't even think to care what her body looks like as she wrenches the door open and crosses into her bedroom.

"You're so *annoying*," Jane says, but she's close behind, shutting the door and pulling August into her, throwing the towel across the room as carelessly as she threw August's glasses that night on the Manhattan Bridge.

She backs August toward the bed, and August can feel warm, shower-fresh skin everywhere, and she's going crazy over it. Jane's waist and hips, the tight swells of her ass and thighs, ribs, breasts, elbows, ankles. She's losing it. She's a lifelong heretic suddenly overwhelmed with blissful gratitude for whatever made this possible. Her mouth is watering, and it tastes like honey, but maybe that's because Jane tastes as sweet as she smells.

Jane gives her a little push, and she lets herself fall into the sheets.

She lies there, watching Jane look around the room—the tiny writing desk stacked with textbooks, the basket of carefully folded laundry by the closet, the potted cactus on the windowsill that Niko gave her for her birthday in September, the maps and timelines that she hasn't yet brought herself to unpin from the walls. The jacket on the chair. August's room is like her: quiet, unfancy, gray in the stormy afternoon, and filled up with Jane.

"Yeah, this'll do," Jane says. "I have some suggestions about decor, but we can talk about that later."

She's still standing a few feet from the bed, naked and never shy, and August doesn't bother pretending not to look at every inch of her for the first time. Jane is obviously, always, inevitably stunning, all long legs and gentle curves and sharp hipbones and tattoos. But August finds that she loves things it never occurred to her to love. The dimples of her knees. The knots of her shoulders. The way her bare toes touch the scuffed floor.

"What?" Jane asks.

"Nothing," August says, rolling over to lay her cheek against the pillow. Jane's eyes track the way her damp hair tumbles down her shoulders and back. "It's cute how you just invited yourself to move in with us."

"Four's unlucky anyway," Jane says, "might as well make it five."

She throws herself at the bed, and August bounces and laughs and lets Jane push her onto her back, already gasping.

"You're always so," she says, kissing the patch of skin behind August's ear, her right hand finding its way, "sensitive."

"Don't—don't make fun of me."

"I'm not making fun of you." She moves one of her fingers in a teasing little circle and August gasps again, one hand fisting in the sheets. "I love that about you. It's fun."

When August opens her eyes, Jane's hovering over her, face gentle and awed. At August. She's looking at August like that. August can literally split time open, apparently, but she still can't believe the way Jane looks at her.

"You know I still love you, right?" August tells her. It falls out of her mouth readily. Losing her made it easy to say. "Even though it's been months for me. I never even came close to stopping."

Jane presses her lips to the center of August's chest.

"Tell me one more time."

August lets out a quiet, eager sound when she moves again. "I love you. I—I love you."

And Jane presses her into the mattress and says, "I'm here. I'm not leaving."

It's luxury. The most basic parameters of privacy—a door, an empty apartment, an afternoon stretching out before them— and that's luxury. No train schedules or nosy commuters. No fluorescent lights. Just touching for the luxury of touch, greedy because they can be. Jane keeps watching her face, and August can't imagine what her expression is doing, but Jane's smiling, and it only winds her up more to know that Jane's getting off on getting her off. August wants more, wants everything she can possibly have, wants to bury herself in it and never come back.

The first one goes quickly—it's been too long and she's missed Jane too much for it to take much more than a hand and a few minutes—and when she's finished shivering through it, Jane kisses her back to her senses.

"God," August says, breaking off, "come up here."

"I am up here," Jane says. "I'm kissing you."

"No." August licks her lips and reaches up to drag one fingertip across the bottom one. *"Here."*

"Oh," Jane exhales. "*Oh,* okay."

Jane kisses her once more, and then she's moving up August's body, shifting on her knees until she's even with August's shoulders, bracing herself with both hands against the wall. August can feel the heat radiating off of her like wet sunlight.

"Ready?" she asks.

"Don't ask stupid questions," August tells her. She's thought about this more times than Jane can imagine.

"I just wanted—*fuck,* okay, stupid question, sorry—fuck, oh, *fuck.*"

August thinks about summertime in New Orleans, cups of ice and sugary syrup, satsuma and strawberry and honeysuckle dripping down her chin and sticking to her fingers, the familiar smother of steam and sweat. Jane rolls her hips, chasing the feeling, soft little moans falling out of her mouth faster and faster until she gives herself over. August's fingernails dig into the flesh of her thighs right where they meet her hips, and she loves this, loves Jane, loves the velvety insides of Jane's legs against her face, loves the way Jane feels on her lips and her tongue, loves how she moves in waves of desperate instinct without a hint of self-consciousness. August could learn how to live without breathing just to stay like this forever.

When it's over—not over, not ever really over with them, but when Jane falls over the edge and can't take any more—Jane kisses her sloppily, drunk and euphoric. She smells like August, and that's a whole different revelation—her body and Jane's and all the ways they can linger on each other.

There never seems to be a beginning or an end to this. Before, it was whatever circumstances demanded, but now it's a mess of touching, one kiss blending into the next, an endless glide, a continuous tide. They both give and take, both have turns gasping and swearing and getting on their knees. It could be hours or days, August thinks, when she has anything in her brain still capable of thought. Jane pushes a pillow under August's hips and hooks August's knees over her own shoulders, and August goes under.

Jane draws her out again, deadly with her mouth and fingers. She moves like art. She finds every piece holding August together and works it loose until she feels like she's spilling out of herself. August's at sea, she's clay in the hands of someone who knows how to make a life out of nothing, she's a girl underneath a girl in a bed they both almost died to get to.

"That's it," Jane whispers when August can barely stand to hear the desperate, dizzy sounds coming out of her own mouth. She's got one hand and her hips between August's thighs, chasing blindly and relentlessly after whatever August's body responds to. Jane fucks her like they're the center of the universe. August is in the stars. "So gorgeous like this, angel, God, I love you—"

August comes again with her hands in Jane's hair, eyes shut, body shaking, and it's not just the touch. Down to her fingertips, singing through her synapses, it's a love too big to be stopped, the unbearable, exquisite fullness of it. Impossible.

Later, when the sun is setting and the streetlights flickering on, August feels Jane's pulse against her and imagines all the wires running over and under the street synced up with it. That isn't how it works anymore. But it feels true anyway.

"You know what's crazy?" Jane says. She looks like she might fall asleep soon.

"What?"

"You're the most important person I've ever met," she says. "And I should have never met you at all."

Time, Myla explains to them later, isn't perfect.

It's not a straight line. It's not neat and tidy. Things get crossed, overlap, splinter. People get lost. It's not a precise science.

So, Jane didn't go back to 1977. They opened a door, and August caught a glimpse through the crack, but Jane didn't stay there. She didn't magically snap into the exact moment of time she left August in either, though. She ended up in the general area of now, the way her socks end up in the general area of the laundry basket when she throws them across August's bedroom.

The first few weeks are rocky. Jane's happy in the way that Jane is often happy—unflappable, gregarious, laughing loud into the night—until suddenly she isn't. She's thankful to be there, but there are moments that startle her out of gratitude. Like when she thinks of someone she wants to tell about a horrible pun she makes over dinner and realizes that person is back in 1977, or when she lingers over the picture of Augie that August has added to the fridge. Almost every night, she lies half-naked in bed, running her fingers over the tattoos on her side, again and again.

"I should have died that night, and I didn't," Jane says one morning, leaning against August's windowsill, looking down at the street. She says this a lot at first, like a meditation. "Either way, I was never going to see them again. At least this way, I get to live."

She's lucky, she says. She got to come back up from underground. She knew a lot of people who never got the chance.

Days go by, and inch by inch, she settles into her new life. And every day, it gets easier.

Though she loves stealing clothes from them all, Jane consents to a trip to H&M for a wardrobe of her own. In return, she convinces August to stop being so uptight about how many things she owns and get a damn bookshelf, which they start to slowly fill: books, photos, Jane's cassette collection, August's notebooks. Myla takes Jane to her favorite record store and starts helping her catch up on contemporary music. She really likes Mitski and Andre 3000.

She dedicates herself to learning everything about life in the twenty-first century and develops fixations on the most random modern inventions. Self-checkout stations at grocery stores freak her out, as do vape pens and almost any kind of social media, but she's fascinated by the Chromecast and Taco Bell beefy five-layer burritos. She spends a whole week mainlining *The* O.C. on Netflix while August is at work and emerges with a soft spot for Ryan Atwood and a lot of questions about early 2000s fashion. She buys a dozen flavors of instant noodles at H-Mart and eats them in front of August's laptop, talking back to mukbangs on YouTube.

They go to brunch with Niko and Myla, dinner with Wes and Isaiah. They spend weeks trying all the foods August never got a chance to bring her on the train—sticky pork ribs, steaming bowls of queso, massive boxes of pizza. Myla's parents find out her roommate has a Chinese girlfriend and mail her a box of homemade almond cookies, and soon Jane's on the phone with Myla's mom every Sunday afternoon, helping her practice her Cantonese. August buys out a whole shelf of strawberry milkshake Pop-Tarts at Target, and they spend the rest of the day dancing around their bedroom in their underwear, shoving pink frosting and sprinkles into their mouths and spreading sugary kisses everywhere.

As soon as Jane gets a MetroCard, she starts spending long days just wandering around Chinatown, occupying a table at a dumpling shop on Mulberry or waiting in line to order bao at

Fay Da, observing the old men playing cards in Columbus Park. Sometimes August goes with her and lets herself be led down Mott, but most of the time Jane goes alone. She always comes home late with her pockets full of sponge cake wrappers and plastic grocery bags heavy with oranges.

Jane becomes part of the apartment seamlessly, as if she's never not been there. She's the new reigning champ of Rolly Bangs, a fixture at Annie Depressant's gigs. She and Niko spend hours discussing gender (Myla wants them to start a podcast, which leads to August explaining podcasts to Jane, and Jane becoming addicted to *Call Your Girlfriend*) and share jeans all the time. One night, August overhears them talking about how far strap-on technology has come since the '70s and takes herself right back to bed. Five days of shipping and handling later, she wakes up deliciously sore and buys Niko a vegan donut as a thank-you.

Wes brings home a tattoo kit from work, and Jane lets him ink her on the living room couch, squeezing the blood out of August's hand. He does two bridges in fine black lines on the inside of her arms, just above the creases of her elbows: the Manhattan Bridge on her left, and on her right, below the anchor, the Golden Gate.

It helps, they discover, for Jane to do things that make her feel connected to her old life. She cooks congee for breakfast like her dad used to, hangs out at Myla's antique shop offering opinions on '60s-era furniture, joins up with demonstrations, brings August with her to volunteer at HIV clinics. When she finds out that most people August's age have never even *heard* of the UpStairs Lounge, she goes on a furious weeklong tear, posting handwritten fliers around the neighborhood until August shows her how to write a Medium post. It goes viral. She keeps writing.

The best nights are when they go dancing. Jane likes music, everything from gigs for half-decent local bands to loud clubs with flashing lights, and August goes along but stringently maintains that she won't dance. It always lasts about half an hour, and suddenly she's in the crowd under Jane's hands, watching her move her hips and stomp her feet and smile up into the haze. She could stay hovering at the bar, but she'd miss this.

Myla pulls some strings she refuses to disclose and matter-of-factly comes home one afternoon with a fake ID for Jane, complete with a photo and a 1995 birthdate. Jane brings it when August takes her to fill out an application at Billy's, and she starts as a line cook the next week, quickly falling into the rhythm of good-natured barbs and backhanded comments with Lucie and Winfield and the rest of the crew. Jerry gives her a good, long look the first time she steps up to the grill next to him, shakes his head, and gets back to his bacon.

Sometimes, when August walks home from the subway, she looks up at her own bedroom window from the street and thinks about hundreds of thousands of people walking past it. One square inch of a picture too big to see all at once. New York is infinite, but it is made up, in very small part, of the room behind the window with her and Jane's books crowding the sill.

August scrapes together the leftovers of her last student loan to buy a queen-sized bed, mattress and box spring and all, and Jane looks like she's in heaven when she flops onto it for the first time, euphoric enough to make August spring for the down comforter too. She's realizing that she'd give Jane pretty much anything she wants. She finds she doesn't really mind.

(Jane does finally make August's dream come true: she assembles the bed. It's exactly as devastating as August always imagined.)

The first night they sleep in it, August wakes up with Jane spooned up against her back, the broken-in fabric of one of Wes's oversized T-shirts soft against her skin. She rolls over and burrows her nose into the dip between Jane's neck and shoulder, breathing her in. She smells sweet, always, somehow, like sugar's in her veins. Last week, August watched her shout down a guy with a racist sign in Times Square and then snap it in half over her knee. But it's still true. Jane is spun sugar. A switchblade girl with a cotton-candy heart.

She stirs a little, stretching in the sheets, squinting at August in the early morning light.

"I'm never gonna get sick of this," she mumbles, reaching out to palm across August's shoulder, her chest.

August blushes and then blinks in surprise.

"Oh my God."

"What?"

She leans in, dragging her fingers through the hair fanned out on the pillow. "You have a gray hair."

"What?"

"Yeah, you have a gray hair! Didn't you say your mom's started super early?"

She's wide awake suddenly, sitting up and throwing off the covers. "Oh, I wanna see!"

August follows her out to the bathroom, the tail of Jane's T-shirt swinging around her bare thighs. There's a bruise on the inside of one, rose petal soft. August left it there.

"It's behind your right ear," August says, watching Jane lean into the mirror to examine her reflection. "Yeah, look, right there."

"Oh my God," she says. "Oh my God. There it is. I didn't have this before."

And it's that, more than anything—more than the new bed,

more than the Pop-Tarts, more than all the times Jane has made her sigh into the pillow. It's a gray hair that makes it feel real, finally. Jane's here. She's staying. She's going to live beside August as long as they want, getting gray hairs and laugh lines, adopting a dog, becoming boring old married people who garden on weekends, a house with windchimes and an untamed yard and a pissed-off HOA. They get to have that.

August nudges up behind her at the sink, and Jane reaches back automatically, tangling their fingers together.

"Brush your teeth," August whispers in her ear. "We have time for a round before breakfast."

Later, August watches her.

There's this thing Jane likes to do when August kneels over her. August will be a few feet down the mattress, straddling her waist or sitting on her heels between Jane's legs, trying to work out where she wants to go first, and Jane will do this thing. She closes her eyes and stretches her arms out on either side of her, skims the back of her knuckles across the sheets, arches her back a little, moves her hips from side to side. Naked as anyone in the world has ever been with a silent, broad, closed-lipped smile on her face, wide open and reveling. Soaking it in like it's the ultimate indulgence to be here in August's bed and under August's attention, unblushing, unafraid, content.

It makes August feel trusted and powerful and capable and admired—basically the whole list of things she's spent twenty-four years trying to figure out how to feel. And so she has a thing she does in return, every single time: she spreads her hands over Jane's skin and says, "I love you."

"Mm-hmm, I know," Jane says, eyes half-open to watch August's hands on her, and that's a familiar routine too. A happy, familiar routine.

A week after she graduates college, August gives Jane a file.

Jane frowns at it, finishing her swig of coffee over the kitchen sink.

"I figured out what I want to do," August says.

"To celebrate your graduation?" Jane asks. "Or, like, with your life?"

She's been agonizing over both a lot lately. It's a fair question.

"Both, kind of." August hops up to sit on the counter. "So, remember when I had my huge meltdown over trying to figure out my purpose in life, and you told me to trust myself?"

"Uh-huh."

"Well, I've been thinking about that. What I trust about myself, what I'm good at. What I like to do whether or not it's *marketable* or whatever. And I've been fighting it for a long time, but the truth is: solving things, finding people. That's my thing."

Jane raises an eyebrow. She's lovely underneath the kitchen lighting, handsome and morning-rumpled. August doesn't think she'll ever stop feeling lucky to see it.

"Finding people?"

"I found you," August says, brushing her fingertips under Jane's chin. "I helped find Augie."

"So, you want to be . . . a private investigator?"

"Kind of," August says. She hops down and starts pacing the kitchen, talking fast. "It's like . . . like when you see a viral tweet where one person is like, 'Here's a picture of this girl I was best friends with for three days on a Carnival cruise, I only remember her first name, Twitter, do your thing,' and three days later it has, like, a hundred thousand retweets and someone manages to find this random person based off almost no information and help two people reunite. People could hire me to do that."

After a long beat, Jane says, "I understood almost nothing you just said."

Right. These days, August occasionally forgets Jane grew up on eight-tracks and landlines.

"*Basically,*" August says, "if someone has a long-lost relative they want to know more about, or a half sibling they never knew existed until their dad got drunk and told them at Thanksgiving, or they want to find that friend from second grade who they only halfway remember . . . I could do that. I'm *great* at that. It doesn't have to be my whole job—I still have Billy's. But I could do this too. And I think, maybe, it can be a good thing. I could make a lot of people happy. Or . . . at least give them some closure."

Jane sets her mug down in the sink and nudges between August's legs to kiss her on the cheek.

"That's an incredible idea, baby," she says, drawing back. She points to the file on the counter. "So, what's this?"

"Okay, so. That. Is kind of . . . my first attempt at this finding people thing. And I want to say, before you open it, there's absolutely no pressure. I don't want you to feel like you have to do anything, especially not before you're ready." Jane picks up the folder and flips it open. "But . . ."

August watches her face shift as she leafs through the pages. She slides a photo out from its paper clip to examine it more closely.

"Is this—?"

"That's your sister," August says, voice only a little shaky.

"Betty. She still lives in the Bay area. She has three kids—two boys, one girl. That's her at her oldest son's wedding. And that's . . . that's her son's husband."

"Oh my God." She paces over to one of the Eames chairs, sitting gingerly on the edge. "August."

"I found your other sister too," August says, hopping down to follow her. She kneels between Jane's bare feet. "And your parents . . . your parents are alive."

Jane stares down at the file, mouth slack, eyes distant. "They're alive."

"I know." August squeezes her knee. "It's a lot. And I'm sorry if it's too much. I know you're still getting used to all this. But . . . I know you. I can see how much you miss them. And I know what it did to my mom to never know. So, if you think you could do it . . . well, we *were* talking about a post-grad road trip."

Jane looks up at her, finally. Her eyes are wet, but she doesn't look upset. Nervous, maybe. Overwhelmed. But not angry.

"What would I even say to them? How could I explain this?"

"I don't know. That's up to you. You could . . . you could tell them that you're Biyu's granddaughter. You could come up with a story for what happened. Or you . . . you could tell them the truth and see where that gets you."

She thinks about it for a long, quiet breath, tracing the shape of her sister with a finger. It's been fifty years since they saw each other.

"And you'll come with me?"

"Yes," August says gently. Jane's hand slides over the back of hers. "Of course I will."

———

A week later, just in time for Christmas, Isaiah drives them to the bus station, Wes in the front seat and the rest of them crammed four-across in the back.

"You're gonna do great," Myla says, leaning across Niko to pinch Jane's cheek. The silver band flashes on her third finger; she and Niko wear matching plain engagement rings now. "They're gonna love you."

"Of course they're gonna love her," Niko says knowingly. "Did you guys pack snacks?"

"Yes, Dad," Jane and August monotone in unison.

"Bring me a souvenir," Wes calls from the front seat.

"Salt and pepper shakers," Isaiah adds. "We need salt and pepper shakers. Shaped like the Golden Gate Bridge."

"We don't need those," Wes says. He's been spending more and more time across the hall at Isaiah's. When he does come home, it's usually to wordlessly leave a dozen homemade cupcakes on the kitchen counter and vanish back into the night.

"But I *want* them," Isaiah whines.

Wes pulls a face. "Okay. Salt and pepper shakers."

They roll into the bus station ten minutes before the bus is set to depart, Jane's hand clenched around their tickets. The other four kiss them sloppy goodbyes and wave them off, and they haul their backpacks up and head for the bus doors.

Jane hasn't worn her ripped jeans or jacket for weeks, settling instead into black skinnies, billowy button-downs, crew neck sweatshirts. But today, her skinnies are paired with the leather jacket from '77, laid across her shoulders like a second skin. She hasn't mentioned it, but August thinks she's hoping it'll help.

"So, this guy," Jane says, "Augie's old boyfriend—he really has my records?"

"Yeah," August says. She called him when Jane bought the bus tickets, and he's agreed to meet up with what he's been told is Jane Su's second cousin. He's also meeting August's mom, who's flying up to spend the holiday in California and get introduced to August's girlfriend. It's a big week. "He said they came in the day Augie left. He never got rid of them."

"I can't wait to see them," Jane says, bouncing restlessly on her heels. "And meet him. And meet your *mom*."

"I'm personally looking forward to this life-changing crispy chicken family recipe you keep telling me about," August replies. Jane's parents' restaurant in Chinatown is still open, it turns out. Jane's sister Barbara runs it.

Jane bites her lip, looking down at the toes of her boots. They're new—heavy black leather. She's still breaking them in.

"You know," Jane says. "My family. If they ... well, if it goes okay, they're gonna call me Biyu."

August shrugs. "I mean, it's your name."

"I've been thinking lately, actually." Jane looks at her. "What would you think about me going by Biyu all the time?"

August smiles. "I'll call you anything you want, Subway Girl."

The line keeps shuffling forward until they're the last ones outside the bus, clutching tickets in clammy palms. Maybe it's insane to try this. Maybe there's no way to know exactly how anything will turn out. Maybe that's okay.

At the door, Jane turns to August. She looks nervous, a little queasy even, but her jaw is set. She lived because she wanted to. There's nothing she can't do.

"There's a very big chance that this could be a disaster," Jane says.

"Never stopped us before," August tells her, and she pulls her up the steps.

———

Letter from Jane Su to August Landry.
Handwritten on a sheet of lined paper
ripped from August's sex notebook, which
Jane was definitely not supposed to know
about, secretly tucked into a jacket pocket
the night of the Save Pancake Billy's House
of Pancakes Pancakepalooza Drag & Art
Extravaganza. Discovered months later on a
bus to San Francisco.

August,

August August August.

August is a time, a place, and a person.

The first time I remember tasting a nectarine, my sisters were too
small to be allowed in the kitchen. It was only my dad and
me in the back of the restaurant, me propped up on a prep table.
He was slicing one up, and I stole a piece, and he always told
me that was the moment he knew I'd be trouble. He taught me
the word for it. I loved the way it felt in my mouth. It was late
summer, warm but not hot, and nectarines were ripe. So, you
know. August is a time.

The first time I felt at home after I left home, New Orleans
was dripping summer down my back. I was leaning against
the wrought iron railing of our balcony, and it was almost hot
enough to burn, but it didn't hurt. A friend I hadn't meant

to make was in the kitchen cooking meat and rice, and he left the window open. The steam kept kissing the humid air, and I thought, they're the same, like the Bay is the same as the River. So, August is a place.

The first time I let myself fall, it wasn't hot at all. It was cold. January. There was ice on the sidewalks—at least, that's what I'd heard. But this girl felt like nectarines and balconies to me. She felt like everything. She felt like a long winter, then a nervous spring, then a sticky summer, and then those last days you never thought you'd get to, the ones that spread themselves out, out, out until they feel like they go on forever. So, August is a person.

I love you. Summer never ends.
Jane

CL new york > brooklyn > community > missed connections

Posted December 29, 2020

Looking for someone? (Brooklyn)

We all have ghosts. People who pass through our lives, there one moment and gone the next—lost friends, family histories faded through time. I'm a freelance researcher and investigator, and I can find people who've slipped through the cracks. Email me. Maybe I can help.

ACKNOWLEDGMENTS

Where to begin?

Like this book, these acknowledgments have gone through multiple drafts. An earlier version was about the anxiety of the sophomore slump, but I decided that one was a bit of a downer. What do I really want to say about this book? That it was hard to write? Of course it was hard to write. It's a romance novel that takes place on the subway. Like, come on.

The truth is, even when this book was trying to kick my ass in a Waffle House parking lot, I loved every second, because it is the weird, fun, horny project of my heart. I still can't quite believe I got to do it.

I love this book. I love August, with her cactus spines and her dreams of a home, and Jane, my firecracker girl who refused to stay buried. I love this story because it's about finding family and finding yourself against all odds, when the world has told you there's no place for you. I love this story because it's an Unbury Your Gays story. I'm so thankful for the chance to tell it. I'm so thankful you, reader, have chosen to read it.

So many more thanks are due here. First and foremost, I have to thank my tireless, thoughtful agent, Sara Megibow, for always being there to support me personally, hold my heart, and fight for my best interests. There's no one I'd trust more to advocate for my work. A million thanks to my editor, Vicki Lame, whose response when I pitched her a lesbian time travel subway rom-com was, "This is so weird. You should do it." To my team at St. Martin's Griffin, including DJ DeSmyter, Meghan Harrington, and Jennie Conway, as well as my wonderful production editor, Melanie Sanders; cover designer, Kerri Resnick; illustrator, Monique Aimee; and Anna Gorovoy, who did incredible work on the interior pages; and sales and marketing and booksellers and bloggers and everyone who had a hand in sending this book out into the world.

To my best friend and most indispensable guide through plotting, Sasha Smith, thank you so much for your mom's potatoes. Endless thanks to my early readers: Elizabeth, Lena, Leah, Season, Agnes, Shanicka, Sierra, Somaya, Isabel, Remy, Anna, Elisabeth, Rosalind, Grace, Leah, Liz (yes, three separate Elizabeths read this book, and yes, two out of three have wives), Lauren (third Elizabeth's wife), Courtney, Vee, Kieryn, Amy, and more. To the authors who so kindly and generously read and blurbed, including Jasmine Guillory, Helen Hoang, Sara Gailey, Cameron Esposito, Julia Whelan, and Meryl Wilsner: I look up to each of you so much, and I'm still so stoked that you liked my book. To my perfect audiobook actress, Natalie Naudus, thank you for bringing my girls to life. So many thanks to my friends in the industry for making all this so much less scary—you know who you are.

To my thoughtful and thorough sensitivity readers, Ivy Fang, Adriana M. Martínez Figueroa, Gladys Qin, and Christina Tucker, thank you for your time and your care. Hugest thanks due to the resources I used for research on this book, including but certainly not limited to *Stone Butch Blues, Tinderbox: The Untold Story of the Up Stairs Lounge Fire and the Rise of Gay Liberation, The Stonewall Reader*, the New York Public Library's

Stonewall 50 installation, Jarek Paul Ervin's article on queer punk in 1970s New York, and the GLBT History Museum in San Francisco.

More thanks than I can express to Lee and Essie, who welcomed me into their home for dinner while I was revising this book and let me in on a real-life story of two women who fell in love in the 1970s and have endured to the present. It meant the world to me. I hope I managed to infuse even a little of what I saw in both of you into this.

To my family, thank you for building me into a person who chases something when I want it. Thank you for the vocabulary to talk about love and the capacity to feel it. To my FoCo fam and my NYC fam, thank you for afternoons in the garden and socially distant picnics in the park, for being a constant foundation of warmth and care.

To K, thank you for believing in me, for always having my back, and for all the sponge cakes. You have given me things I thought would only ever exist in fiction for me. I love you.

To the queer reader, thank you for existing. So much of this story is about building a community. I'm so happy to be in community with you. Be defiant. Love yourself hard. Take the energy in these pages and get involved in your direct physical community. Take care of one another. Know that you are wanted and loved and awaited by millions of us.

To every reader, I'm one of many, many but not enough queer voices in fiction. Each of them deserves to be heard. When you close this book, seek out a queer author you've never read before and buy their book. Don't begin and end with any one work. There are so many to love, and supporting them creates a space for even more queer authors to print their words. Also, support your local Black-owned diner or your local Chinatown or your local drag bar.

Thank you so much for letting this book exist. For seeing me. For seeing this story. I'll see you in the next one. Until then, fight like hell and be good to those you love.

ABOUT THE AUTHOR

Casey McQuiston is a *New York Times* bestselling author of romantic comedies and a pie enthusiast. She writes books about smart people with bad manners falling in love. Born and raised in South Louisiana, she now lives in New York City with her poodle mix/personal assistant, Pepper.